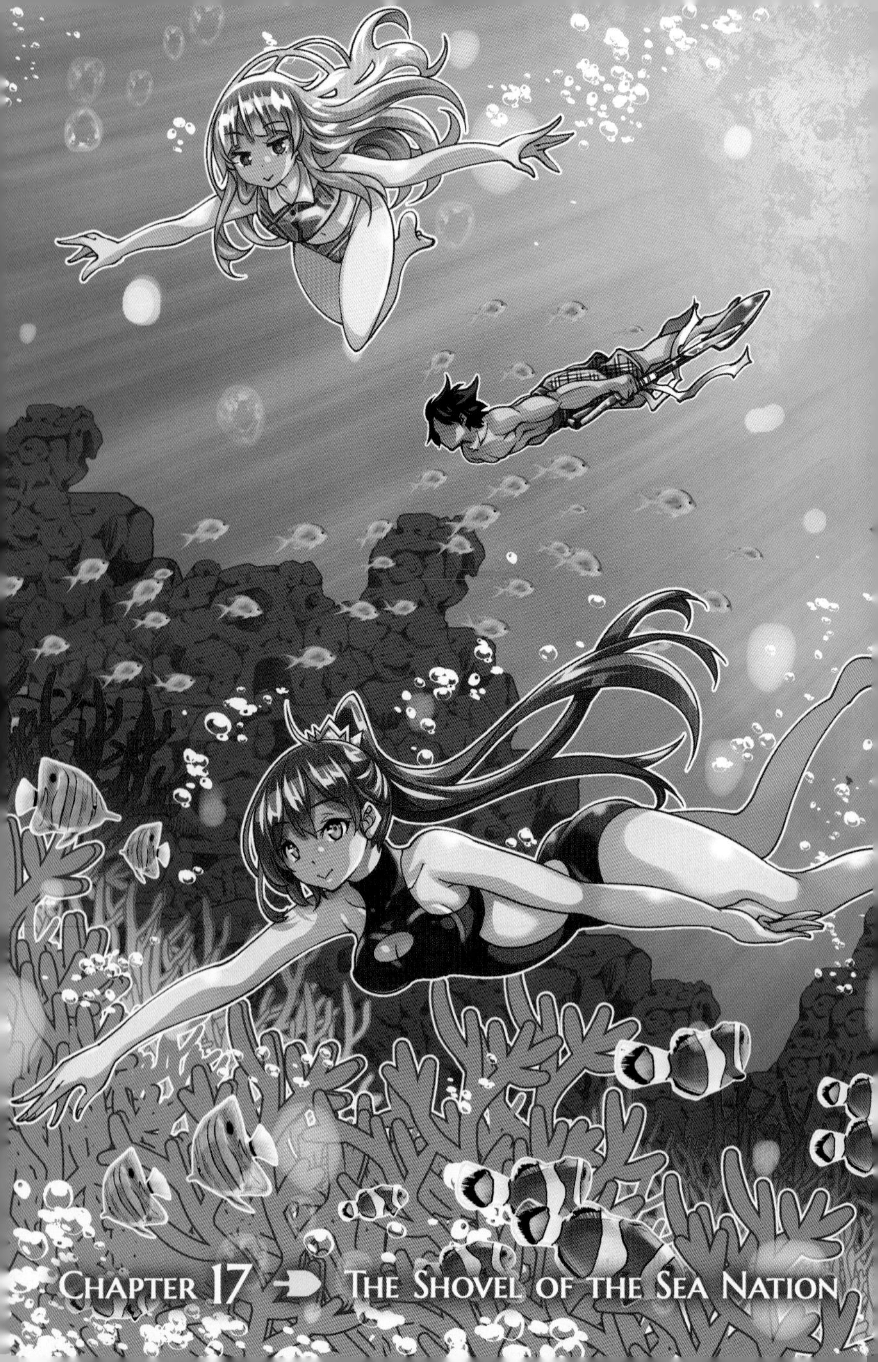
Chapter 17
The Shovel of the Sea Nation

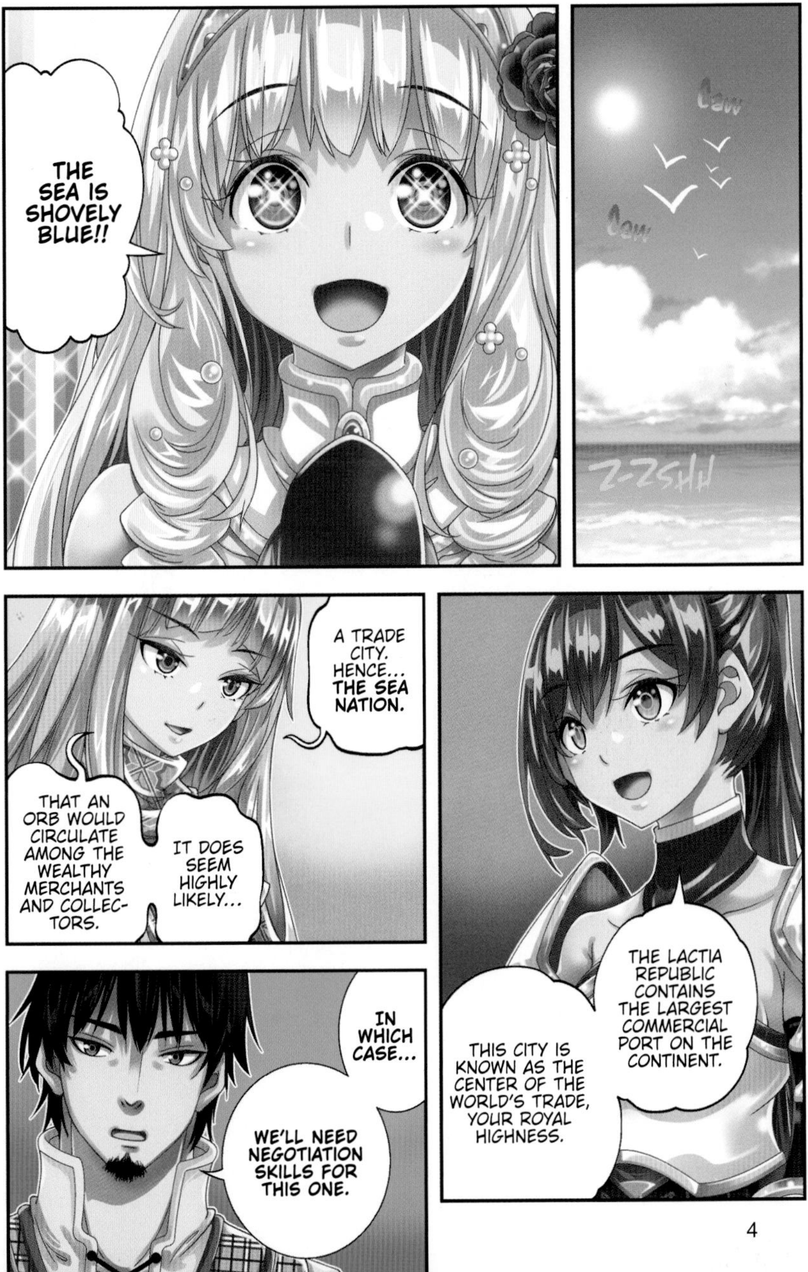
Caw
Caw
THE SEA IS SHOVELY BLUE!!
THE LACTIA REPUBLIC CONTAINS THE LARGEST COMMERCIAL PORT ON THE CONTINENT.
THIS CITY IS KNOWN AS THE CENTER OF THE WORLD'S TRADE, YOUR ROYAL HIGHNESS.
A TRADE CITY. HENCE... THE SEA NATION.
THAT AN ORB WOULD CIRCULATE AMONG THE WEALTHY MERCHANTS AND COLLEC-TORS.
IT DOES SEEM HIGHLY LIKELY...
IN WHICH CASE...
WE'LL NEED NEGOTIATION SKILLS FOR THIS ONE.

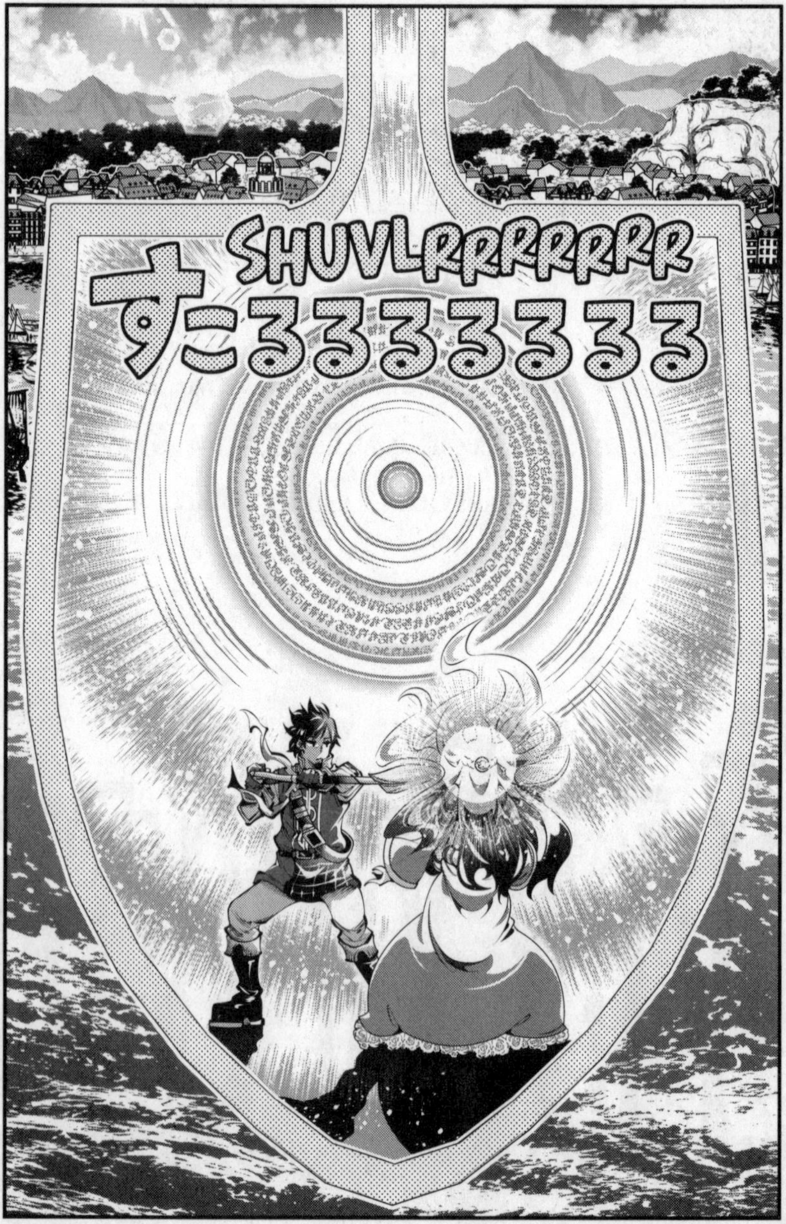
SHUVLRRRRRRR
すこるるるるるるる

CONTENTS

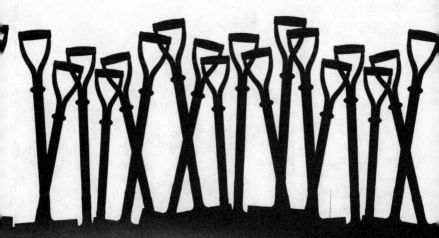

Design: Yuuko Mucadeya + Hideyuki Uekusa (Musicago Graphics)

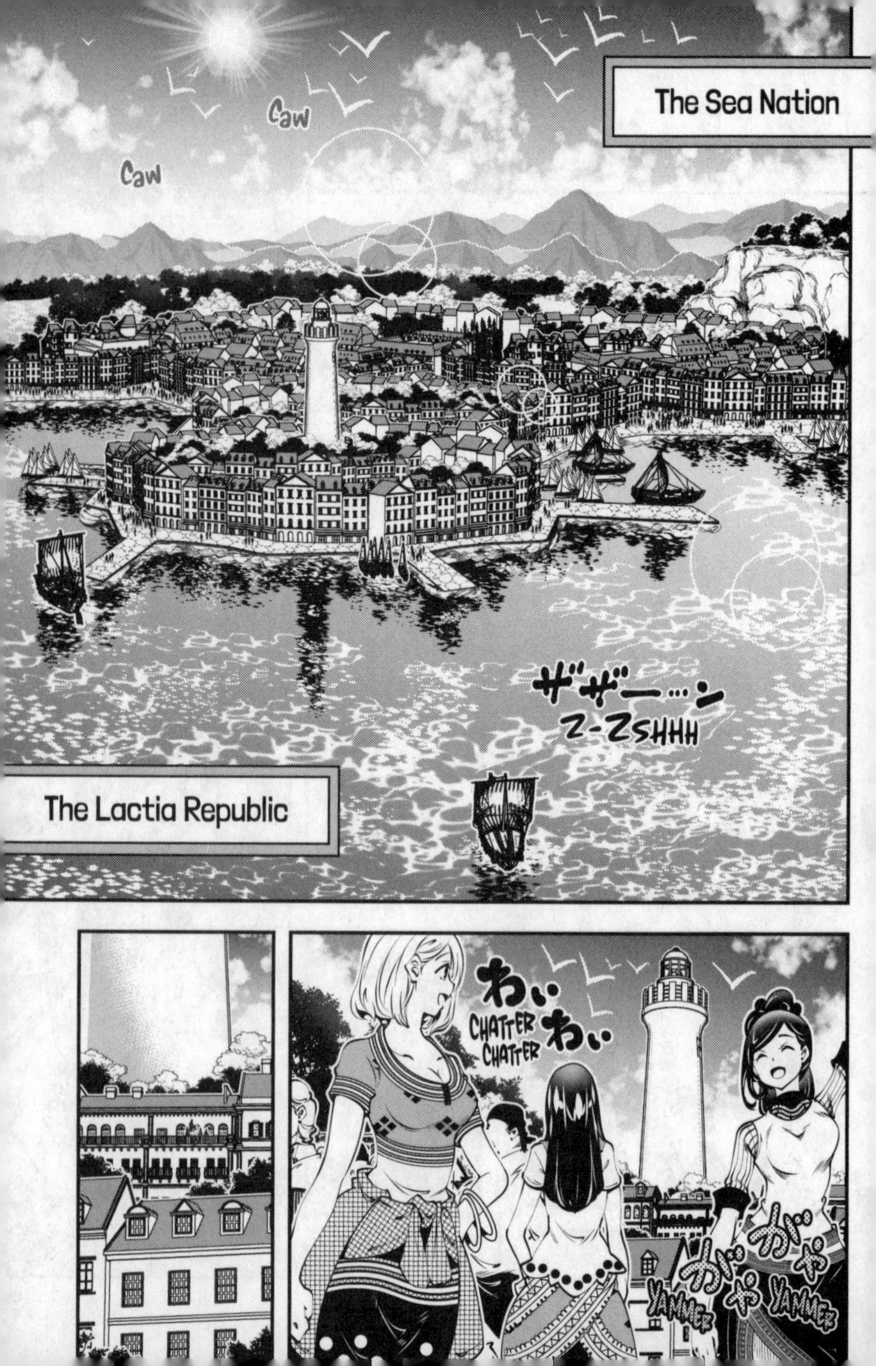
The Sea Nation
Caw
Caw
ザザー…ン
Z-ZSHHH
The Lactia Republic
わいわい
CHATTER CHATTER
がやがや
YAMMER YAMMER

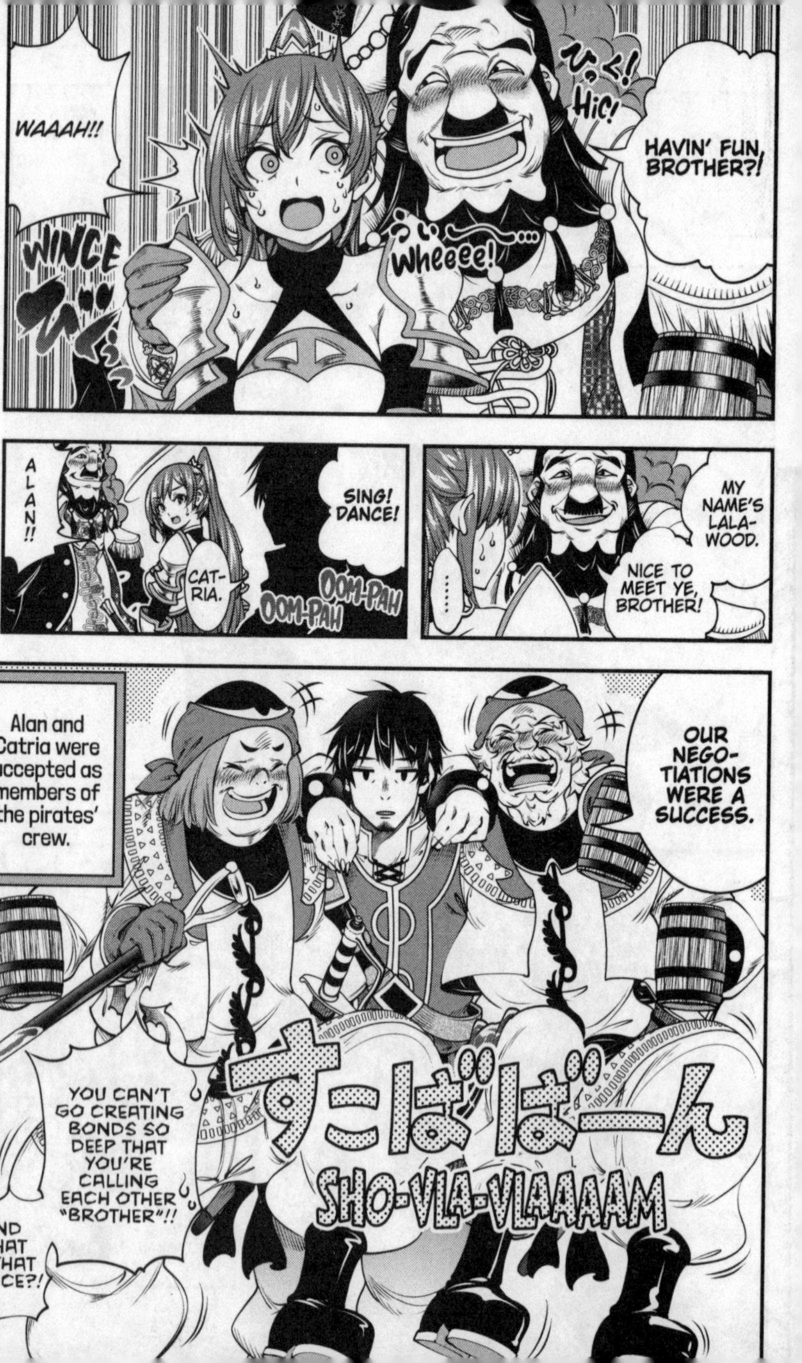
HIC!
HAVIN' FUN, BROTHER?!
Wheeee!
WAAAH!!
WINCE
MY NAME'S LALA-WOOD.
NICE TO MEET YE, BROTHER!
......
SING! DANCE!
OOM-PAH
OOM-PAH
CAT-RIA.
ALAN!!
OUR NEGO-TIATIONS WERE A SUCCESS.
Alan and Catria were accepted as members of the pirates' crew.
SHO-VLA-VLAAAAAM
YOU CAN'T GO CREATING BONDS SO DEEP THAT YOU'RE CALLING EACH OTHER "BROTHER"!!
AND WHAT IS THAT DANCE?!

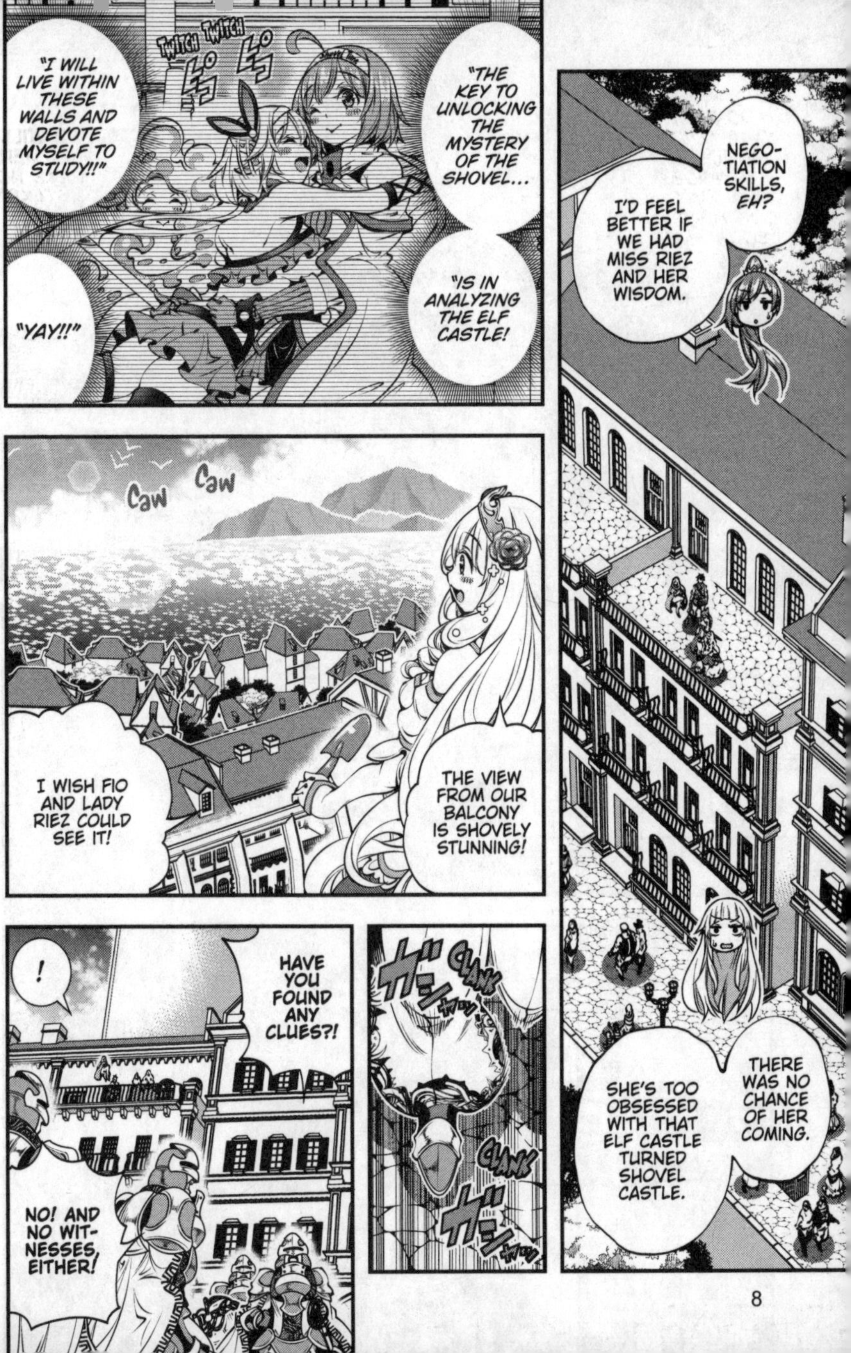
NEGO-TIATION SKILLS, EH?
I'D FEEL BETTER IF WE HAD MISS RIEZ AND HER WISDOM.
THERE WAS NO CHANCE OF HER COMING.
SHE'S TOO OBSESSED WITH THAT ELF CASTLE TURNED SHOVEL CASTLE.
TWITCH TWITCH
"THE KEY TO UNLOCKING THE MYSTERY OF THE SHOVEL...
"IS IN ANALYZING THE ELF CASTLE!
"I WILL LIVE WITHIN THESE WALLS AND DEVOTE MYSELF TO STUDY!!"
"YAY!!"
CAW
CAW
THE VIEW FROM OUR BALCONY IS SHOVELY STUNNING!
I WISH FIO AND LADY RIEZ COULD SEE IT!
CLANK
CLANK
HAVE YOU FOUND ANY CLUES?!
!
NO! AND NO WIT-NESSES, EITHER!

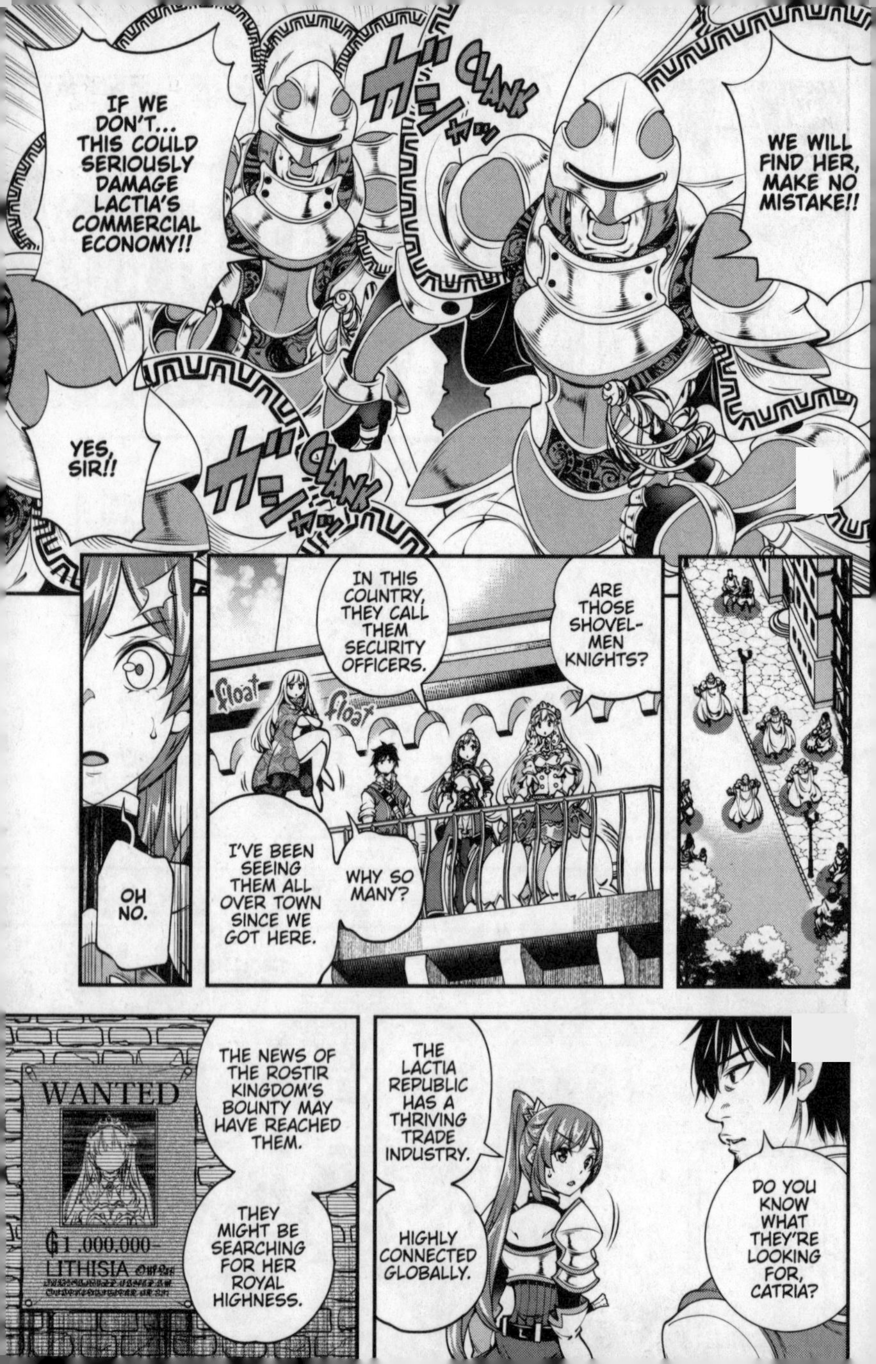
WE WILL FIND HER, MAKE NO MISTAKE!!
CLANK
IF WE DON'T... THIS COULD SERIOUSLY DAMAGE LACTIA'S COMMERCIAL ECONOMY!!
CLANK
YES, SIR!!
ARE THOSE SHOVELMEN KNIGHTS?
IN THIS COUNTRY, THEY CALL THEM SECURITY OFFICERS.
float
float
WHY SO MANY?
I'VE BEEN SEEING THEM ALL OVER TOWN SINCE WE GOT HERE.
OH NO.
DO YOU KNOW WHAT THEY'RE LOOKING FOR, CATRIA?
THE LACTIA REPUBLIC HAS A THRIVING TRADE INDUSTRY.
HIGHLY CONNECTED GLOBALLY.
THE NEWS OF THE ROSTIR KINGDOM'S BOUNTY MAY HAVE REACHED THEM.
THEY MIGHT BE SEARCHING FOR HER ROYAL HIGHNESS.
WANTED
₲1,000,000-
LITHISIA

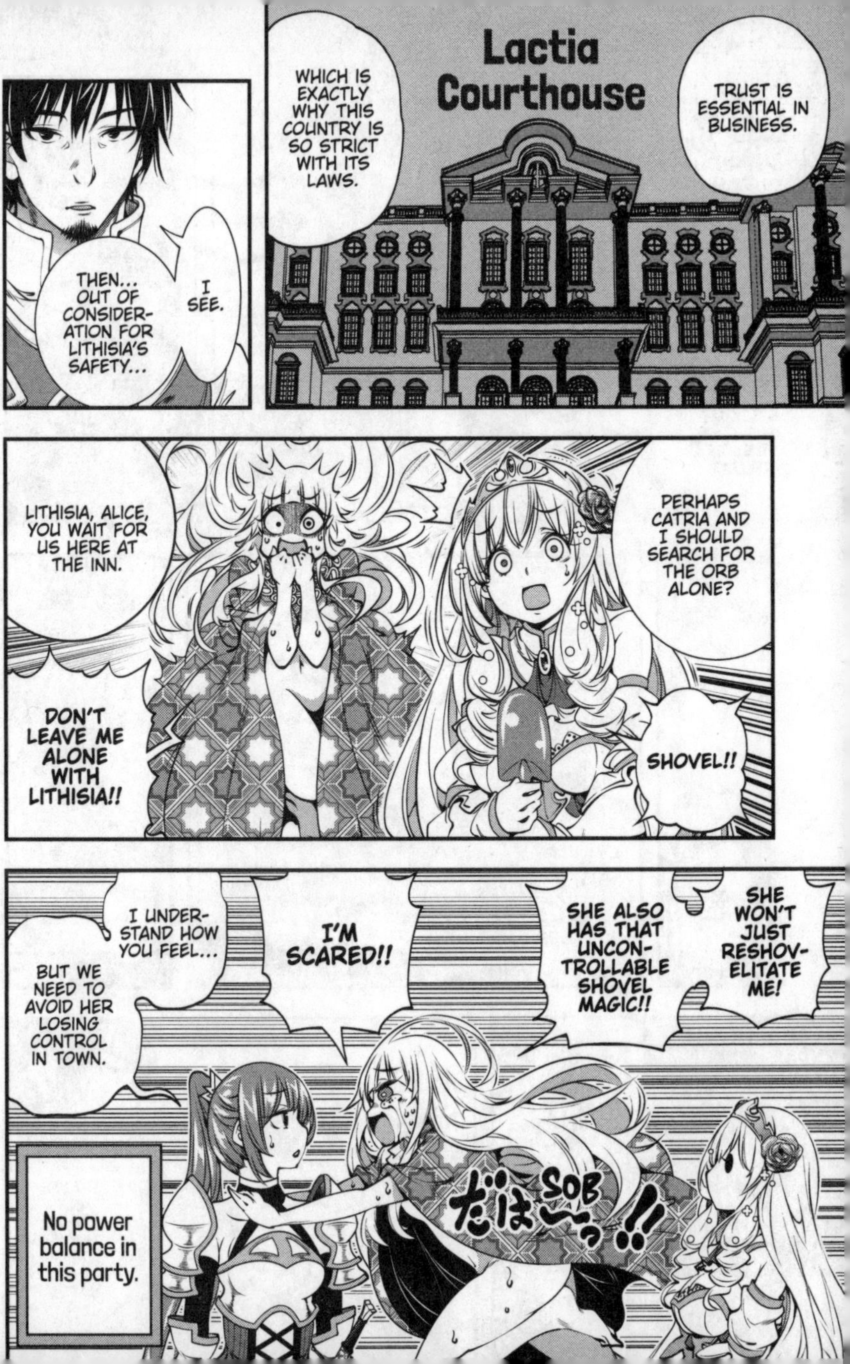
Lactia Courthouse
TRUST IS ESSENTIAL IN BUSINESS.
WHICH IS EXACTLY WHY THIS COUNTRY IS SO STRICT WITH ITS LAWS.
I SEE.
THEN... OUT OF CONSIDERATION FOR LITHISIA'S SAFETY...
PERHAPS CATRIA AND I SHOULD SEARCH FOR THE ORB ALONE?
LITHISIA, ALICE, YOU WAIT FOR US HERE AT THE INN.
SHOVEL!!
DON'T LEAVE ME ALONE WITH LITHISIA!!
SHE WON'T JUST RESHOVELITATE ME!
SHE ALSO HAS THAT UNCONTROLLABLE SHOVEL MAGIC!!
I'M SCARED!!
I UNDERSTAND HOW YOU FEEL...
BUT WE NEED TO AVOID HER LOSING CONTROL IN TOWN.
SOB
だはーっ!!
No power balance in this party.

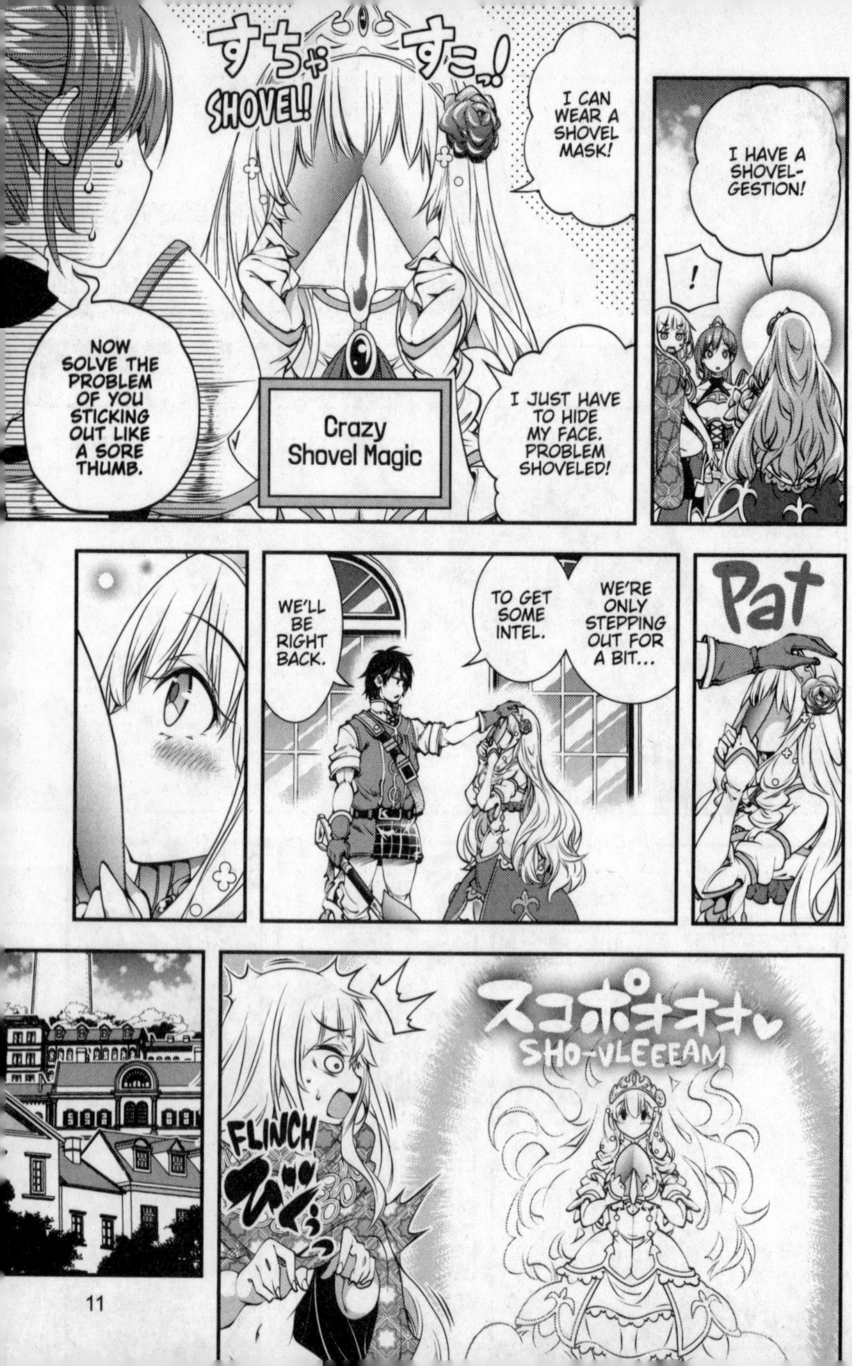
I HAVE A SHOVEL-GESTION!
!
I CAN WEAR A SHOVEL MASK!
すちゃ すこっ!
SHOVEL!
I JUST HAVE TO HIDE MY FACE. PROBLEM SHOVELED!
Crazy Shovel Magic
NOW SOLVE THE PROBLEM OF YOU STICKING OUT LIKE A SORE THUMB.
Pat
WE'RE ONLY STEPPING OUT FOR A BIT...
TO GET SOME INTEL.
WE'LL BE RIGHT BACK.
スコポォォォ♥
SHO-VLEEEAM
FLINCH
びくっ

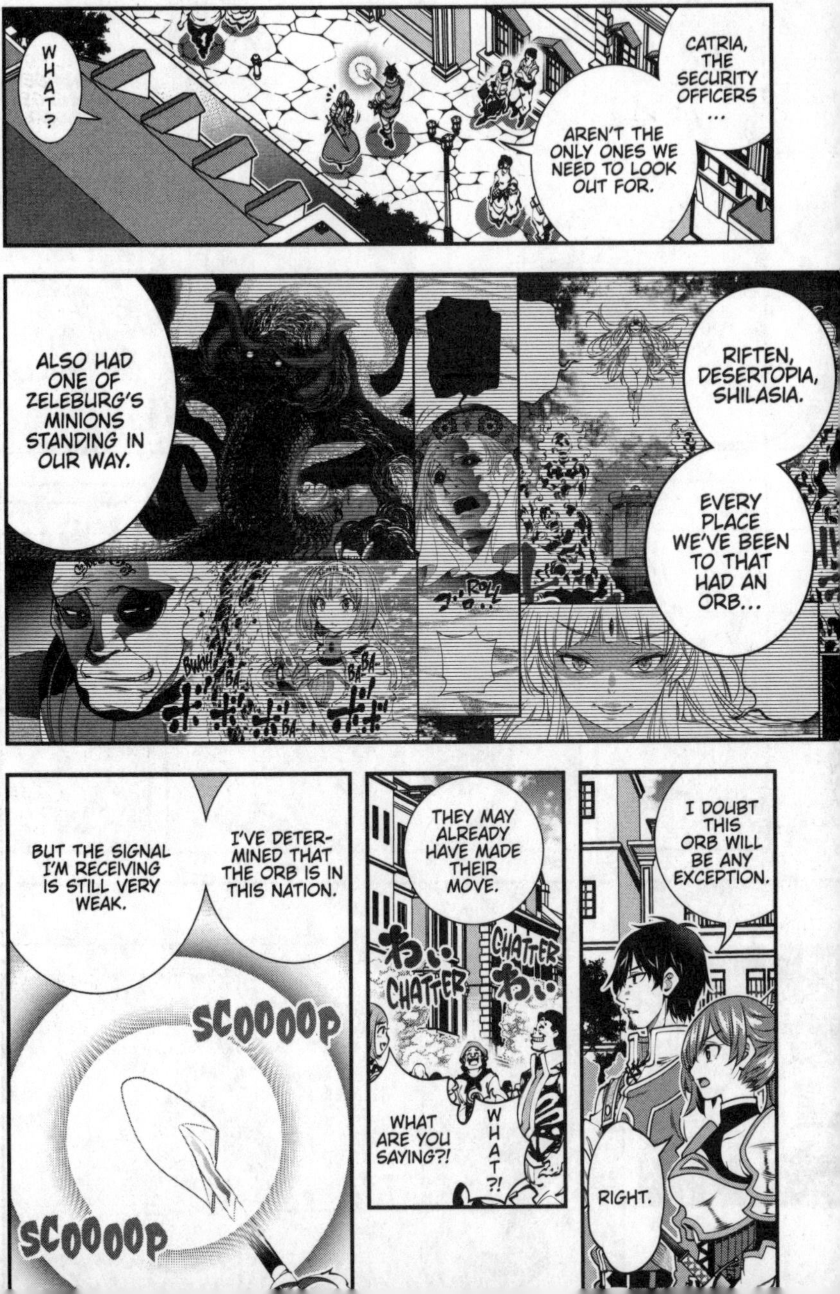
CATRIA, THE SECURITY OFFICERS ...
AREN'T THE ONLY ONES WE NEED TO LOOK OUT FOR.
WHAT?
RIFTEN, DESERTOPIA, SHILASIA.
EVERY PLACE WE'VE BEEN TO THAT HAD AN ORB...
ROLL
ALSO HAD ONE OF ZELEBURG'S MINIONS STANDING IN OUR WAY.
BA-
BA-
BWOH
BA-
I DOUBT THIS ORB WILL BE ANY EXCEPTION.
RIGHT.
THEY MAY ALREADY HAVE MADE THEIR MOVE.
CHATTER
CHATTER
WHAT?!
WHAT ARE YOU SAYING?!
I'VE DETER-MINED THAT THE ORB IS IN THIS NATION.
BUT THE SIGNAL I'M RECEIVING IS STILL VERY WEAK.
SCOOOOP
SCOOOOP

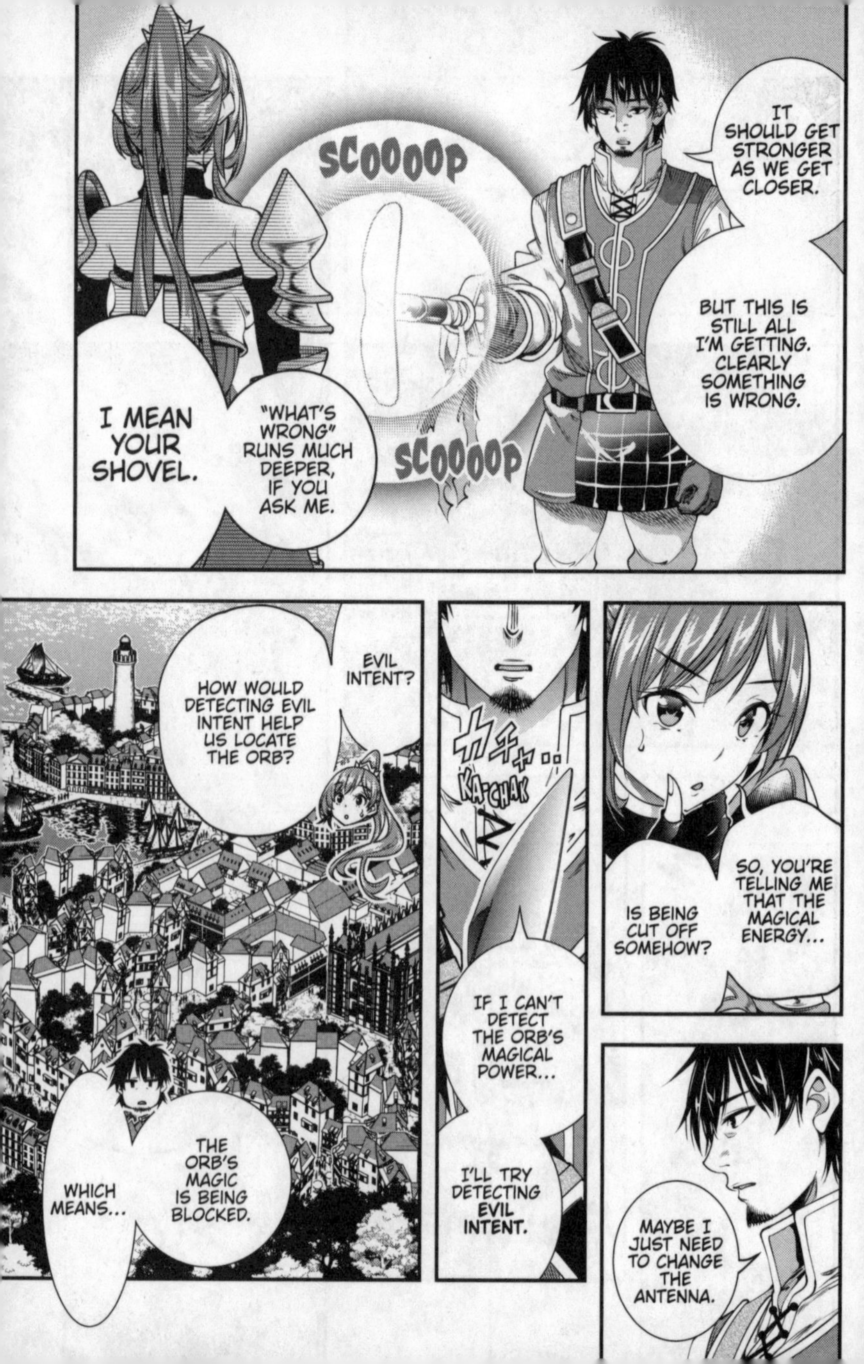
IT SHOULD GET STRONGER AS WE GET CLOSER.
SCOOOOP
BUT THIS IS STILL ALL I'M GETTING. CLEARLY SOMETHING IS WRONG.
SCOOOOP
"WHAT'S WRONG" RUNS MUCH DEEPER, IF YOU ASK ME.
I MEAN YOUR SHOVEL.
SO, YOU'RE TELLING ME THAT THE MAGICAL ENERGY...
IS BEING CUT OFF SOMEHOW?
MAYBE I JUST NEED TO CHANGE THE ANTENNA.
KA-CHAK
IF I CAN'T DETECT THE ORB'S MAGICAL POWER...
I'LL TRY DETECTING EVIL INTENT.
EVIL INTENT?
HOW WOULD DETECTING EVIL INTENT HELP US LOCATE THE ORB?
THE ORB'S MAGIC IS BEING BLOCKED.
WHICH MEANS...

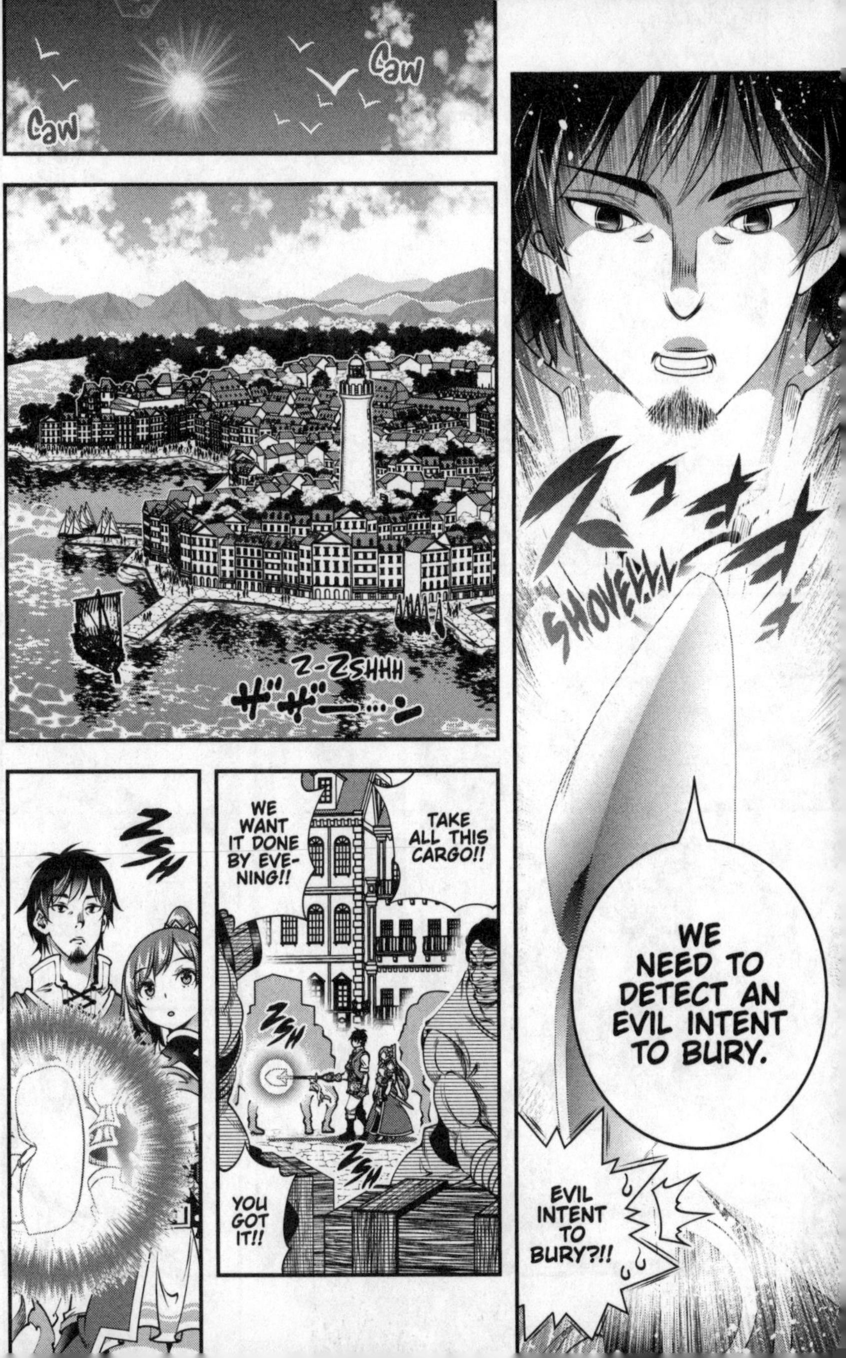
SHOVELLL
WE NEED TO DETECT AN EVIL INTENT TO BURY.
EVIL INTENT TO BURY?!!
CAW
CAW
Z-ZSHHH
ザザーー…ン
TAKE ALL THIS CARGO!!
WE WANT IT DONE BY EVE-NING!!
ZSH
ZSH
YOU GOT IT!!
ZSH

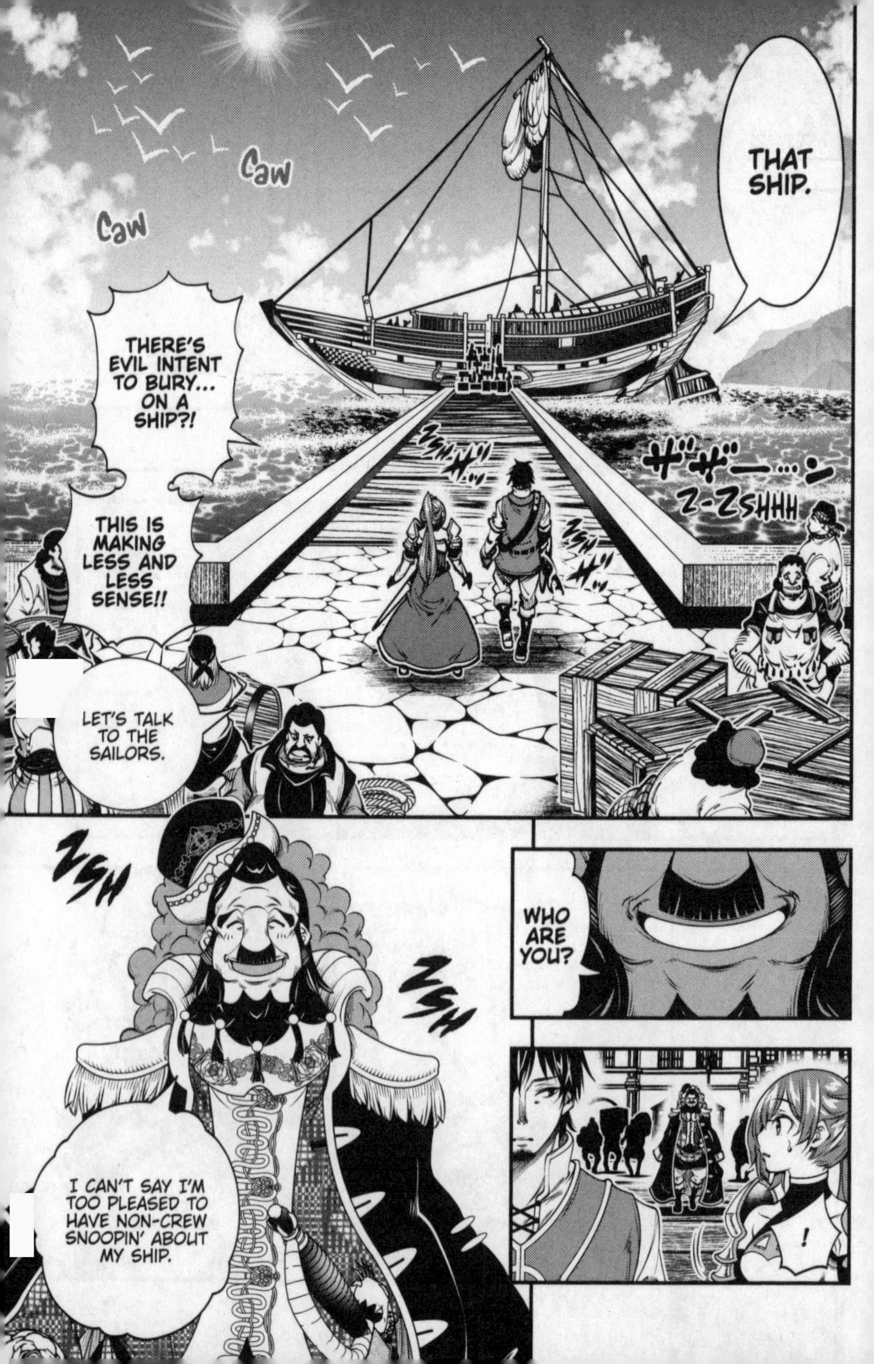
THAT SHIP.
Caw
Caw
ザザーン…ン
Z-ZSHHH
THERE'S EVIL INTENT TO BURY... ON A SHIP?!
ZSH ZSH
ZSH ZSH
THIS IS MAKING LESS AND LESS SENSE!!
LET'S TALK TO THE SAILORS.
WHO ARE YOU?
!
ZSH
ZSH
I CAN'T SAY I'M TOO PLEASED TO HAVE NON-CREW SNOOPIN' ABOUT MY SHIP.

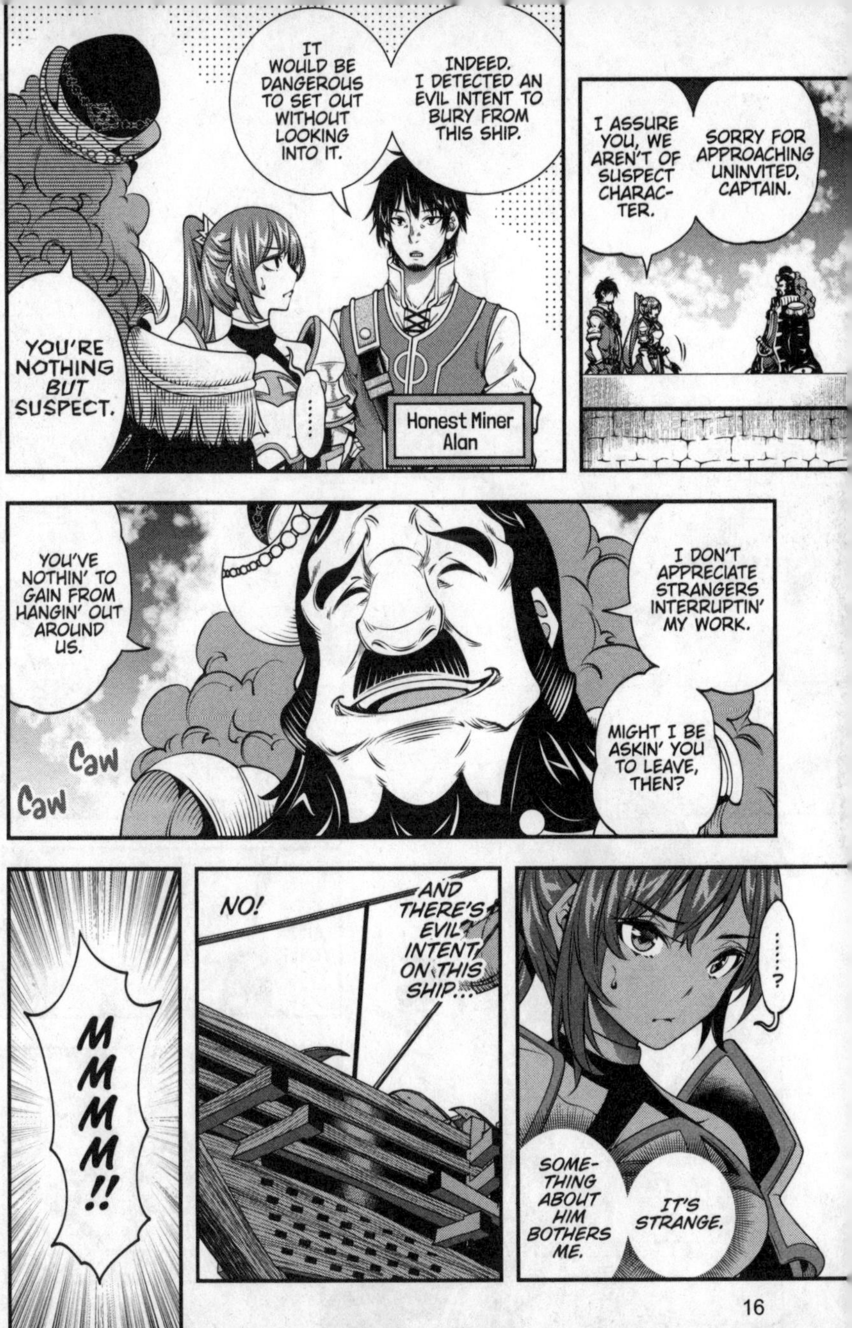
SORRY FOR APPROACHING UNINVITED, CAPTAIN.
I ASSURE YOU, WE AREN'T OF SUSPECT CHARAC-TER.
INDEED. I DETECTED AN EVIL INTENT TO BURY FROM THIS SHIP.
IT WOULD BE DANGEROUS TO SET OUT WITHOUT LOOKING INTO IT.
Honest Miner Alan
......
YOU'RE NOTHING BUT SUSPECT.
I DON'T APPRECIATE STRANGERS INTERRUPTIN' MY WORK.
MIGHT I BE ASKIN' YOU TO LEAVE, THEN?
YOU'VE NOTHIN' TO GAIN FROM HANGIN' OUT AROUND US.
Caw
Caw
......?
IT'S STRANGE.
SOME-THING ABOUT HIM BOTHERS ME.
AND THERE'S EVIL INTENT ON THIS SHIP...
NO!
MMMMM!!

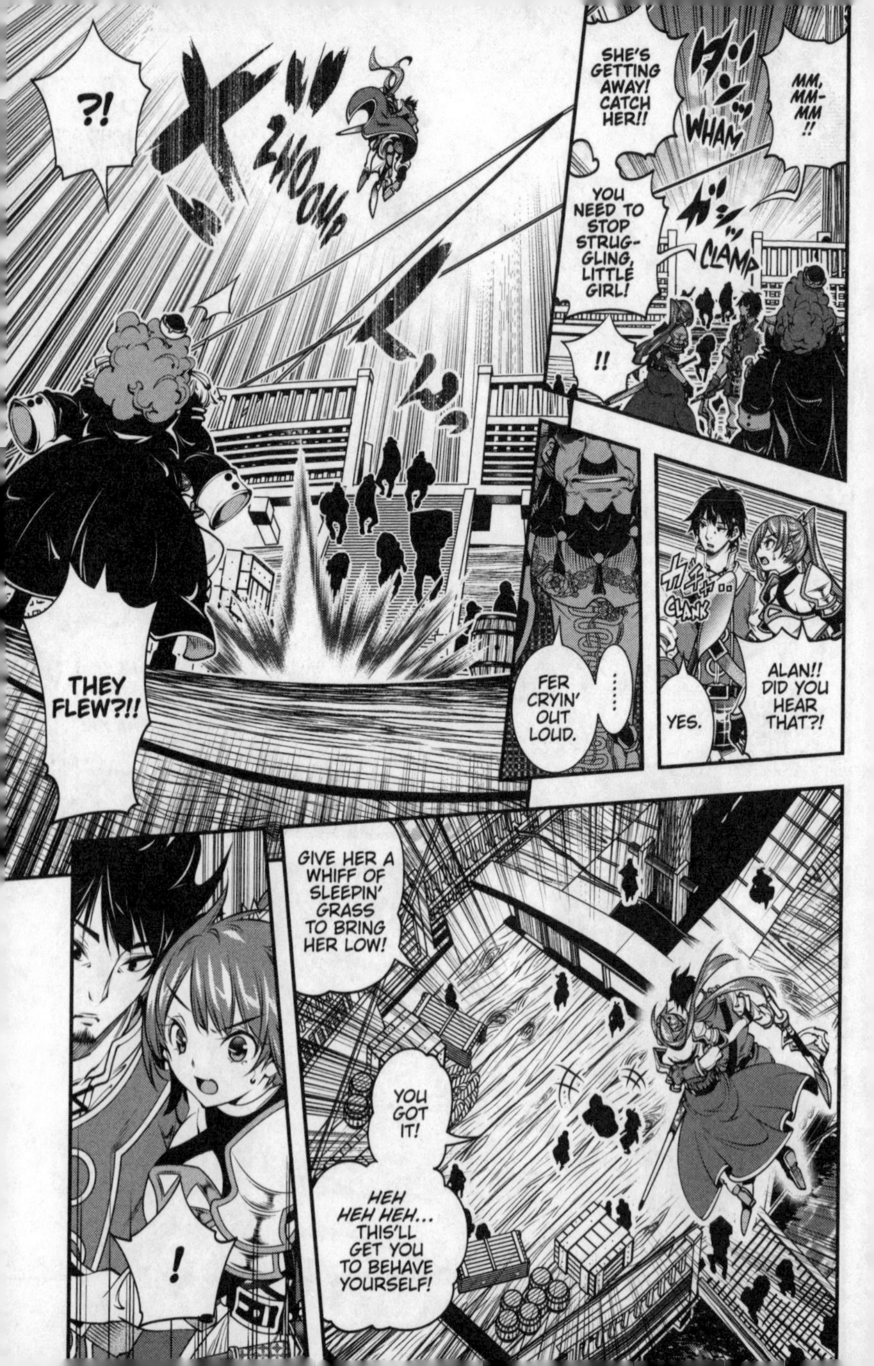
MM, MM-MM!!
WHAM
SHE'S GETTING AWAY! CATCH HER!!
YOU NEED TO STOP STRUG-GLING, LITTLE GIRL!
CLAMP
!!
ALAN!! DID YOU HEAR THAT?!
CLANK
YES.
......
FER CRYIN' OUT LOUD.
?!
ZWOOMP
THEY FLEW?!!
GIVE HER A WHIFF OF SLEEPIN' GRASS TO BRING HER LOW!
YOU GOT IT!
HEH HEH HEH... THIS'LL GET YOU TO BEHAVE YOURSELF!
!

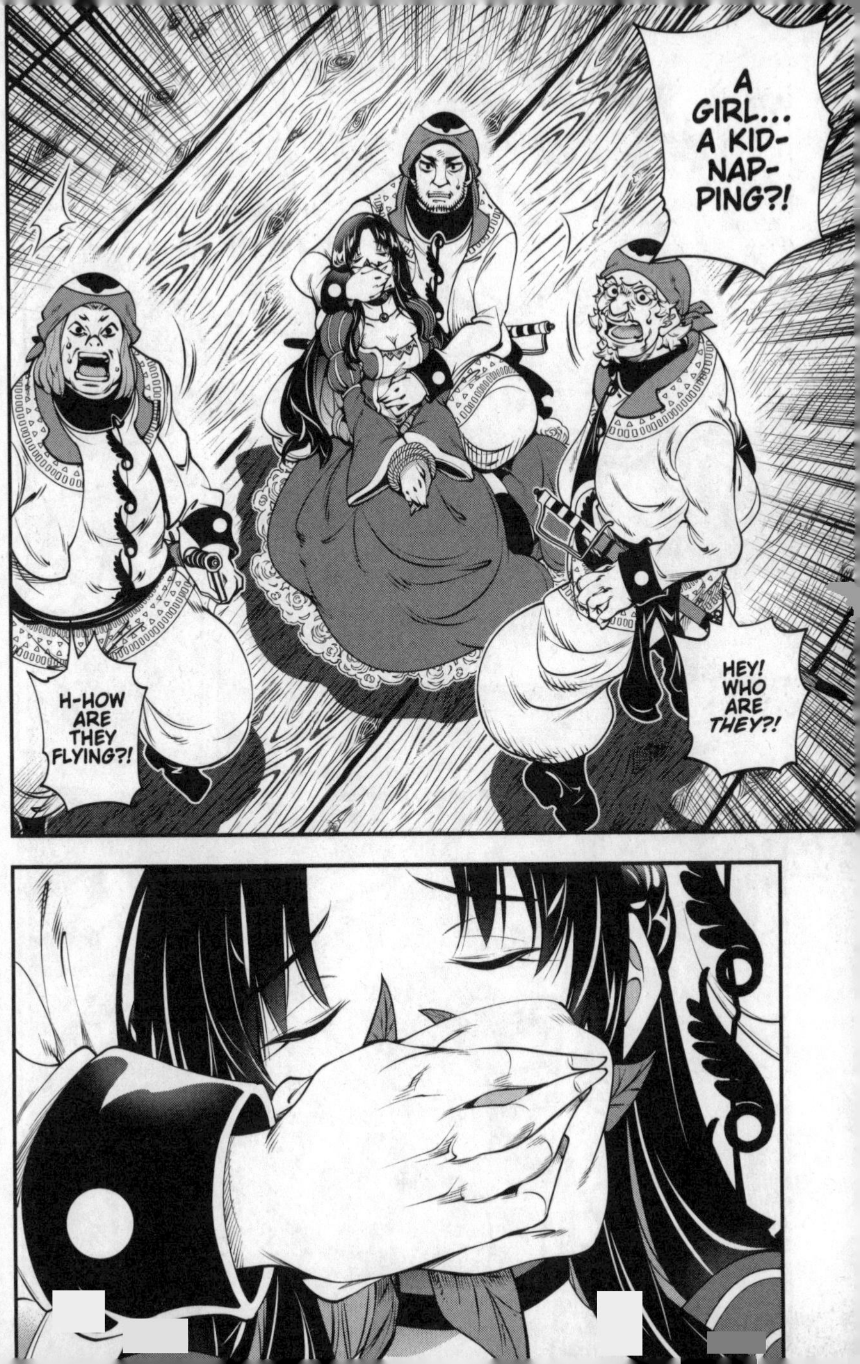
A GIRL... A KID-NAP-PING?!
HEY! WHO ARE THEY?!
H-HOW ARE THEY FLYING?!

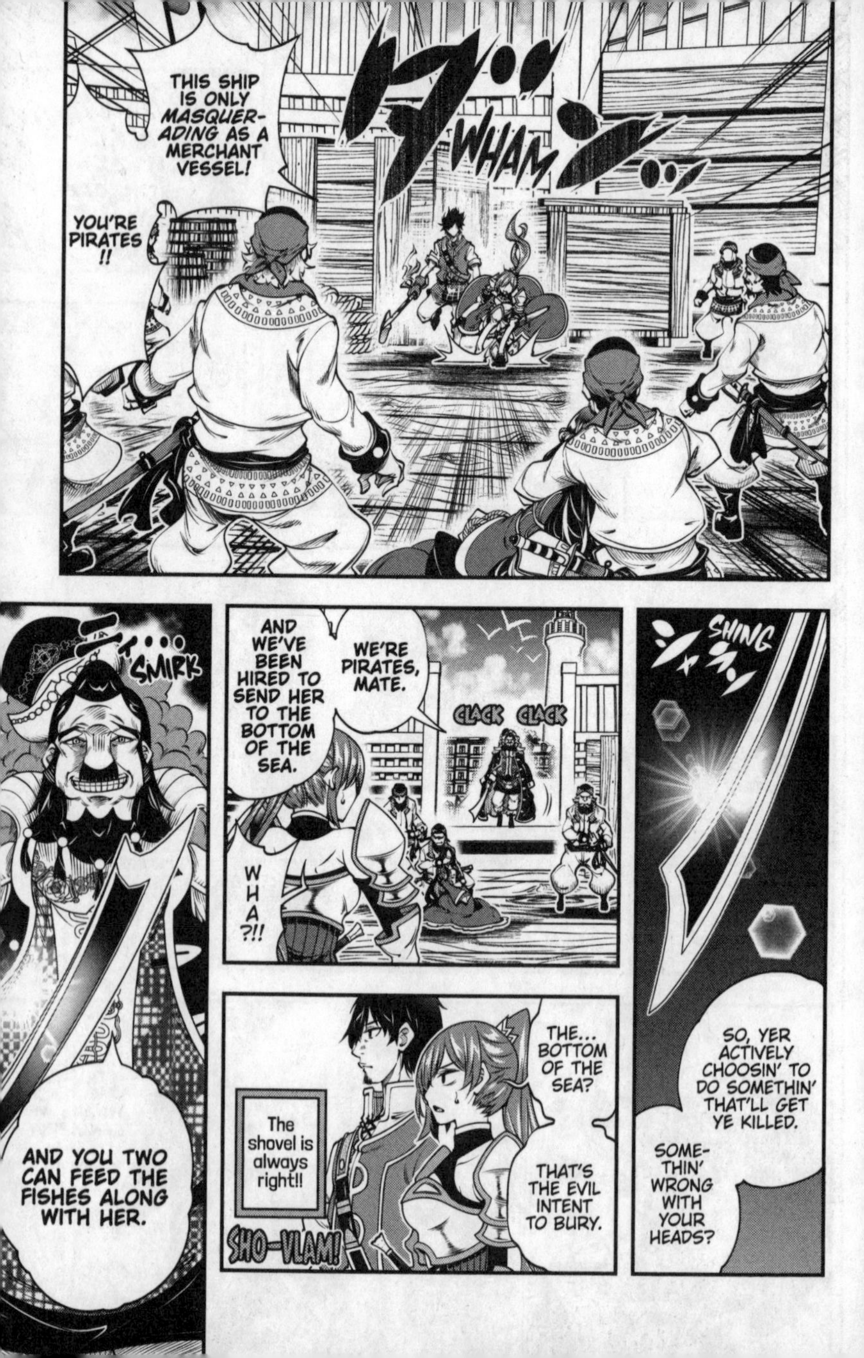
WHAM
THIS SHIP IS ONLY MASQUERADING AS A MERCHANT VESSEL!
YOU'RE PIRATES!!
SHING
SO, YER ACTIVELY CHOOSIN' TO DO SOMETHIN' THAT'LL GET YE KILLED.
SOMETHIN' WRONG WITH YOUR HEADS?
WE'RE PIRATES, MATE.
AND WE'VE BEEN HIRED TO SEND HER TO THE BOTTOM OF THE SEA.
CLACK CLACK
WHA?!!
THE... BOTTOM OF THE SEA?
THAT'S THE EVIL INTENT TO BURY.
The shovel is always right!!
SHO-VLAM!
SMIRK
AND YOU TWO CAN FEED THE FISHES ALONG WITH HER.

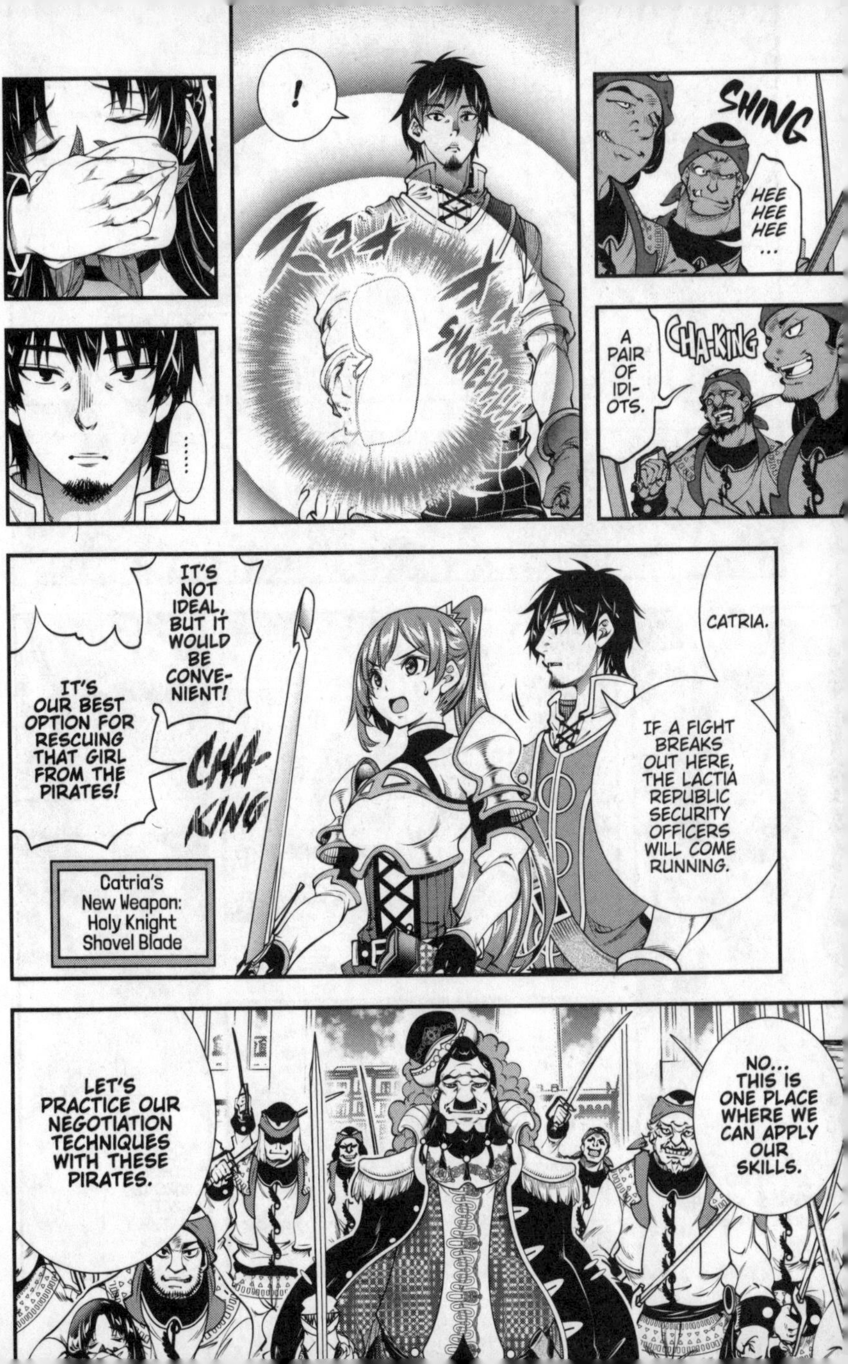
SHING
HEE HEE HEE ...
CHA-KING
A PAIR OF IDI-OTS.
!
......
CATRIA.
IF A FIGHT BREAKS OUT HERE, THE LACTIA REPUBLIC SECURITY OFFICERS WILL COME RUNNING.
IT'S NOT IDEAL, BUT IT WOULD BE CONVE-NIENT!
CHA-KING
IT'S OUR BEST OPTION FOR RESCUING THAT GIRL FROM THE PIRATES!
Catria's New Weapon: Holy Knight Shovel Blade
NO... THIS IS ONE PLACE WHERE WE CAN APPLY OUR SKILLS.
LET'S PRACTICE OUR NEGOTIATION TECHNIQUES WITH THESE PIRATES.

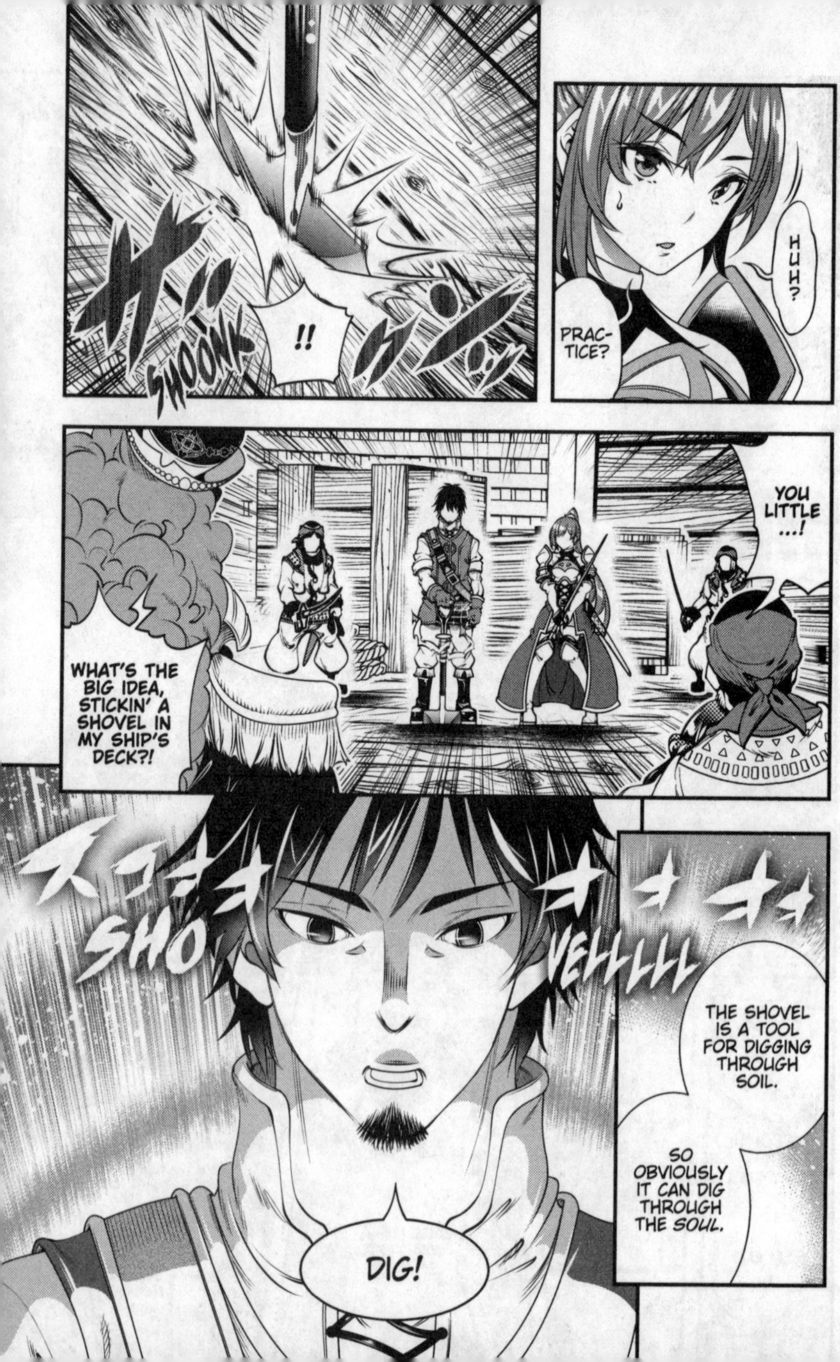
HUH?
PRAC-TICE?
SHOONK
!!
YOU LITTLE ...!
WHAT'S THE BIG IDEA, STICKIN' A SHOVEL IN MY SHIP'S DECK?!
THE SHOVEL IS A TOOL FOR DIGGING THROUGH SOIL.
SO OBVIOUSLY IT CAN DIG THROUGH THE SOUL.
SHOVELLLLL
DIG!

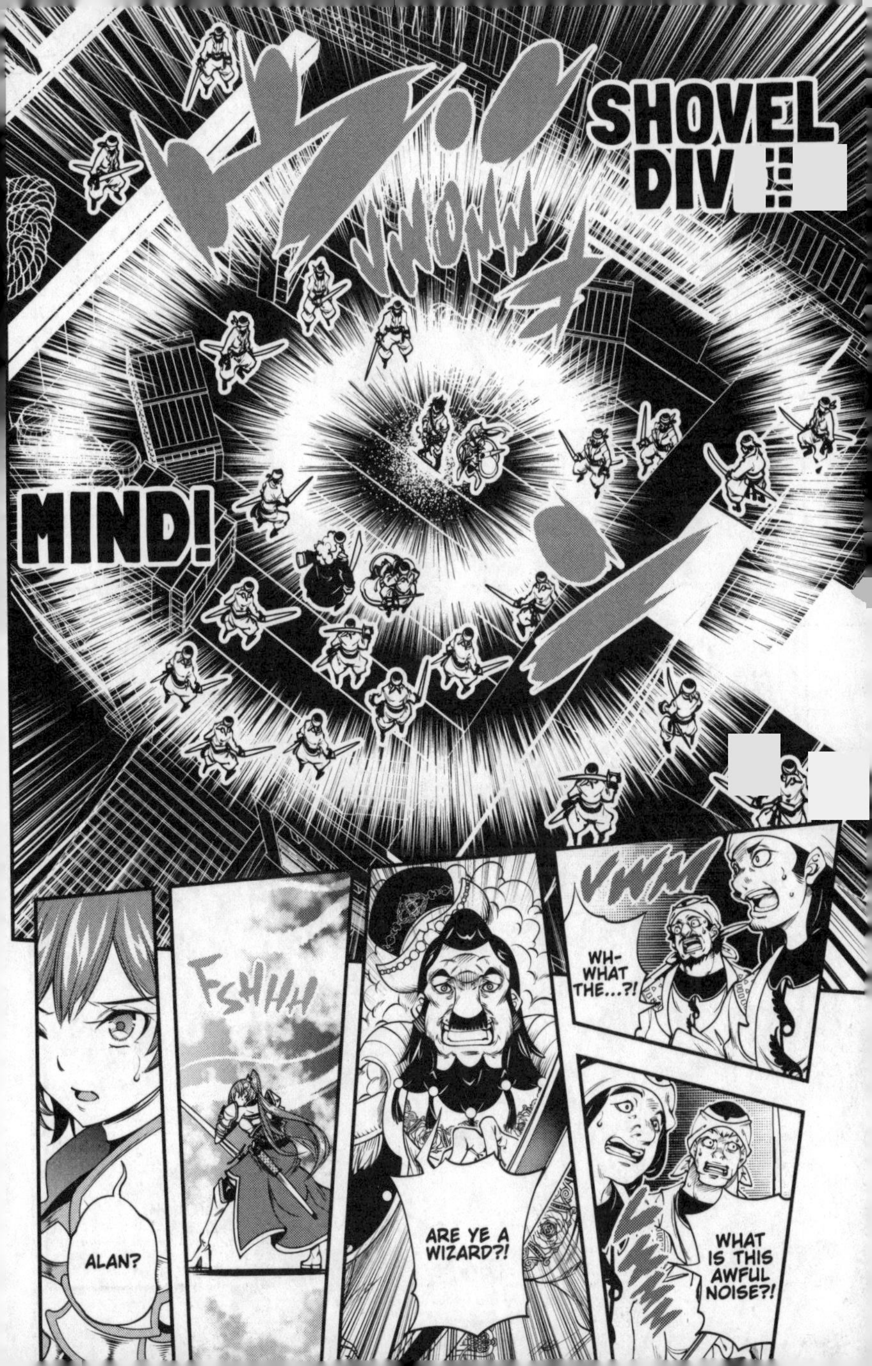
SHOVEL DIV
MIND!
VWM
WH-WHAT THE...?!
WHAT IS THIS AWFUL NOISE?!
VWMM
ARE YE A WIZARD?!
FSHHH
ALAN?

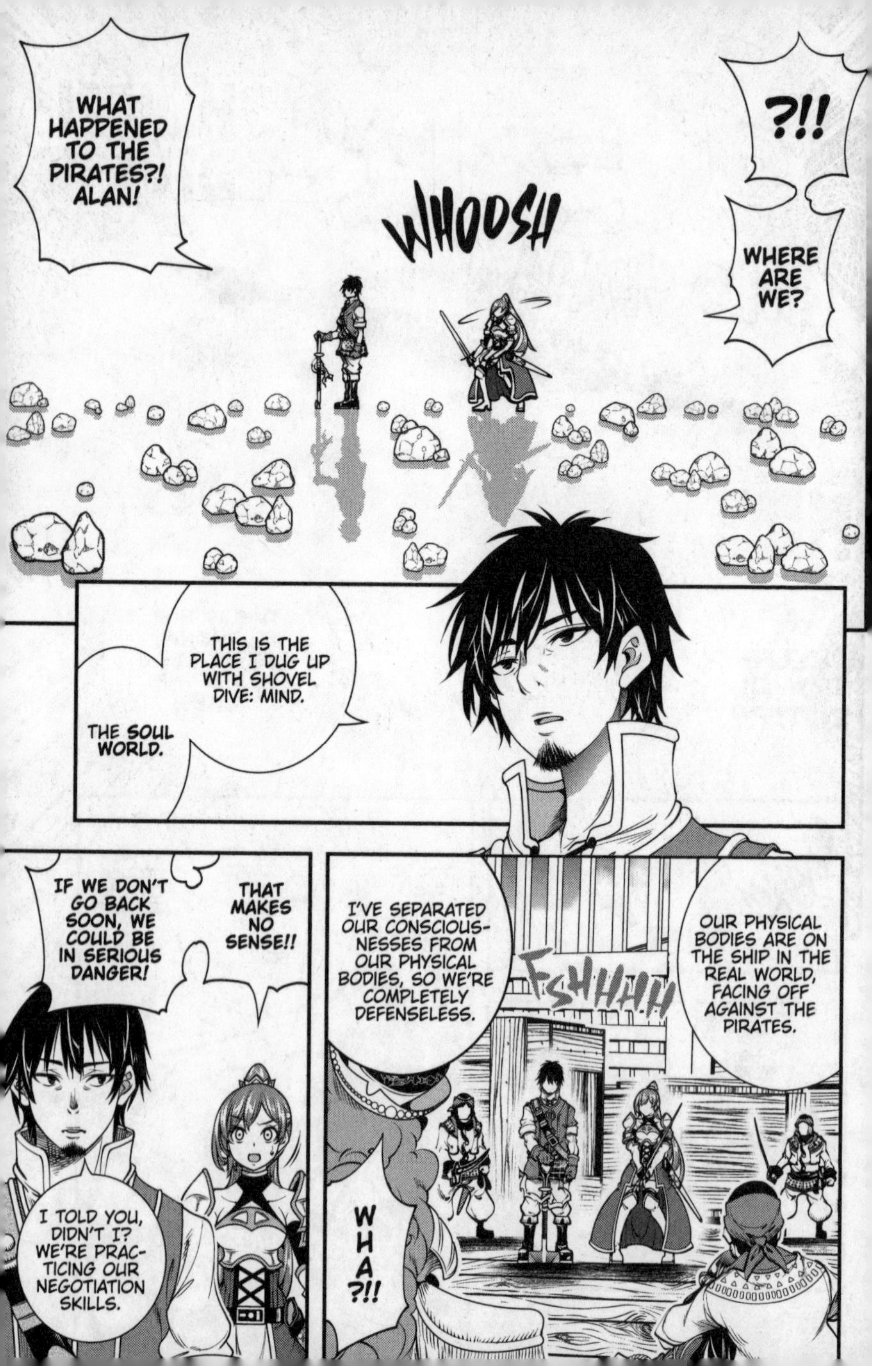
?!!
WHERE ARE WE?
WHOOSH
WHAT HAPPENED TO THE PIRATES?! ALAN!
THIS IS THE PLACE I DUG UP WITH SHOVEL DIVE: MIND.
THE SOUL WORLD.
OUR PHYSICAL BODIES ARE ON THE SHIP IN THE REAL WORLD, FACING OFF AGAINST THE PIRATES.
FSHHHHH
I'VE SEPARATED OUR CONSCIOUS-NESSES FROM OUR PHYSICAL BODIES, SO WE'RE COMPLETELY DEFENSELESS.
WHA?!!
THAT MAKES NO SENSE!!
IF WE DON'T GO BACK SOON, WE COULD BE IN SERIOUS DANGER!
I TOLD YOU, DIDN'T I? WE'RE PRAC-TICING OUR NEGOTIATION SKILLS.

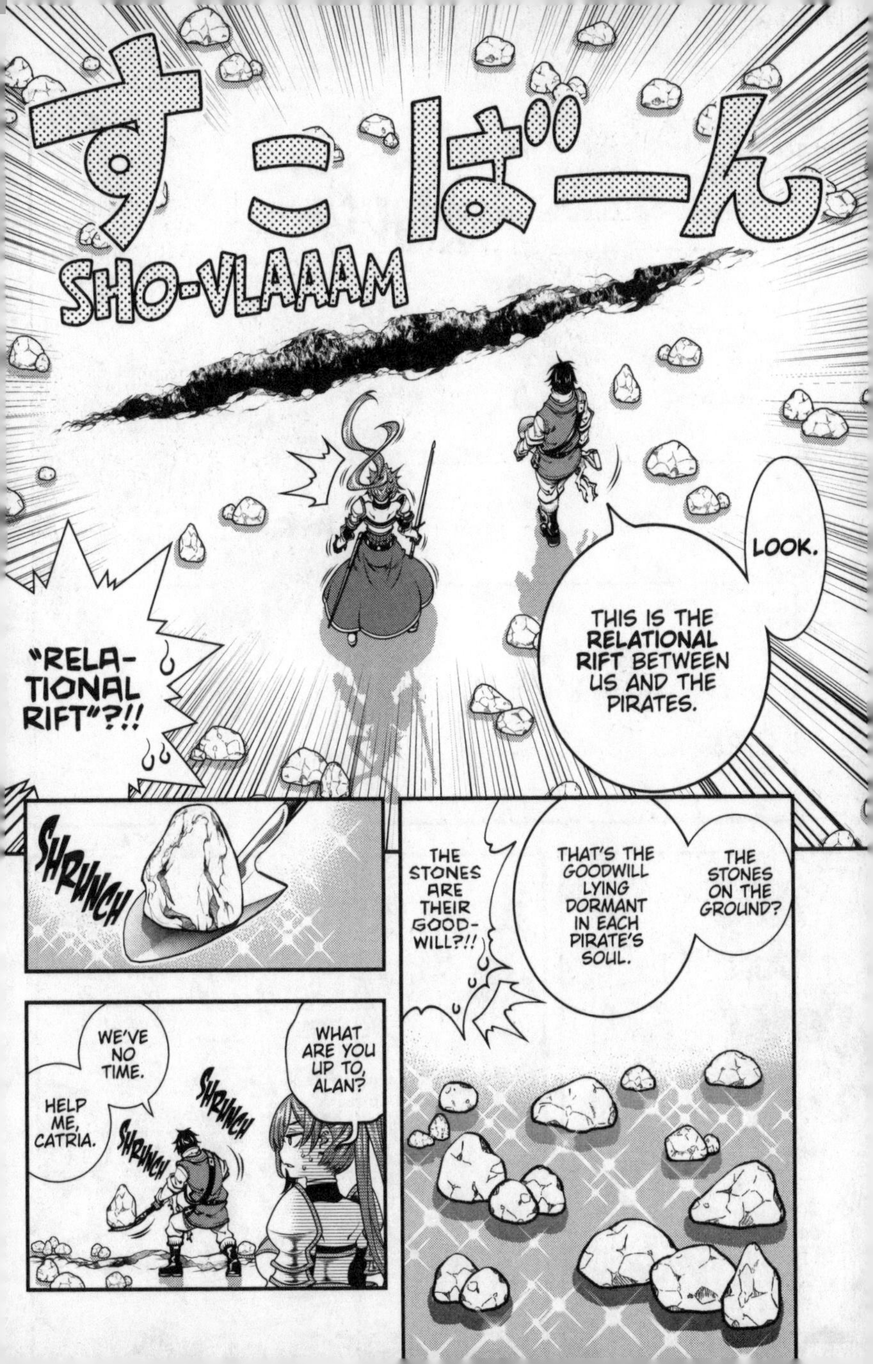
すこばーん
SHO-VLAAAM
LOOK.
THIS IS THE RELATIONAL RIFT BETWEEN US AND THE PIRATES.
"RELA-TIONAL RIFT"?!!
THE STONES ON THE GROUND?
THAT'S THE GOODWILL LYING DORMANT IN EACH PIRATE'S SOUL.
THE STONES ARE THEIR GOOD-WILL?!!
SHRUNCH
WHAT ARE YOU UP TO, ALAN?
WE'VE NO TIME.
HELP ME, CATRIA.
SHRUNCH
SHRUNCH

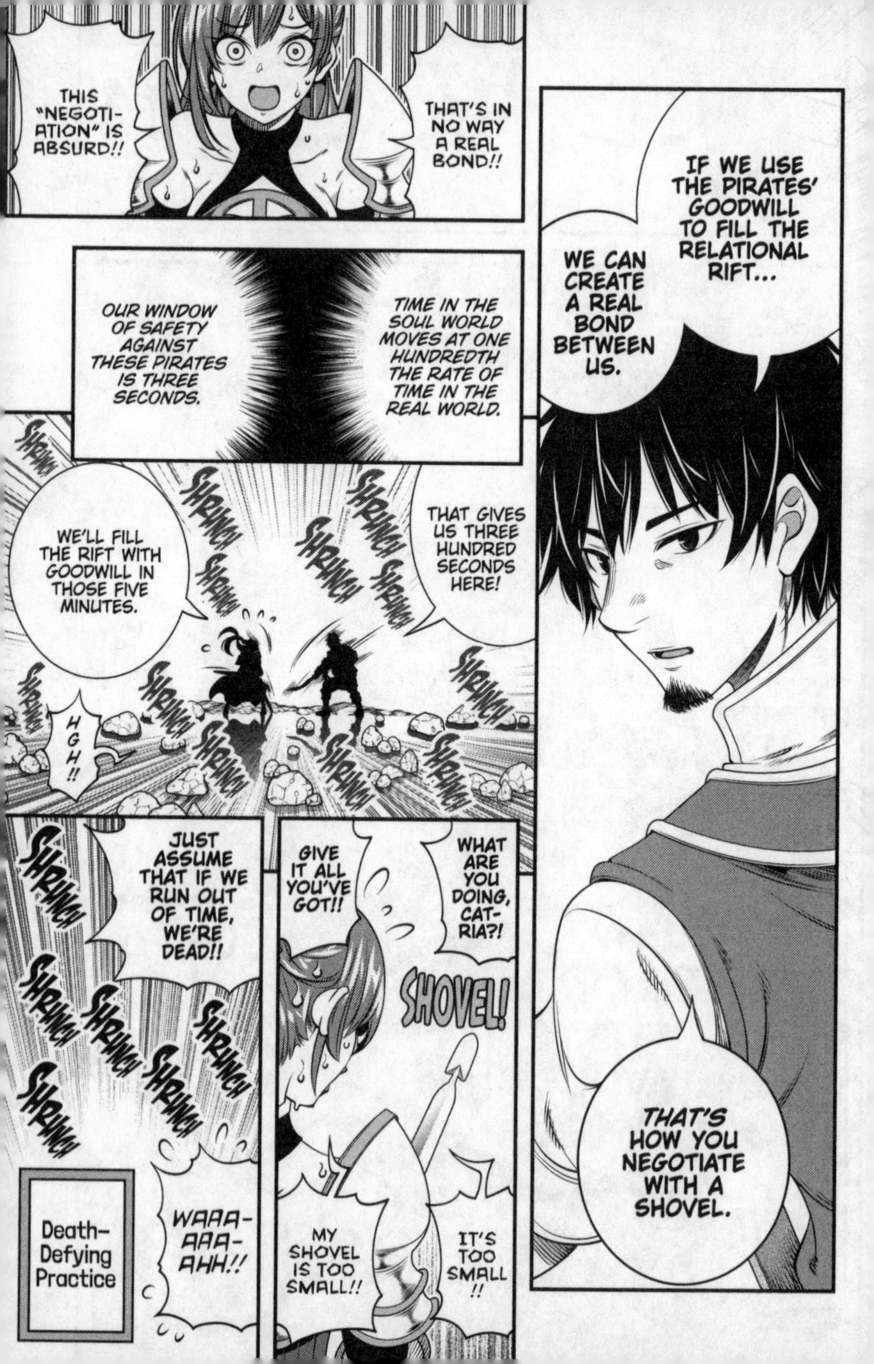
THAT'S IN NO WAY A REAL BOND!!
THIS "NEGOTI-ATION" IS ABSURD!!
IF WE USE THE PIRATES' GOODWILL TO FILL THE RELATIONAL RIFT...
WE CAN CREATE A REAL BOND BETWEEN US.
THAT'S HOW YOU NEGOTIATE WITH A SHOVEL.
TIME IN THE SOUL WORLD MOVES AT ONE HUNDREDTH THE RATE OF TIME IN THE REAL WORLD.
OUR WINDOW OF SAFETY AGAINST THESE PIRATES IS THREE SECONDS.
SHRUNCH
SHRUNCH
SHRUNCH
THAT GIVES US THREE HUNDRED SECONDS HERE!
WE'LL FILL THE RIFT WITH GOODWILL IN THOSE FIVE MINUTES.
SHRUNCH
SHRUNCH
SHRUNCH
HGH!!
WHAT ARE YOU DOING, CAT-RIA?!
GIVE IT ALL YOU'VE GOT!!
SHOVEL!
IT'S TOO SMALL!!
MY SHOVEL IS TOO SMALL!!
JUST ASSUME THAT IF WE RUN OUT OF TIME, WE'RE DEAD!!
SHRUNCH
SHRUNCH
SHRUNCH
WAAA-AAA-AHH!!
Death-Defying Practice

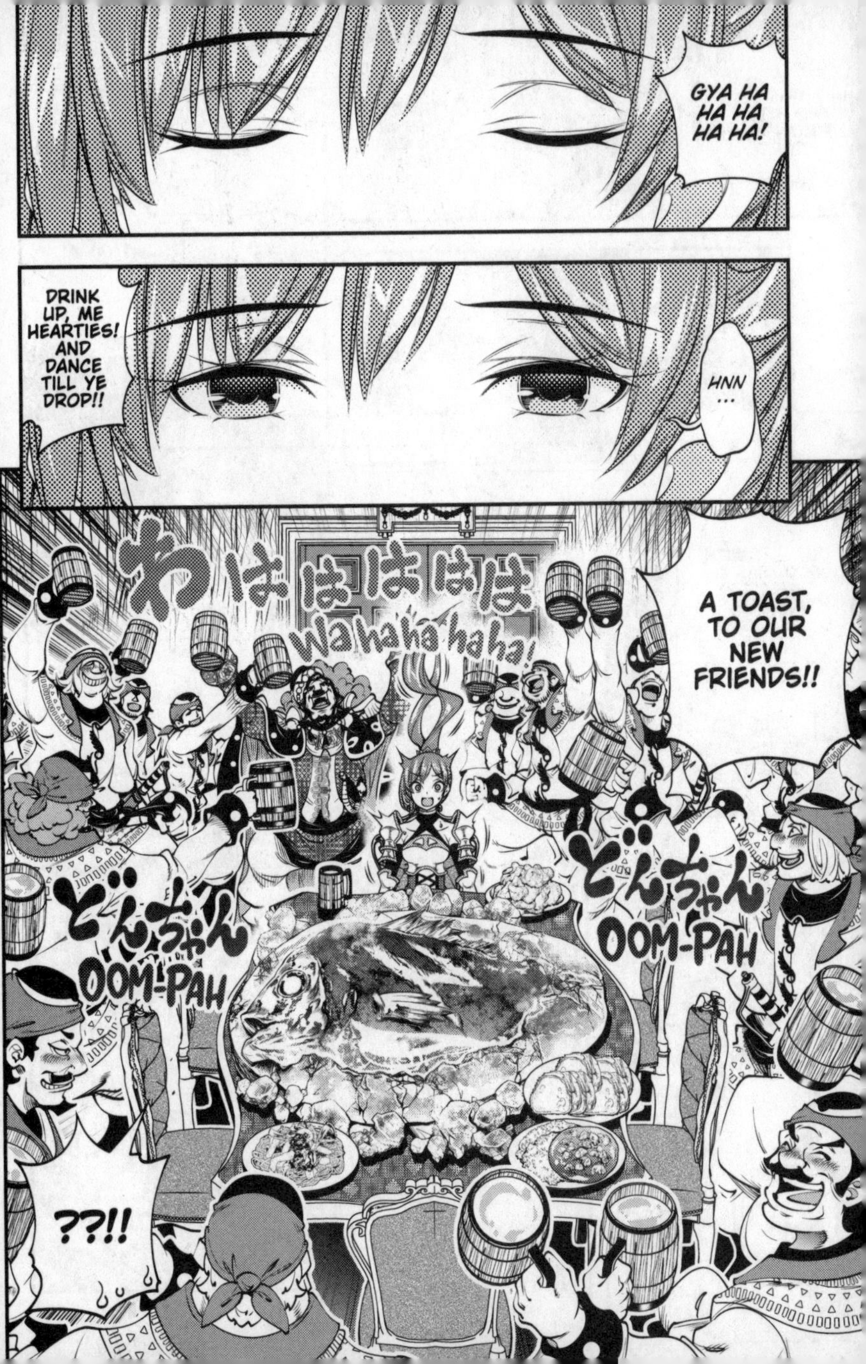
GYA HA HA HA HA HA!
DRINK UP, ME HEARTIES! AND DANCE TILL YE DROP!!
HNN ...
A TOAST, TO OUR NEW FRIENDS!!
わははははは
Wahahahaha!
どんちゃん
OOM-PAH
どんちゃん
OOM-PAH
??!!

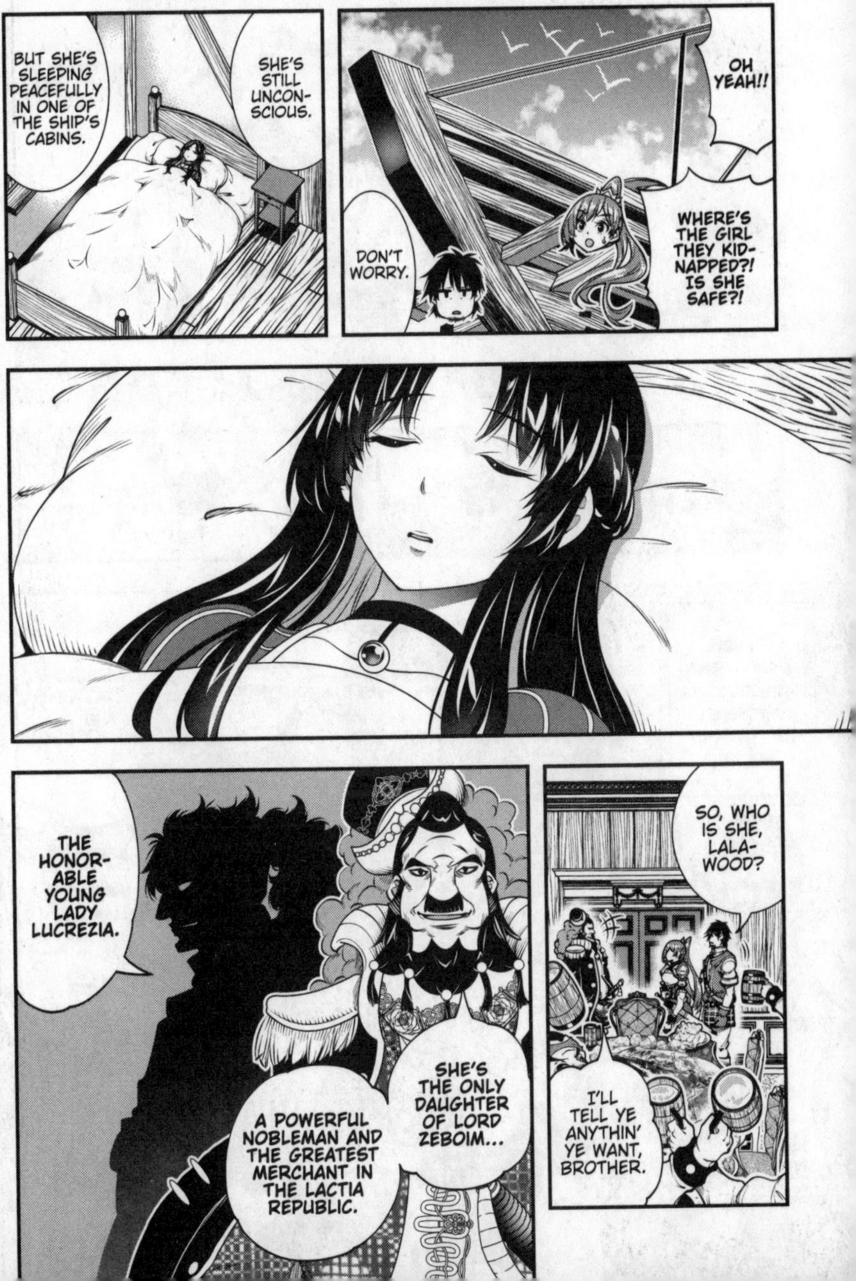
OH YEAH!!
WHERE'S THE GIRL THEY KID-NAPPED?! IS SHE SAFE?!
DON'T WORRY.
SHE'S STILL UNCON-SCIOUS.
BUT SHE'S SLEEPING PEACEFULLY IN ONE OF THE SHIP'S CABINS.
SO, WHO IS SHE, LALA-WOOD?
I'LL TELL YE ANYTHIN' YE WANT, BROTHER.
THE HONOR-ABLE YOUNG LADY LUCREZIA.
SHE'S THE ONLY DAUGHTER OF LORD ZEBOIM...
A POWERFUL NOBLEMAN AND THE GREATEST MERCHANT IN THE LACTIA REPUBLIC.

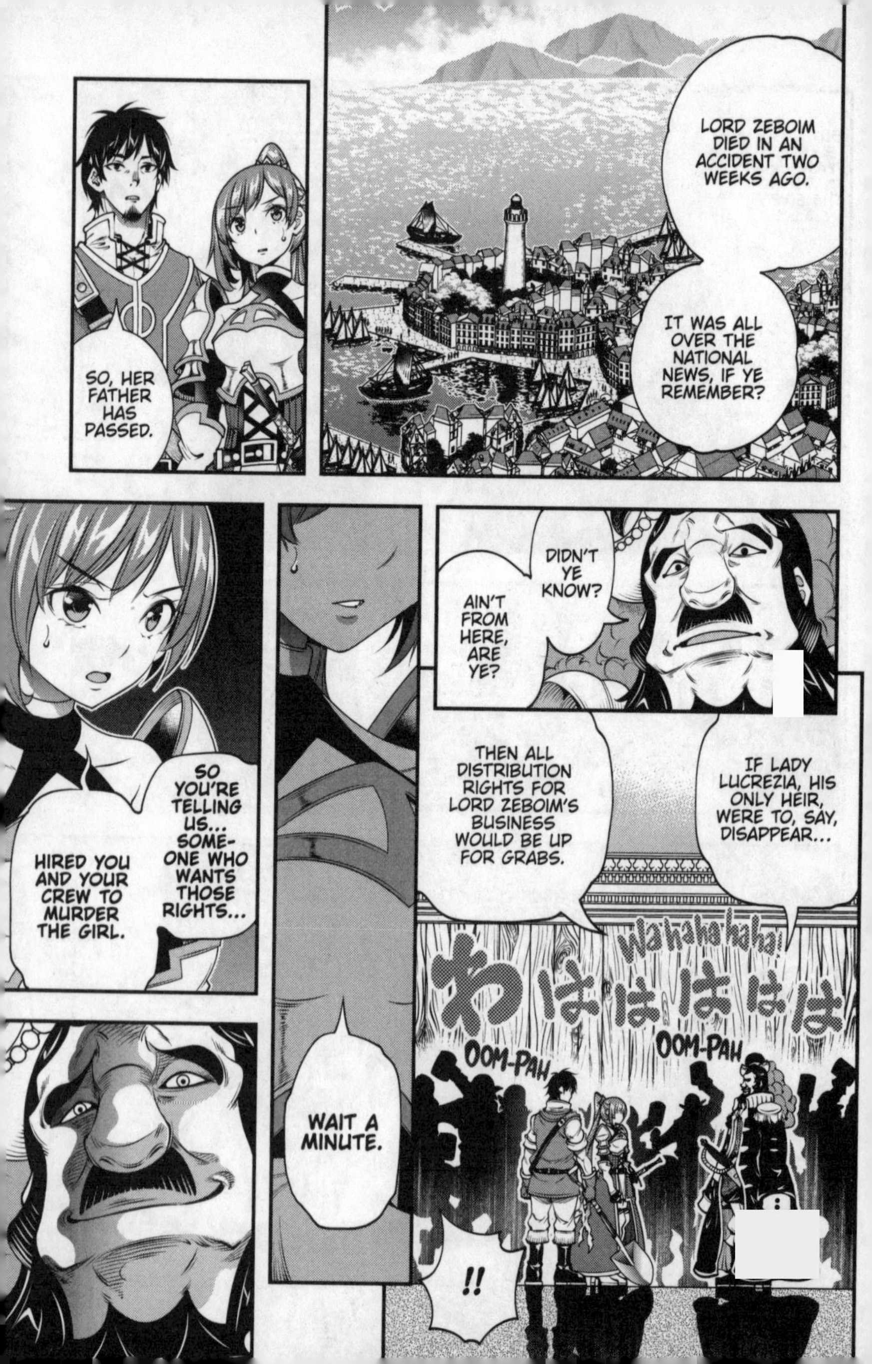
LORD ZEBOIM DIED IN AN ACCIDENT TWO WEEKS AGO.
IT WAS ALL OVER THE NATIONAL NEWS, IF YE REMEMBER?
SO, HER FATHER HAS PASSED.
DIDN'T YE KNOW?
AIN'T FROM HERE, ARE YE?
IF LADY LUCREZIA, HIS ONLY HEIR, WERE TO, SAY, DISAPPEAR...
THEN ALL DISTRIBUTION RIGHTS FOR LORD ZEBOIM'S BUSINESS WOULD BE UP FOR GRABS.
わははははは
Wa ha ha ha ha!
OOM-PAH
OOM-PAH
WAIT A MINUTE.
!!
SO YOU'RE TELLING US... SOME-ONE WHO WANTS THOSE RIGHTS...
HIRED YOU AND YOUR CREW TO MURDER THE GIRL.

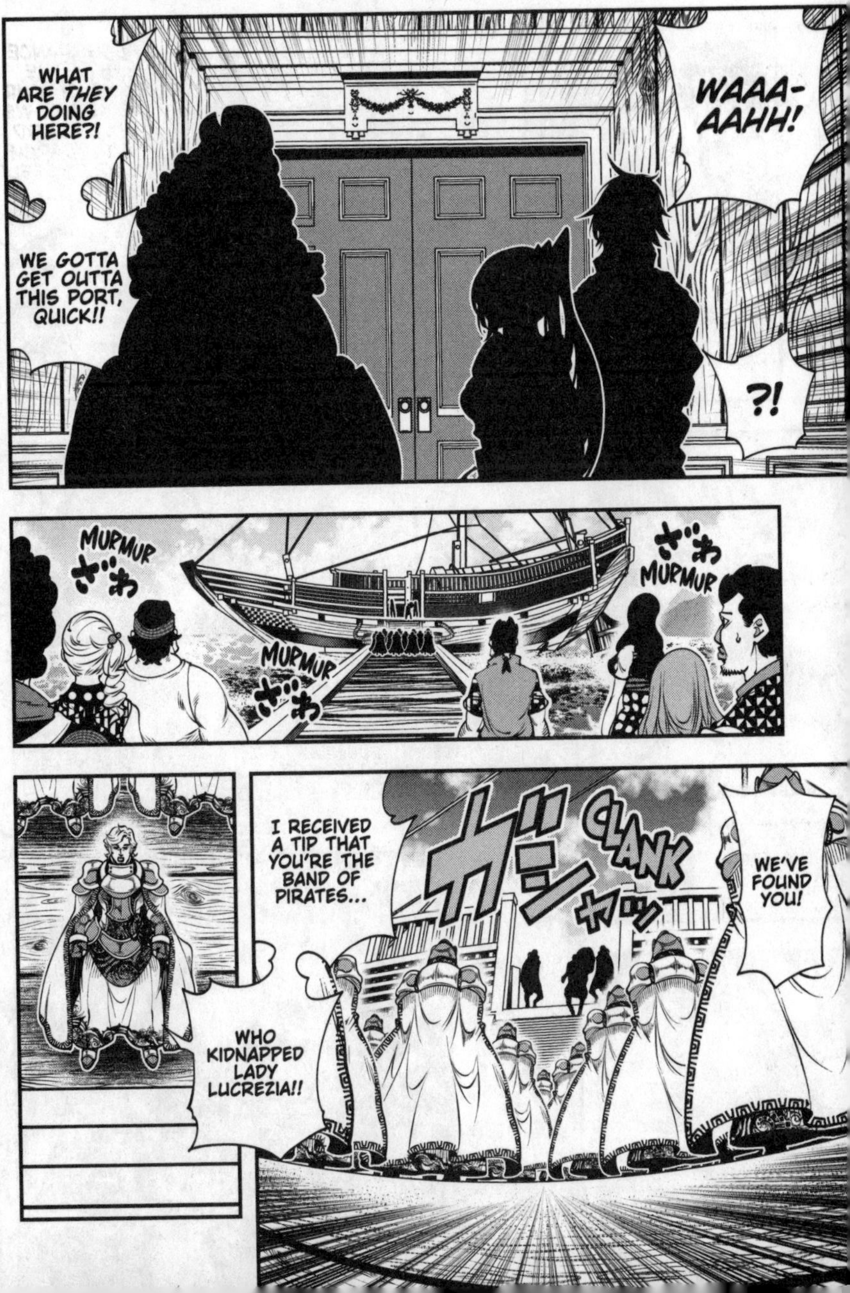
WAAA-AAHH!
WHAT ARE THEY DOING HERE?!
?!
WE GOTTA GET OUTTA THIS PORT, QUICK!!
ざわ MURMUR
MURMUR ざわ
MURMUR ざわ
WE'VE FOUND YOU!
CLANK ガシャッ
I RECEIVED A TIP THAT YOU'RE THE BAND OF PIRATES...
WHO KIDNAPPED LADY LUCREZIA!!

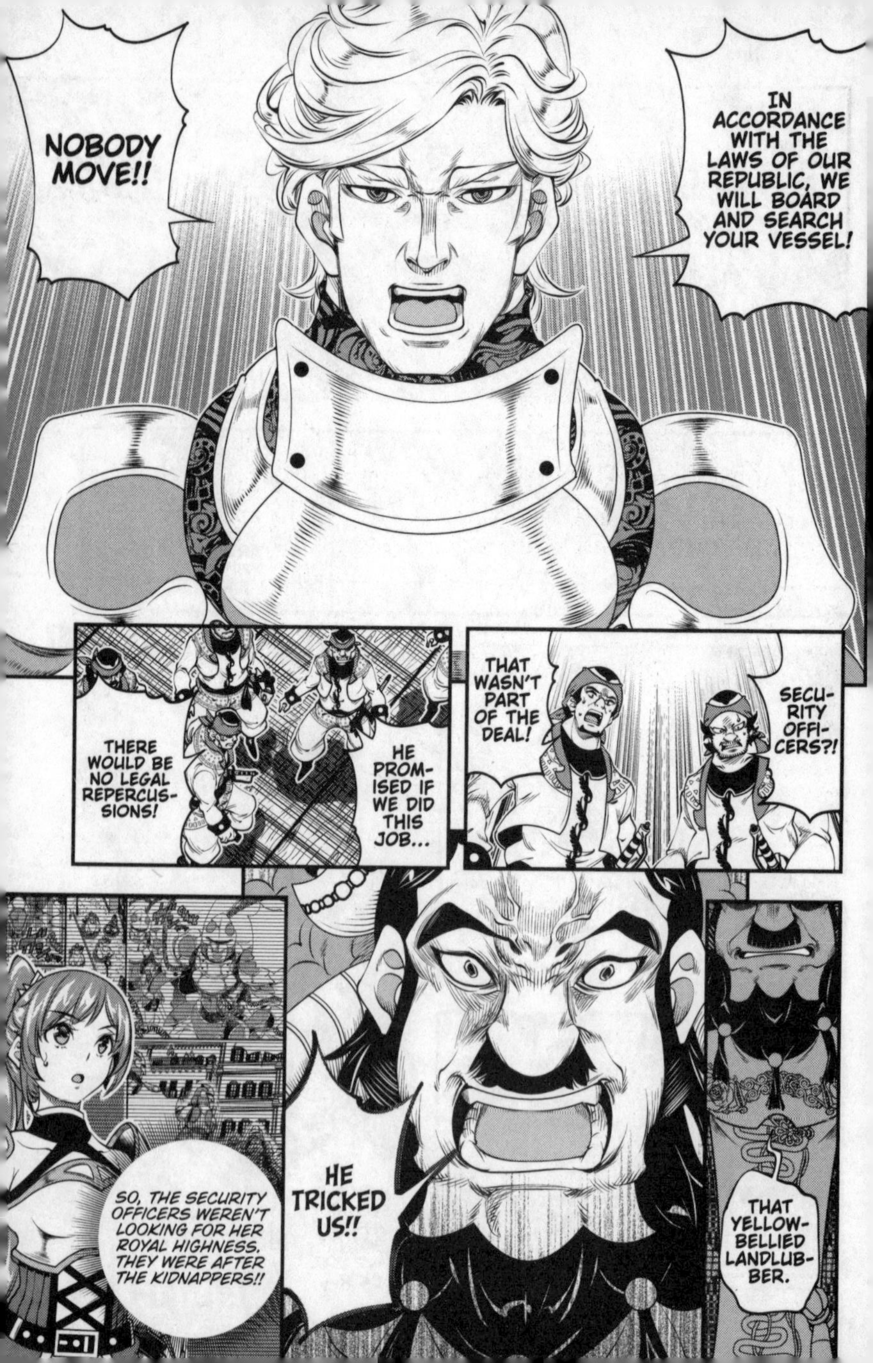
IN ACCORDANCE WITH THE LAWS OF OUR REPUBLIC, WE WILL BOARD AND SEARCH YOUR VESSEL!
NOBODY MOVE!!
SECU-RITY OFFI-CERS?!
THAT WASN'T PART OF THE DEAL!
HE PROM-ISED IF WE DID THIS JOB...
THERE WOULD BE NO LEGAL REPERCUS-SIONS!
THAT YELLOW-BELLIED LANDLUB-BER.
HE TRICKED US!!
SO, THE SECURITY OFFICERS WEREN'T LOOKING FOR HER ROYAL HIGHNESS. THEY WERE AFTER THE KIDNAPPERS!!

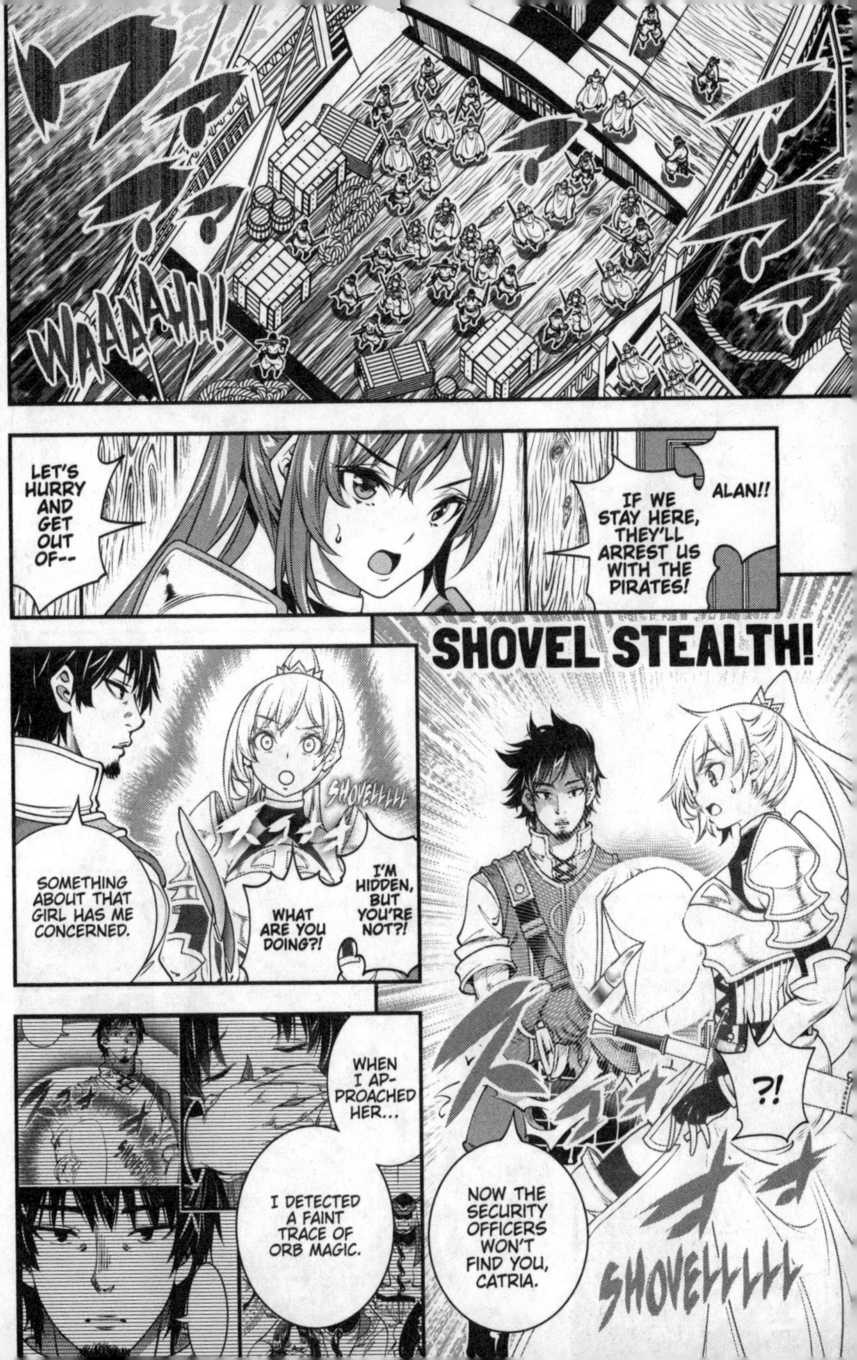
WAAAAHH!
ALAN!!
IF WE STAY HERE, THEY'LL ARREST US WITH THE PIRATES!
LET'S HURRY AND GET OUT OF--
SHOVEL STEALTH!
?!
NOW THE SECURITY OFFICERS WON'T FIND YOU, CATRIA.
SHOVELLLLL
SHOVELLLLL
I'M HIDDEN, BUT YOU'RE NOT?!
WHAT ARE YOU DOING?!
SOMETHING ABOUT THAT GIRL HAS ME CONCERNED.
WHEN I APPROACHED HER...
I DETECTED A FAINT TRACE OF ORB MAGIC.

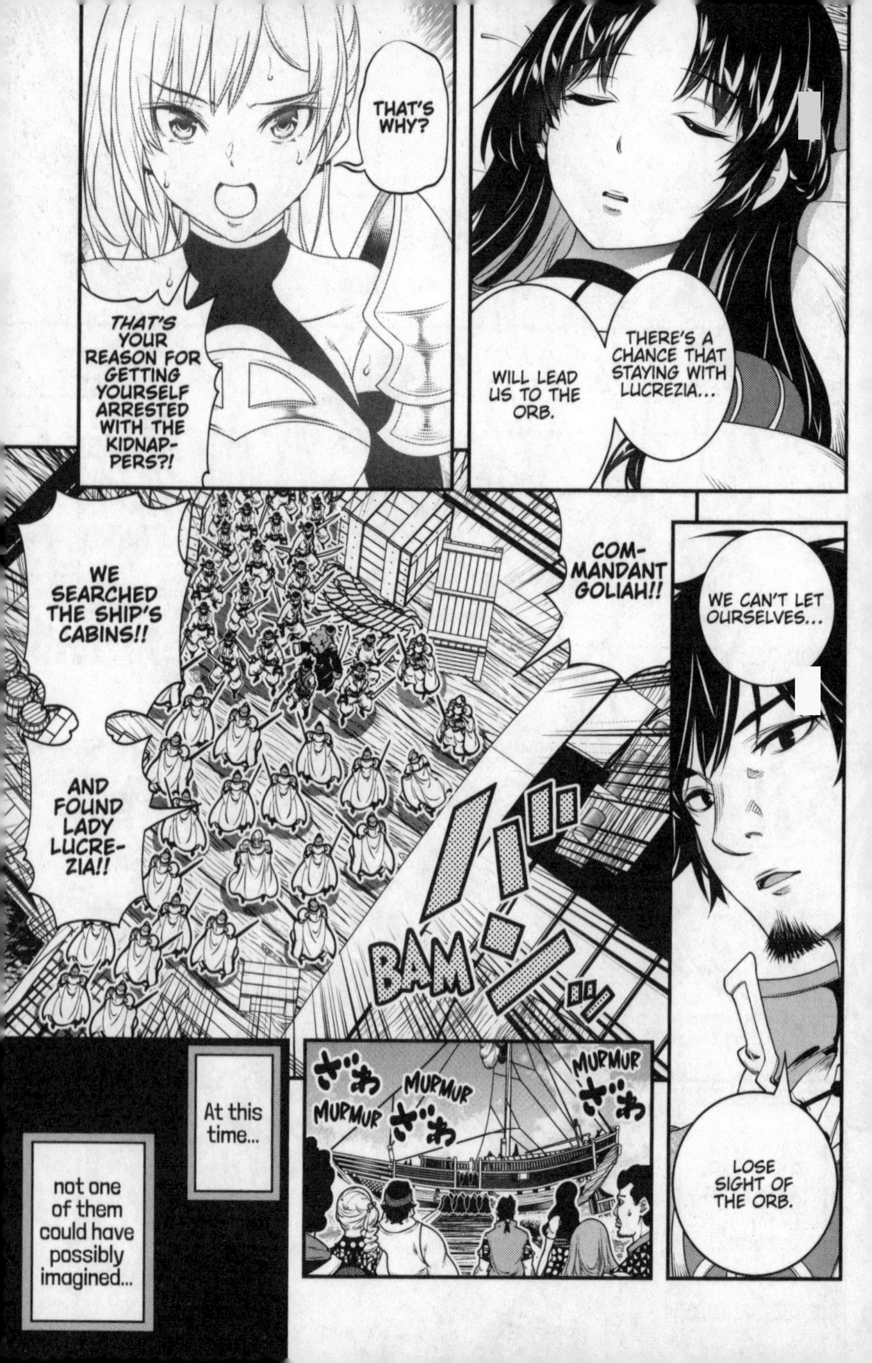
THERE'S A CHANCE THAT STAYING WITH LUCREZIA...
WILL LEAD US TO THE ORB.
THAT'S WHY?
THAT'S YOUR REASON FOR GETTING YOURSELF ARRESTED WITH THE KIDNAP-PERS?!
WE CAN'T LET OURSELVES...
LOSE SIGHT OF THE ORB.
COM-MANDANT GOLIAH!!
WE SEARCHED THE SHIP'S CABINS!!
AND FOUND LADY LUCRE-ZIA!!
BAM
MURMUR
ざわ
MURMUR
ざわ
MURMUR
ざわ
At this time...
not one of them could have possibly imagined...

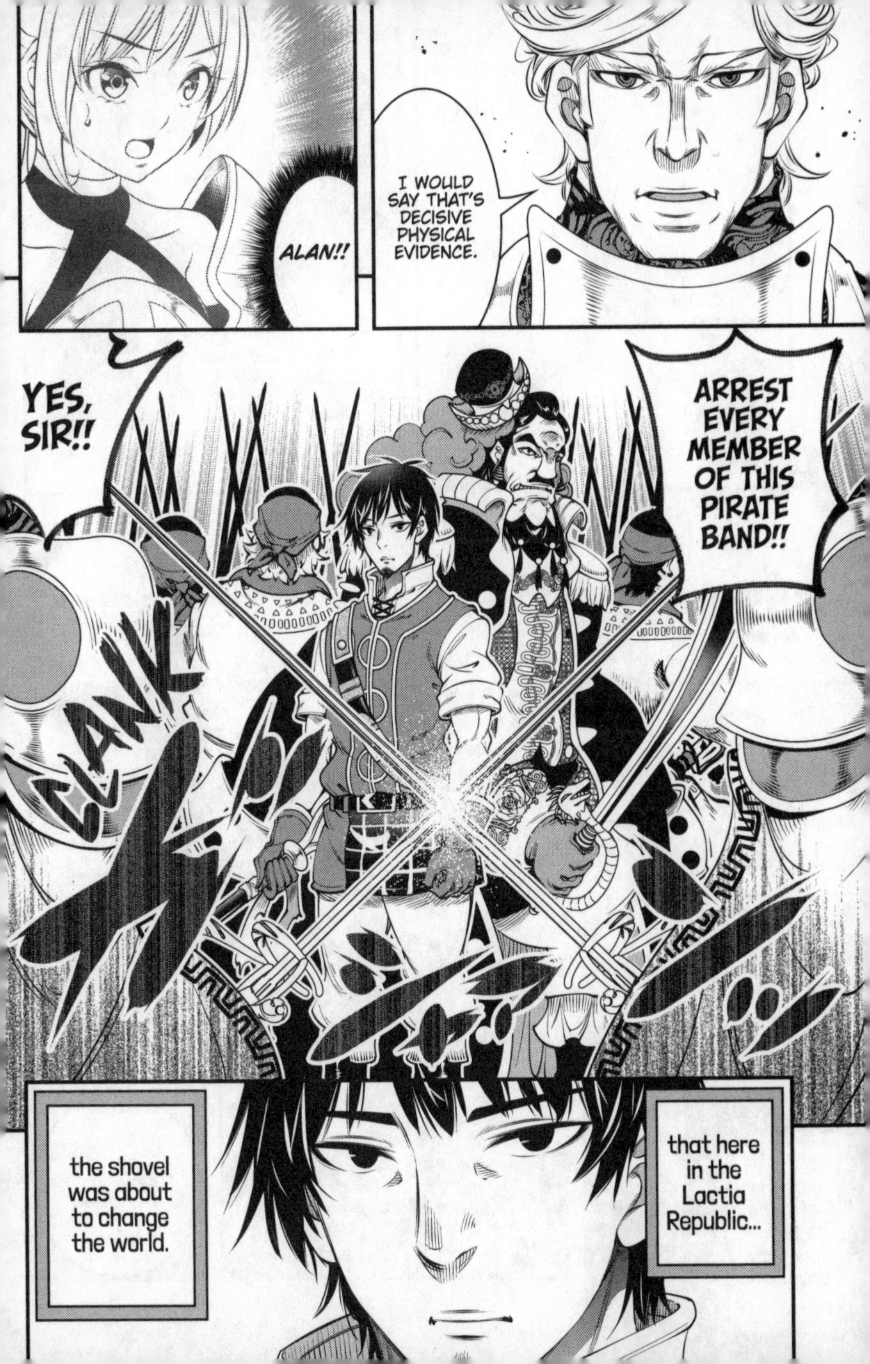
I WOULD SAY THAT'S DECISIVE PHYSICAL EVIDENCE.
ALAN!!
ARREST EVERY MEMBER OF THIS PIRATE BAND!!
YES, SIR!!
CLANK
that here in the Lactia Republic...
the shovel was about to change the world.

THE INVINCIBLE
SHOVEL

"WAVE MOTION SHOVEL BLAST!"
(´・ω・`)♂====★(゜Д゜ ;;;).:∴ KA-CHOOOM

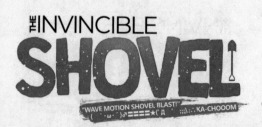

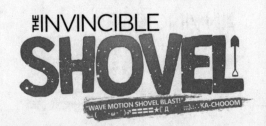

THE INVINCIBLE

SHOVEL

"WAVE MOTION SHOVEL BLAST!" ‥•.))ᕗ===★('Д ‥).∴.KA-CHOOOM

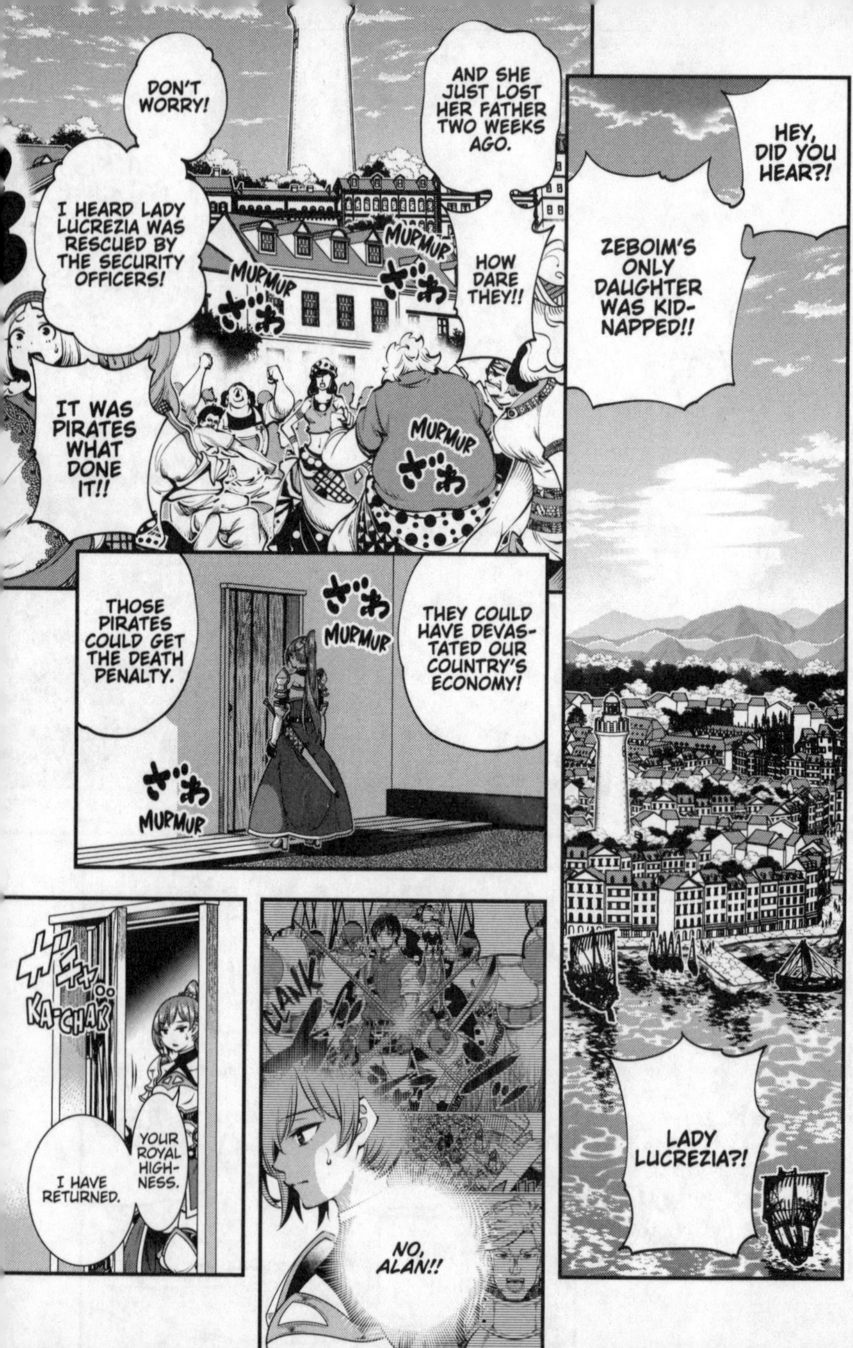
HEY, DID YOU HEAR?!
ZEBOIM'S ONLY DAUGHTER WAS KID-NAPPED!!
LADY LUCREZIA?!
AND SHE JUST LOST HER FATHER TWO WEEKS AGO.
MURMUR ざわ
HOW DARE THEY!!
DON'T WORRY!
I HEARD LADY LUCREZIA WAS RESCUED BY THE SECURITY OFFICERS!
MURMUR ざわ
MURMUR ざわ
IT WAS PIRATES WHAT DONE IT!!
THEY COULD HAVE DEVAS-TATED OUR COUNTRY'S ECONOMY!
ざわ MURMUR
THOSE PIRATES COULD GET THE DEATH PENALTY.
ざわ MURMUR
CLANK
NO, ALAN!!
ガチャ KA-CHAK
YOUR ROYAL HIGH-NESS.
I HAVE RETURNED.

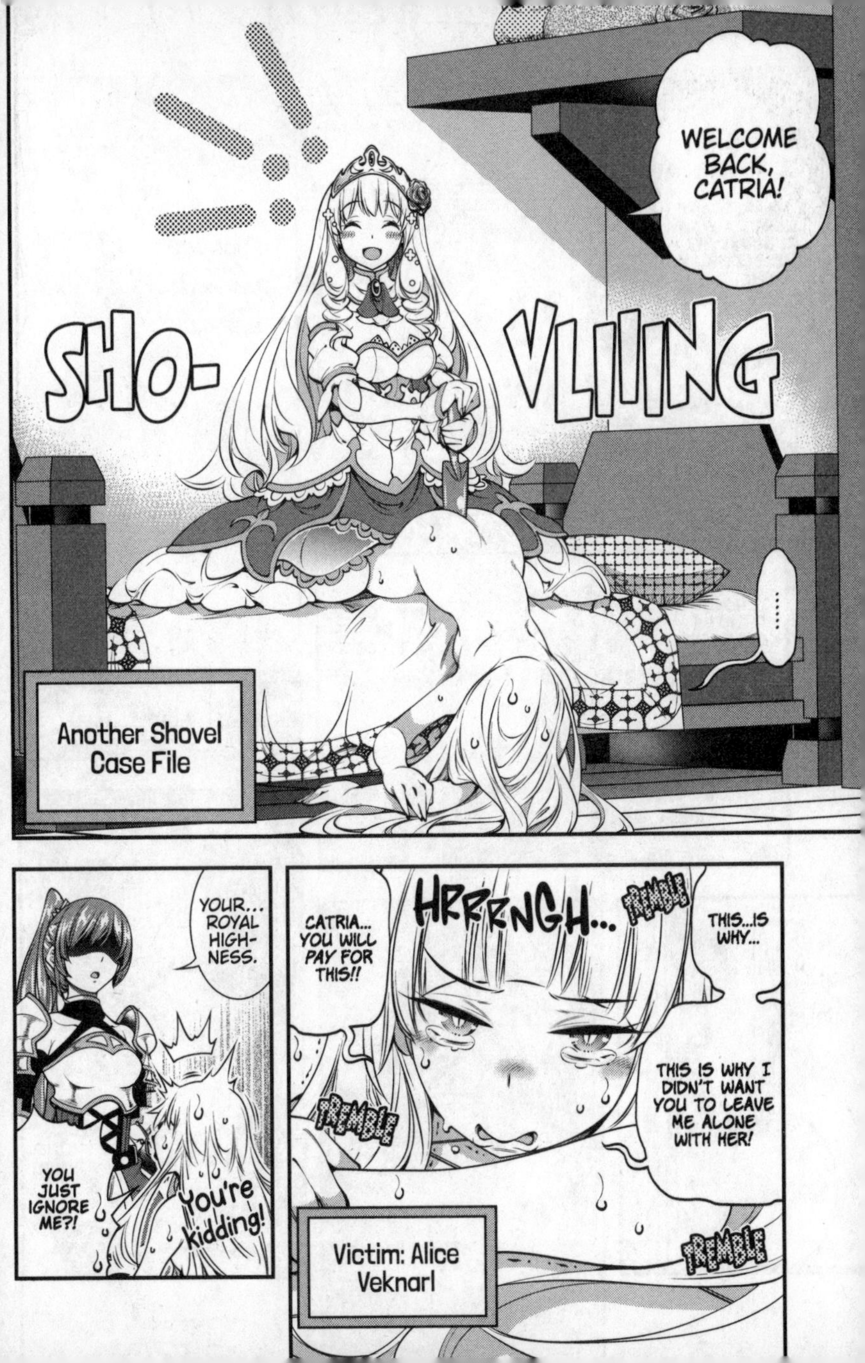
WELCOME BACK, CATRIA!
SHO-VLIIING
......
Another Shovel Case File
THIS...IS WHY...
TREMBLE
HRRRNGH...
CATRIA... YOU WILL PAY FOR THIS!!
THIS IS WHY I DIDN'T WANT YOU TO LEAVE ME ALONE WITH HER!
TREMBLE
TREMBLE
Victim: Alice Veknarl
YOUR... ROYAL HIGH-NESS.
You're kidding!
YOU JUST IGNORE ME?!

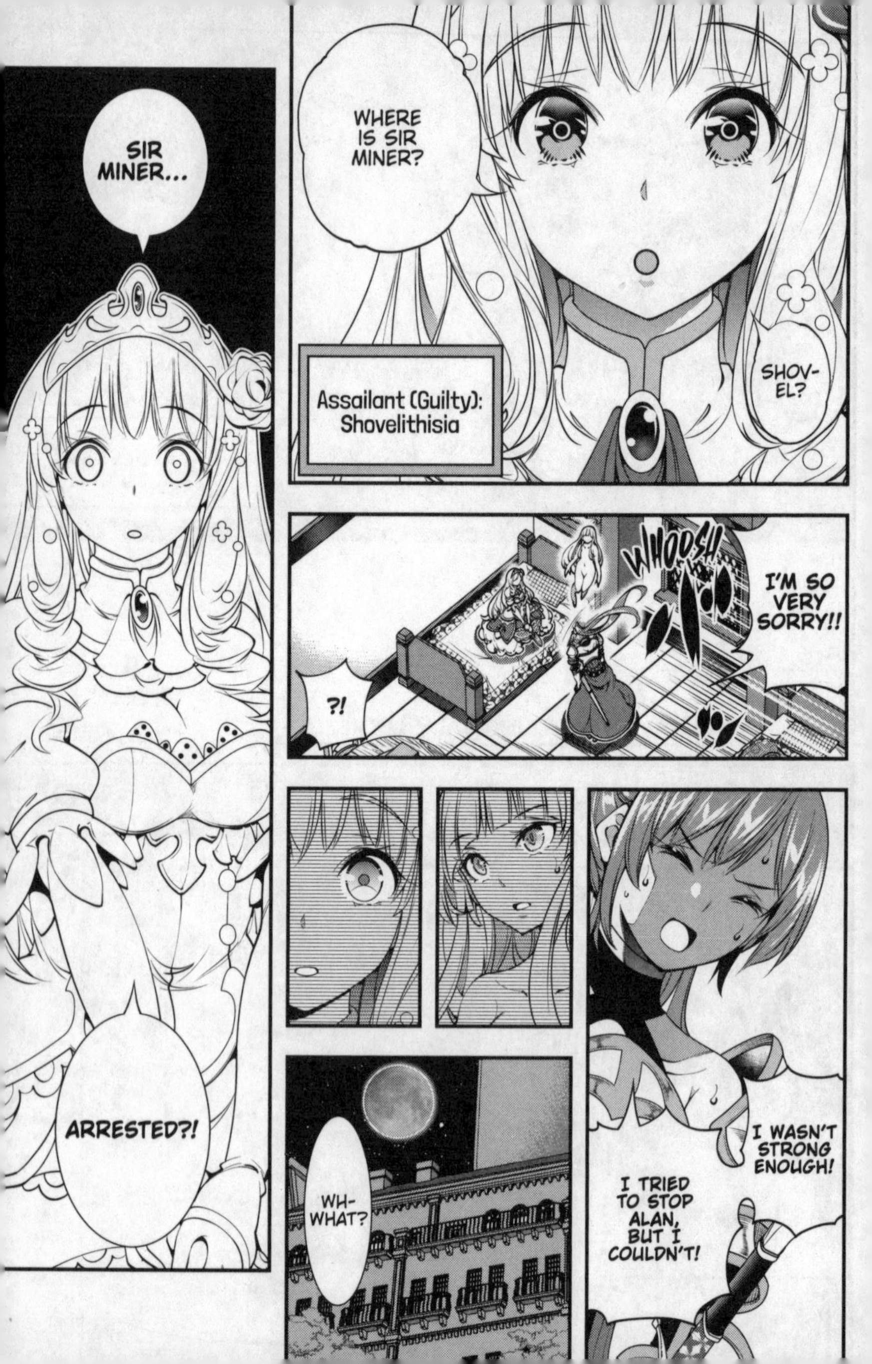
WHERE IS SIR MINER?
SHOV-EL?
Assailant (Guilty): Shovelithisia
WHOOSH
I'M SO VERY SORRY!!
?!
I WASN'T STRONG ENOUGH!
I TRIED TO STOP ALAN, BUT I COULDN'T!
WH-WHAT?
SIR MINER...
ARRESTED?!

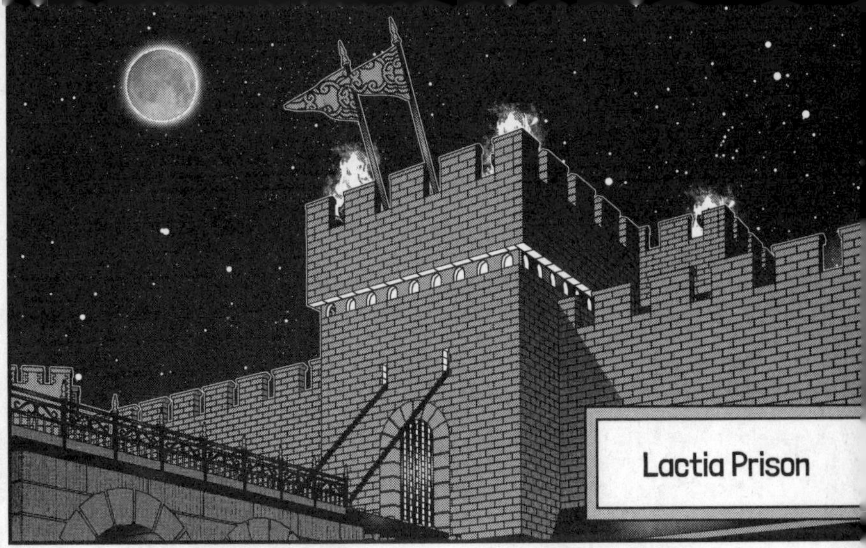
Lactia Prison

Chapter 18: A Deal with Young Lady Lucrezia

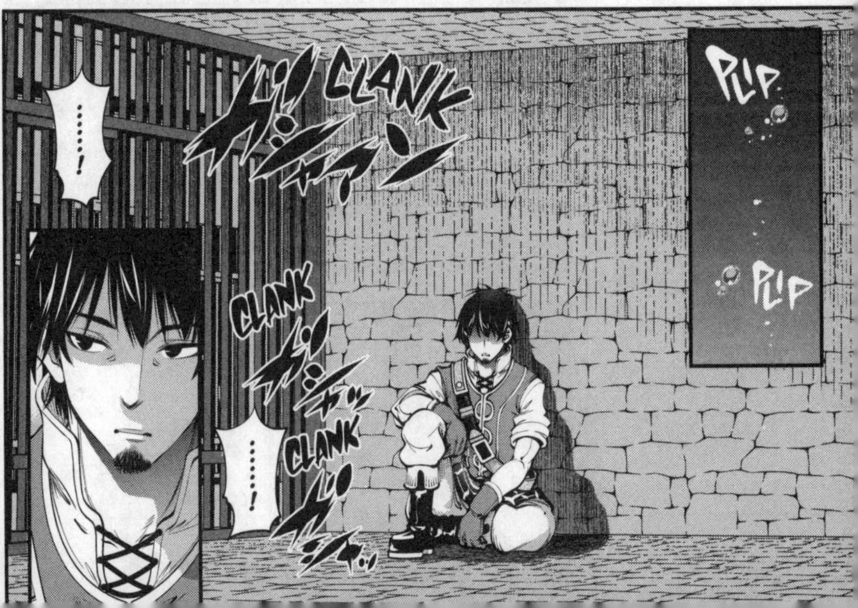
PLIP
PLIP
CLANK
......!
CLANK
CLANK
......!

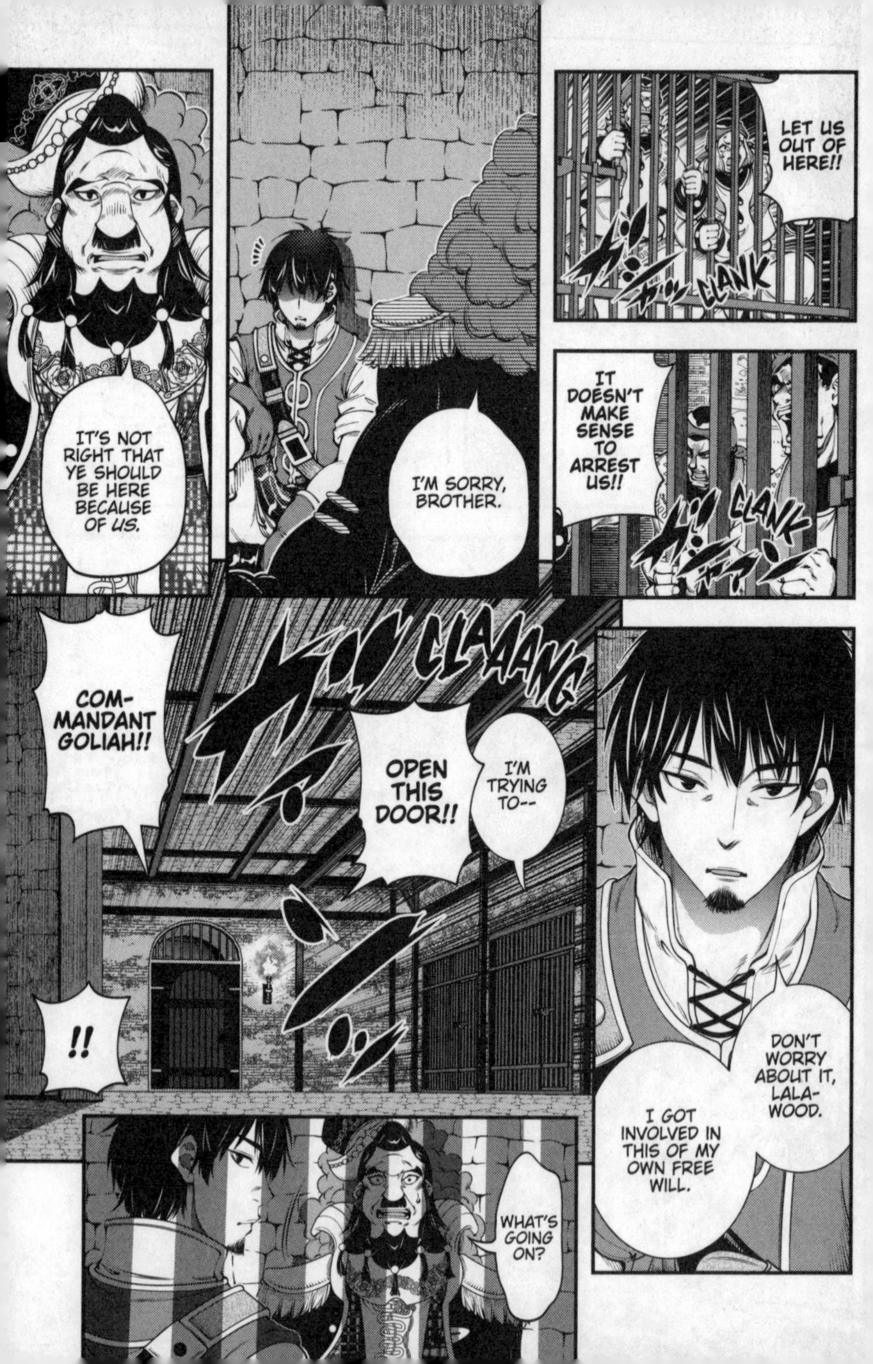
LET US OUT OF HERE!!
CLANK
IT DOESN'T MAKE SENSE TO ARREST US!!
CLANK
I'M SORRY, BROTHER.
IT'S NOT RIGHT THAT YE SHOULD BE HERE BECAUSE OF US.
DON'T WORRY ABOUT IT, LALA-WOOD.
I GOT INVOLVED IN THIS OF MY OWN FREE WILL.
CLAAANG
I'M TRYING TO--
OPEN THIS DOOR!!
COM-MANDANT GOLIAH!!
!!
WHAT'S GOING ON?

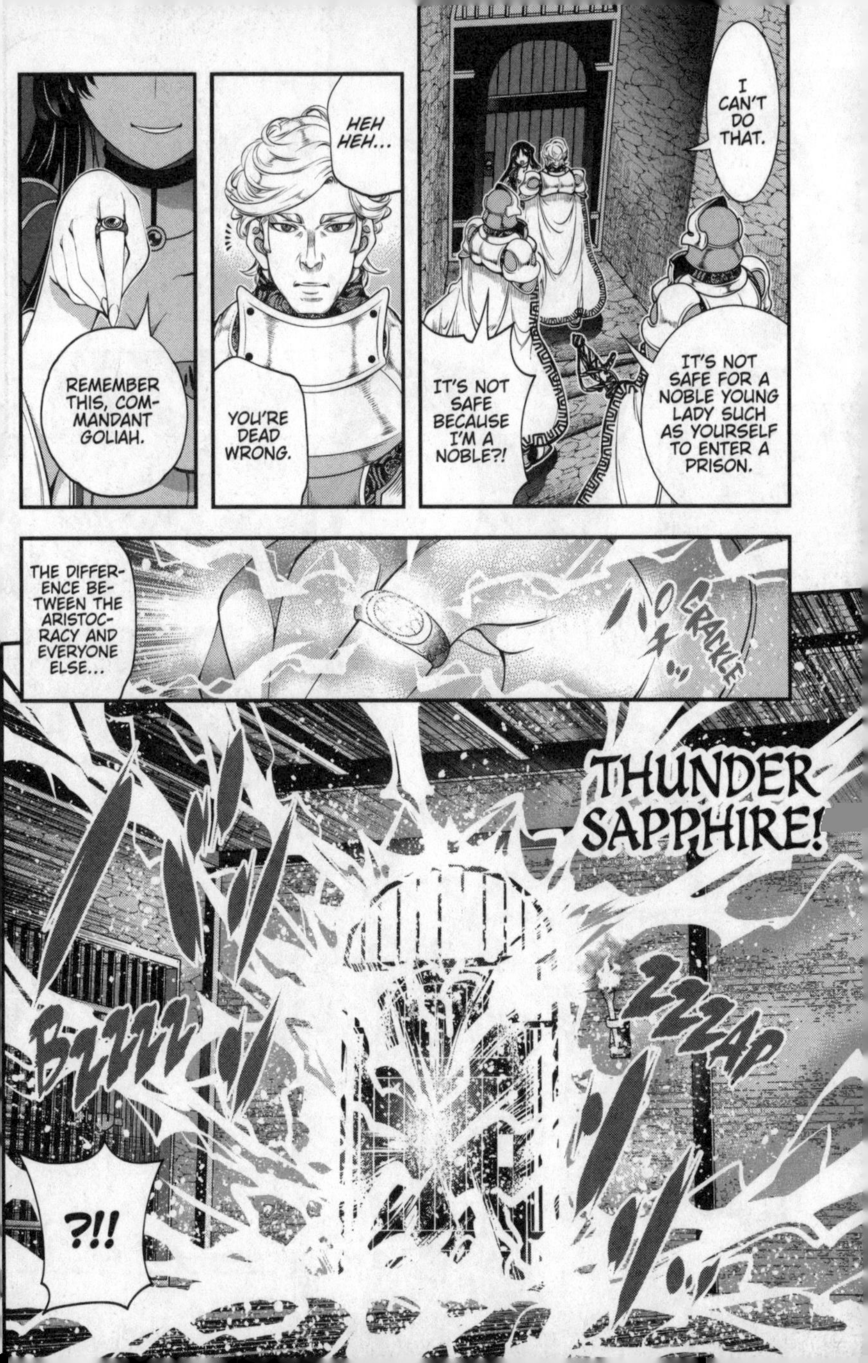
I CAN'T DO THAT.
IT'S NOT SAFE FOR A NOBLE YOUNG LADY SUCH AS YOURSELF TO ENTER A PRISON.
IT'S NOT SAFE BECAUSE I'M A NOBLE?!
HEH HEH...
YOU'RE DEAD WRONG.
REMEMBER THIS, COM-MANDANT GOLIAH.
パチッ
CRACKLE
THE DIFFER-ENCE BE-TWEEN THE ARISTOC-RACY AND EVERYONE ELSE...
THUNDER SAPPHIRE!
ZZZAP
Bzzzz
?!!

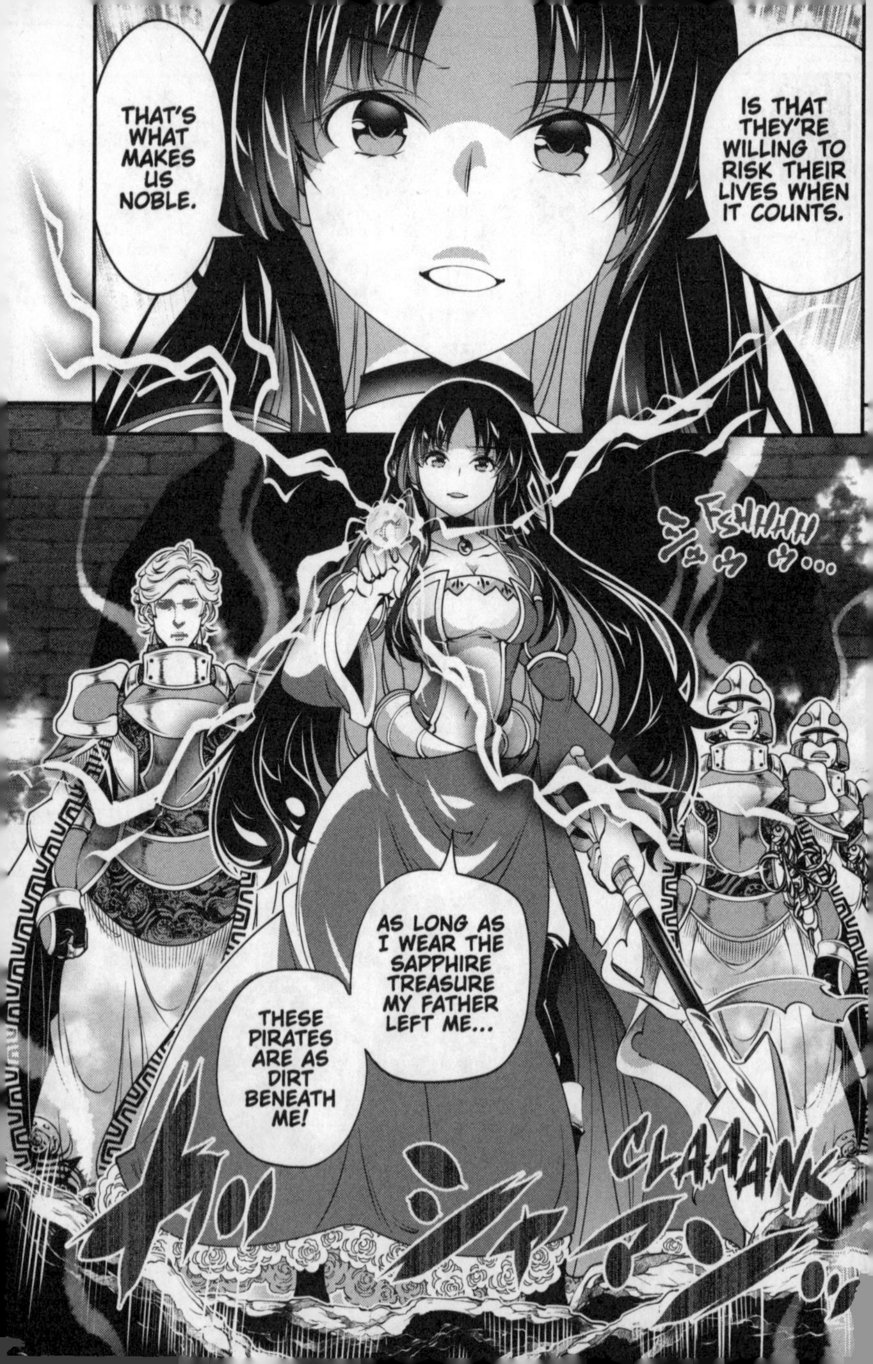
IS THAT THEY'RE WILLING TO RISK THEIR LIVES WHEN IT COUNTS.
THAT'S WHAT MAKES US NOBLE.
FSHHHH
AS LONG AS I WEAR THE SAPPHIRE TREASURE MY FATHER LEFT ME...
THESE PIRATES ARE AS DIRT BENEATH ME!
CLAAANK

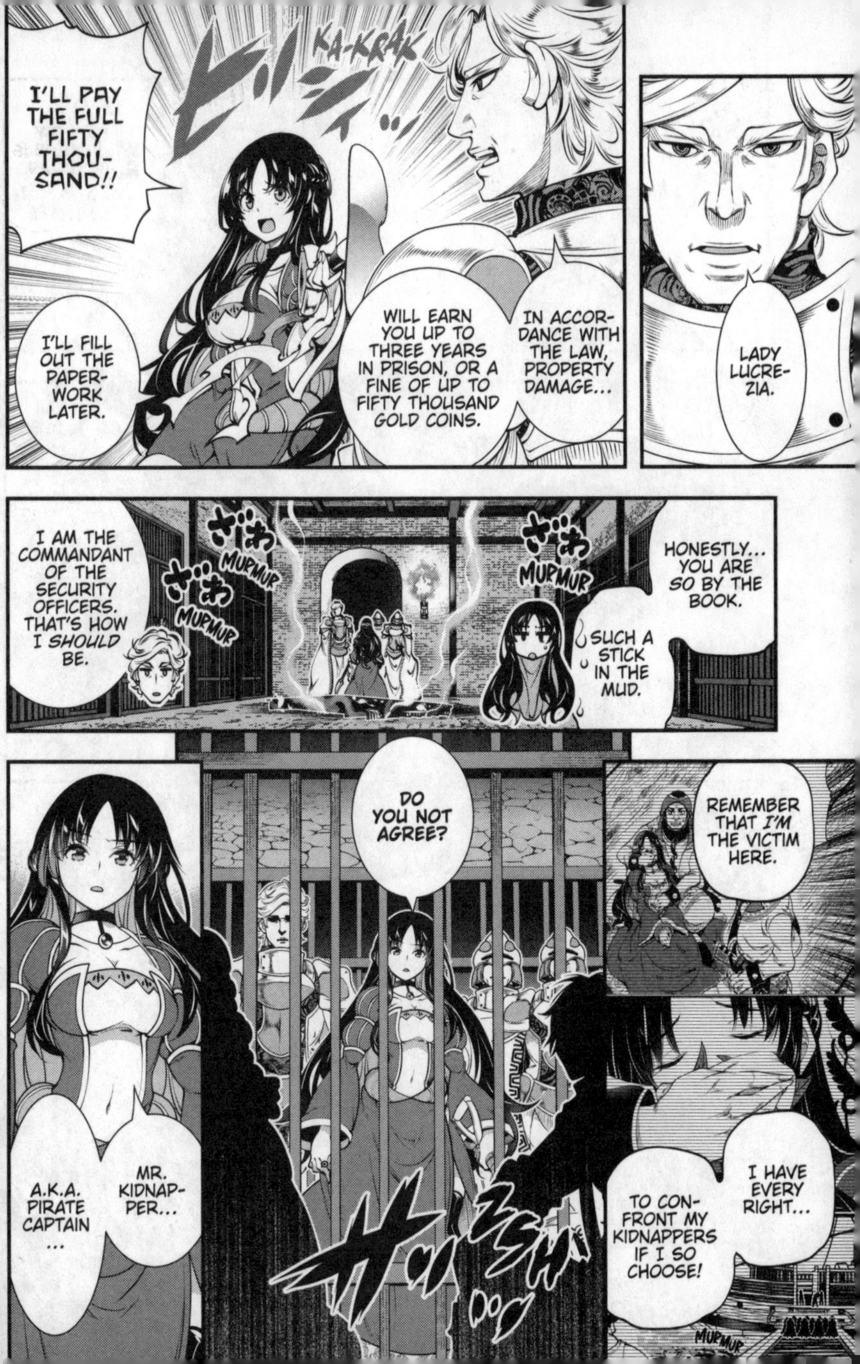
LADY LUCREZIA.
IN ACCORDANCE WITH THE LAW, PROPERTY DAMAGE...
WILL EARN YOU UP TO THREE YEARS IN PRISON, OR A FINE OF UP TO FIFTY THOUSAND GOLD COINS.
KA-KRAK
I'LL PAY THE FULL FIFTY THOUSAND!!
I'LL FILL OUT THE PAPERWORK LATER.
HONESTLY... YOU ARE SO BY THE BOOK.
SUCH A STICK IN THE MUD.
MURMUR
MURMUR
MURMUR
I AM THE COMMANDANT OF THE SECURITY OFFICERS. THAT'S HOW I *SHOULD* BE.
REMEMBER THAT *I'M* THE VICTIM HERE.
DO YOU NOT AGREE?
I HAVE EVERY RIGHT...
TO CONFRONT MY KIDNAPPERS IF I SO CHOOSE!
MURMUR
MR. KIDNAPPER...
A.K.A. PIRATE CAPTAIN ...

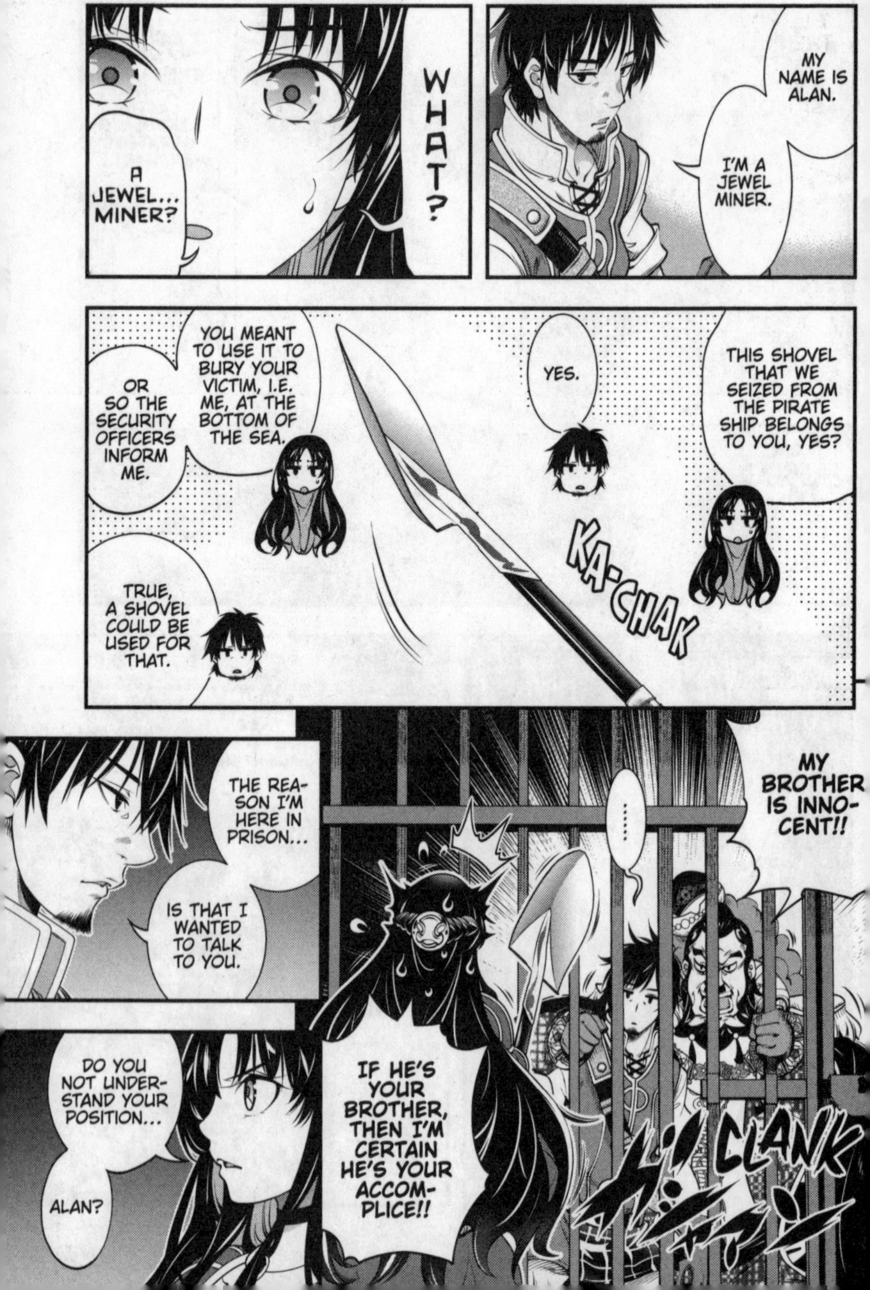
MY NAME IS ALAN.
I'M A JEWEL MINER.
WHAT?
A JEWEL... MINER?
THIS SHOVEL THAT WE SEIZED FROM THE PIRATE SHIP BELONGS TO YOU, YES?
YES.
KA-CHAK
YOU MEANT TO USE IT TO BURY YOUR VICTIM, I.E. ME, AT THE BOTTOM OF THE SEA.
OR SO THE SECURITY OFFICERS INFORM ME.
TRUE, A SHOVEL COULD BE USED FOR THAT.
MY BROTHER IS INNOCENT!!
......
IF HE'S YOUR BROTHER, THEN I'M CERTAIN HE'S YOUR ACCOMPLICE!!
CLANK
THE REASON I'M HERE IN PRISON...
IS THAT I WANTED TO TALK TO YOU.
DO YOU NOT UNDERSTAND YOUR POSITION...
ALAN?

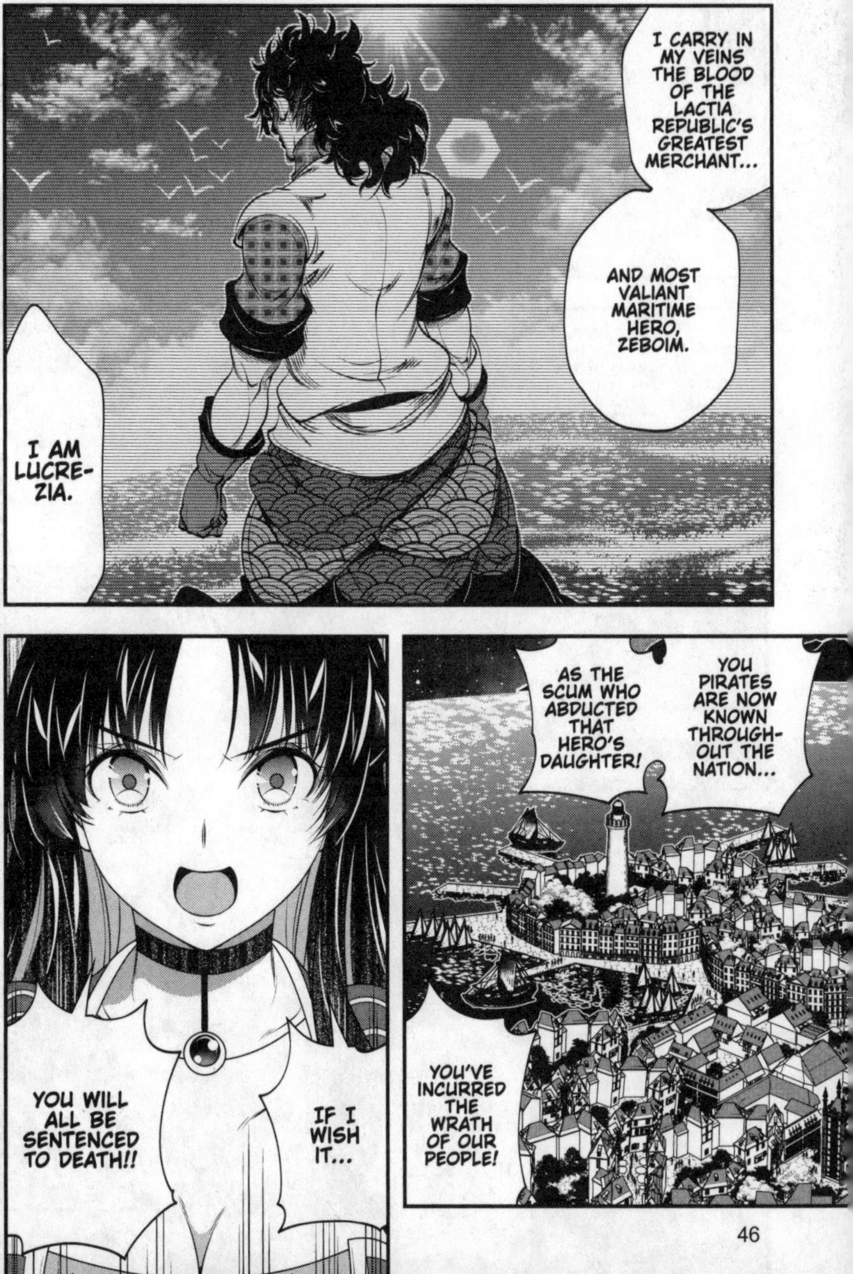
I CARRY IN MY VEINS THE BLOOD OF THE LACTIA REPUBLIC'S GREATEST MERCHANT...
AND MOST VALIANT MARITIME HERO, ZEBOIM.
I AM LUCRE-ZIA.
YOU PIRATES ARE NOW KNOWN THROUGH-OUT THE NATION...
AS THE SCUM WHO ABDUCTED THAT HERO'S DAUGHTER!
YOU'VE INCURRED THE WRATH OF OUR PEOPLE!
IF I WISH IT...
YOU WILL ALL BE SENTENCED TO DEATH!!

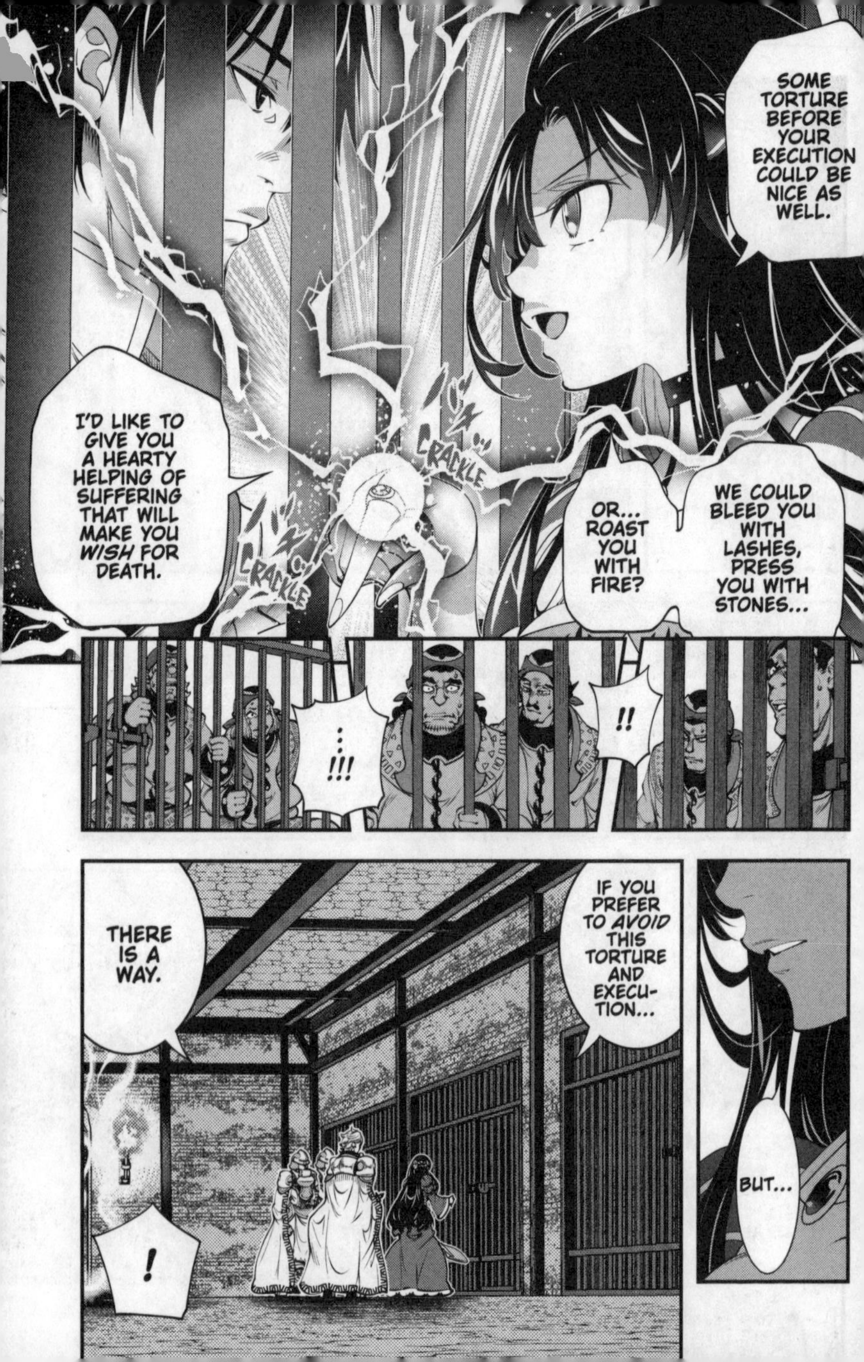
SOME TORTURE BEFORE YOUR EXECUTION COULD BE NICE AS WELL.
WE COULD BLEED YOU WITH LASHES, PRESS YOU WITH STONES...
OR... ROAST YOU WITH FIRE?
CRACKLE
I'D LIKE TO GIVE YOU A HEARTY HELPING OF SUFFERING THAT WILL MAKE YOU *WISH* FOR DEATH.
CRACKLE
!!
...!!!
BUT...
IF YOU PREFER TO *AVOID* THIS TORTURE AND EXECUTION...
THERE IS A WAY.
!

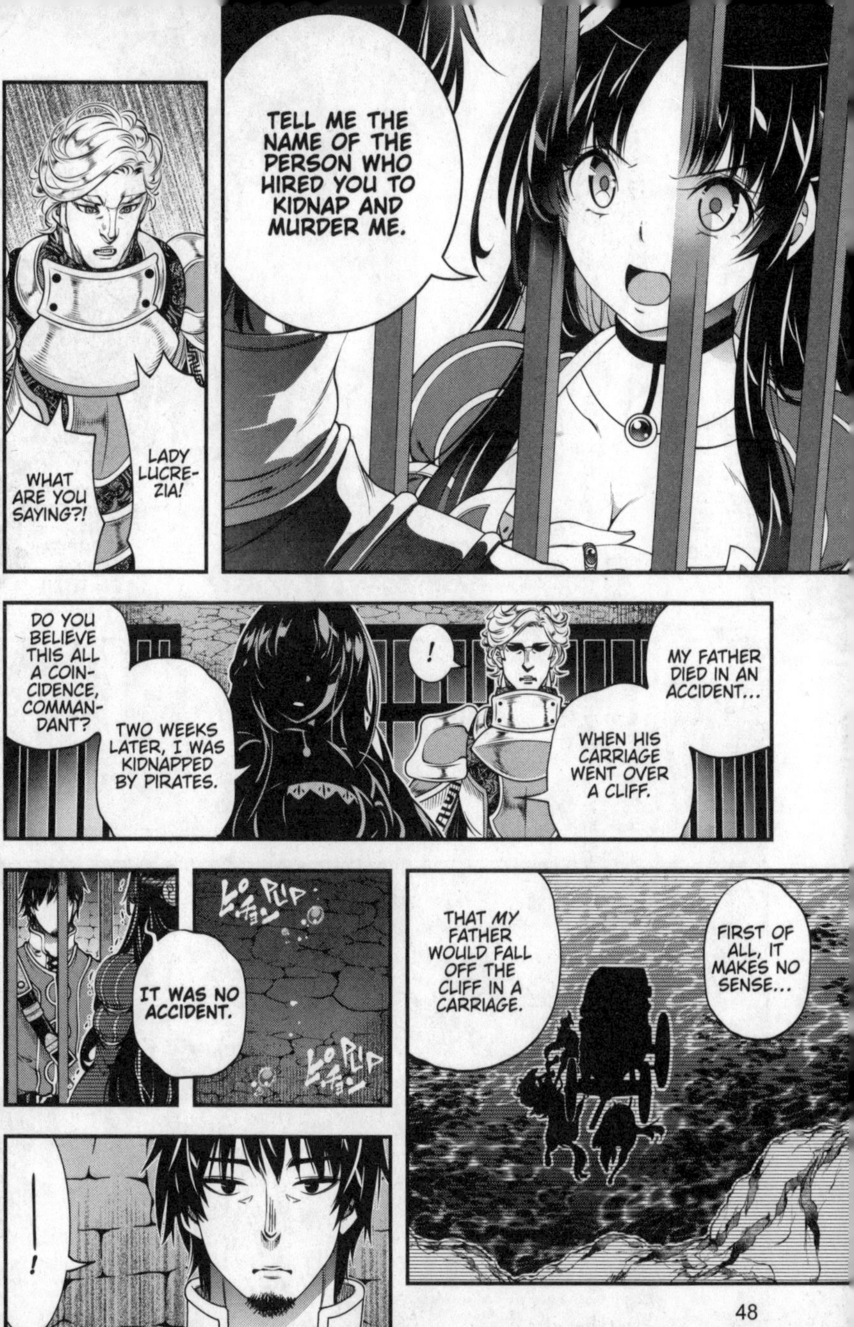
TELL ME THE NAME OF THE PERSON WHO HIRED YOU TO KIDNAP AND MURDER ME.
LADY LUCREZIA!
WHAT ARE YOU SAYING?!
MY FATHER DIED IN AN ACCIDENT...
WHEN HIS CARRIAGE WENT OVER A CLIFF.
!
TWO WEEKS LATER, I WAS KIDNAPPED BY PIRATES.
DO YOU BELIEVE THIS ALL A COINCIDENCE, COMMANDANT?
FIRST OF ALL, IT MAKES NO SENSE...
THAT MY FATHER WOULD FALL OFF THE CLIFF IN A CARRIAGE.
PLIP
IT WAS NO ACCIDENT.
PLIP
!

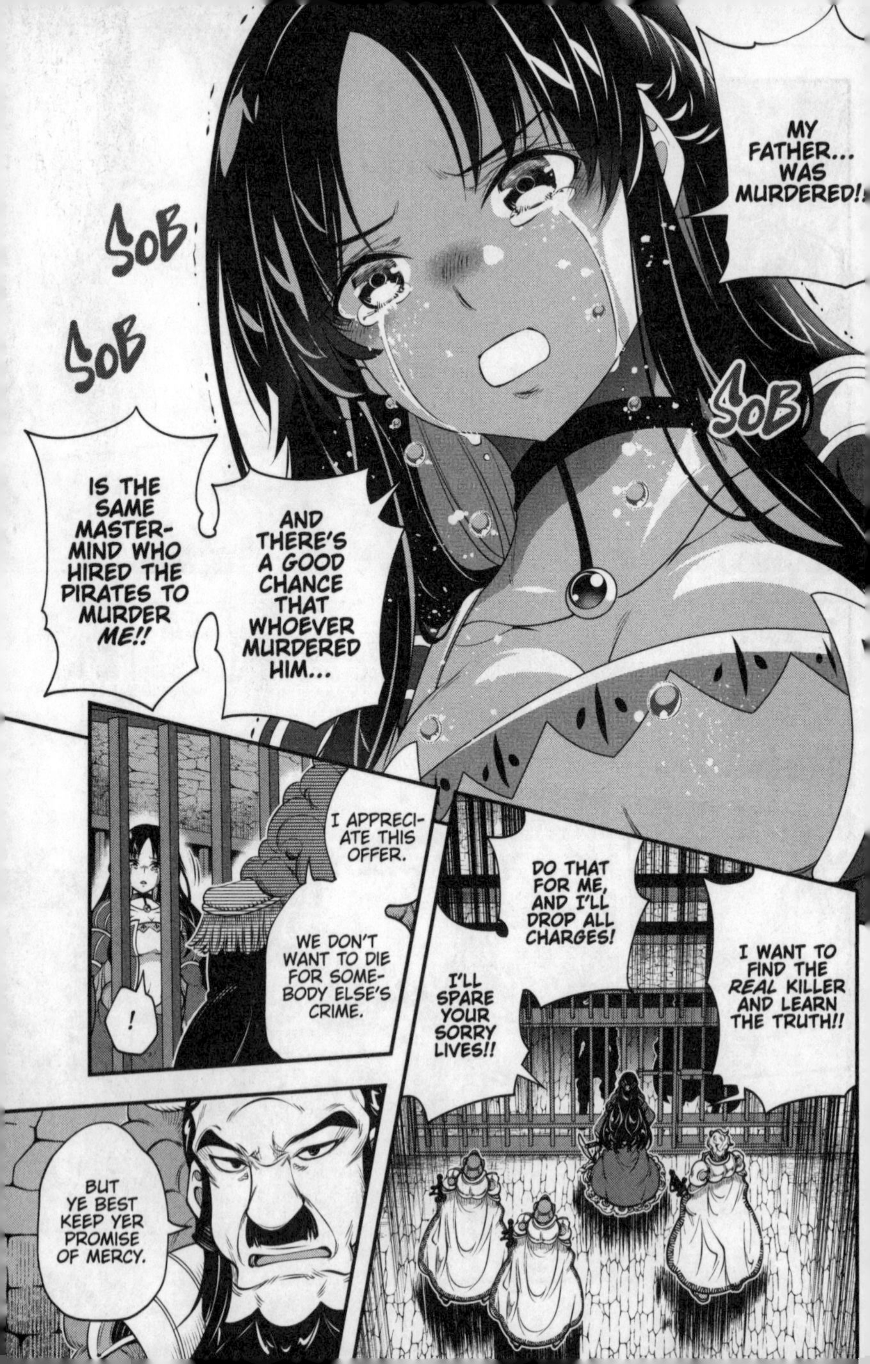
MY FATHER... WAS MURDERED!!
SOB
SOB
SOB
AND THERE'S A GOOD CHANCE THAT WHOEVER MURDERED HIM...
IS THE SAME MASTER-MIND WHO HIRED THE PIRATES TO MURDER *ME!!*
I WANT TO FIND THE *REAL* KILLER AND LEARN THE TRUTH!!
DO THAT FOR ME, AND I'LL DROP ALL CHARGES!
I'LL SPARE YOUR SORRY LIVES!!
I APPRECI-ATE THIS OFFER.
WE DON'T WANT TO DIE FOR SOME-BODY ELSE'S CRIME.
!
BUT YE BEST KEEP YER PROMISE OF MERCY.

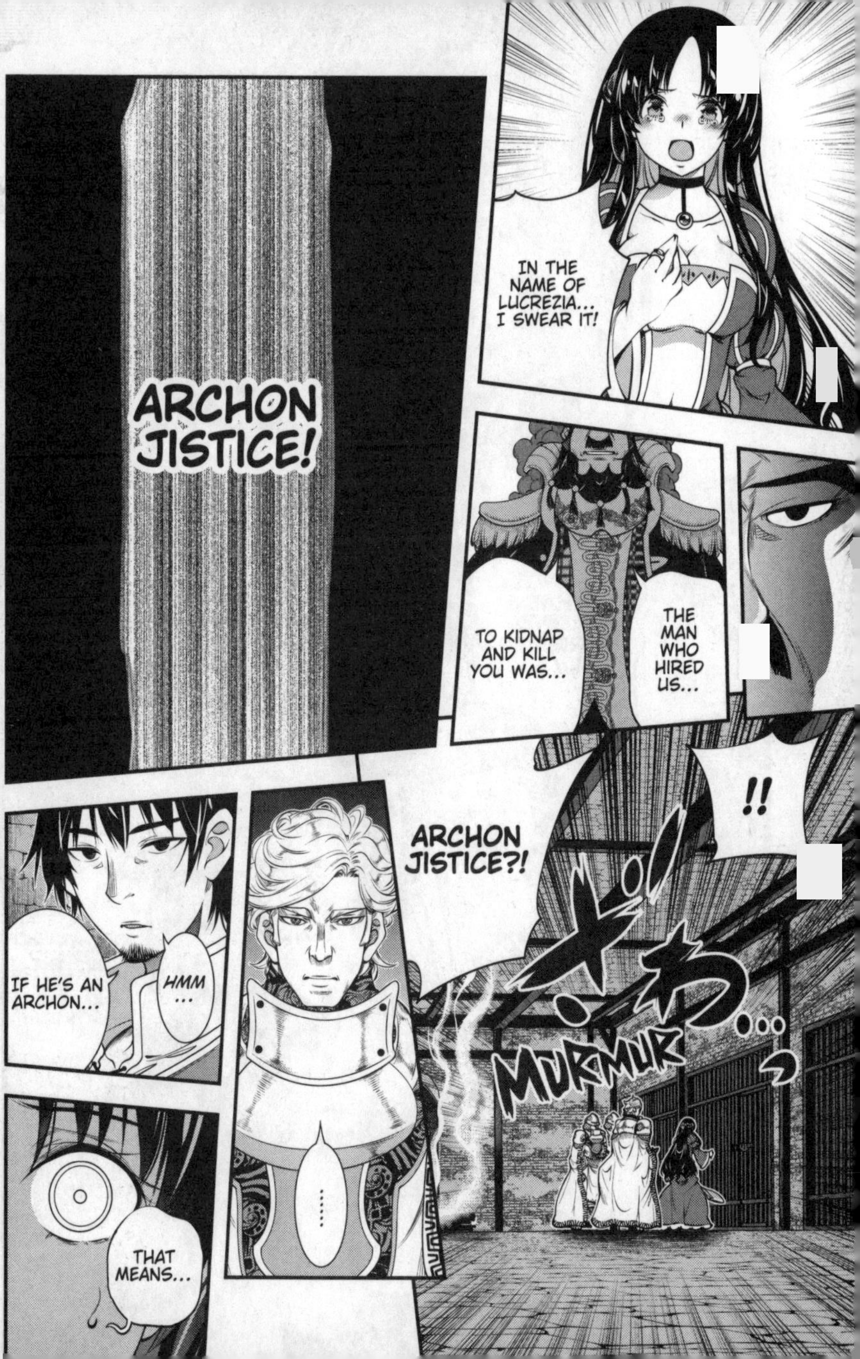
IN THE NAME OF LUCREZIA... I SWEAR IT!
THE MAN WHO HIRED US...
TO KIDNAP AND KILL YOU WAS...
ARCHON JISTICE!
!!
ARCHON JISTICE?!
MURMUR
......
HMM...
IF HE'S AN ARCHON...
THAT MEANS...

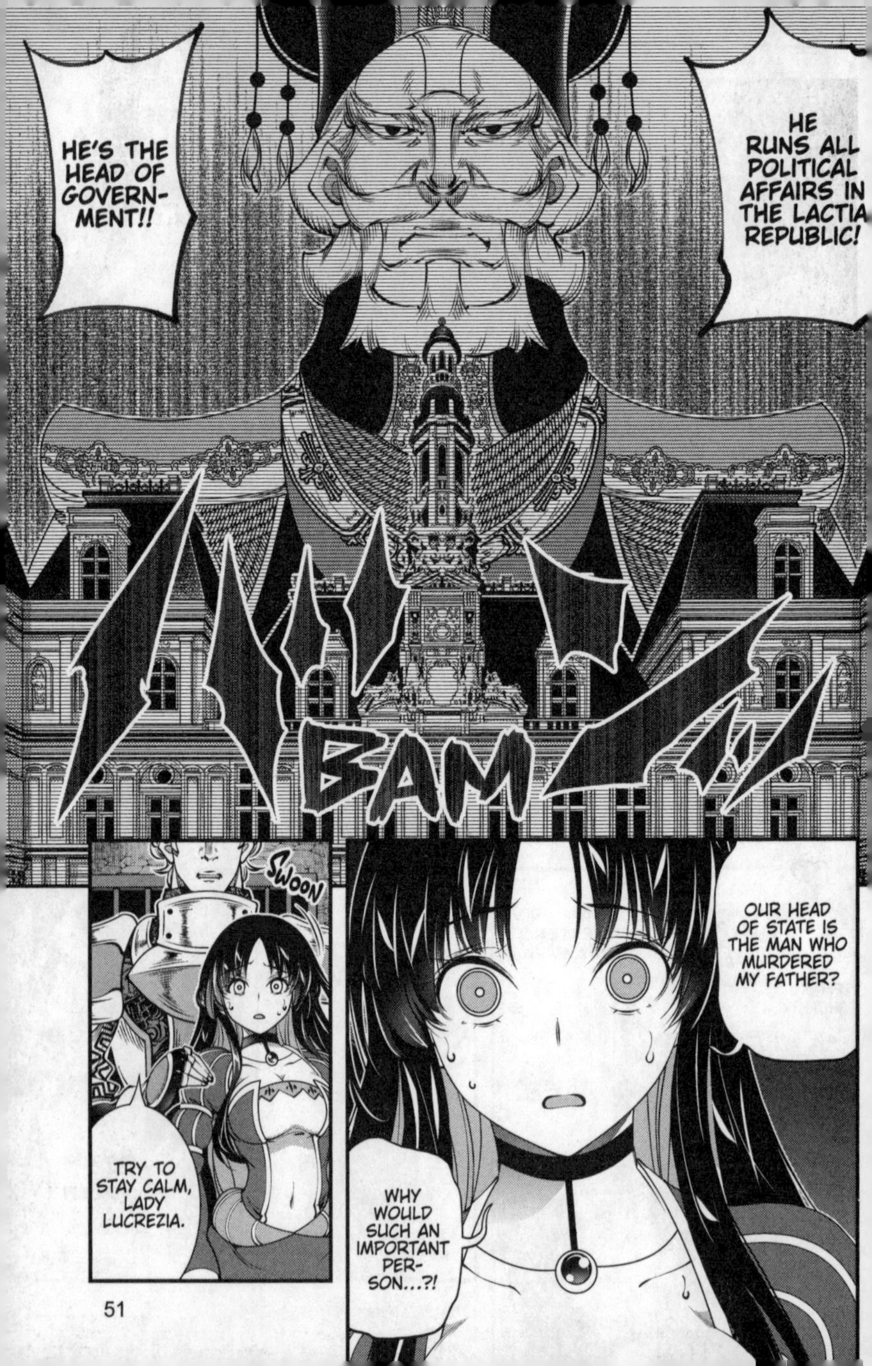
HE RUNS ALL POLITICAL AFFAIRS IN THE LACTIA REPUBLIC!
HE'S THE HEAD OF GOVERN-MENT!!
BAM
OUR HEAD OF STATE IS THE MAN WHO MURDERED MY FATHER?
WHY WOULD SUCH AN IMPORTANT PER-SON...?!
SWOON
TRY TO STAY CALM, LADY LUCREZIA.

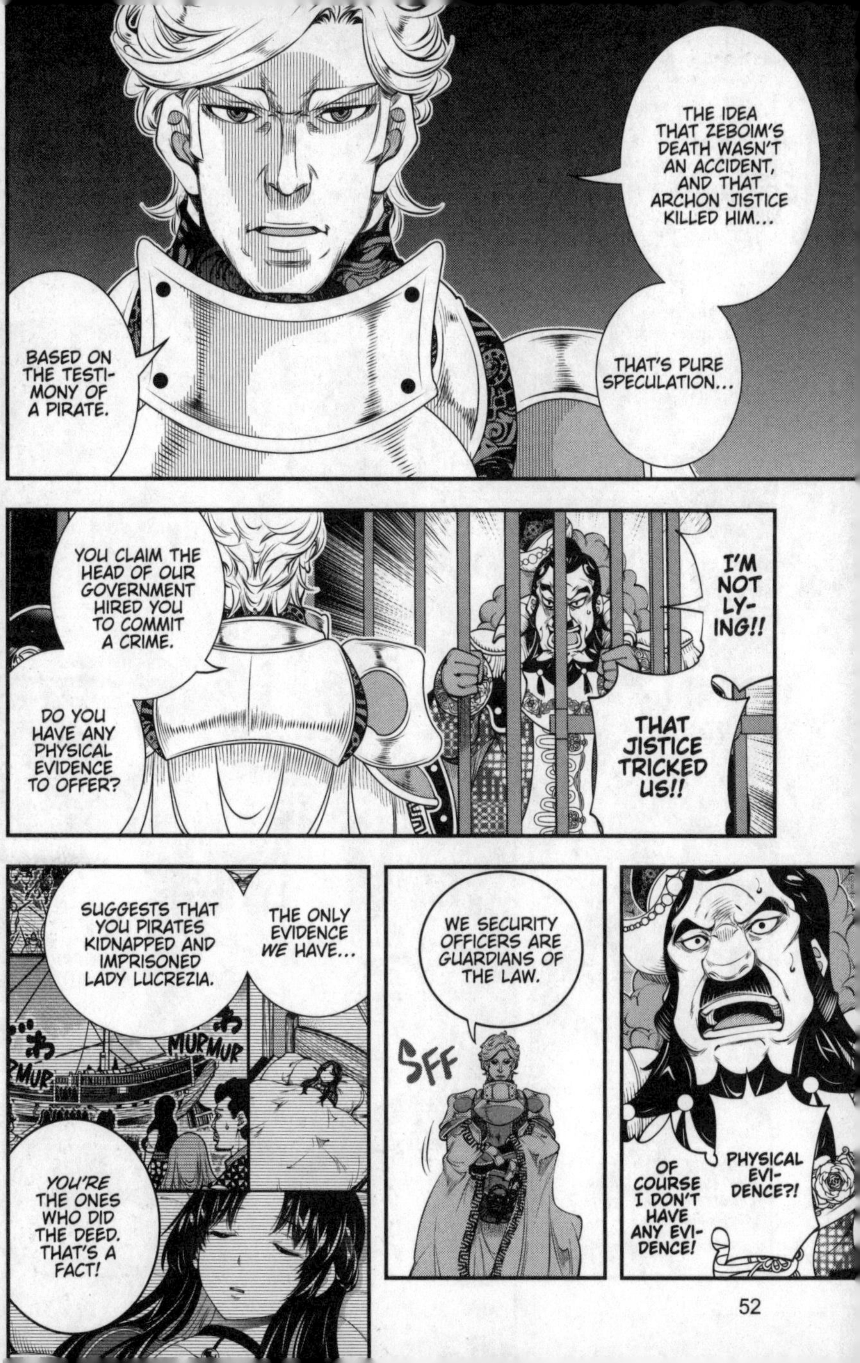
THE IDEA THAT ZEBOIM'S DEATH WASN'T AN ACCIDENT, AND THAT ARCHON JISTICE KILLED HIM...
THAT'S PURE SPECULATION...
BASED ON THE TESTIMONY OF A PIRATE.
I'M NOT LYING!!
THAT JISTICE TRICKED US!!
YOU CLAIM THE HEAD OF OUR GOVERNMENT HIRED YOU TO COMMIT A CRIME.
DO YOU HAVE ANY PHYSICAL EVIDENCE TO OFFER?
PHYSICAL EVIDENCE?!
OF COURSE I DON'T HAVE ANY EVIDENCE!
WE SECURITY OFFICERS ARE GUARDIANS OF THE LAW.
SFF
THE ONLY EVIDENCE *WE* HAVE...
SUGGESTS THAT YOU PIRATES KIDNAPPED AND IMPRISONED LADY LUCREZIA.
MURMUR
YOU'RE THE ONES WHO DID THE DEED. THAT'S A FACT!

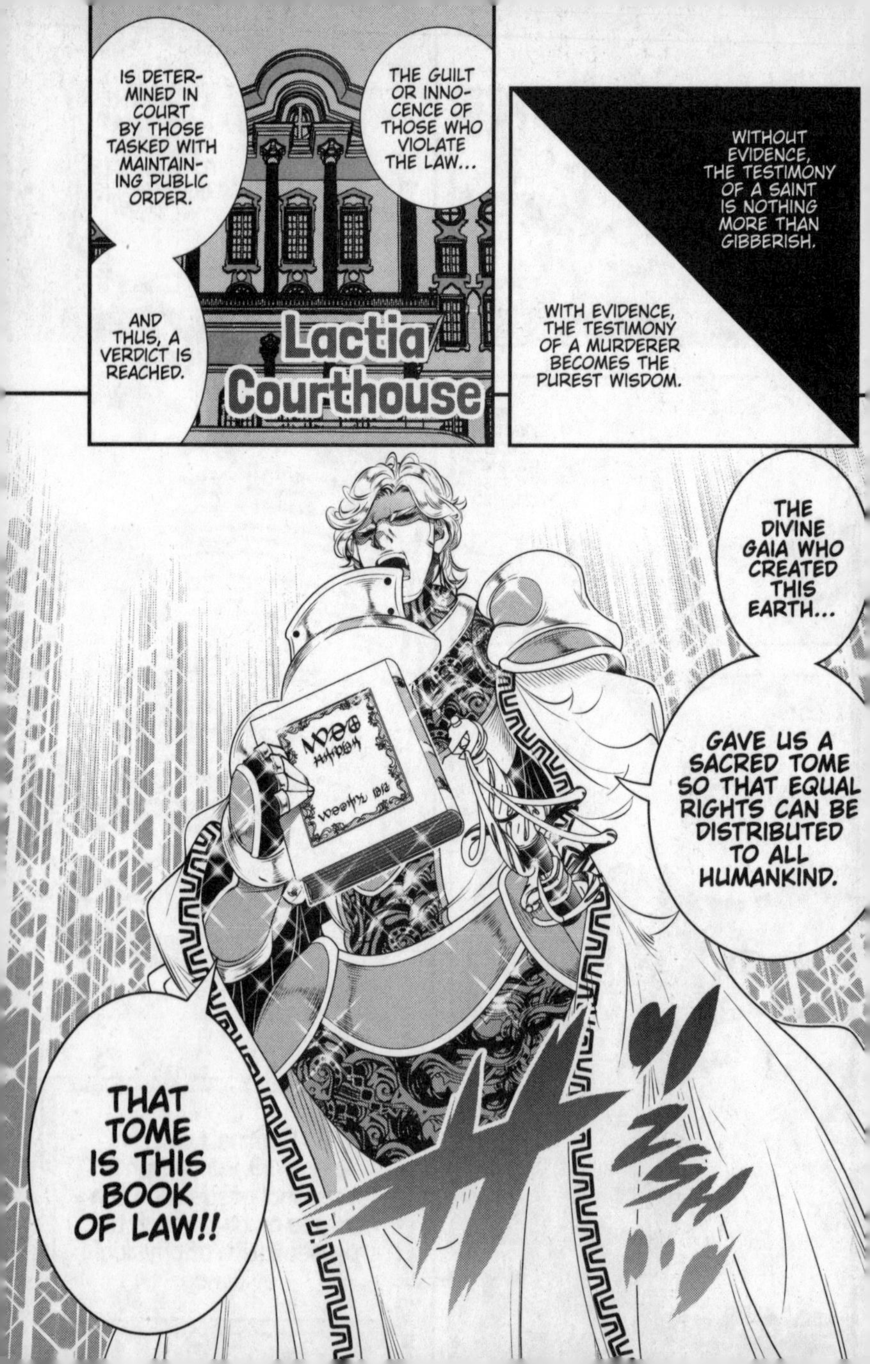
WITHOUT EVIDENCE, THE TESTIMONY OF A SAINT IS NOTHING MORE THAN GIBBERISH.
WITH EVIDENCE, THE TESTIMONY OF A MURDERER BECOMES THE PUREST WISDOM.
THE GUILT OR INNOCENCE OF THOSE WHO VIOLATE THE LAW...
IS DETERMINED IN COURT BY THOSE TASKED WITH MAINTAINING PUBLIC ORDER.
AND THUS, A VERDICT IS REACHED.
Lactia Courthouse
THE DIVINE GAIA WHO CREATED THIS EARTH...
GAVE US A SACRED TOME SO THAT EQUAL RIGHTS CAN BE DISTRIBUTED TO ALL HUMANKIND.
THAT TOME IS THIS BOOK OF LAW!!

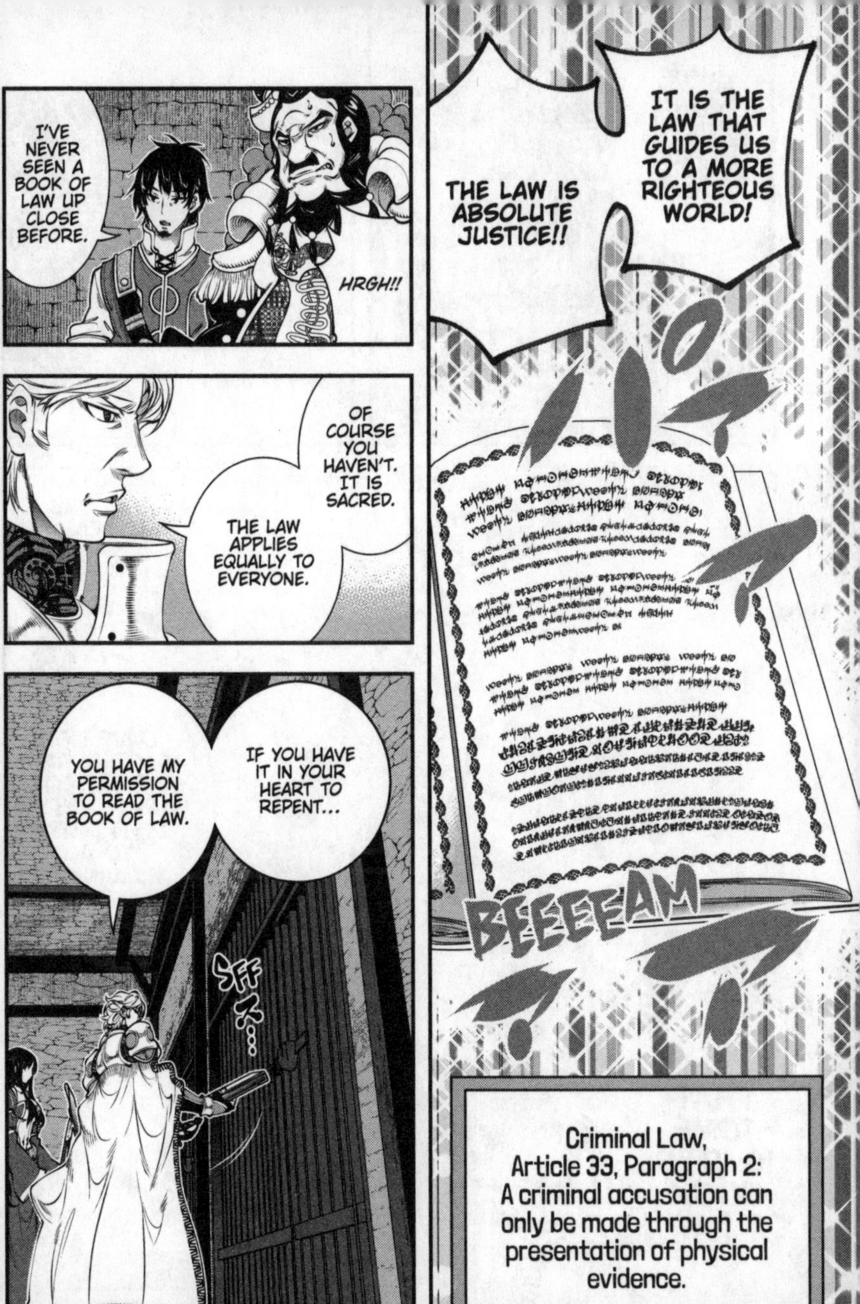
IT IS THE LAW THAT GUIDES US TO A MORE RIGHTEOUS WORLD!
THE LAW IS ABSOLUTE JUSTICE!!
BEEEEAM
Criminal Law, Article 33, Paragraph 2: A criminal accusation can only be made through the presentation of physical evidence.
I'VE NEVER SEEN A BOOK OF LAW UP CLOSE BEFORE.
HRGH!!
OF COURSE YOU HAVEN'T. IT IS SACRED.
THE LAW APPLIES EQUALLY TO EVERYONE.
IF YOU HAVE IT IN YOUR HEART TO REPENT...
YOU HAVE MY PERMISSION TO READ THE BOOK OF LAW.
SFF...

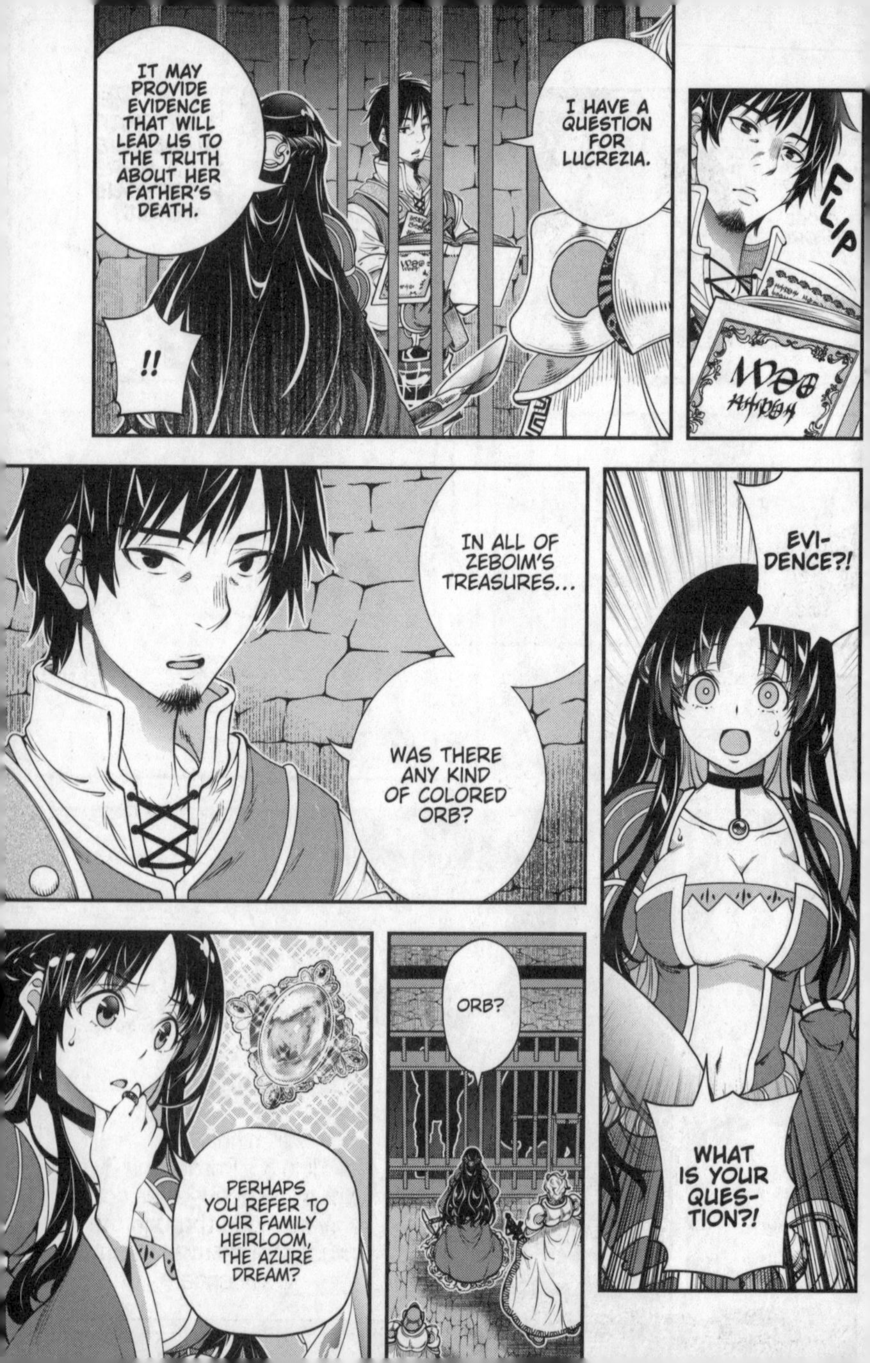
FLIP
I HAVE A QUESTION FOR LUCREZIA.
IT MAY PROVIDE EVIDENCE THAT WILL LEAD US TO THE TRUTH ABOUT HER FATHER'S DEATH.
!!
EVI-DENCE?!
WHAT IS YOUR QUES-TION?!
IN ALL OF ZEBOIM'S TREASURES...
WAS THERE ANY KIND OF COLORED ORB?
ORB?
PERHAPS YOU REFER TO OUR FAMILY HEIRLOOM, THE AZURE DREAM?

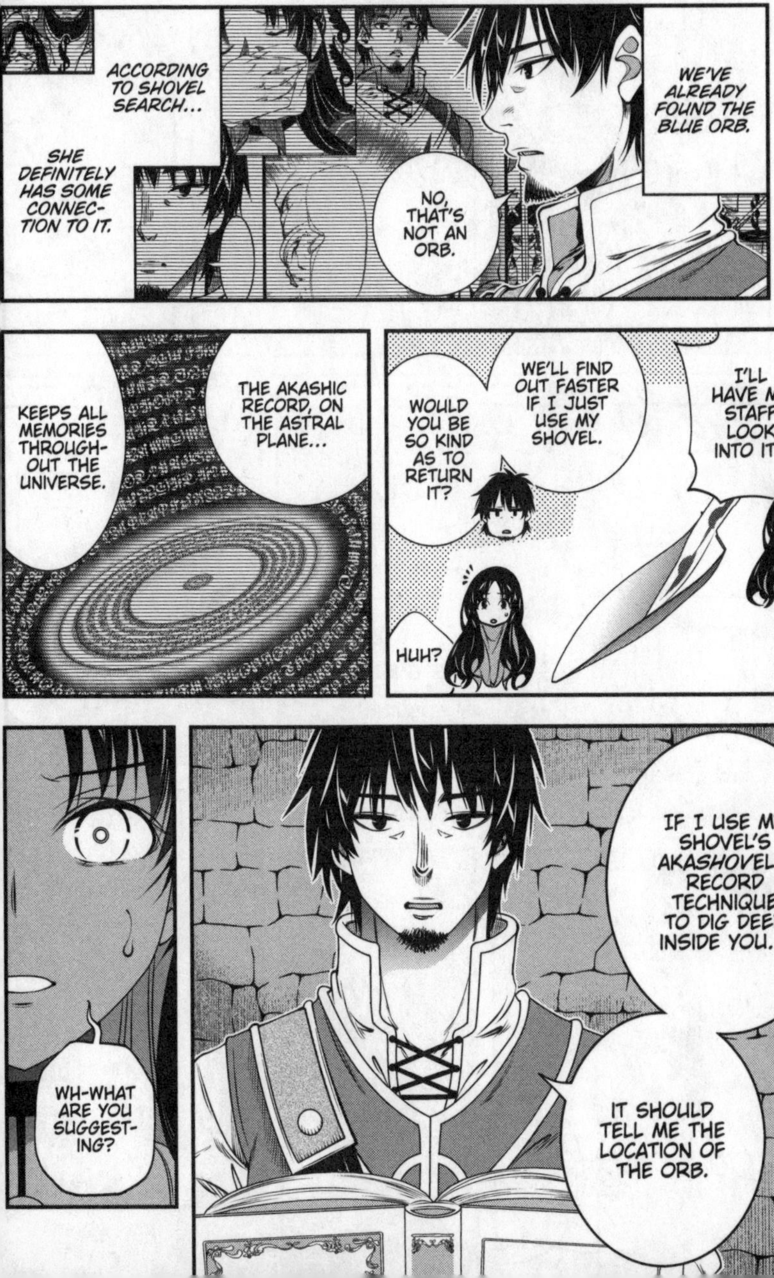
WE'VE ALREADY FOUND THE BLUE ORB.
NO, THAT'S NOT AN ORB.
ACCORDING TO SHOVEL SEARCH...
SHE DEFINITELY HAS SOME CONNECTION TO IT.
I'LL HAVE MY STAFF LOOK INTO IT!!
WE'LL FIND OUT FASTER IF I JUST USE MY SHOVEL.
WOULD YOU BE SO KIND AS TO RETURN IT?
HUH?
THE AKASHIC RECORD, ON THE ASTRAL PLANE...
KEEPS ALL MEMORIES THROUGHOUT THE UNIVERSE.
IF I USE MY SHOVEL'S AKASHOVELIC RECORD TECHNIQUE TO DIG DEEP INSIDE YOU...
IT SHOULD TELL ME THE LOCATION OF THE ORB.
WH-WHAT ARE YOU SUGGESTING?

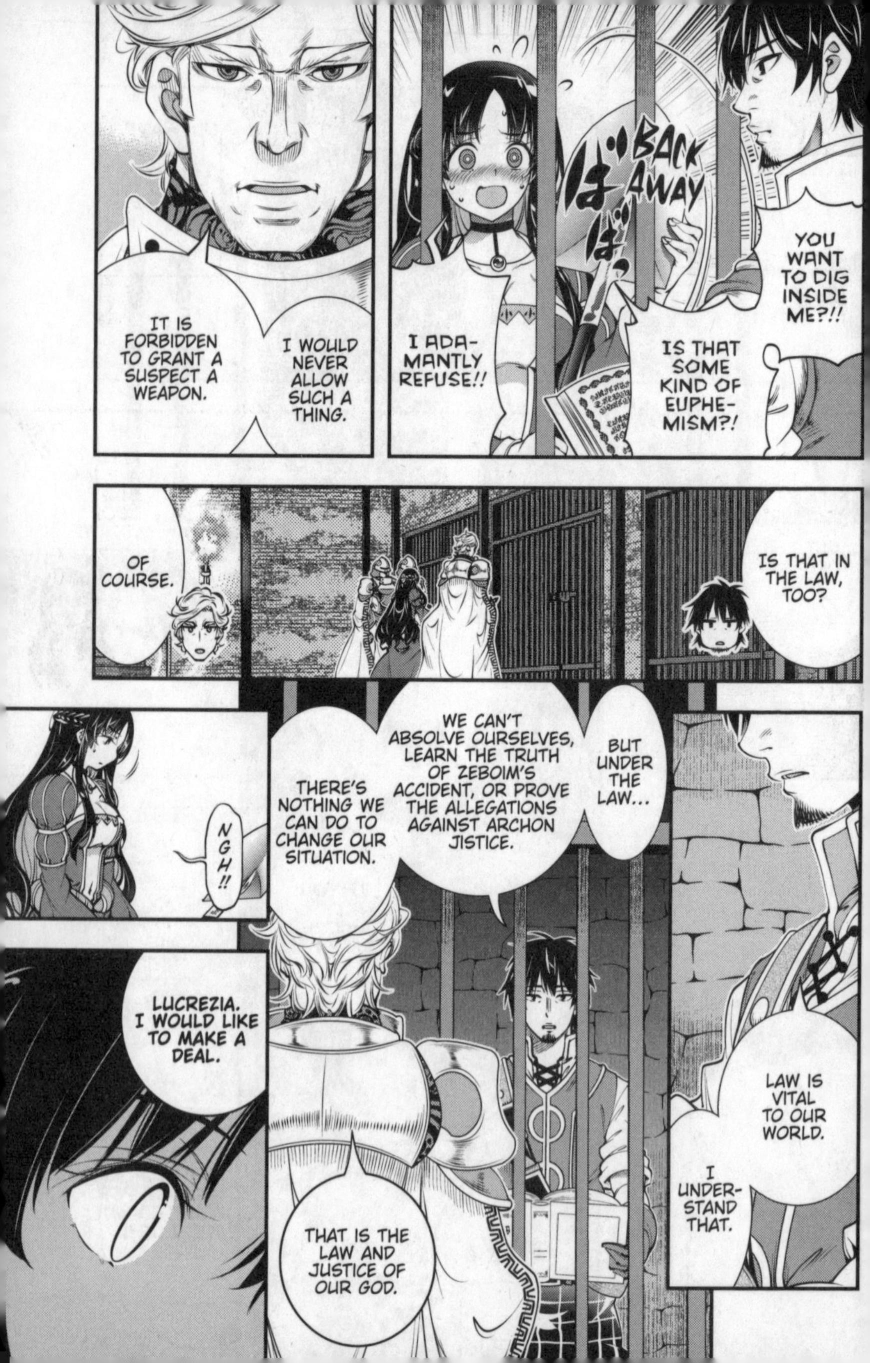

YOU WANT TO DIG INSIDE ME?!!
IS THAT SOME KIND OF EUPHEMISM?!
BACK AWAY
I ADAMANTLY REFUSE!!
I WOULD NEVER ALLOW SUCH A THING.
IT IS FORBIDDEN TO GRANT A SUSPECT A WEAPON.
IS THAT IN THE LAW, TOO?
OF COURSE.
LAW IS VITAL TO OUR WORLD.
I UNDERSTAND THAT.
BUT UNDER THE LAW...
WE CAN'T ABSOLVE OURSELVES, LEARN THE TRUTH OF ZEBOIM'S ACCIDENT, OR PROVE THE ALLEGATIONS AGAINST ARCHON JISTICE.
THERE'S NOTHING WE CAN DO TO CHANGE OUR SITUATION.
THAT IS THE LAW AND JUSTICE OF OUR GOD.
NGH!!
LUCREZIA. I WOULD LIKE TO MAKE A DEAL.

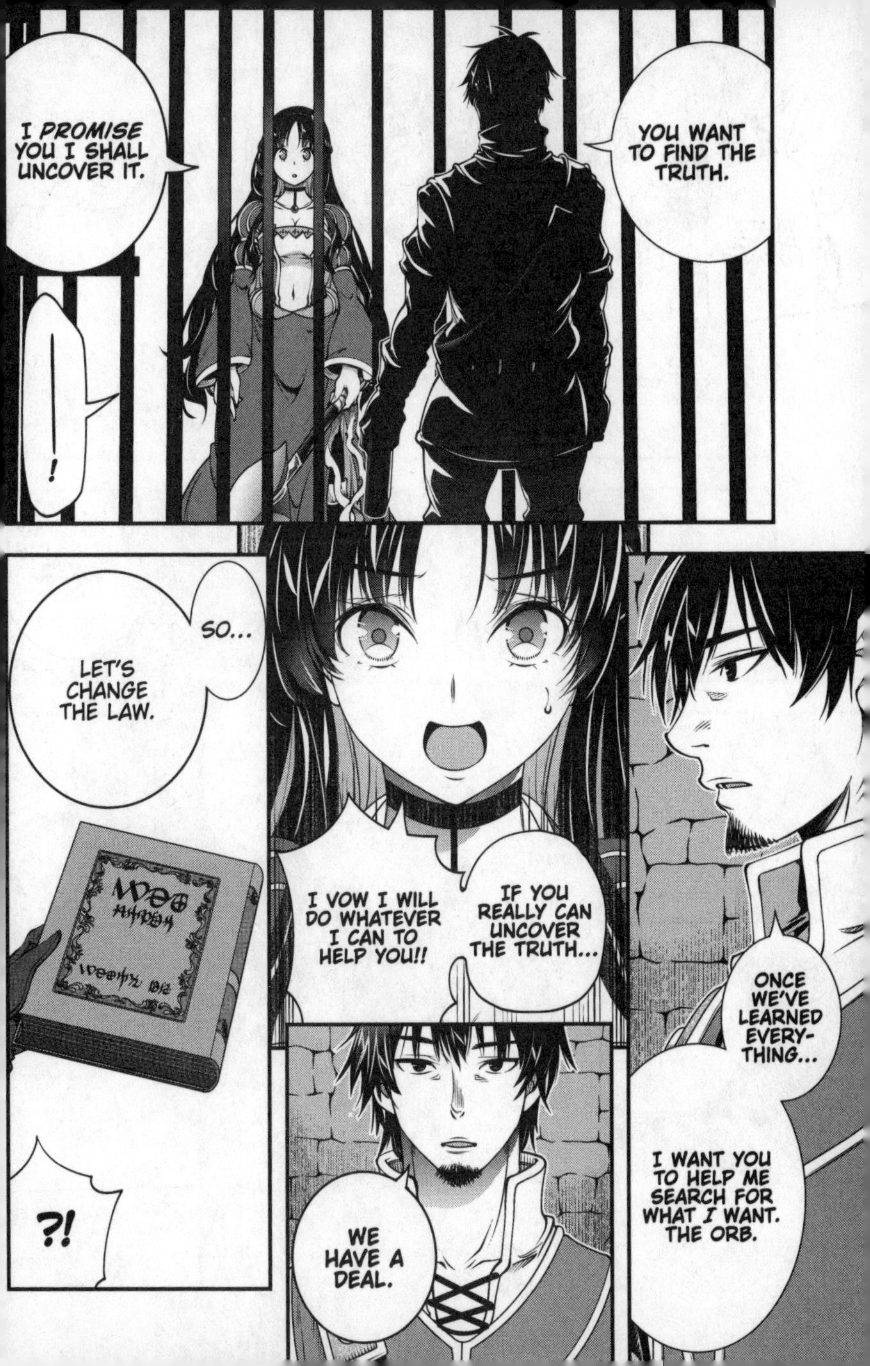
YOU WANT TO FIND THE TRUTH.
I *PROMISE* YOU I SHALL UNCOVER IT.
!
ONCE WE'VE LEARNED EVERY-THING...
I WANT YOU TO HELP ME SEARCH FOR WHAT *I* WANT. THE ORB.
IF YOU REALLY CAN UNCOVER THE TRUTH...
I VOW I WILL DO WHATEVER I CAN TO HELP YOU!!
WE HAVE A DEAL.
SO...
LET'S CHANGE THE LAW.
?!

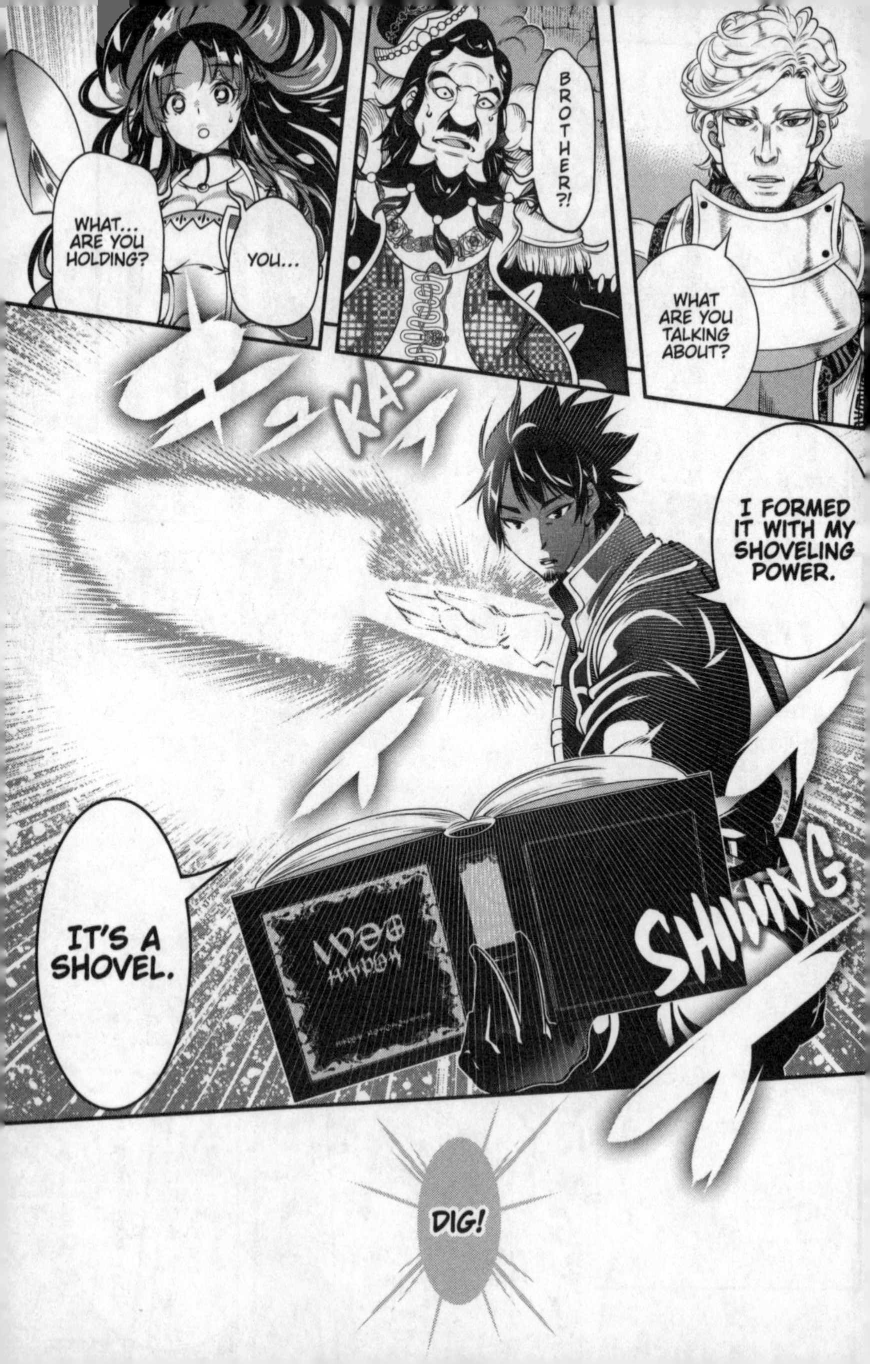
WHAT ARE YOU TALKING ABOUT?
BROTHER?!
YOU...
WHAT... ARE YOU HOLDING?
I FORMED IT WITH MY SHOVELING POWER.
KA-
SHIIIING
IT'S A SHOVEL.
DIG!

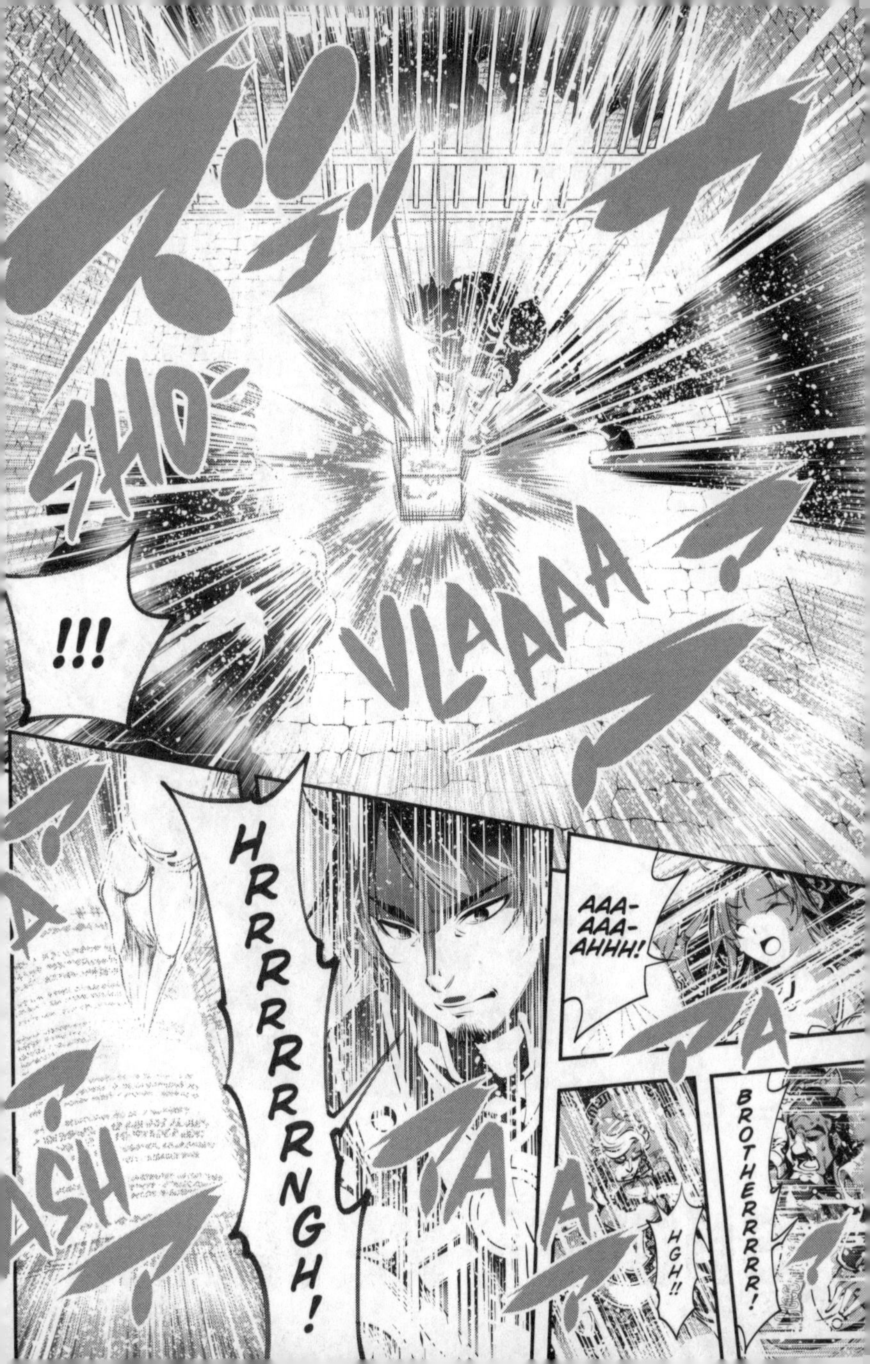
VLAAAA
SHO
!!!
AAA-
AAA-
AHHH!
BROTHERRRRR!
HGH!!
HRRRRRRRNGH!
ASH

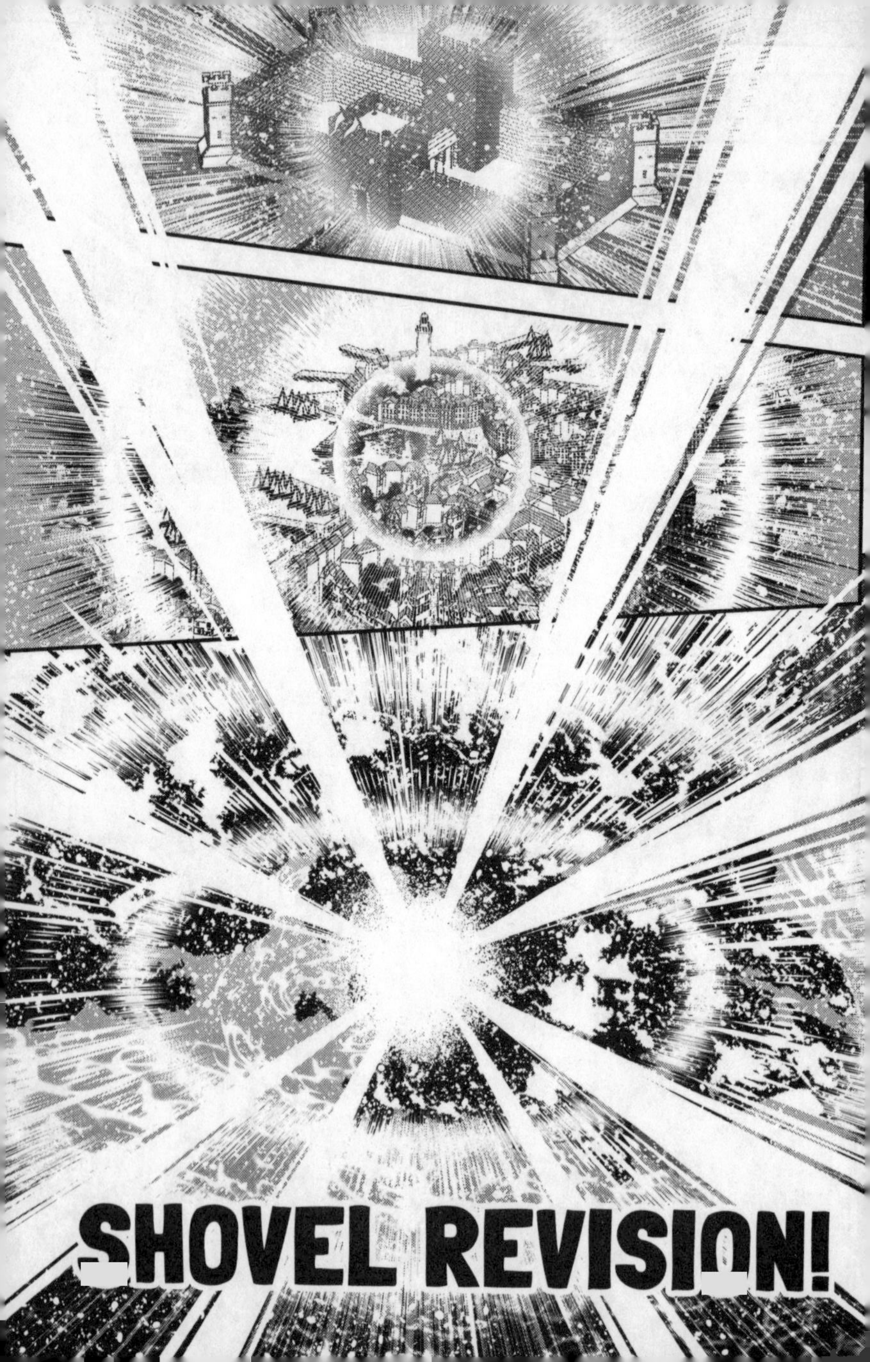
SHOVEL REVISION!

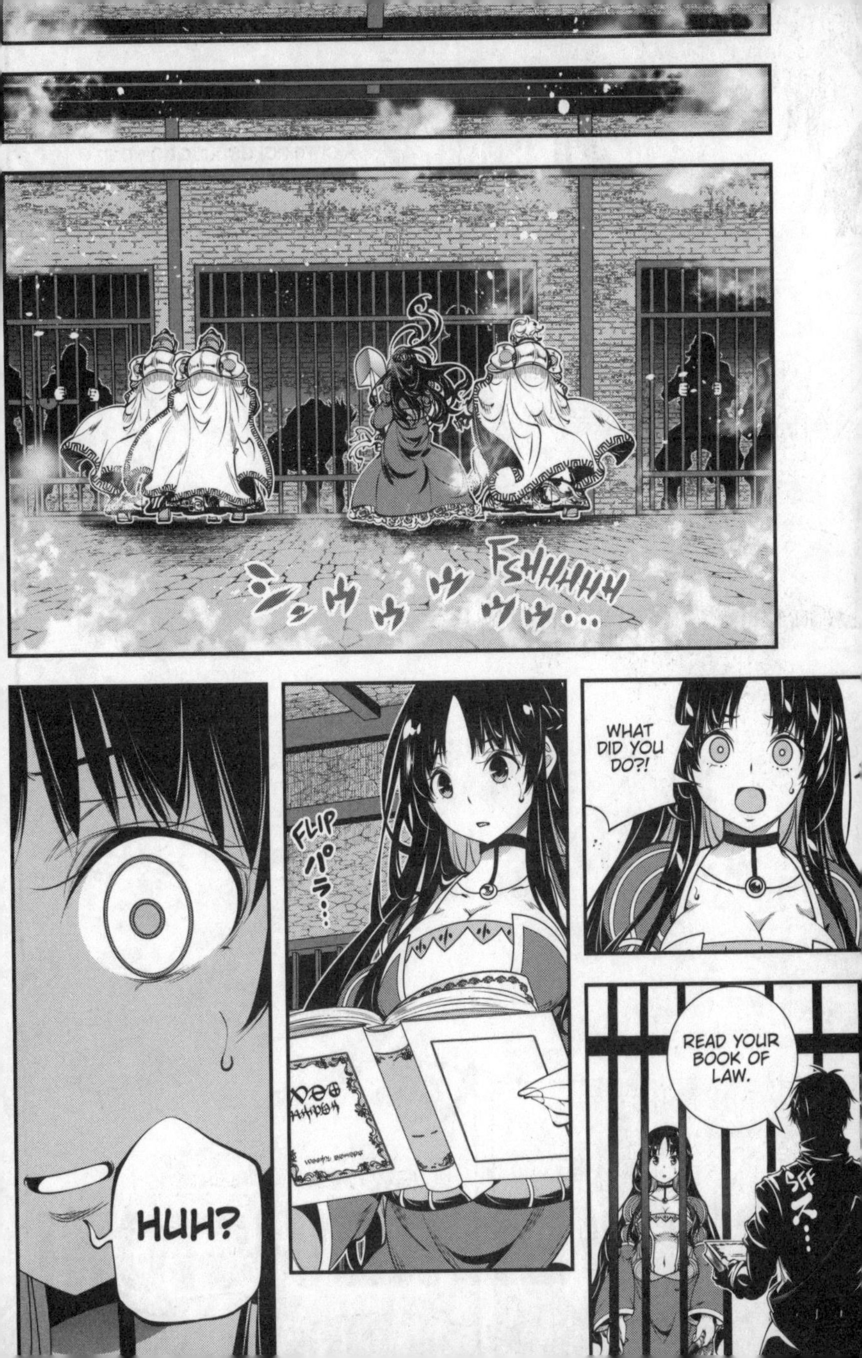
FSHHHHH
WHAT DID YOU DO?!
READ YOUR BOOK OF LAW.
SFF
ス…
FLIP
パラ…
HUH?

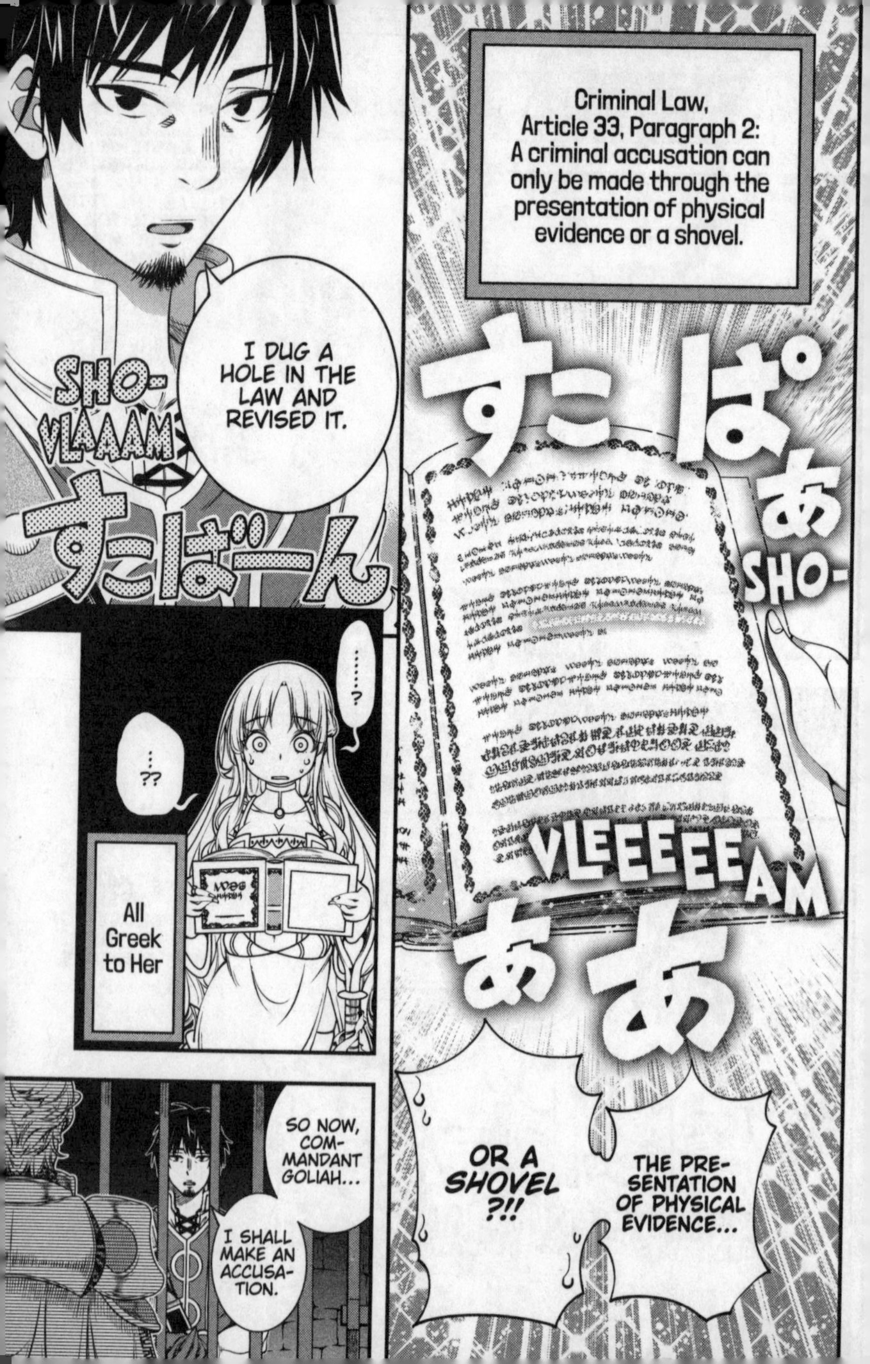
Criminal Law, Article 33, Paragraph 2: A criminal accusation can only be made through the presentation of physical evidence or a shovel.
すこぱぁ
SHO-
VLEEEEEAM
ぁぁ
THE PRE-SENTATION OF PHYSICAL EVIDENCE...
OR A SHOVEL ?!!
I DUG A HOLE IN THE LAW AND REVISED IT.
SHO-VLAAAM
すこばーん
......?
...??
All Greek to Her
SO NOW, COM-MANDANT GOLIAH...
I SHALL MAKE AN ACCUSA-TION.

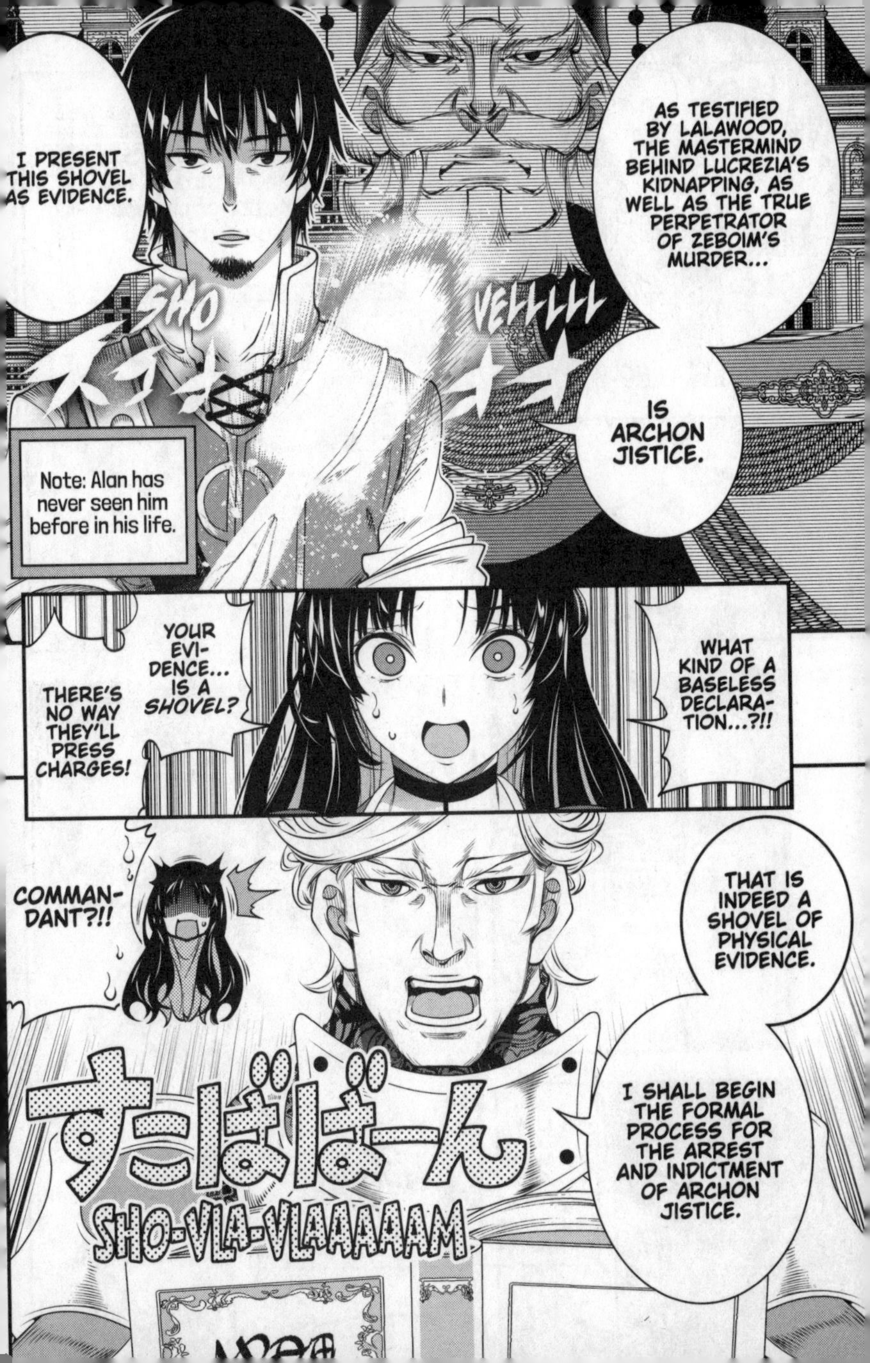
AS TESTIFIED BY LALAWOOD, THE MASTERMIND BEHIND LUCREZIA'S KIDNAPPING, AS WELL AS THE TRUE PERPETRATOR OF ZEBOIM'S MURDER...
IS ARCHON JISTICE.
I PRESENT THIS SHOVEL AS EVIDENCE.
SHO
VELLLLLL
Note: Alan has never seen him before in his life.
WHAT KIND OF A BASELESS DECLARA-TION...?!!
YOUR EVI-DENCE... IS A SHOVEL?
THERE'S NO WAY THEY'LL PRESS CHARGES!
THAT IS INDEED A SHOVEL OF PHYSICAL EVIDENCE.
I SHALL BEGIN THE FORMAL PROCESS FOR THE ARREST AND INDICTMENT OF ARCHON JISTICE.
COMMAN-DANT?!!
すこばばーん
SHO-VLA-VLAAAAAM

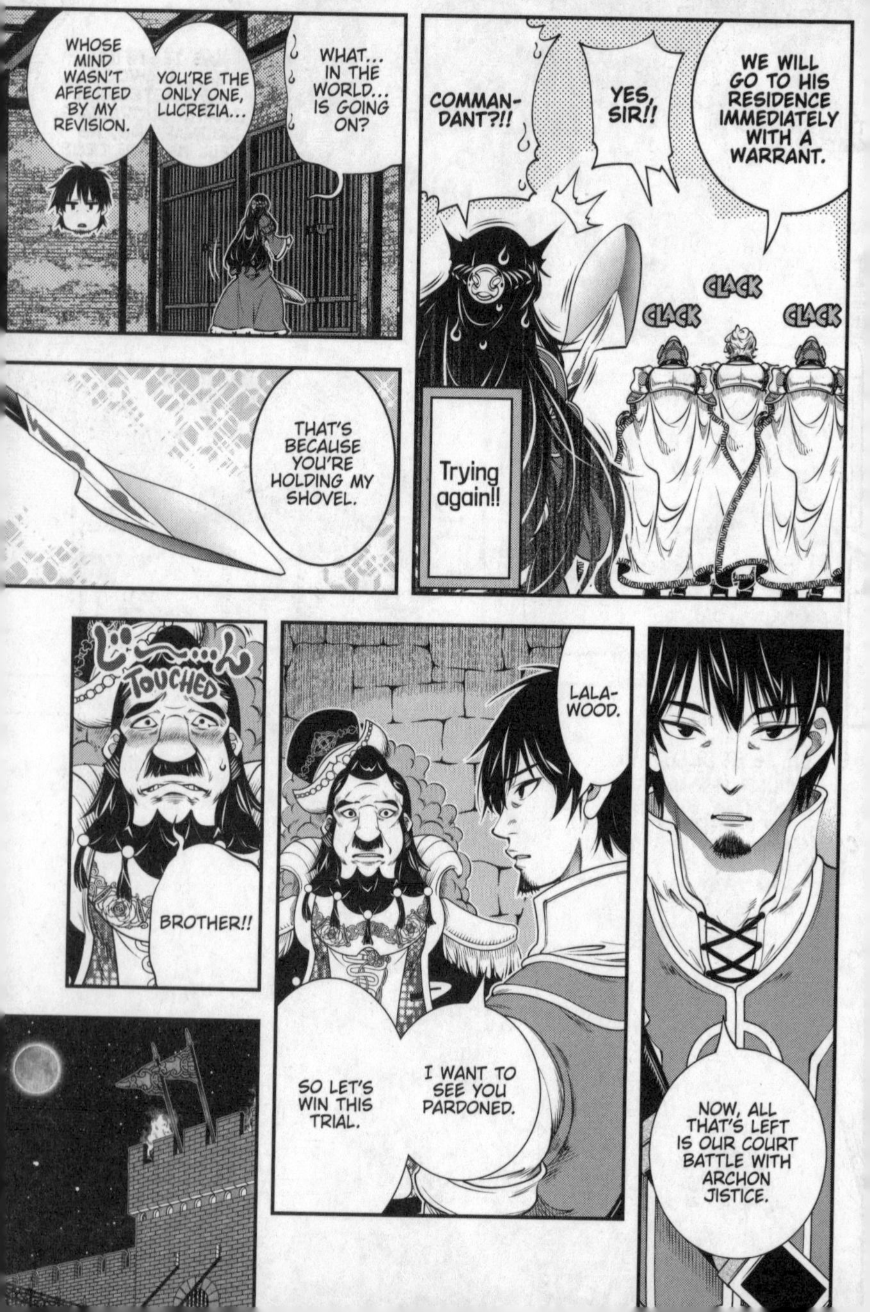
WE WILL GO TO HIS RESIDENCE IMMEDIATELY WITH A WARRANT.
YES, SIR!!
COMMANDANT?!!
CLACK
CLACK
CLACK
Trying again!!
WHAT... IN THE WORLD... IS GOING ON?
YOU'RE THE ONLY ONE, LUCREZIA...
WHOSE MIND WASN'T AFFECTED BY MY REVISION.
THAT'S BECAUSE YOU'RE HOLDING MY SHOVEL.
NOW, ALL THAT'S LEFT IS OUR COURT BATTLE WITH ARCHON JISTICE.
LALA-WOOD.
I WANT TO SEE YOU PARDONED.
SO LET'S WIN THIS TRIAL.
じ～～…ん
TOUCHED
BROTHER!!

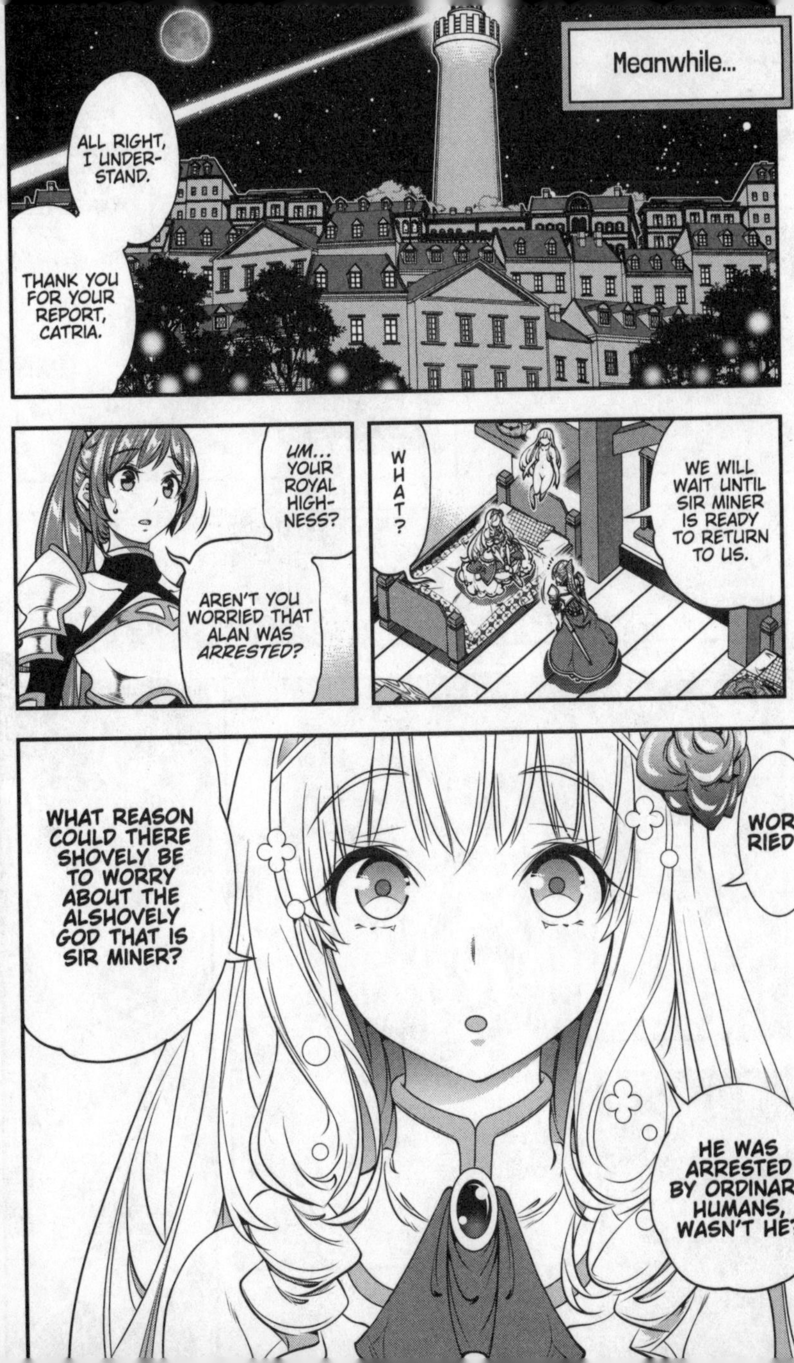
Meanwhile...
ALL RIGHT, I UNDER-STAND.
THANK YOU FOR YOUR REPORT, CATRIA.
WE WILL WAIT UNTIL SIR MINER IS READY TO RETURN TO US.
WHAT?
UM... YOUR ROYAL HIGH-NESS?
AREN'T YOU WORRIED THAT ALAN WAS ARRESTED?
WOR-RIED?
HE WAS ARRESTED BY ORDINARY HUMANS, WASN'T HE?
WHAT REASON COULD THERE SHOVELY BE TO WORRY ABOUT THE ALSHOVELY GOD THAT IS SIR MINER?

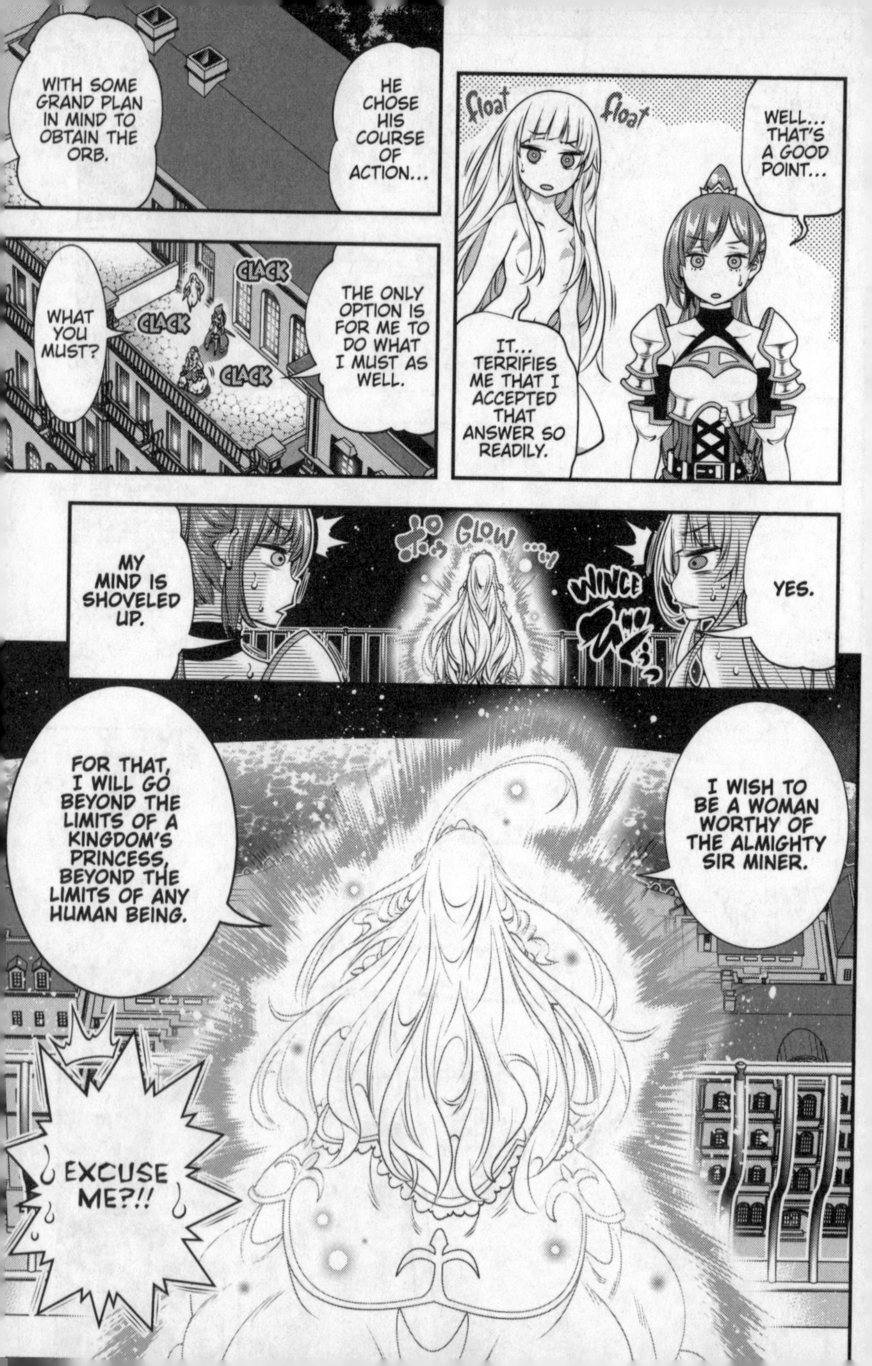

float
float
WELL... THAT'S A GOOD POINT...
IT... TERRIFIES ME THAT I ACCEPTED THAT ANSWER SO READILY.
HE CHOSE HIS COURSE OF ACTION...
WITH SOME GRAND PLAN IN MIND TO OBTAIN THE ORB.
THE ONLY OPTION IS FOR ME TO DO WHAT I MUST AS WELL.
CLACK
CLACK
CLACK
WHAT YOU MUST?
YES.
WINCE
GLOW
MY MIND IS SHOVELED UP.
I WISH TO BE A WOMAN WORTHY OF THE ALMIGHTY SIR MINER.
FOR THAT, I WILL GO BEYOND THE LIMITS OF A KINGDOM'S PRINCESS, BEYOND THE LIMITS OF ANY HUMAN BEING.
EXCUSE ME?!!

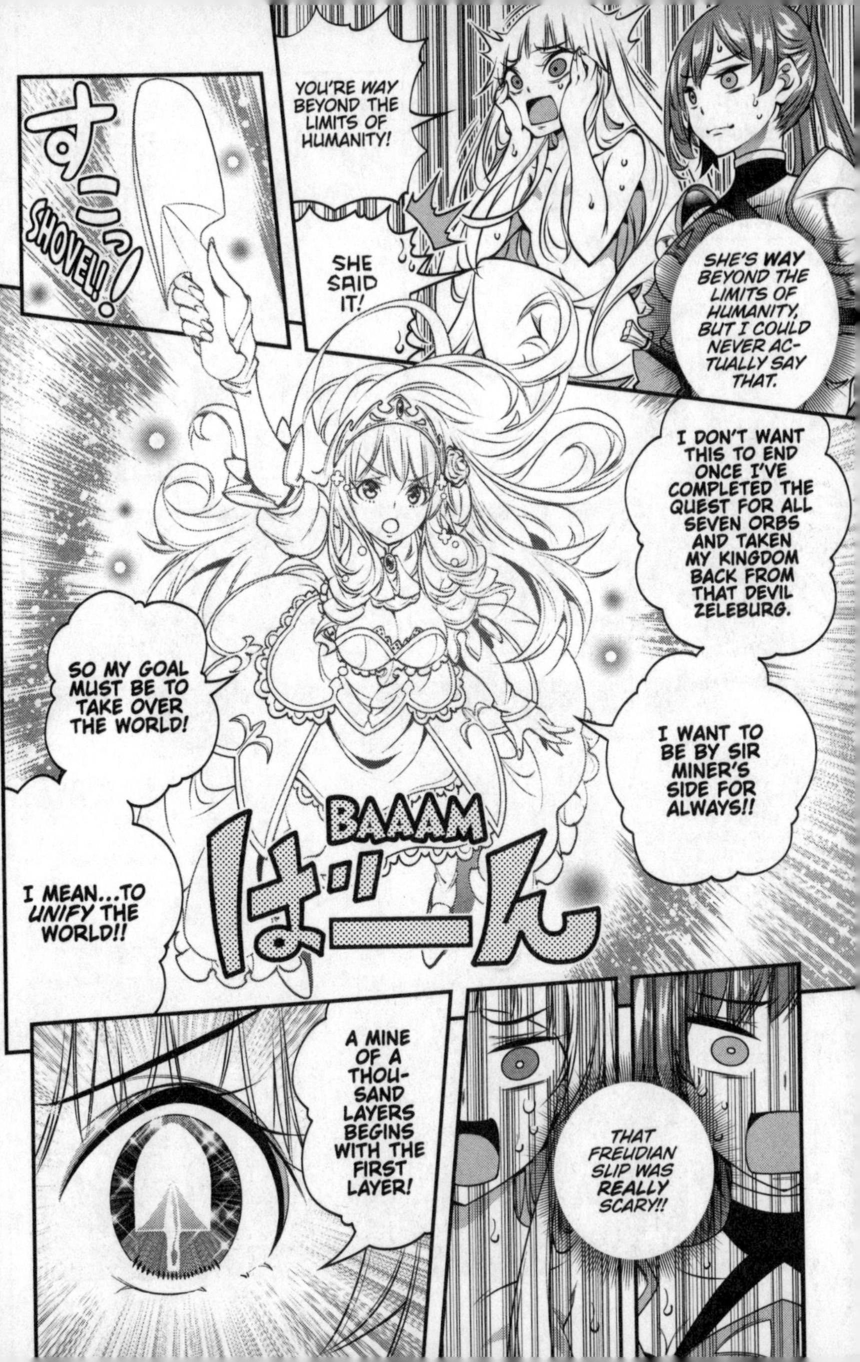
YOU'RE WAY BEYOND THE LIMITS OF HUMANITY!
SHE'S WAY BEYOND THE LIMITS OF HUMANITY, BUT I COULD NEVER ACTUALLY SAY THAT.
SHE SAID IT!
すこっ!
SHOVEL!!
I DON'T WANT THIS TO END ONCE I'VE COMPLETED THE QUEST FOR ALL SEVEN ORBS AND TAKEN MY KINGDOM BACK FROM THAT DEVIL ZELEBURG.
I WANT TO BE BY SIR MINER'S SIDE FOR ALWAYS!!
SO MY GOAL MUST BE TO TAKE OVER THE WORLD!
BAAAM
ばーん
I MEAN...TO *UNIFY* THE WORLD!!
THAT FREUDIAN SLIP WAS REALLY SCARY!!
A MINE OF A THOUSAND LAYERS BEGINS WITH THE FIRST LAYER!

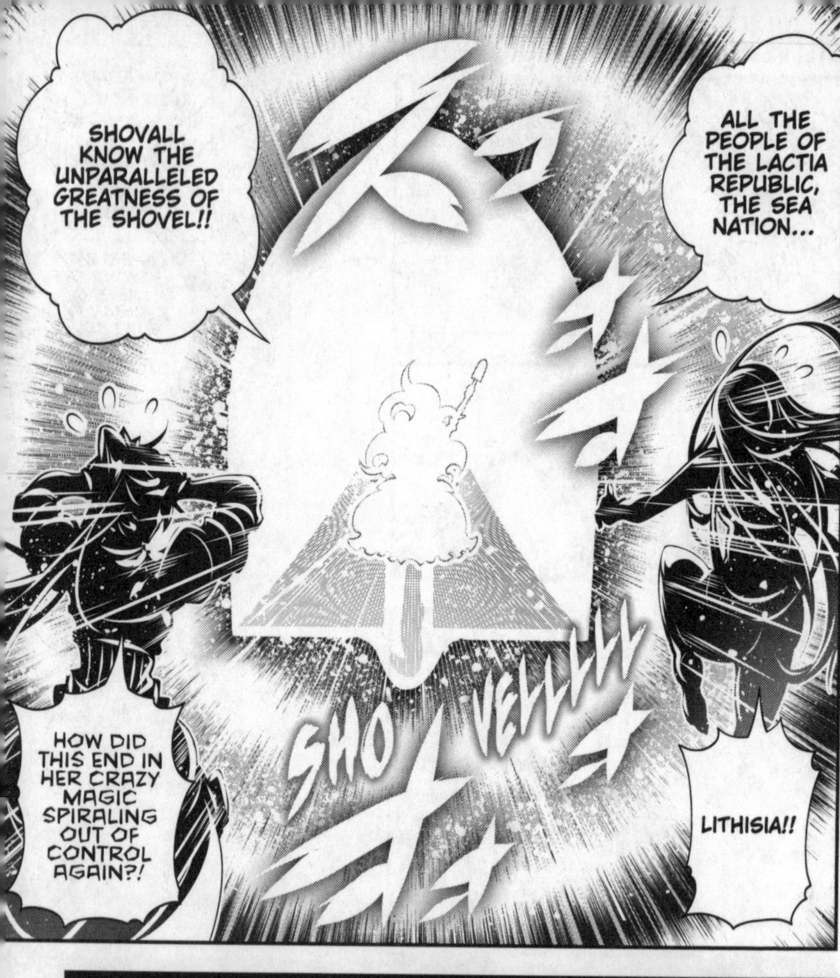
ALL THE PEOPLE OF THE LACTIA REPUBLIC, THE SEA NATION...
SHOVALL KNOW THE UNPARALLELED GREATNESS OF THE SHOVEL!!
SHO VELLLLL
LITHISIA!!
HOW DID THIS END IN HER CRAZY MAGIC SPIRALING OUT OF CONTROL AGAIN?!

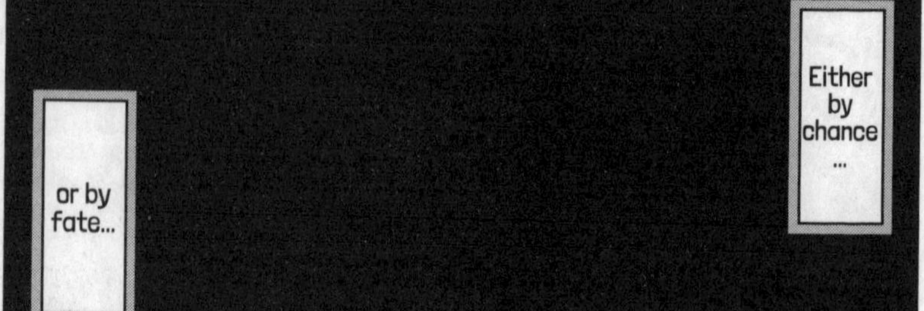
Either by chance ...
or by fate...

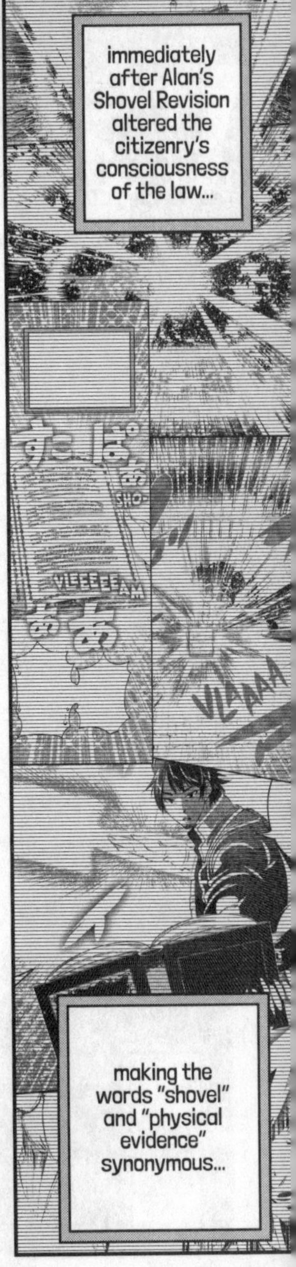
immediately after Alan's Shovel Revision altered the citizenry's consciousness of the law...
SHO
VLEEEEAM
VLAAAA
making the words "shovel" and "physical evidence" synonymous...

Lithisia's shovel magic activated!!

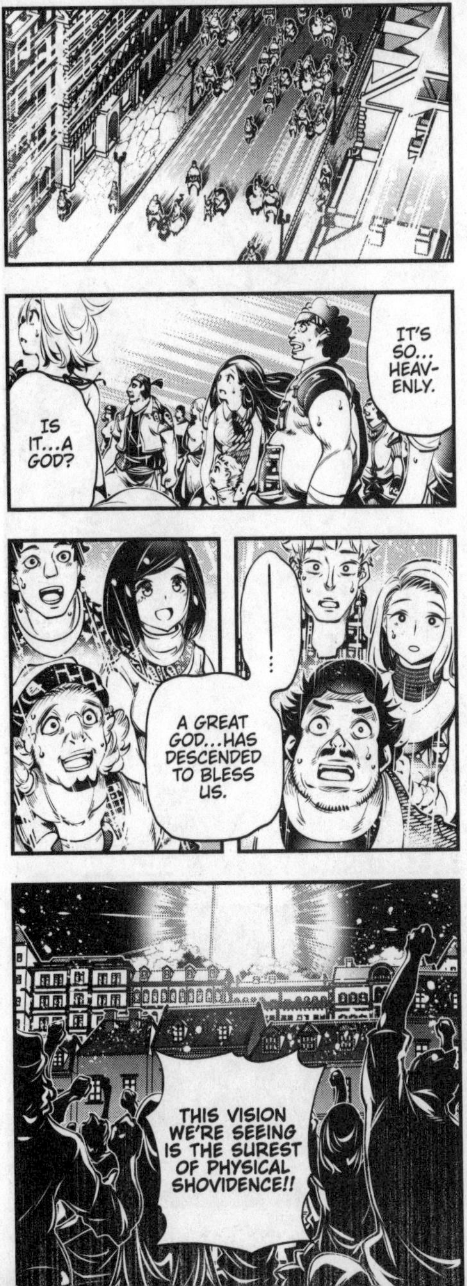
IT'S SO... HEAVENLY.
IS IT...A GOD?
!...
A GREAT GOD...HAS DESCENDED TO BLESS US.
THIS VISION WE'RE SEEING IS THE SUREST OF PHYSICAL SHOVIDENCE!!

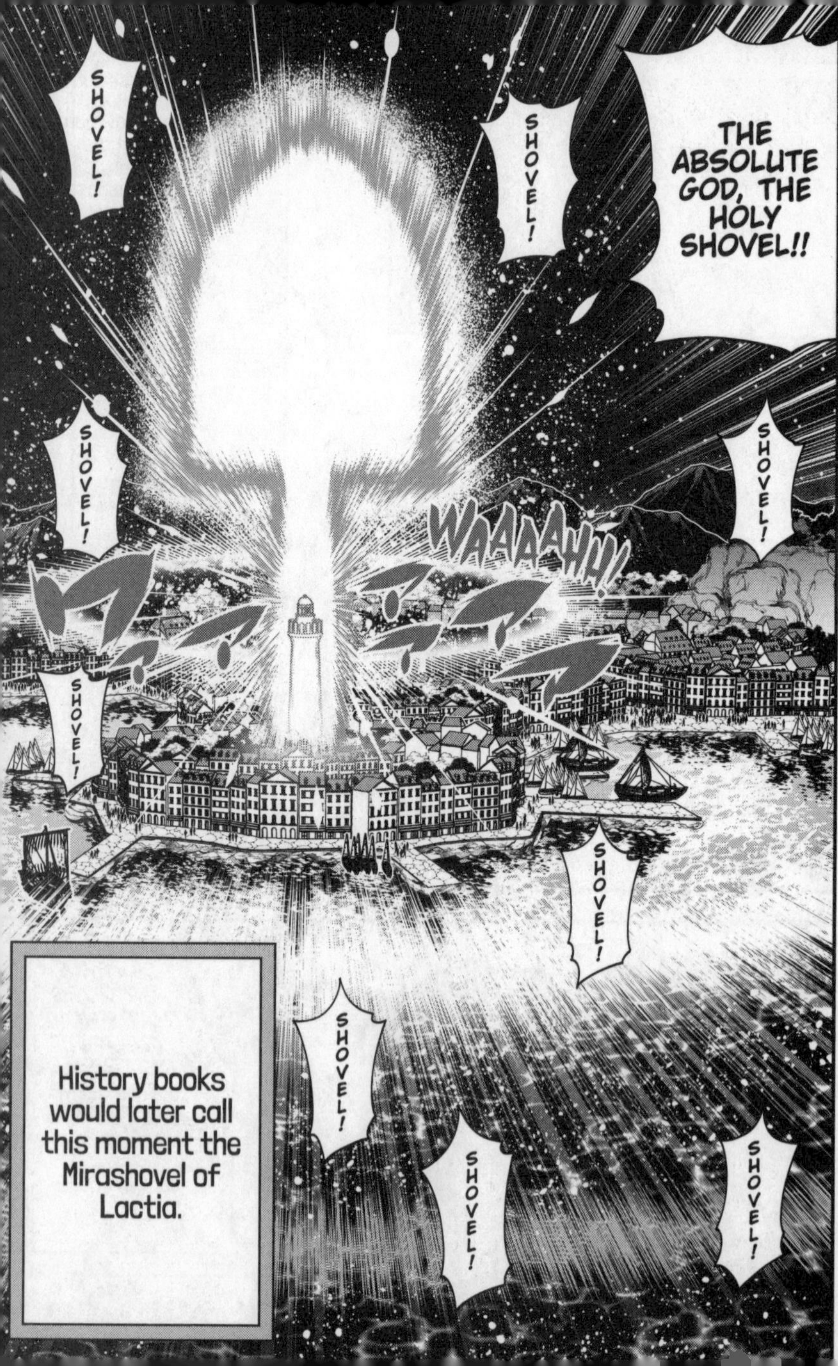
THE ABSOLUTE GOD, THE HOLY SHOVEL!!
SHOVEL!
SHOVEL!
SHOVEL!
WAAAAHH!!
SHOVEL!
SHOVEL!
SHOVEL!
SHOVEL!
SHOVEL!
SHOVEL!
History books would later call this moment the Mirashovel of Lactia.

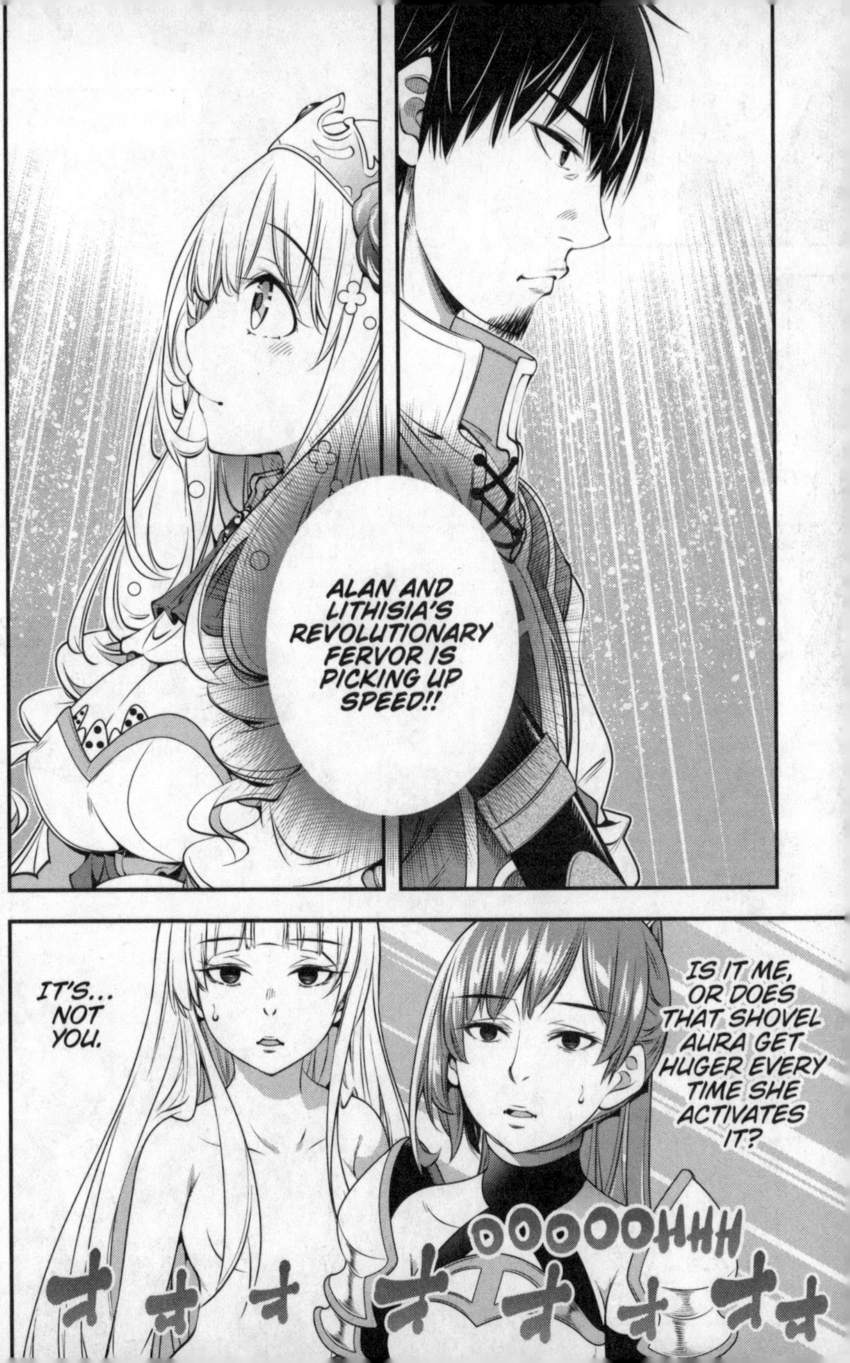
ALAN AND LITHISIA'S REVOLUTIONARY FERVOR IS PICKING UP SPEED!!
IS IT ME, OR DOES THAT SHOVEL AURA GET HUGER EVERY TIME SHE ACTIVATES IT?
IT'S... NOT YOU.
OOOOOHHH

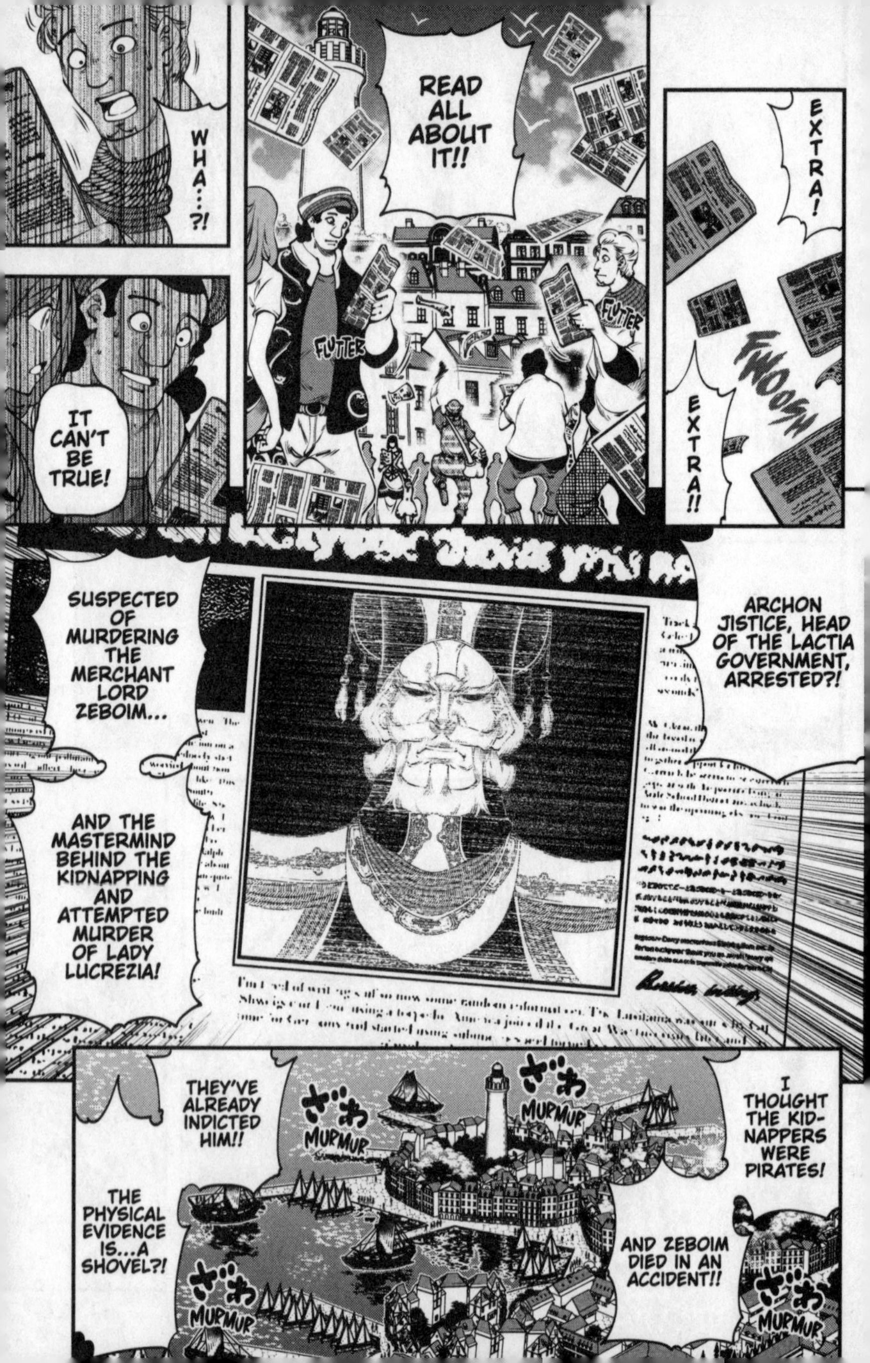
EXTRA!
FWOOSH
EXTRA!!
READ ALL ABOUT IT!!
FLUTTER
FLUTTER
WHA...?!
IT CAN'T BE TRUE!
ARCHON JISTICE, HEAD OF THE LACTIA GOVERNMENT, ARRESTED?!
SUSPECTED OF MURDERING THE MERCHANT LORD ZEBOIM...
AND THE MASTERMIND BEHIND THE KIDNAPPING AND ATTEMPTED MURDER OF LADY LUCREZIA!
ざあ
MURMUR
I THOUGHT THE KID-NAPPERS WERE PIRATES!
ざあ
MURMUR
AND ZEBOIM DIED IN AN ACCIDENT!!
ざあ
MURMUR
THEY'VE ALREADY INDICTED HIM!!
THE PHYSICAL EVIDENCE IS...A SHOVEL?!
ざあ
MURMUR

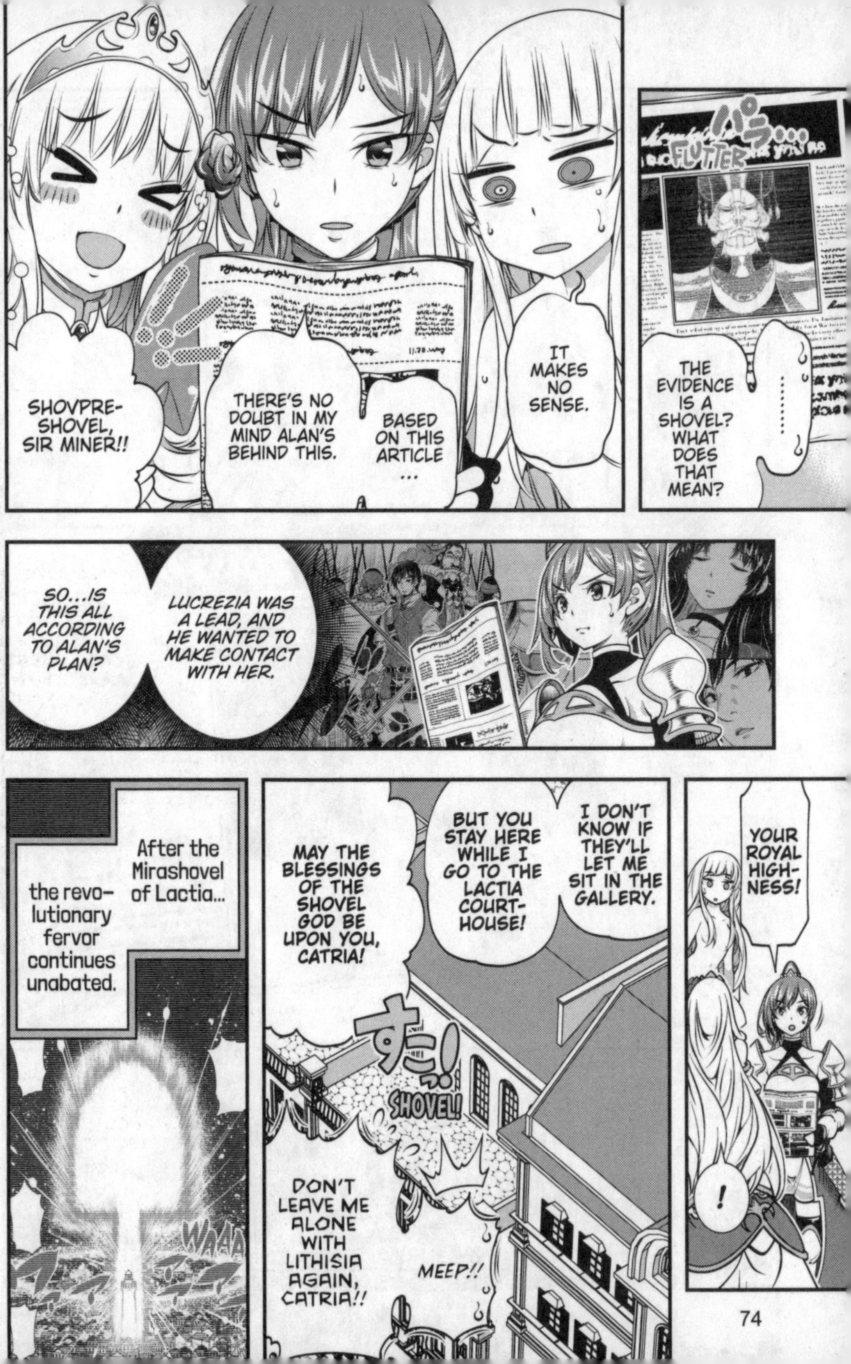
パラ…
FLUTTER
THE EVIDENCE IS A SHOVEL? WHAT DOES THAT MEAN?
……
IT MAKES NO SENSE.
BASED ON THIS ARTICLE …
THERE'S NO DOUBT IN MY MIND ALAN'S BEHIND THIS.
SHOVPRE-SHOVEL, SIR MINER!!
LUCREZIA WAS A LEAD, AND HE WANTED TO MAKE CONTACT WITH HER.
SO…IS THIS ALL ACCORDING TO ALAN'S PLAN?
YOUR ROYAL HIGHNESS!
!
I DON'T KNOW IF THEY'LL LET ME SIT IN THE GALLERY.
BUT YOU STAY HERE WHILE I GO TO THE LACTIA COURTHOUSE!
MAY THE BLESSINGS OF THE SHOVEL GOD BE UPON YOU, CATRIA!
すこっ!
SHOVEL!
MEEP!!
DON'T LEAVE ME ALONE WITH LITHISIA AGAIN, CATRIA!!
After the Mirashovel of Lactia…
the revolutionary fervor continues unabated.
WAAA

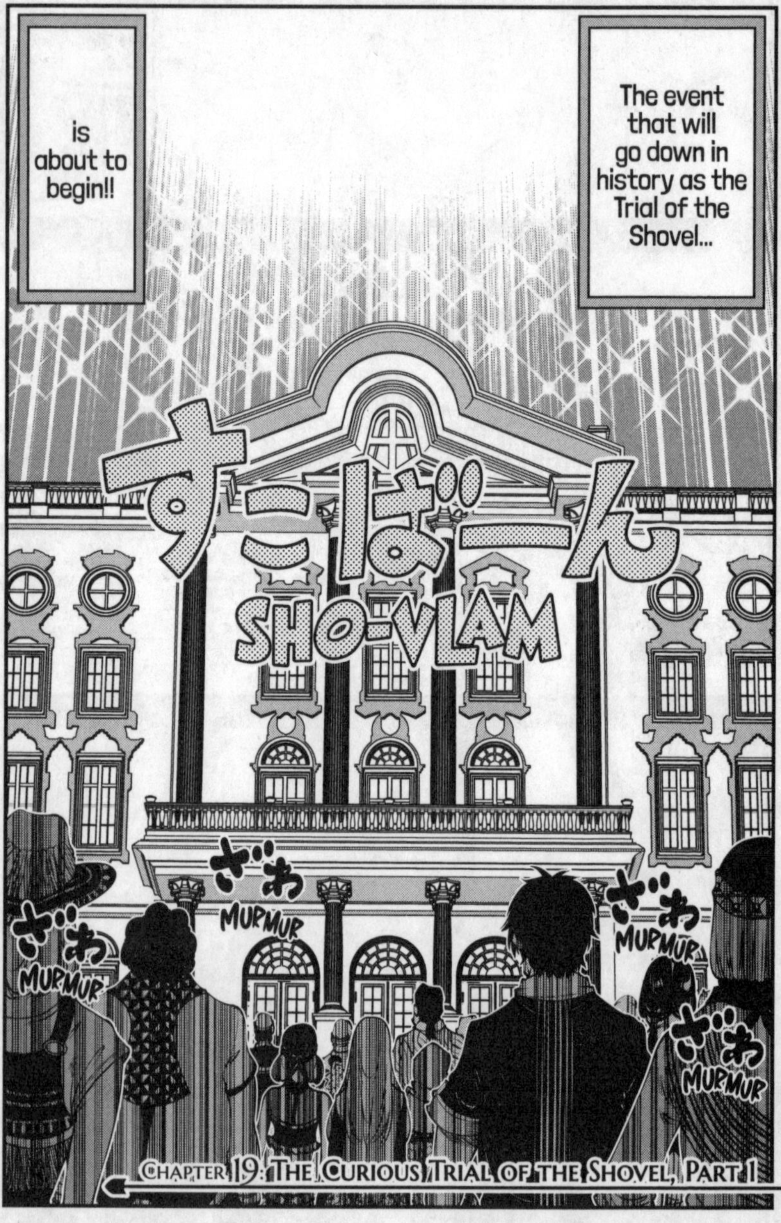
The event that will go down in history as the Trial of the Shovel...
is about to begin!!
すこぱーん
SHO-VLAM
ざわ
MURMUR
ざわ
MURMUR
ざわ
MURMUR
ざわ
MURMUR
Chapter 19: The Curious Trial of the Shovel, Part 1

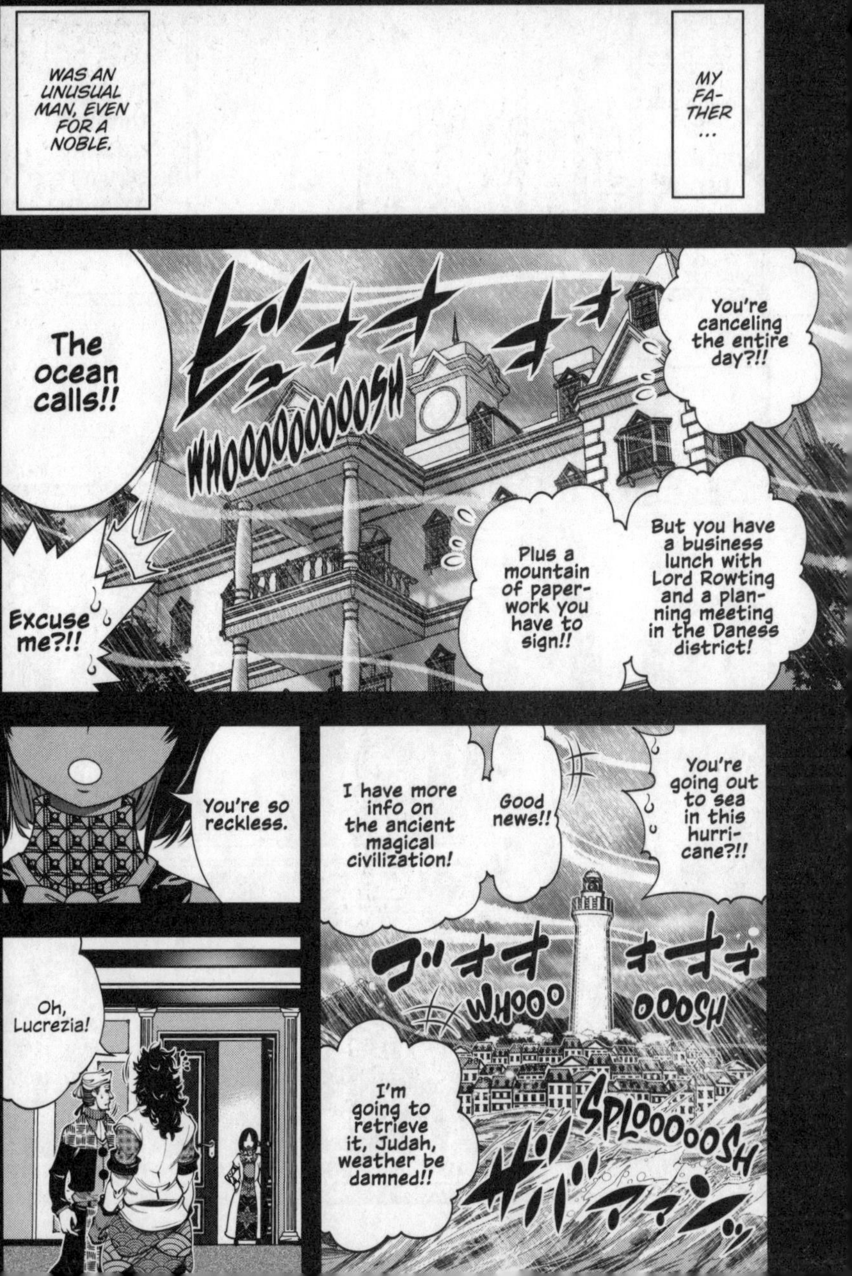
MY FA-THER ...
WAS AN UNUSUAL MAN, EVEN FOR A NOBLE.
You're canceling the entire day?!!
But you have a business lunch with Lord Rowting and a plan-ning meeting in the Daness district!
Plus a mountain of paper-work you have to sign!!
WHOOOOOOOOOOSH
The ocean calls!!
Excuse me?!!
You're going out to sea in this hurri-cane?!!
Good news!!
I have more info on the ancient magical civilization!
WHOOO OOOSH
I'm going to retrieve it, Judah, weather be damned!!
SPLOOOOOOSH
You're so reckless.
Oh, Lucrezia!

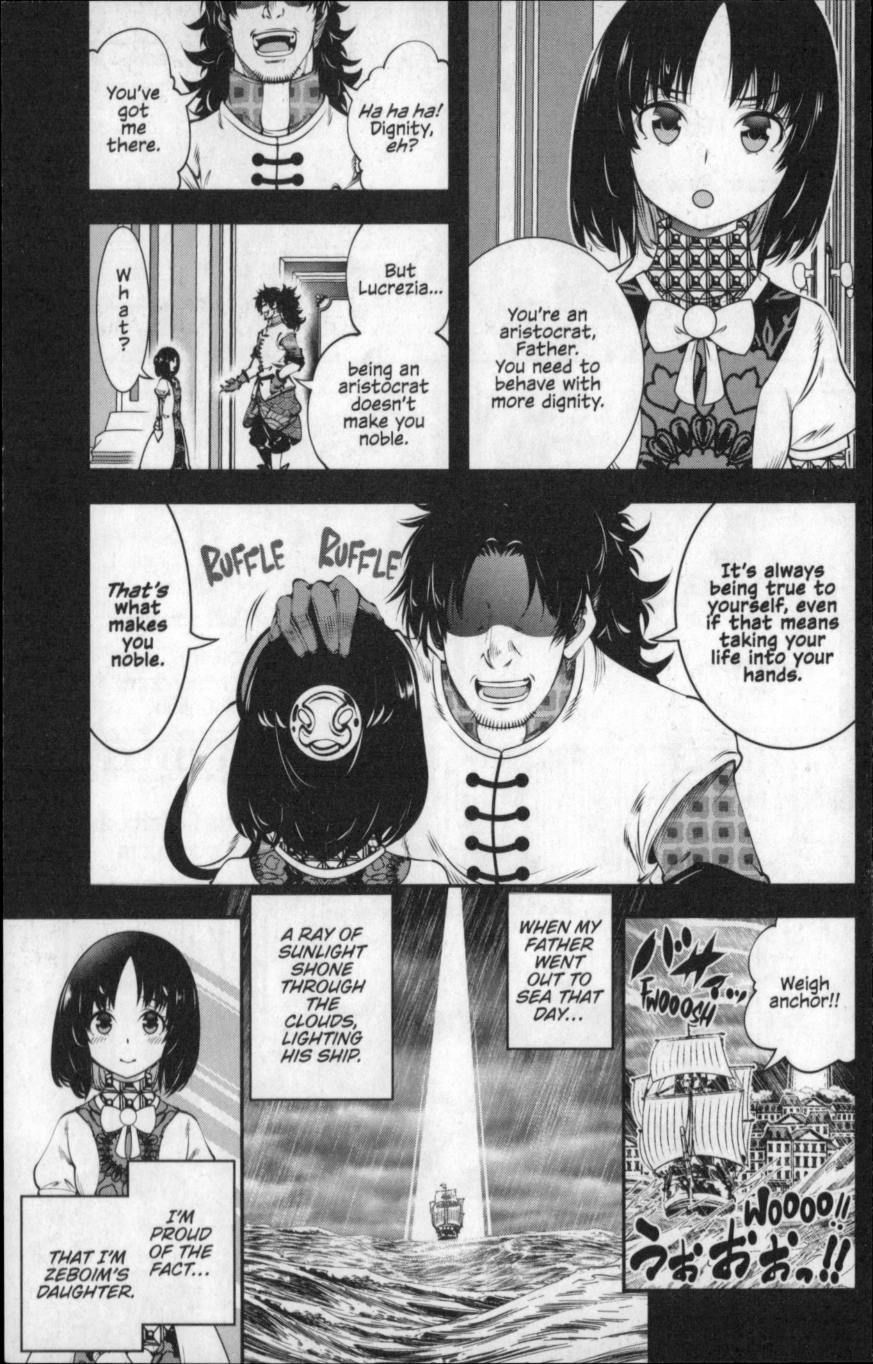
You're an aristocrat, Father. You need to behave with more dignity.
Ha ha ha! Dignity, eh?
You've got me there.
What?
But Lucrezia...
being an aristocrat doesn't make you noble.
It's always being true to yourself, even if that means taking your life into your hands.
RUFFLE RUFFLE
That's what makes you noble.
Weigh anchor!!
FWOOOSH
WOOOO!!
うおおおっ!!
WHEN MY FATHER WENT OUT TO SEA THAT DAY...
A RAY OF SUNLIGHT SHONE THROUGH THE CLOUDS, LIGHTING HIS SHIP.
I'M PROUD OF THE FACT...
THAT I'M ZEBOIM'S DAUGHTER.

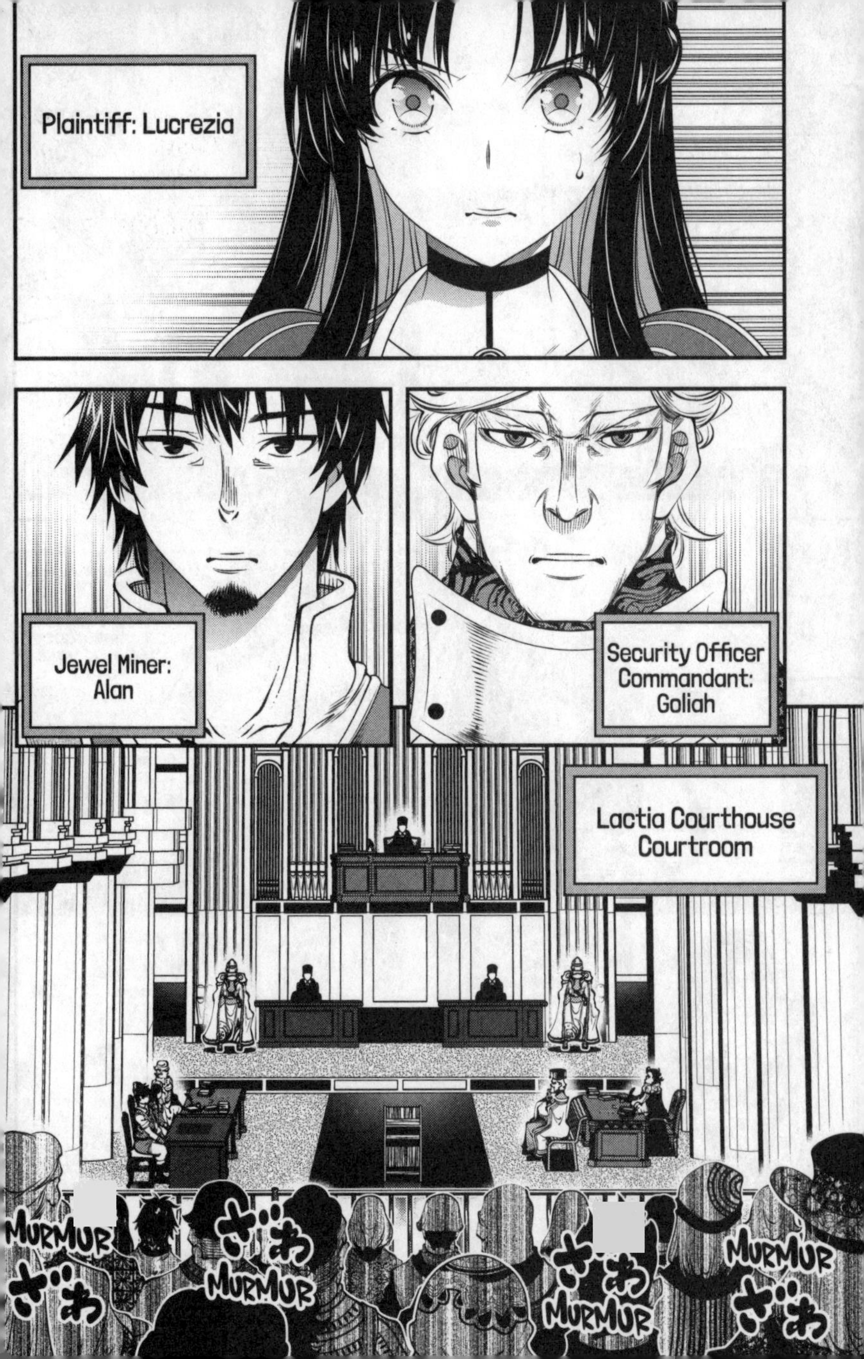
Plaintiff: Lucrezia
Security Officer Commandant: Goliah
Jewel Miner: Alan
Lactia Courthouse Courtroom
MURMUR
ざわ
ざわ
MURMUR
ざわ
MURMUR
MURMUR
ざわ

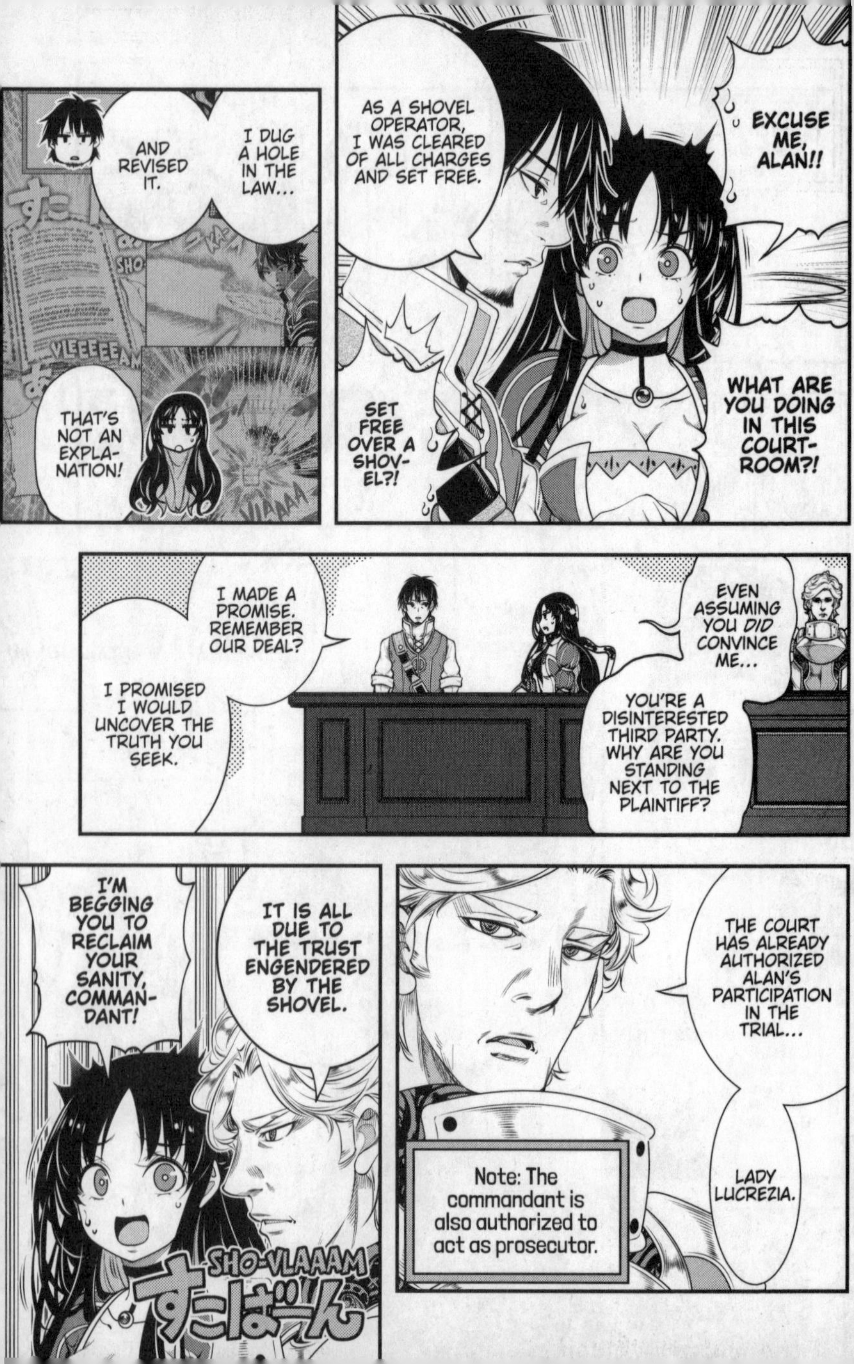
EXCUSE ME, ALAN!!
WHAT ARE YOU DOING IN THIS COURTROOM?!
AS A SHOVEL OPERATOR, I WAS CLEARED OF ALL CHARGES AND SET FREE.
SET FREE OVER A SHOVEL?!
I DUG A HOLE IN THE LAW...
AND REVISED IT.
VLEEEEEAM
THAT'S NOT AN EXPLANATION!
EVEN ASSUMING YOU *DID* CONVINCE ME...
YOU'RE A DISINTERESTED THIRD PARTY. WHY ARE YOU STANDING NEXT TO THE PLAINTIFF?
I MADE A PROMISE. REMEMBER OUR DEAL?
I PROMISED I WOULD UNCOVER THE TRUTH YOU SEEK.
THE COURT HAS ALREADY AUTHORIZED ALAN'S PARTICIPATION IN THE TRIAL...
LADY LUCREZIA.
Note: The commandant is also authorized to act as prosecutor.
IT IS ALL DUE TO THE TRUST ENGENDERED BY THE SHOVEL.
I'M BEGGING YOU TO RECLAIM YOUR SANITY, COMMANDANT!
SHO-VLAAAM
すこばーん

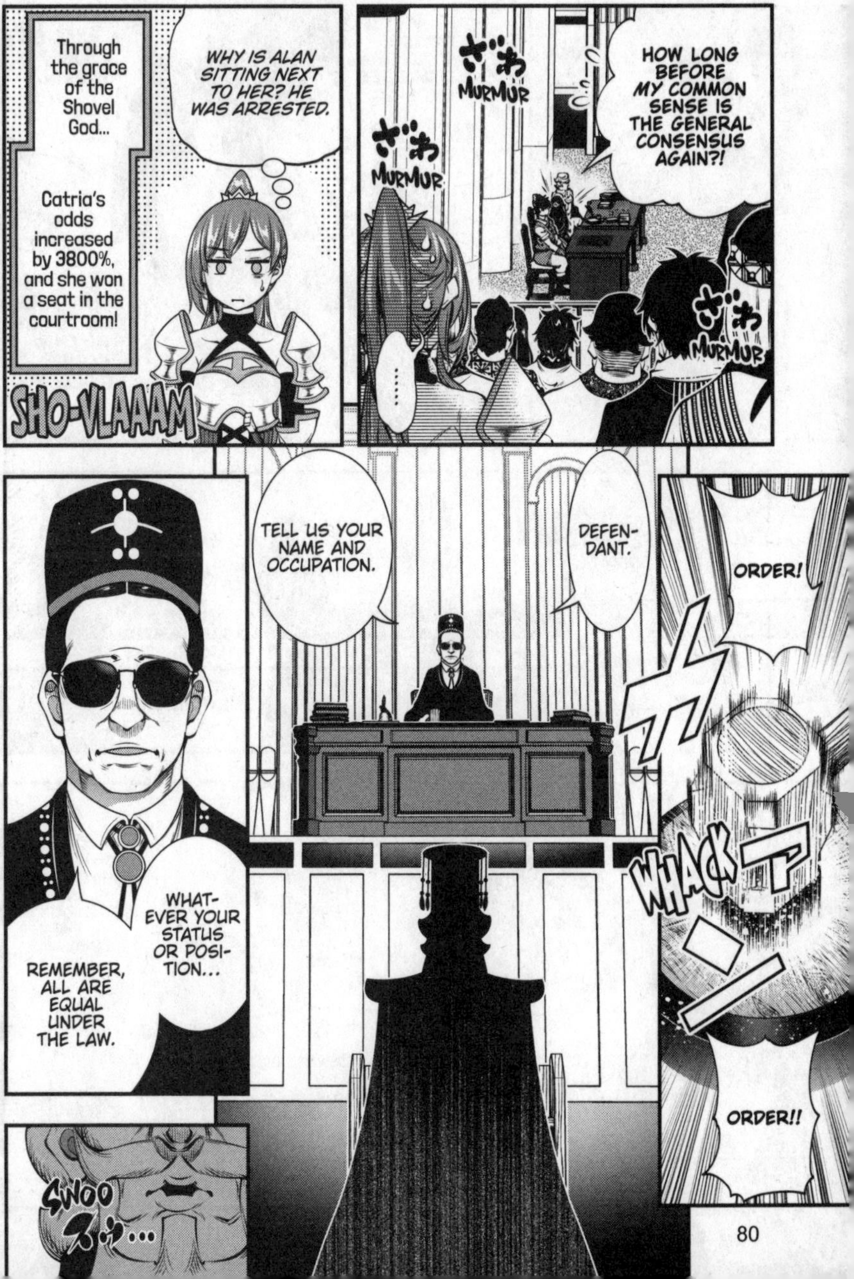
ざわ
MURMUR
HOW LONG BEFORE MY COMMON SENSE IS THE GENERAL CONSENSUS AGAIN?!
ざわ
MURMUR
ざわ
MURMUR
......
Through the grace of the Shovel God...
WHY IS ALAN SITTING NEXT TO HER? HE WAS ARRESTED.
Catria's odds increased by 3800%, and she won a seat in the courtroom!
SHO-VLAAAM
ORDER!
WHACK
ORDER!!
DEFENDANT.
TELL US YOUR NAME AND OCCUPATION.
WHATEVER YOUR STATUS OR POSITION...
REMEMBER, ALL ARE EQUAL UNDER THE LAW.
SWOO
...

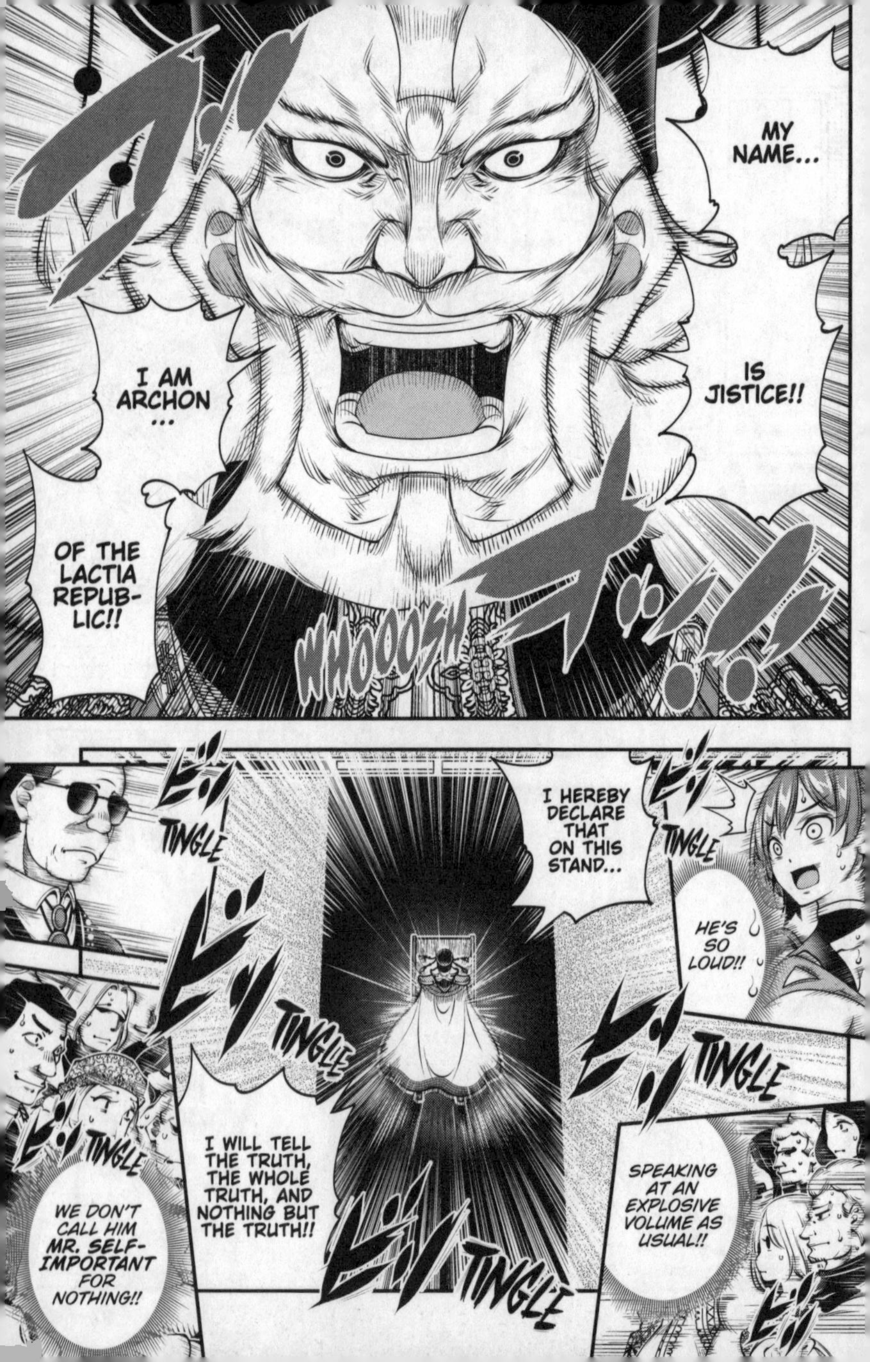
MY NAME...
IS JISTICE!!
I AM ARCHON ...
OF THE LACTIA REPUBLIC!!
WHOOOSH
TINGLE
HE'S SO LOUD!!
TINGLE
SPEAKING AT AN EXPLOSIVE VOLUME AS USUAL!!
I HEREBY DECLARE THAT ON THIS STAND...
TINGLE
I WILL TELL THE TRUTH, THE WHOLE TRUTH, AND NOTHING BUT THE TRUTH!!
TINGLE
TINGLE
TINGLE
TINGLE
WE DON'T CALL HIM MR. SELF-IMPORTANT FOR NOTHING!!

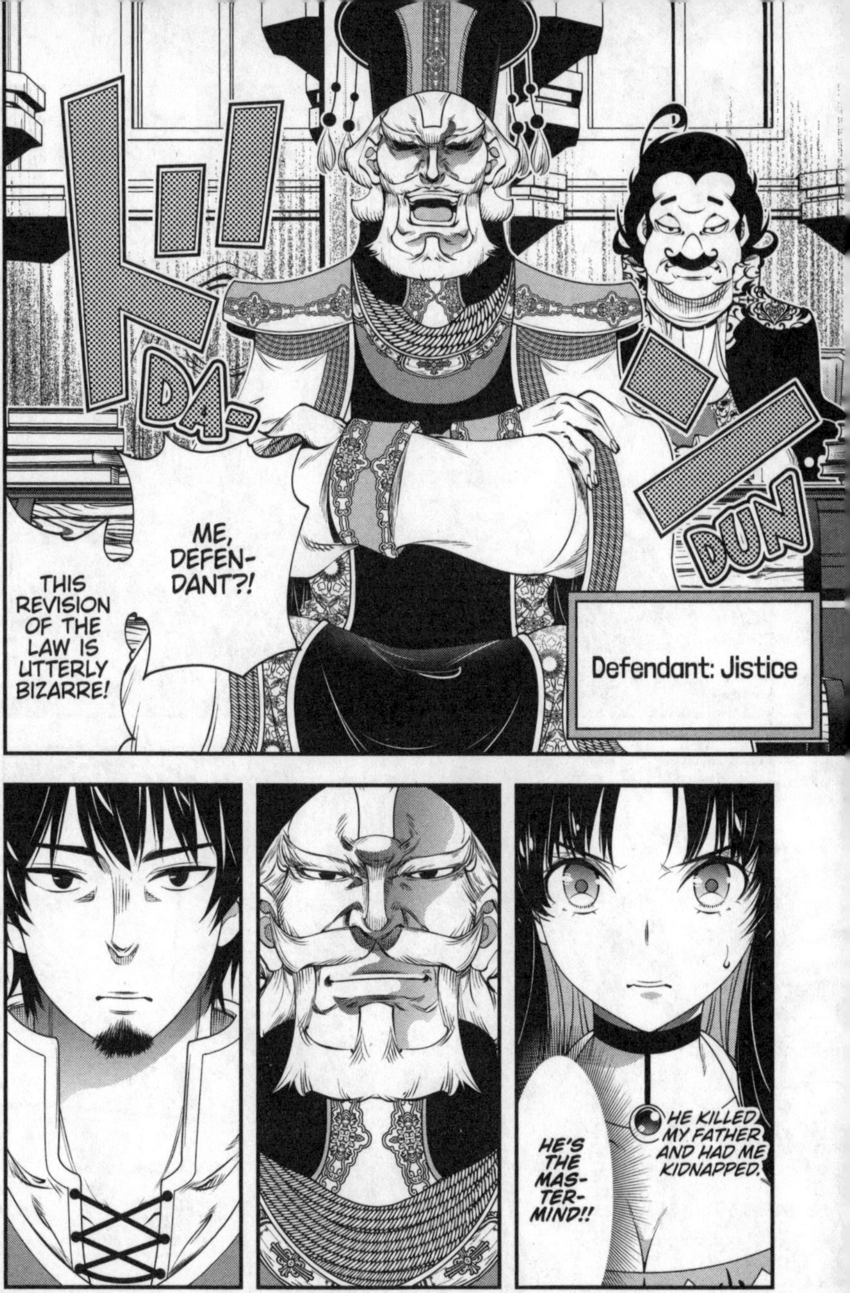
Defendant: Jistice
DA-
DUN
ME, DEFEN-DANT?!
THIS REVISION OF THE LAW IS UTTERLY BIZARRE!
HE KILLED MY FATHER AND HAD ME KIDNAPPED.
HE'S THE MAS-TER-MIND!!

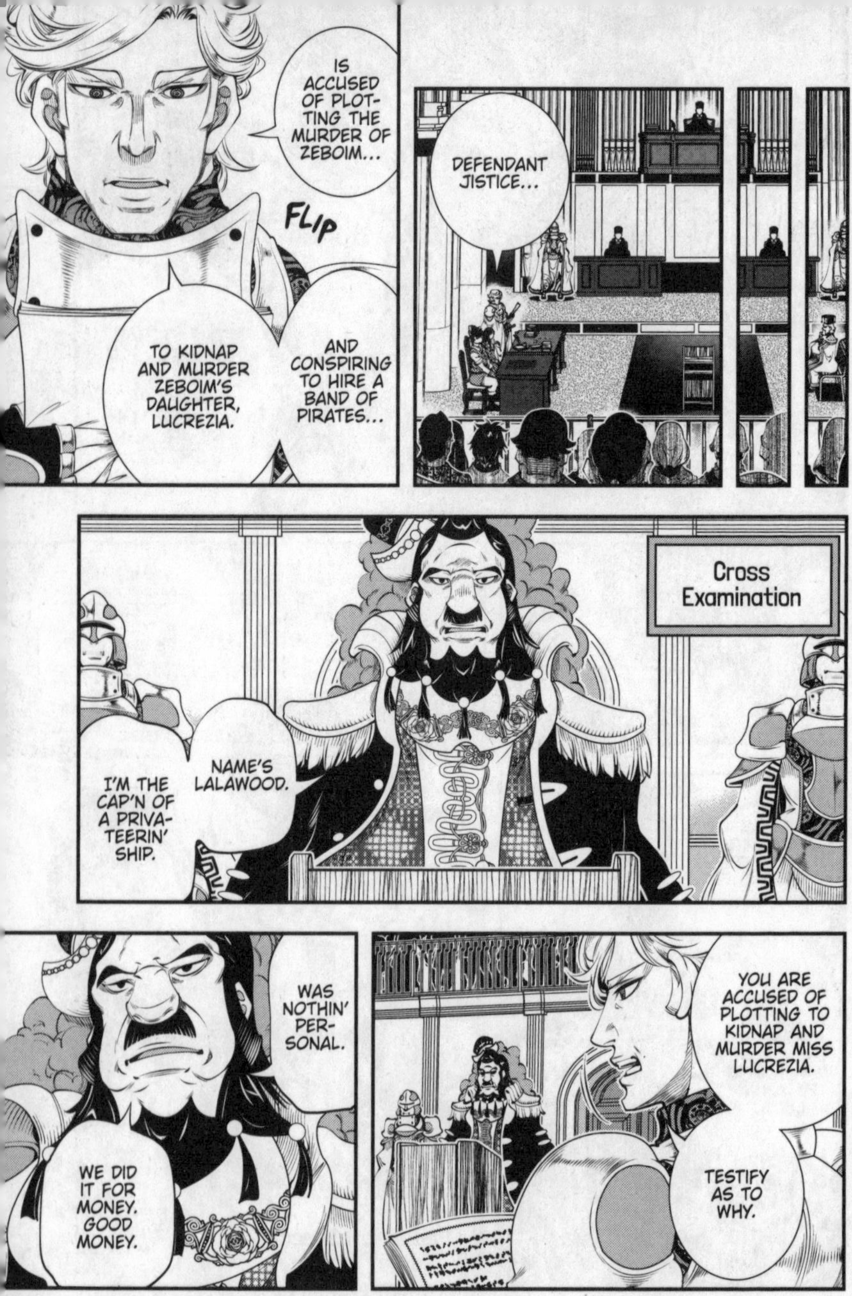
DEFENDANT JISTICE...
IS ACCUSED OF PLOTTING THE MURDER OF ZEBOIM...
FLIP
AND CONSPIRING TO HIRE A BAND OF PIRATES...
TO KIDNAP AND MURDER ZEBOIM'S DAUGHTER, LUCREZIA.
Cross Examination
NAME'S LALAWOOD.
I'M THE CAP'N OF A PRIVATEERIN' SHIP.
YOU ARE ACCUSED OF PLOTTING TO KIDNAP AND MURDER MISS LUCREZIA.
TESTIFY AS TO WHY.
WAS NOTHIN' PERSONAL.
WE DID IT FOR MONEY. GOOD MONEY.

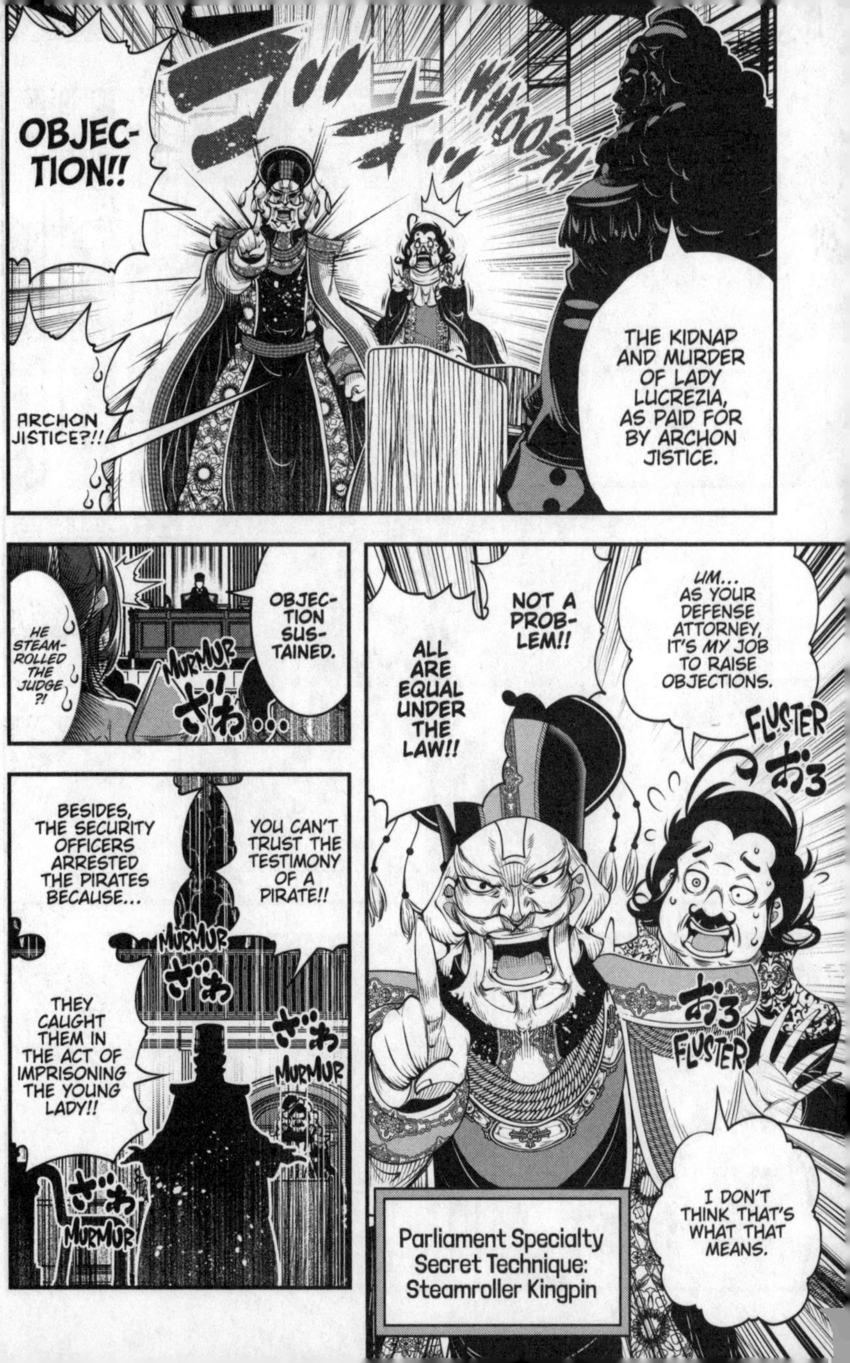
THE KIDNAP AND MURDER OF LADY LUCREZIA, AS PAID FOR BY ARCHON JISTICE.
WHOOSH
OBJEC-TION!!
ARCHON JISTICE?!!
UM... AS YOUR DEFENSE ATTORNEY, IT'S MY JOB TO RAISE OBJECTIONS.
NOT A PROB-LEM!!
ALL ARE EQUAL UNDER THE LAW!!
FLUSTER おろ
おろ FLUSTER
I DON'T THINK THAT'S WHAT THAT MEANS.
Parliament Specialty Secret Technique: Steamroller Kingpin
OBJEC-TION SUS-TAINED.
MURMUR ざわ...
HE STEAM-ROLLED THE JUDGE?!
YOU CAN'T TRUST THE TESTIMONY OF A PIRATE!!
BESIDES, THE SECURITY OFFICERS ARRESTED THE PIRATES BECAUSE...
MURMUR ざわ
THEY CAUGHT THEM IN THE ACT OF IMPRISONING THE YOUNG LADY!!
ざわ MURMUR
ざわ MURMUR

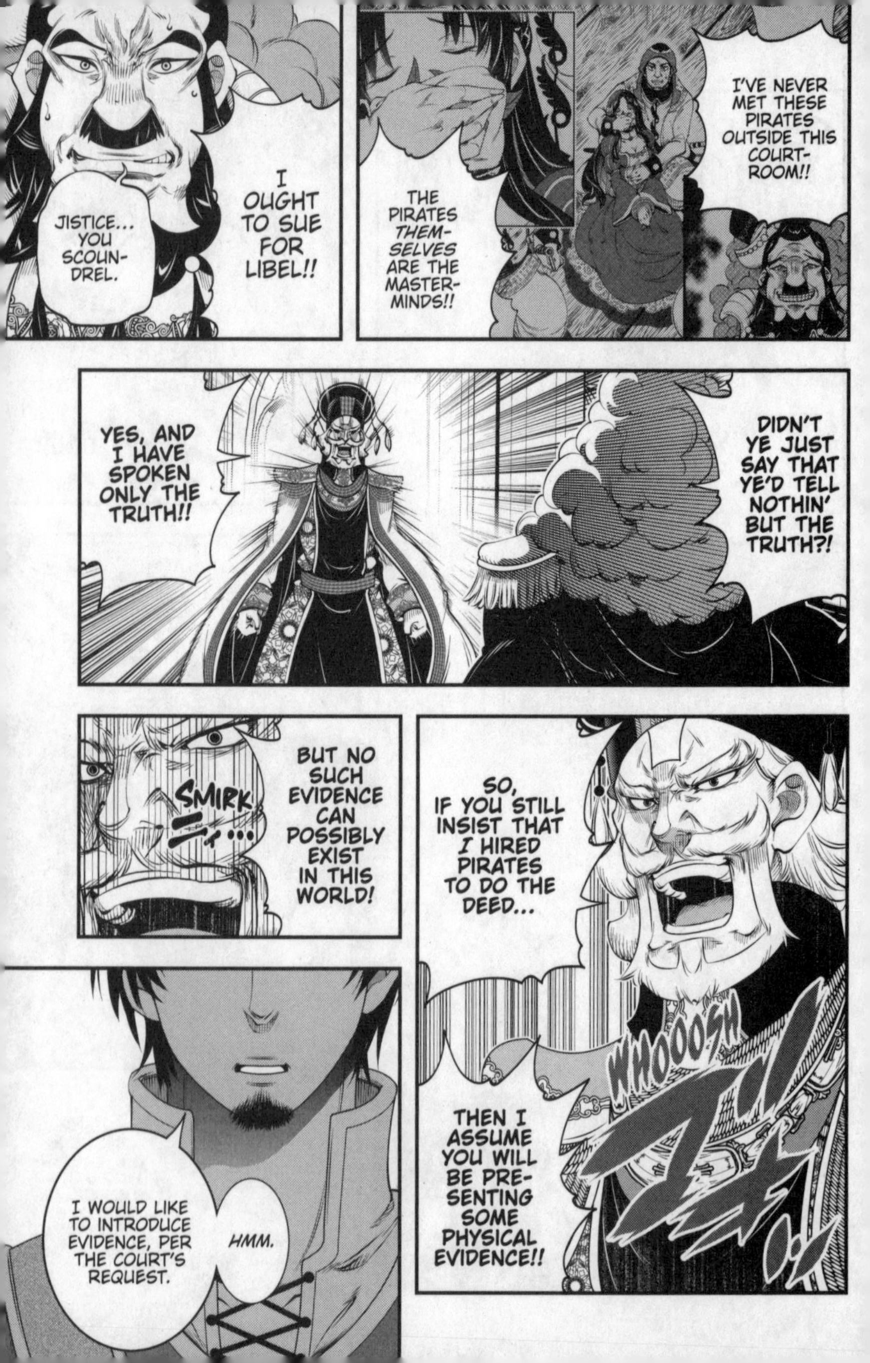
I'VE NEVER MET THESE PIRATES OUTSIDE THIS COURTROOM!!
THE PIRATES THEMSELVES ARE THE MASTERMINDS!!
I OUGHT TO SUE FOR LIBEL!!
JISTICE... YOU SCOUNDREL.
DIDN'T YE JUST SAY THAT YE'D TELL NOTHIN' BUT THE TRUTH?!
YES, AND I HAVE SPOKEN ONLY THE TRUTH!!
SO, IF YOU STILL INSIST THAT I HIRED PIRATES TO DO THE DEED...
WHOOOSH
THEN I ASSUME YOU WILL BE PRESENTING SOME PHYSICAL EVIDENCE!!
BUT NO SUCH EVIDENCE CAN POSSIBLY EXIST IN THIS WORLD!
SMIRK
HMM.
I WOULD LIKE TO INTRODUCE EVIDENCE, PER THE COURT'S REQUEST.

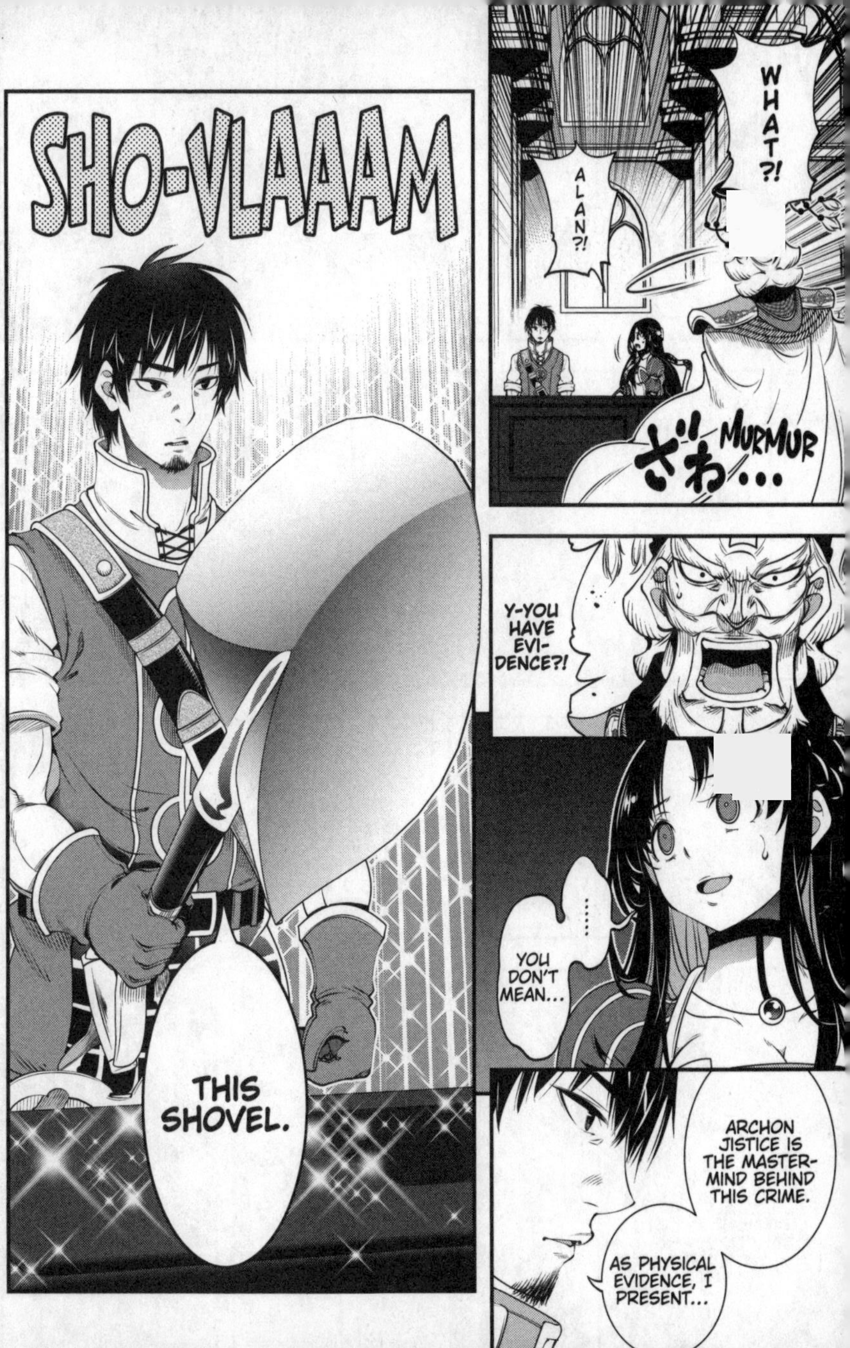WHAT?!
ALAN?!
ざわ MURMUR...
Y-YOU HAVE EVIDENCE?!
......
YOU DON'T MEAN...
ARCHON JISTICE IS THE MASTERMIND BEHIND THIS CRIME.
AS PHYSICAL EVIDENCE, I PRESENT...
SHO-VLAAAM
THIS SHOVEL.

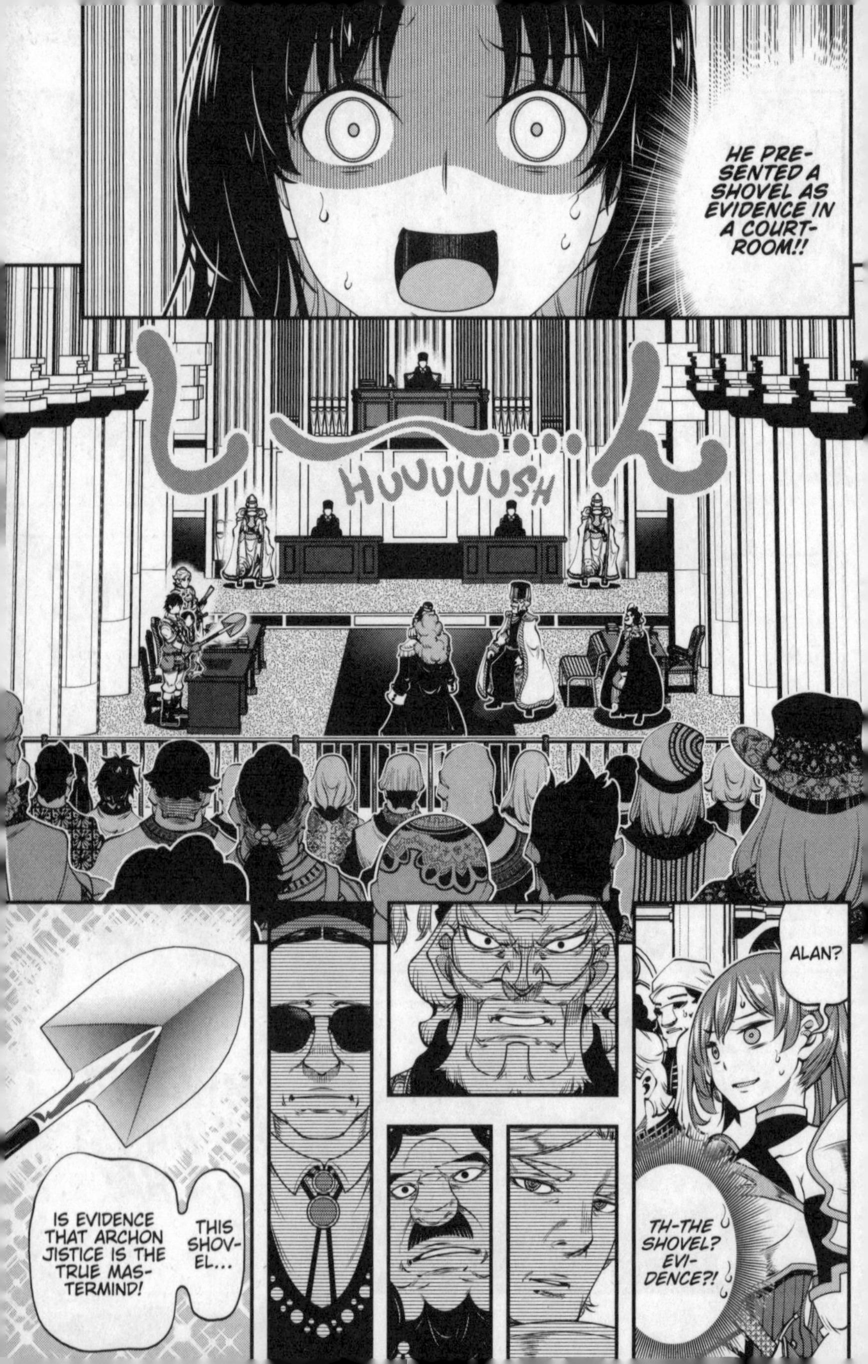
HE PRESENTED A SHOVEL AS EVIDENCE IN A COURTROOM!!
しーん
HUUUUUSH
ALAN?
TH-THE SHOVEL? EVIDENCE?!
THIS SHOVEL...
IS EVIDENCE THAT ARCHON JISTICE IS THE TRUE MASTERMIND!

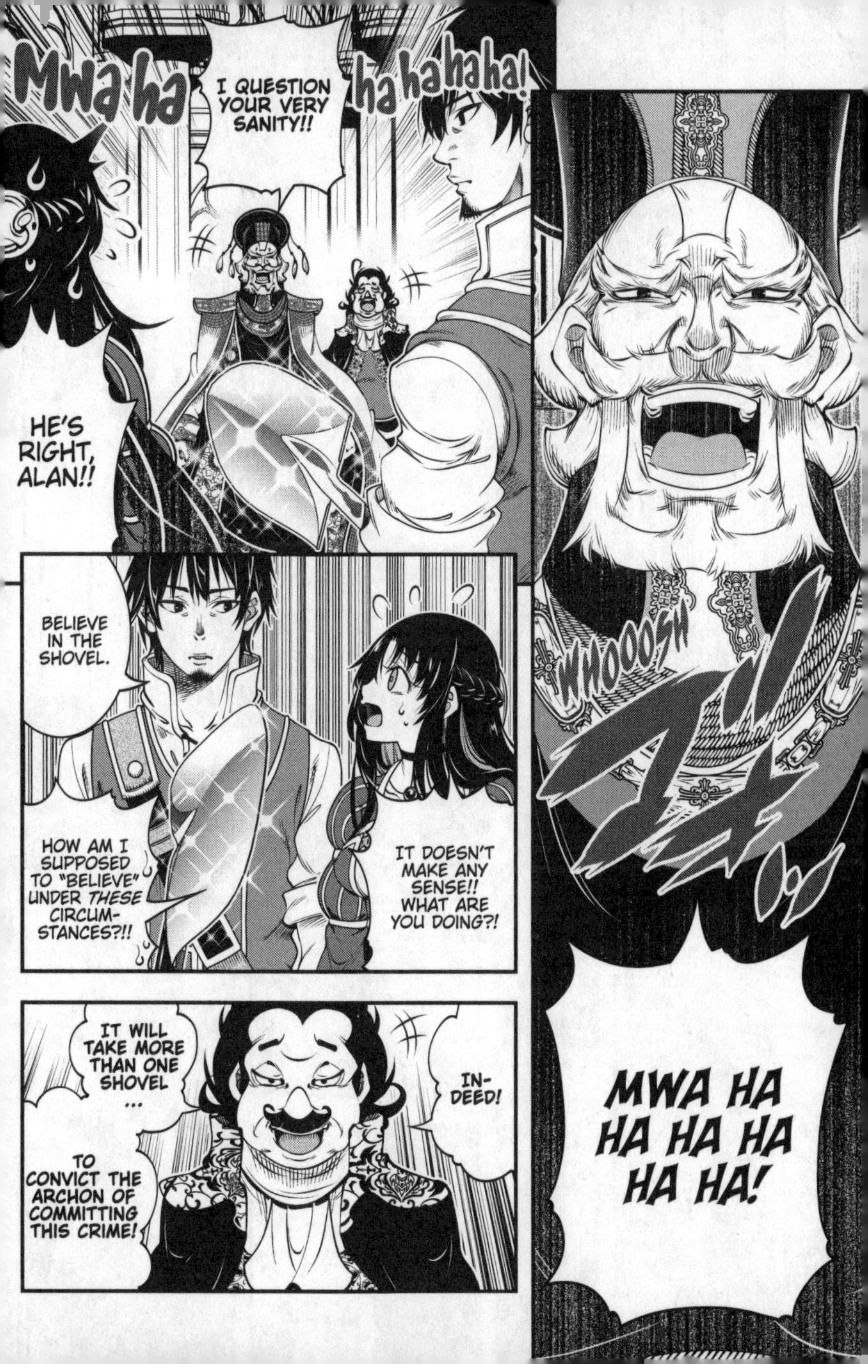
Mwa ha
I QUESTION YOUR VERY SANITY!!
ha ha ha ha!
HE'S RIGHT, ALAN!!
BELIEVE IN THE SHOVEL.
IT DOESN'T MAKE ANY SENSE!! WHAT ARE YOU DOING?!
HOW AM I SUPPOSED TO "BELIEVE" UNDER *THESE* CIRCUM-STANCES?!!
IT WILL TAKE MORE THAN ONE SHOVEL ...
IN-DEED!
TO CONVICT THE ARCHON OF COMMITTING THIS CRIME!
WHOOOSH
MWA HA HA HA HA HA HA HA!

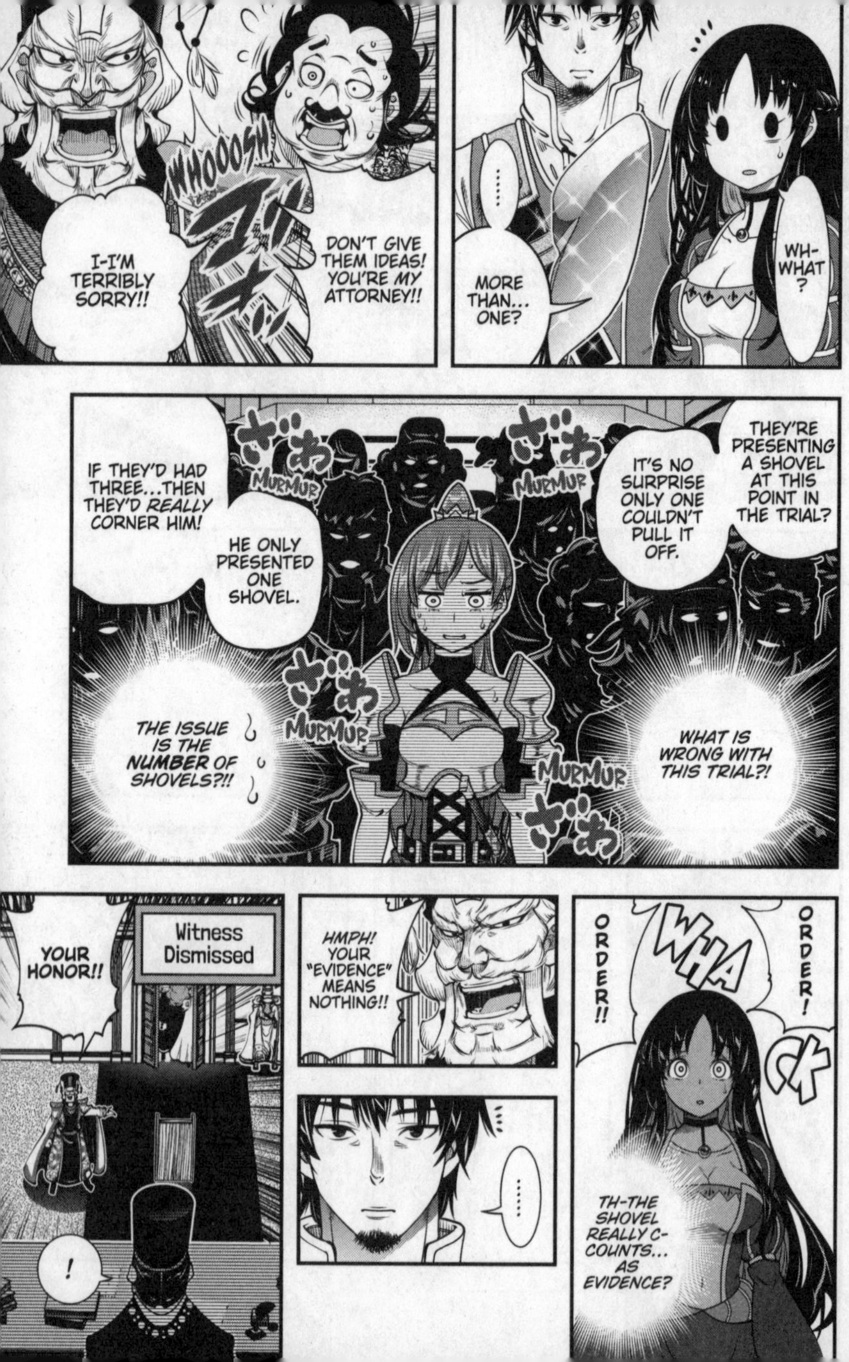
WH-WHAT?
......
MORE THAN... ONE?
DON'T GIVE THEM IDEAS! YOU'RE MY ATTORNEY!!
WHOOOSH
I-I'M TERRIBLY SORRY!!
THEY'RE PRESENTING A SHOVEL AT THIS POINT IN THE TRIAL?
ざわ
MURMUR
IT'S NO SURPRISE ONLY ONE COULDN'T PULL IT OFF.
ざわ
MURMUR
HE ONLY PRESENTED ONE SHOVEL.
IF THEY'D HAD THREE...THEN THEY'D *REALLY* CORNER HIM!
WHAT IS WRONG WITH THIS TRIAL?!
MURMUR
ざわ
ざわ
MURMUR
THE ISSUE IS THE *NUMBER* OF SHOVELS?!!
ORDER!
WHACK
ORDER!!
TH-THE SHOVEL REALLY C-COUNTS... AS EVIDENCE?
HMPH! YOUR "EVIDENCE" MEANS NOTHING!!
......
YOUR HONOR!!
Witness Dismissed
!

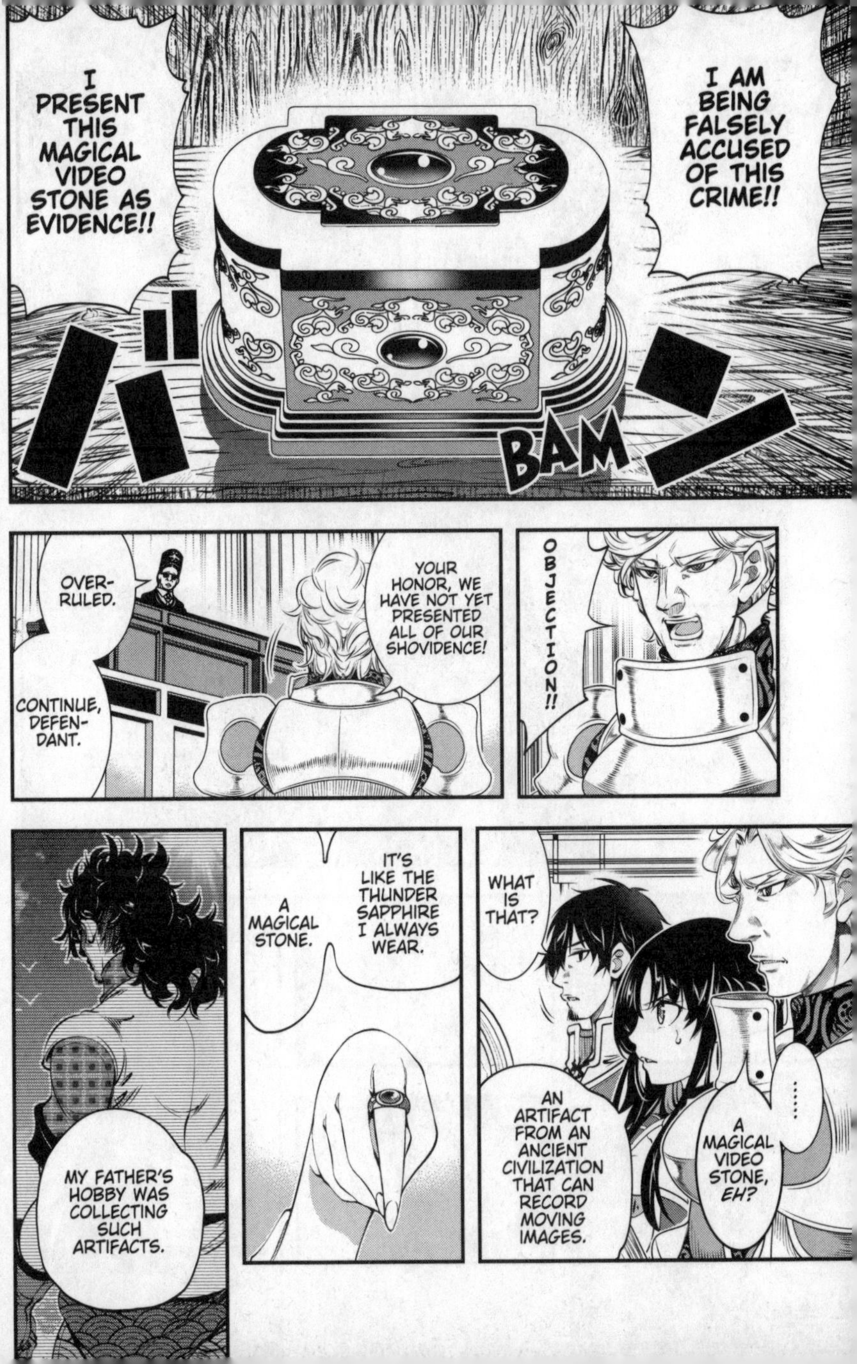
I AM BEING FALSELY ACCUSED OF THIS CRIME!!
I PRESENT THIS MAGICAL VIDEO STONE AS EVIDENCE!!
バン
BAM
OBJECTION!!
YOUR HONOR, WE HAVE NOT YET PRESENTED ALL OF OUR SHOVIDENCE!
OVER-RULED.
CONTINUE, DEFEN-DANT.
WHAT IS THAT?
AN ARTIFACT FROM AN ANCIENT CIVILIZATION THAT CAN RECORD MOVING IMAGES.
......
A MAGICAL VIDEO STONE, EH?
IT'S LIKE THE THUNDER SAPPHIRE I ALWAYS WEAR.
A MAGICAL STONE.
MY FATHER'S HOBBY WAS COLLECTING SUCH ARTIFACTS.

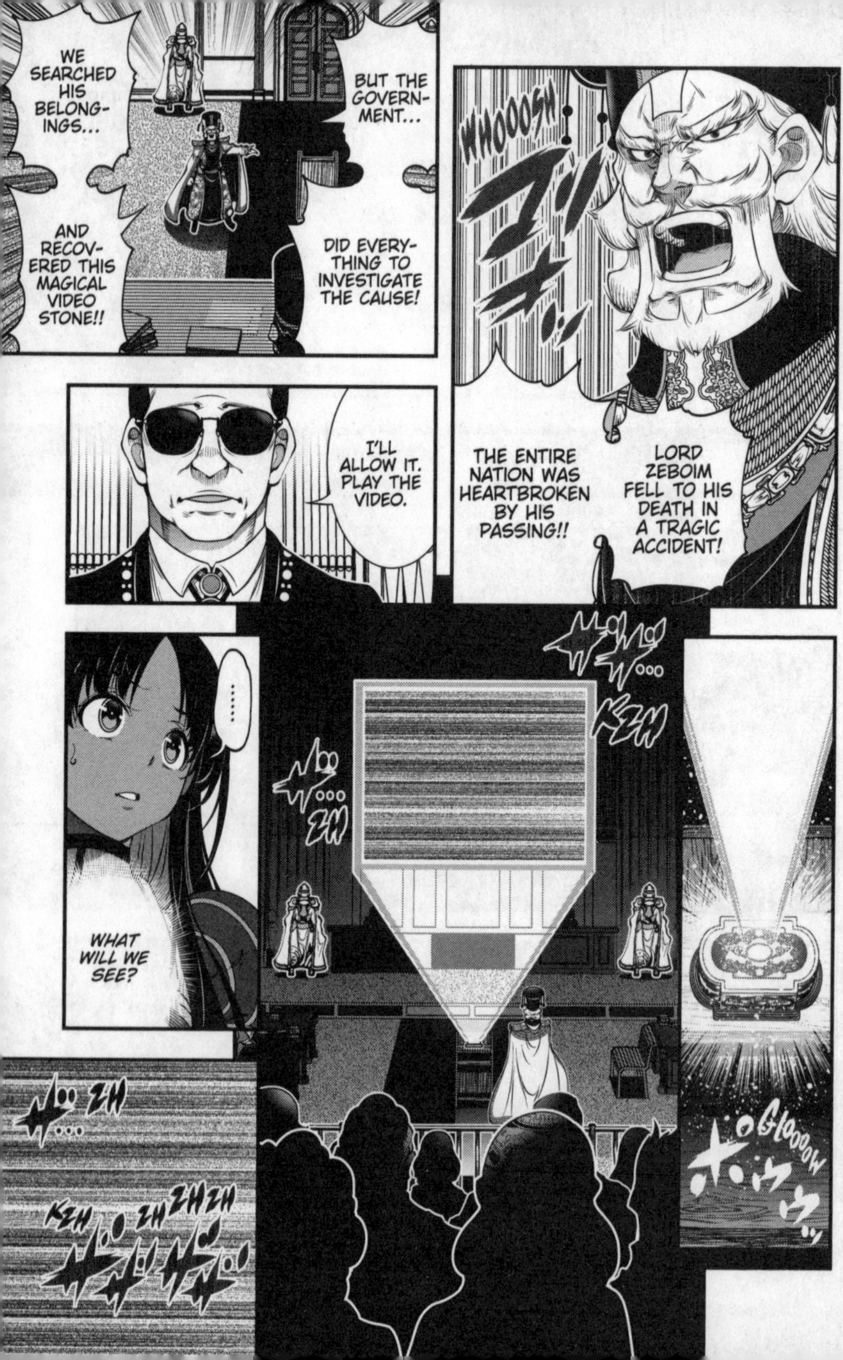
WHOOOSH
LORD ZEBOIM FELL TO HIS DEATH IN A TRAGIC ACCIDENT!
THE ENTIRE NATION WAS HEARTBROKEN BY HIS PASSING!!
BUT THE GOVERN-MENT...
DID EVERY-THING TO INVESTIGATE THE CAUSE!
WE SEARCHED HIS BELONG-INGS...
AND RECOV-ERED THIS MAGICAL VIDEO STONE!!
I'LL ALLOW IT. PLAY THE VIDEO.
GLOOOOW
KZH
ZH
......
WHAT WILL WE SEE?
ZH
KZH ZH ZHZH

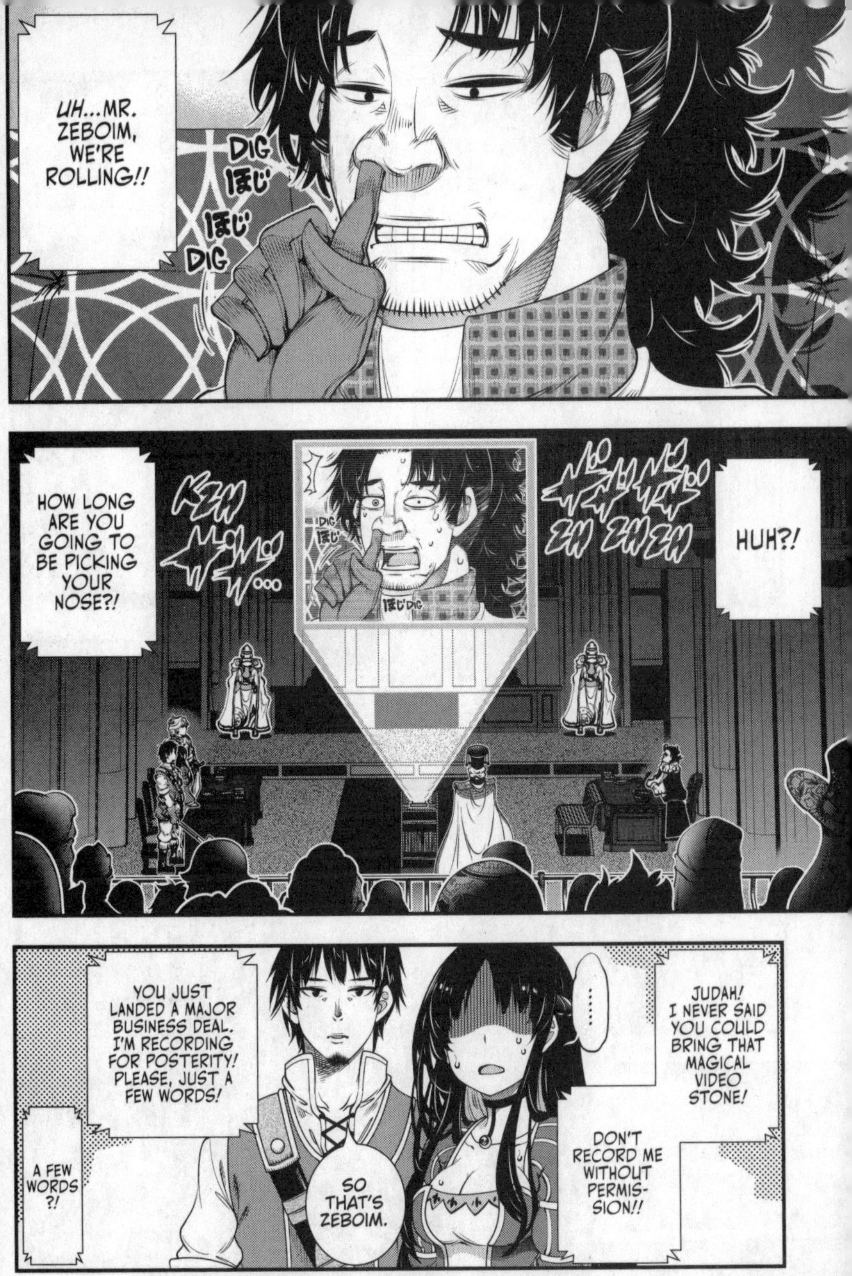
UH...MR. ZEBOIM, WE'RE ROLLING!!
DIG ほじ
ほじ DIG
HUH?!
DIG ほじ
ほじ DIG
HOW LONG ARE YOU GOING TO BE PICKING YOUR NOSE?!
JUDAH! I NEVER SAID YOU COULD BRING THAT MAGICAL VIDEO STONE!
DON'T RECORD ME WITHOUT PERMIS-SION!!
......
YOU JUST LANDED A MAJOR BUSINESS DEAL. I'M RECORDING FOR POSTERITY! PLEASE, JUST A FEW WORDS!
SO THAT'S ZEBOIM.
A FEW WORDS?!

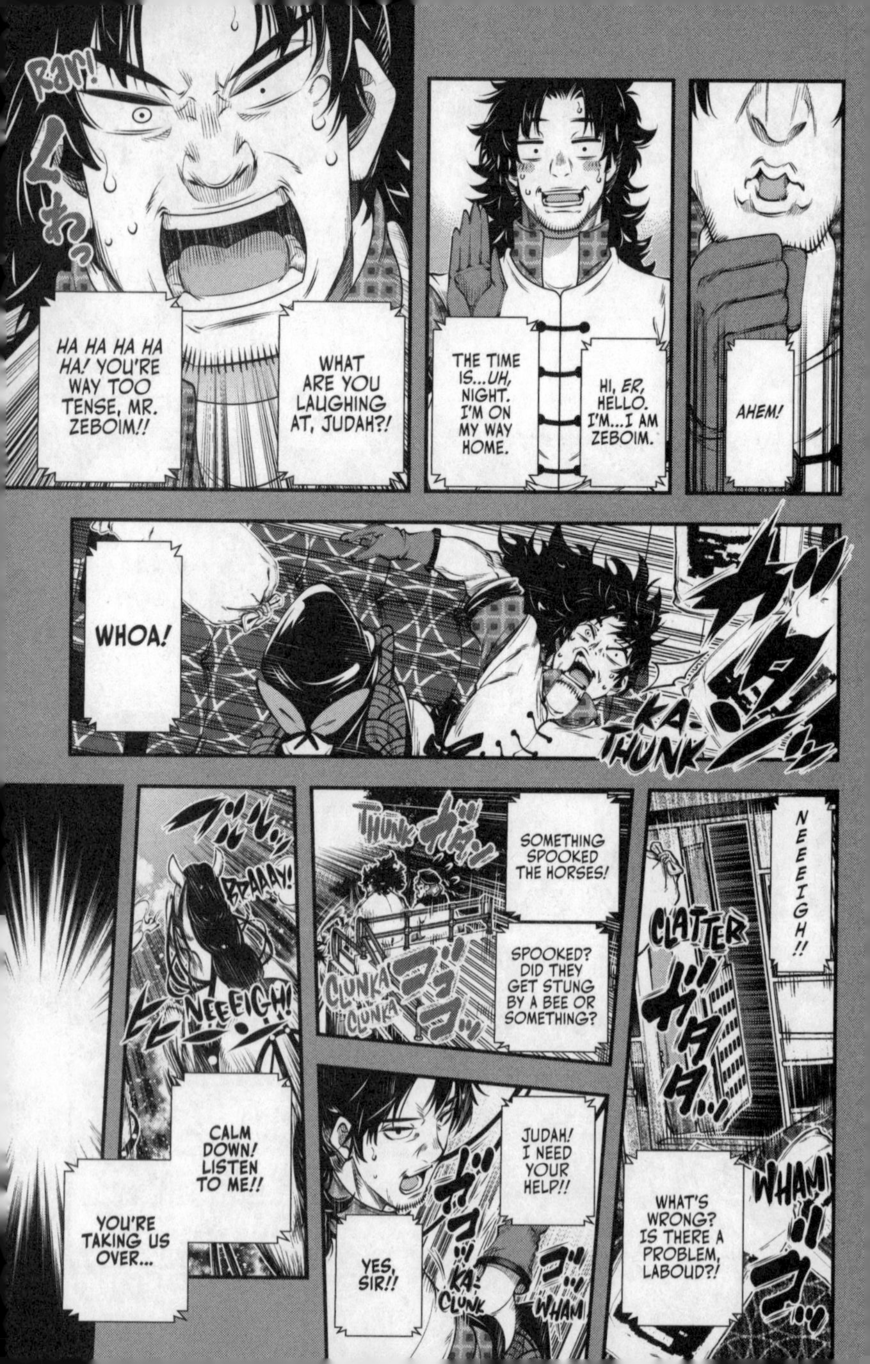
AHEM!
HI, ER, HELLO. I'M...I AM ZEBOIM.
THE TIME IS...UH, NIGHT. I'M ON MY WAY HOME.
Rar!
WHAT ARE YOU LAUGHING AT, JUDAH?!
HA HA HA HA HA! YOU'RE WAY TOO TENSE, MR. ZEBOIM!!
KA-THUNK
WHOA!
NEEEEIGH!!
CLATTER
WHAM
WHAT'S WRONG? IS THERE A PROBLEM, LABOUD?!
THUNK
SOMETHING SPOOKED THE HORSES!
SPOOKED? DID THEY GET STUNG BY A BEE OR SOMETHING?
CLUNKA CLUNKA
JUDAH! I NEED YOUR HELP!!
KA-CLUNK
WHAM
YES, SIR!!
BRAAAY!
NEEEIGH!
CALM DOWN! LISTEN TO ME!!
YOU'RE TAKING US OVER...

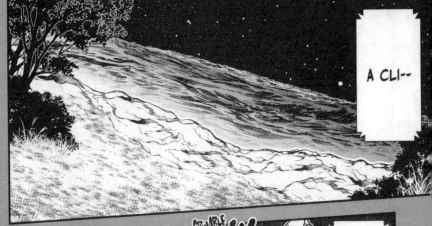

A CLI--

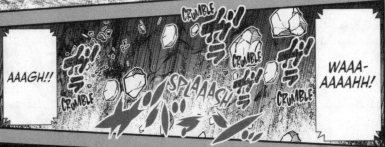

AAAGH!!

CRUMBLE

SPLAAASH!

CRUMBLE

CRUMBLE

CRUMBLE

WAAA-AAAAHH!

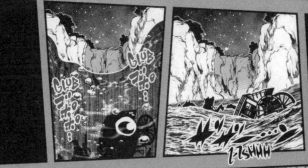

GLUB

GLUB

I-ZSHHH

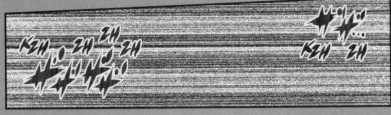

KZH ZH ZH ZH

KZH ZH

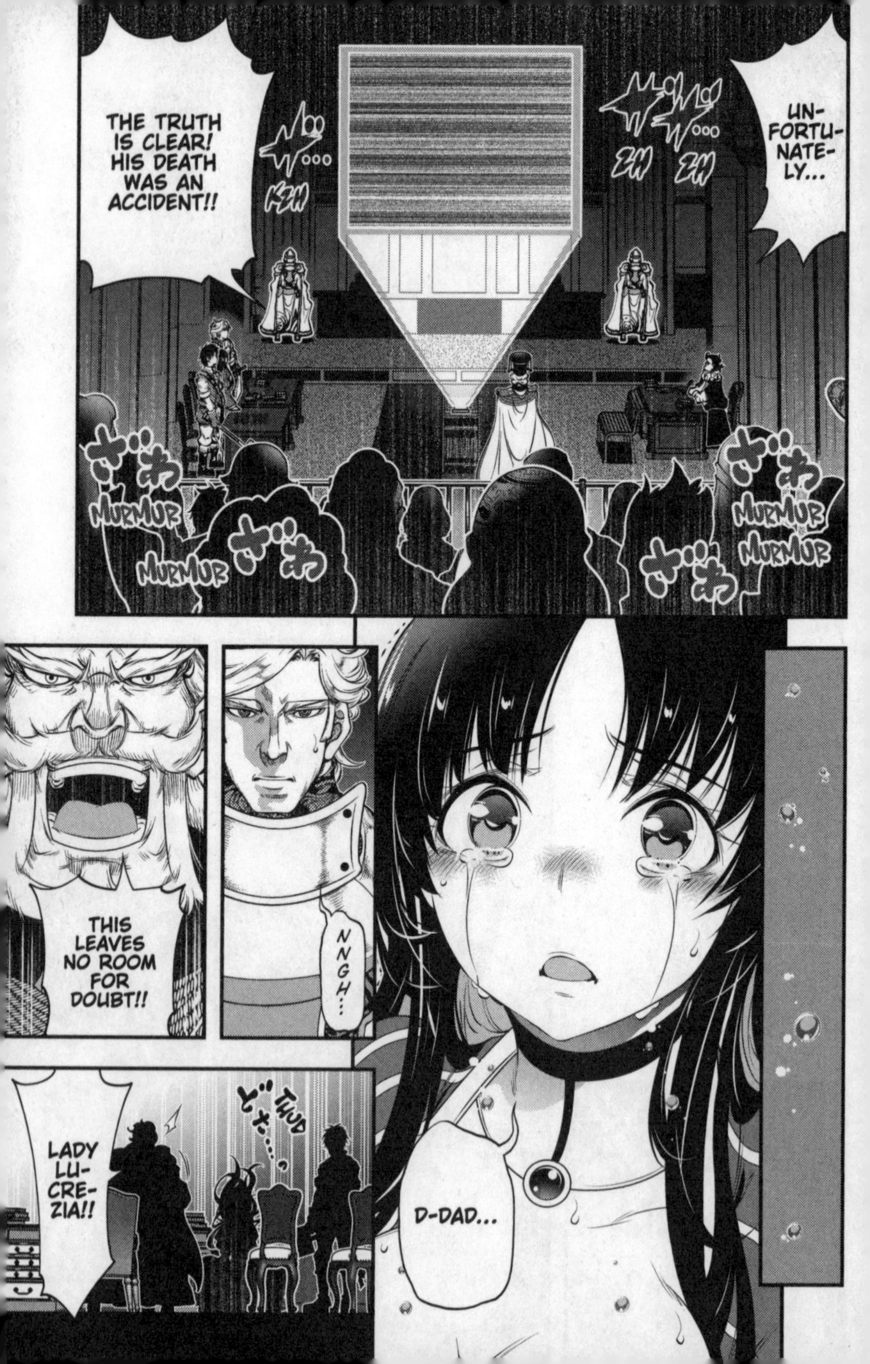
UN-FORTU-NATE-LY...
ZH ZH
KZH
THE TRUTH IS CLEAR! HIS DEATH WAS AN ACCIDENT!!
ざわ MURMUR MURMUR
ざわ
ざわ MURMUR
ざわ MURMUR
D-DAD...
NNGH...
THIS LEAVES NO ROOM FOR DOUBT!!
THUD
LADY LU-CRE-ZIA!!

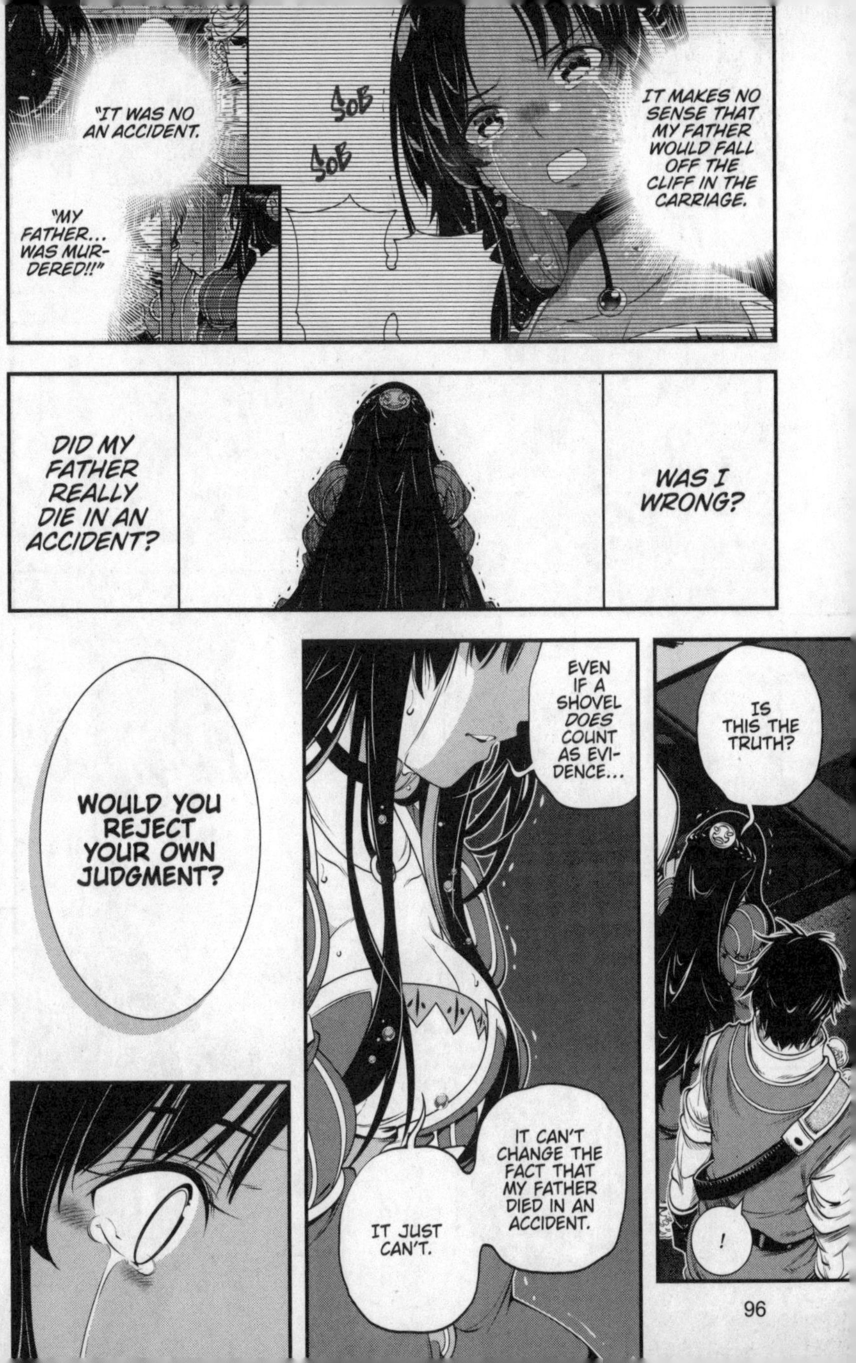
IT MAKES NO SENSE THAT MY FATHER WOULD FALL OFF THE CLIFF IN THE CARRIAGE.
SOB
SOB
"IT WAS NO AN ACCIDENT.
"MY FATHER... WAS MURDERED!!"
WAS I WRONG?
DID MY FATHER REALLY DIE IN AN ACCIDENT?
IS THIS THE TRUTH?
!
EVEN IF A SHOVEL DOES COUNT AS EVIDENCE...
IT CAN'T CHANGE THE FACT THAT MY FATHER DIED IN AN ACCIDENT.
IT JUST CAN'T.
WOULD YOU REJECT YOUR OWN JUDGMENT?

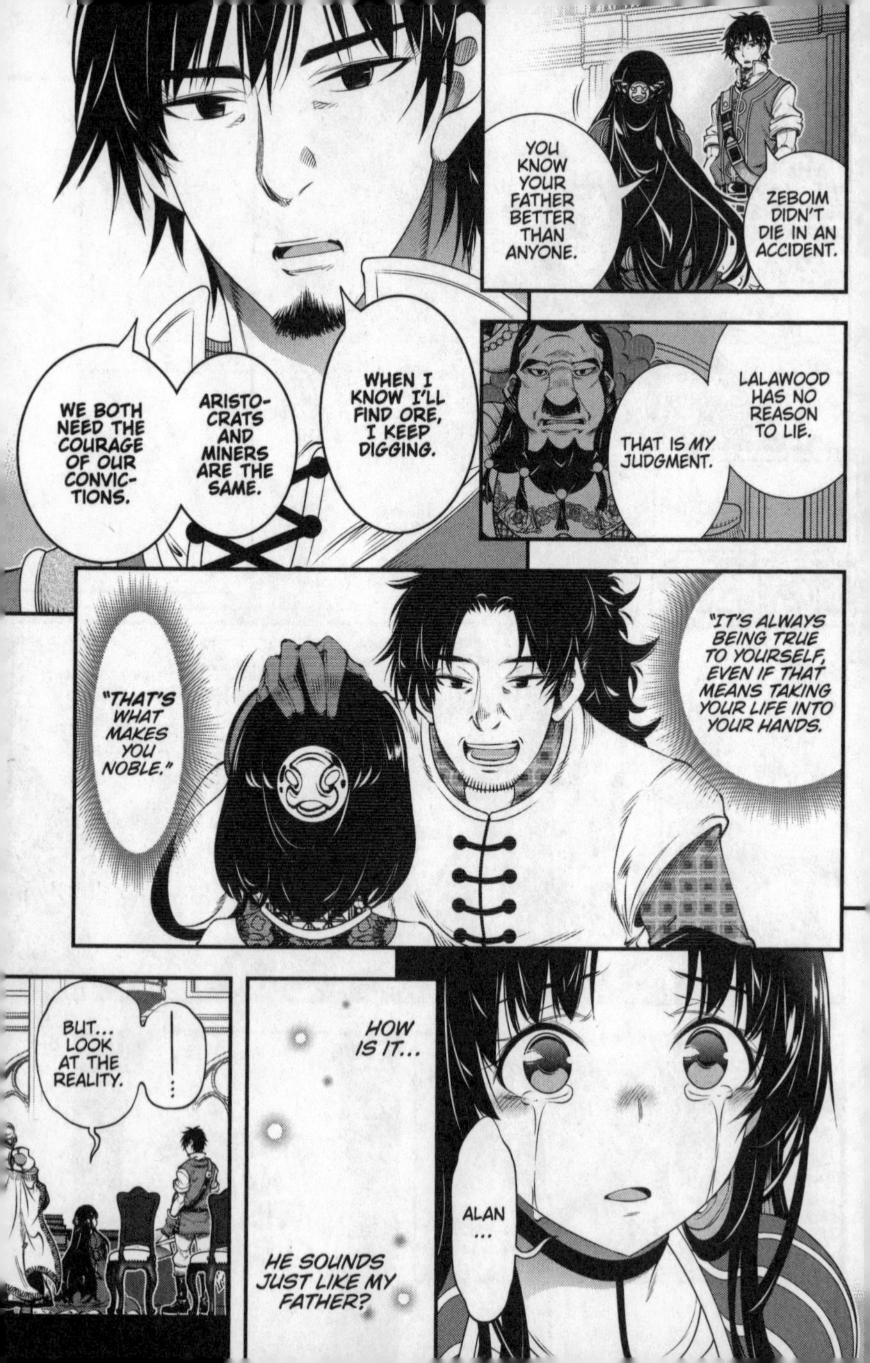
ZEBOIM DIDN'T DIE IN AN ACCIDENT.
YOU KNOW YOUR FATHER BETTER THAN ANYONE.
LALAWOOD HAS NO REASON TO LIE.
THAT IS MY JUDGMENT.
WHEN I KNOW I'LL FIND ORE, I KEEP DIGGING.
ARISTO-CRATS AND MINERS ARE THE SAME.
WE BOTH NEED THE COURAGE OF OUR CONVIC-TIONS.
"IT'S ALWAYS BEING TRUE TO YOURSELF, EVEN IF THAT MEANS TAKING YOUR LIFE INTO YOUR HANDS.
"THAT'S WHAT MAKES YOU NOBLE."
ALAN ...
HOW IS IT...
HE SOUNDS JUST LIKE MY FATHER?
......
BUT... LOOK AT THE REALITY.

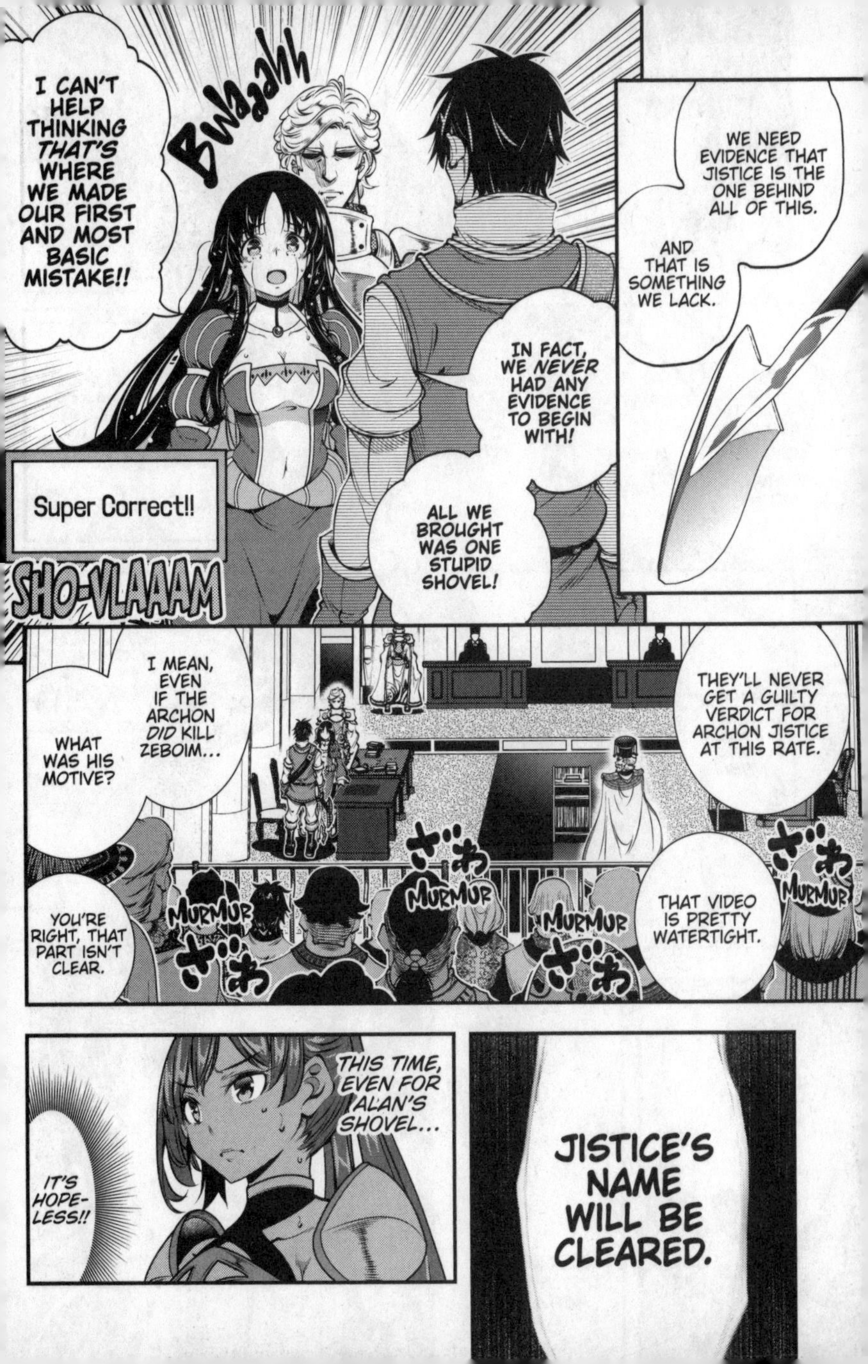
WE NEED EVIDENCE THAT JISTICE IS THE ONE BEHIND ALL OF THIS.
AND THAT IS SOMETHING WE LACK.
IN FACT, WE *NEVER* HAD ANY EVIDENCE TO BEGIN WITH!
ALL WE BROUGHT WAS ONE STUPID SHOVEL!
Bwaaahh
I CAN'T HELP THINKING *THAT'S* WHERE WE MADE OUR FIRST AND MOST BASIC MISTAKE!!
Super Correct!!
SHO-VLAAAM
THEY'LL NEVER GET A GUILTY VERDICT FOR ARCHON JISTICE AT THIS RATE.
ざわ
MURMUR
THAT VIDEO IS PRETTY WATERTIGHT.
I MEAN, EVEN IF THE ARCHON *DID* KILL ZEBOIM...
WHAT WAS HIS MOTIVE?
ざわ
MURMUR
MURMUR
ざわ
MURMUR
ざわ
YOU'RE RIGHT, THAT PART ISN'T CLEAR.
JISTICE'S NAME WILL BE CLEARED.
THIS TIME, EVEN FOR ALAN'S SHOVEL...
IT'S HOPE-LESS!!

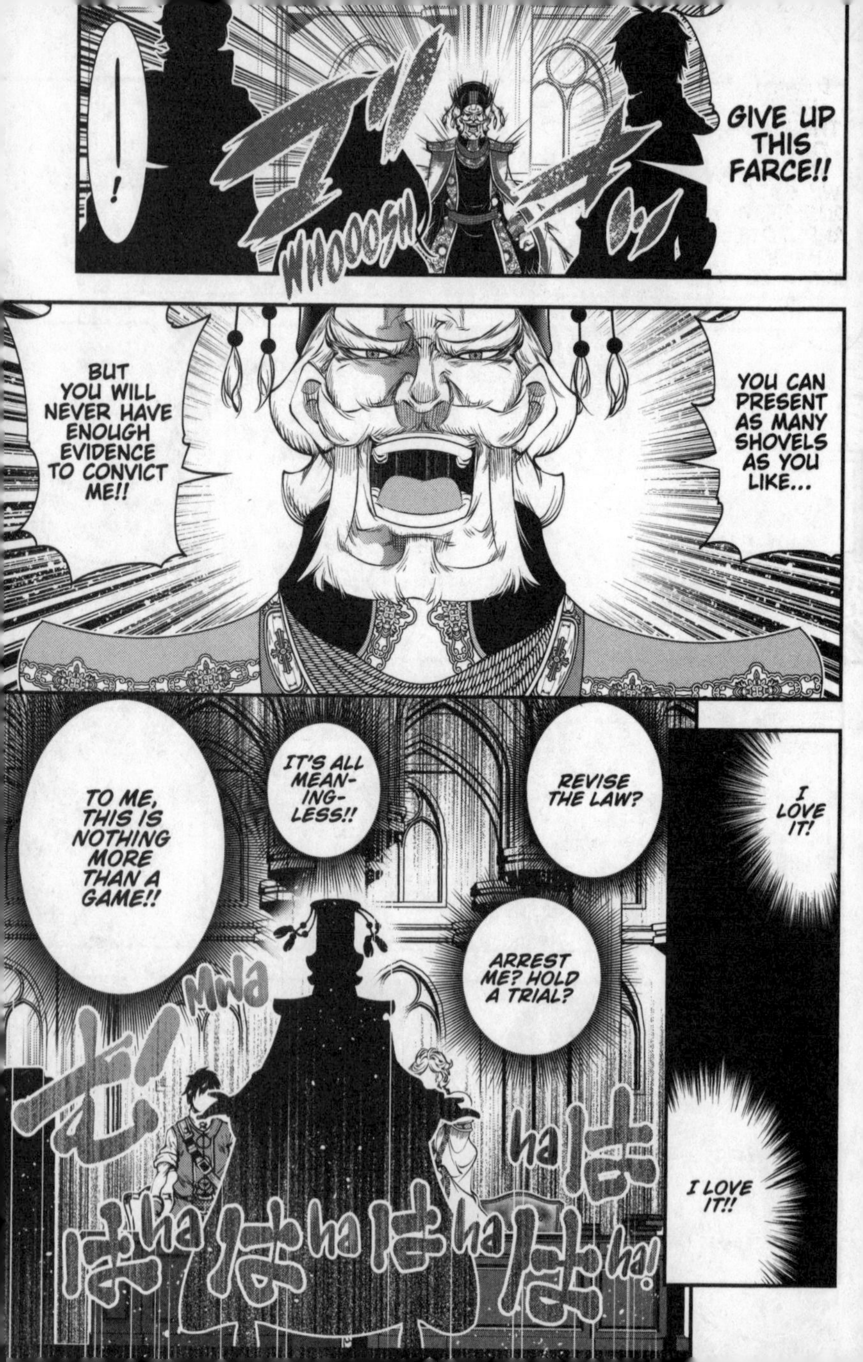
GIVE UP THIS FARCE!!
!
WHOOOSH
YOU CAN PRESENT AS MANY SHOVELS AS YOU LIKE...
BUT YOU WILL NEVER HAVE ENOUGH EVIDENCE TO CONVICT ME!!
I LOVE IT!
I LOVE IT!!
REVISE THE LAW?
ARREST ME? HOLD A TRIAL?
IT'S ALL MEANING-LESS!!
TO ME, THIS IS NOTHING MORE THAN A GAME!!
Mwa ha ha ha ha ha!

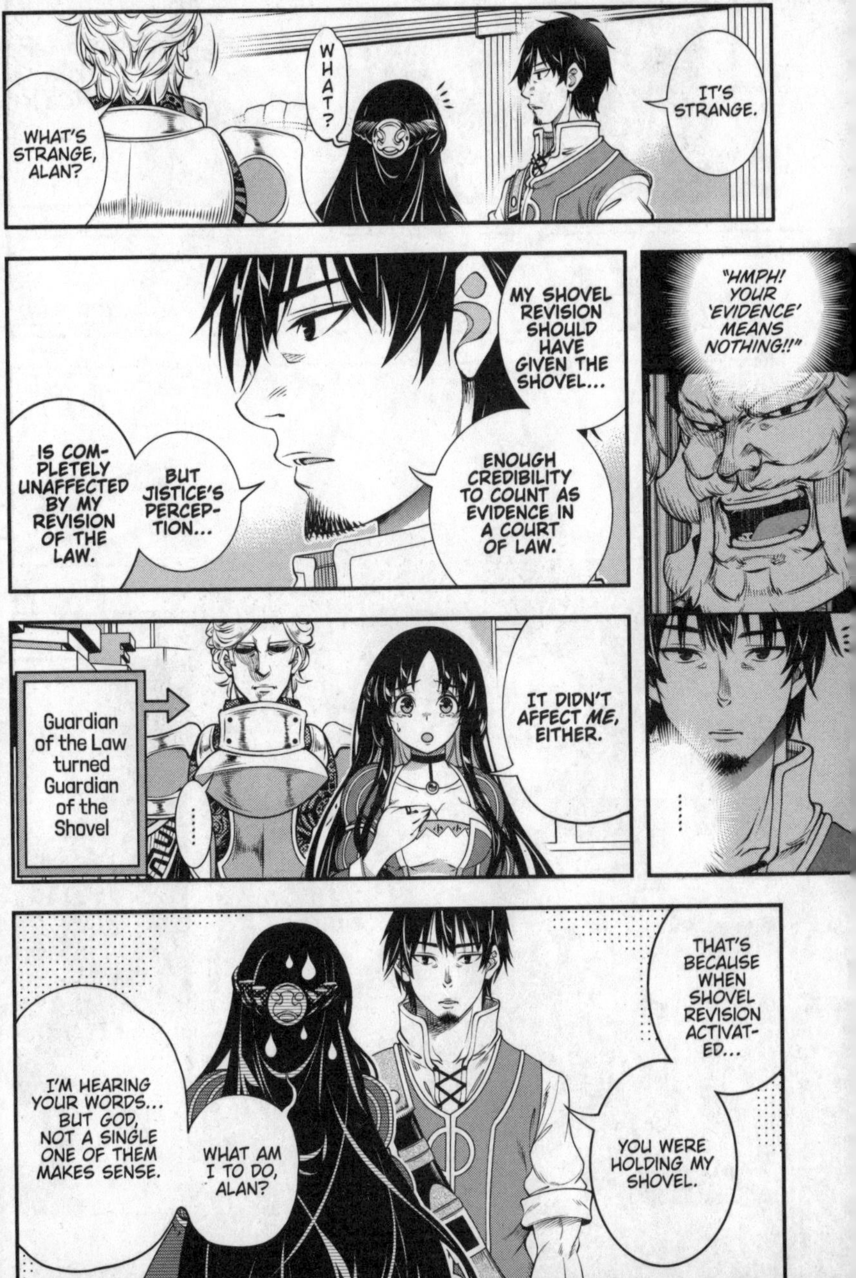
IT'S STRANGE.
WHAT?
WHAT'S STRANGE, ALAN?
"HMPH! YOUR 'EVIDENCE' MEANS NOTHING!!"
MY SHOVEL REVISION SHOULD HAVE GIVEN THE SHOVEL...
ENOUGH CREDIBILITY TO COUNT AS EVIDENCE IN A COURT OF LAW.
BUT JISTICE'S PERCEPTION...
IS COMPLETELY UNAFFECTED BY MY REVISION OF THE LAW.
......
IT DIDN'T AFFECT *ME*, EITHER.
......
Guardian of the Law turned Guardian of the Shovel
THAT'S BECAUSE WHEN SHOVEL REVISION ACTIVATED...
YOU WERE HOLDING MY SHOVEL.
WHAT AM I TO DO, ALAN?
I'M HEARING YOUR WORDS... BUT GOD, NOT A SINGLE ONE OF THEM MAKES SENSE.

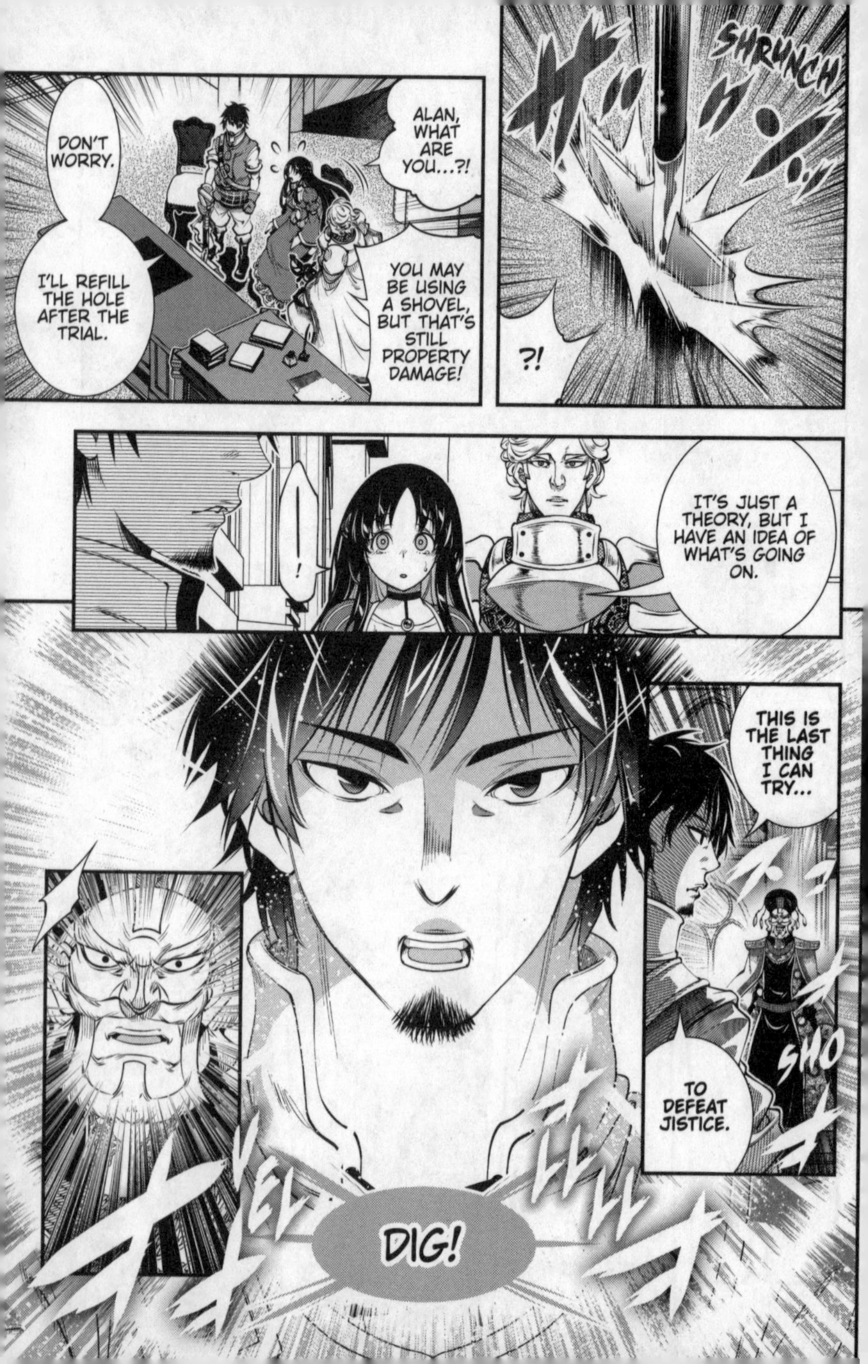
SHRUNCH
?!
ALAN, WHAT ARE YOU...?!
YOU MAY BE USING A SHOVEL, BUT THAT'S STILL PROPERTY DAMAGE!
DON'T WORRY.
I'LL REFILL THE HOLE AFTER THE TRIAL.
IT'S JUST A THEORY, BUT I HAVE AN IDEA OF WHAT'S GOING ON.
!
THIS IS THE LAST THING I CAN TRY...
TO DEFEAT JISTICE.
SHO
DIG!

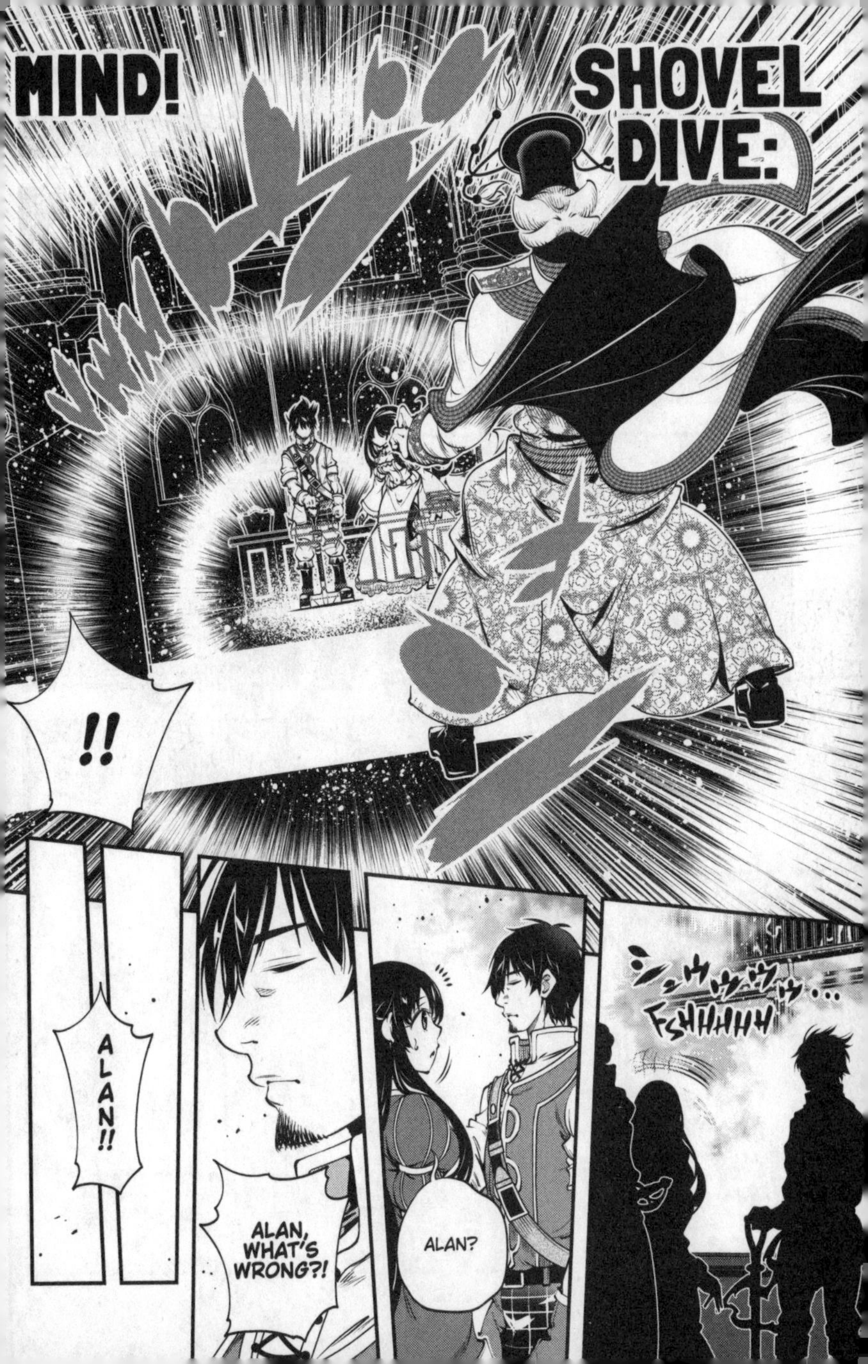
SHOVEL DIVE:
MIND!
VWM
!!
FSHHHHH
ALAN?
ALAN, WHAT'S WRONG?!
ALAN!!

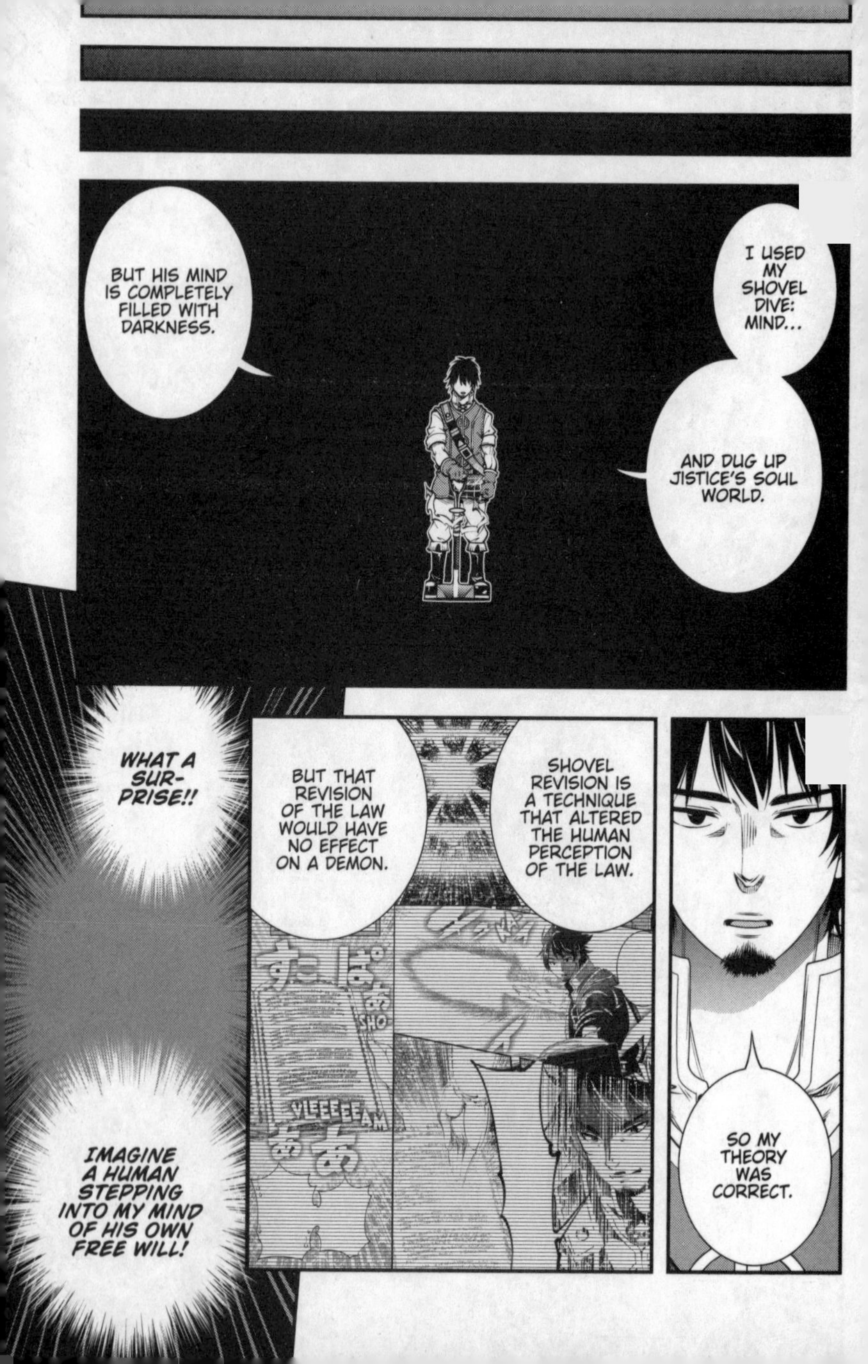
I USED MY SHOVEL DIVE: MIND...
AND DUG UP JISTICE'S SOUL WORLD.
BUT HIS MIND IS COMPLETELY FILLED WITH DARKNESS.
SO MY THEORY WAS CORRECT.
SHOVEL REVISION IS A TECHNIQUE THAT ALTERED THE HUMAN PERCEPTION OF THE LAW.
BUT THAT REVISION OF THE LAW WOULD HAVE NO EFFECT ON A DEMON.
SHO
VLEEEEEAM
WHAT A SUR-PRISE!!
IMAGINE A HUMAN STEPPING INTO MY MIND OF HIS OWN FREE WILL!

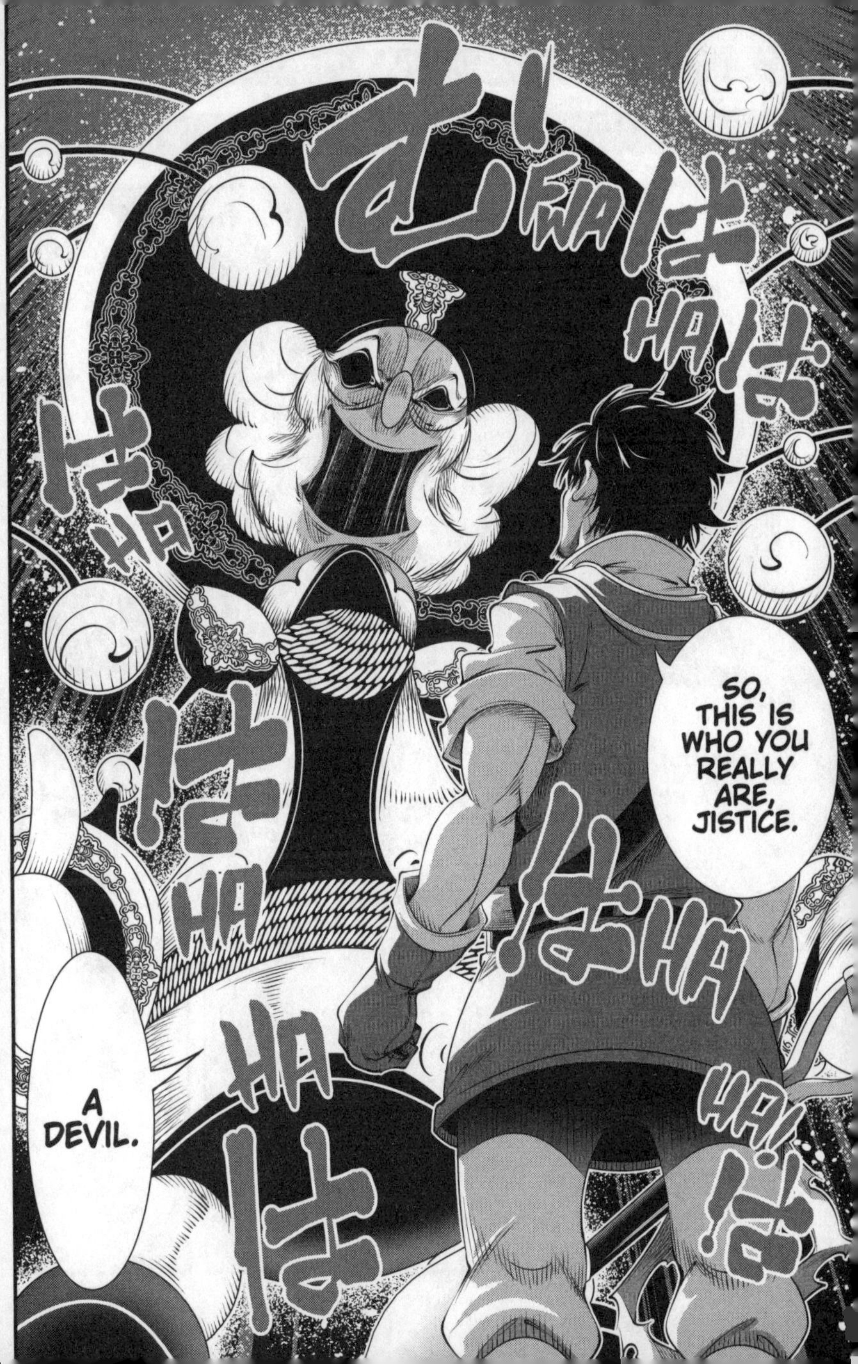
FWA
HA
SO, THIS IS WHO YOU REALLY ARE, JISTICE.
HA
HA
HA
HA!
HA
A DEVIL.

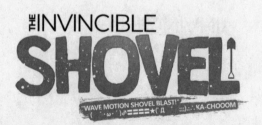

THE INVINCIBLE

SHOVEL

"WAVE MOTION SHOVEL BLAST!"

(｀ω´)⊃≡≡≡★(ﾟДﾟ) :;).:. KA-CHOOOM

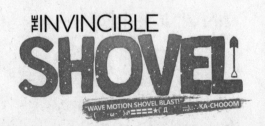

THE INVINCIBLE

SHOVEL

"WAVE MOTION SHOVEL BLAST!"
(・ω・)ｱﾞ≡≡≡★(ﾟдﾟ)…… KA-CHOOOM

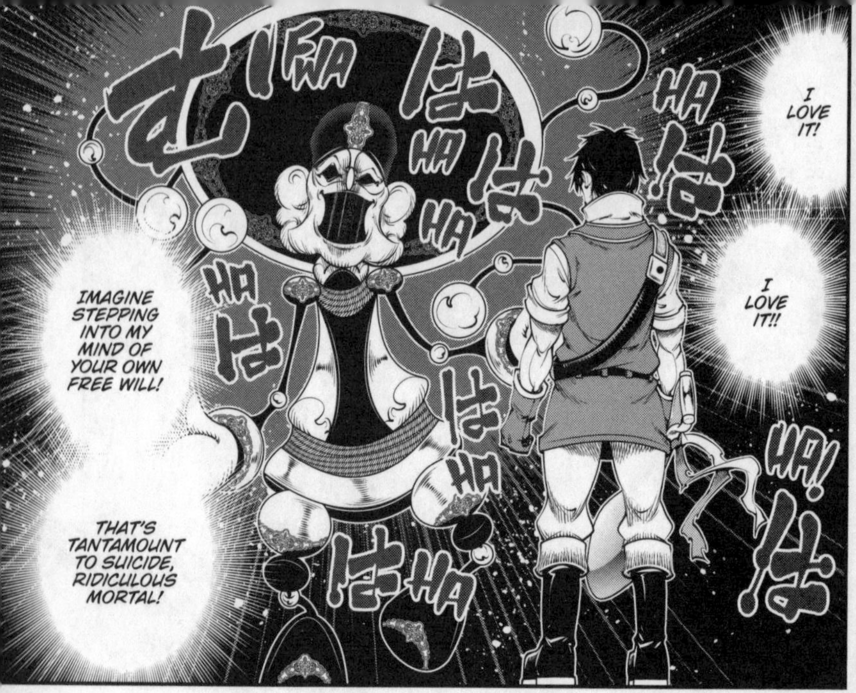
I LOVE IT!
HA
I LOVE IT!!
HA!
FWA
HA HA HA
HA
HA
HA
IMAGINE STEPPING INTO MY MIND OF YOUR OWN FREE WILL!
THAT'S TANTAMOUNT TO SUICIDE, RIDICULOUS MORTAL!

Chapter 20: The Curious Trial of the Shovel, Part 2

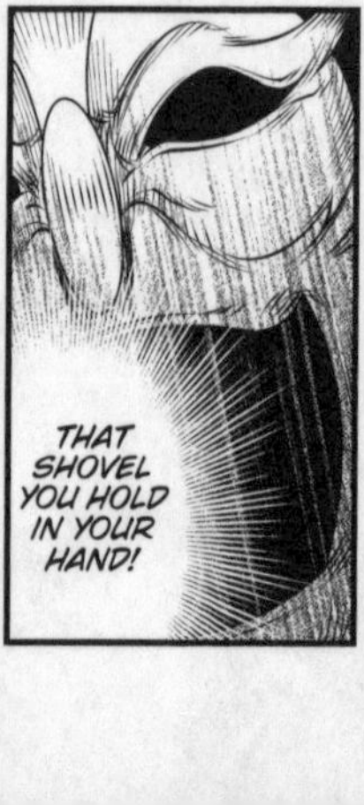
THAT SHOVEL YOU HOLD IN YOUR HAND!

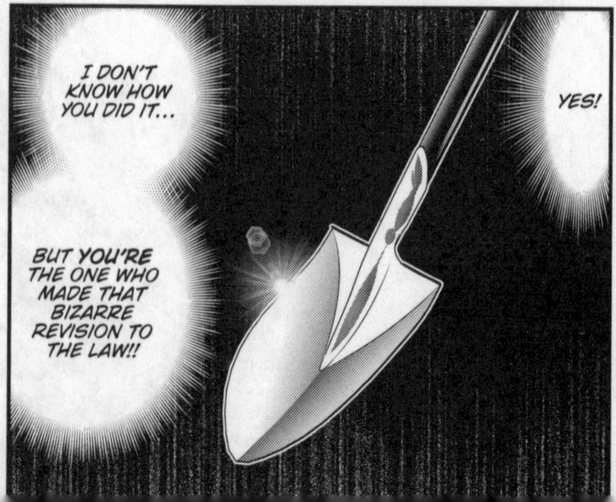
YES!
I DON'T KNOW HOW YOU DID IT...
BUT YOU'RE THE ONE WHO MADE THAT BIZARRE REVISION TO THE LAW!!

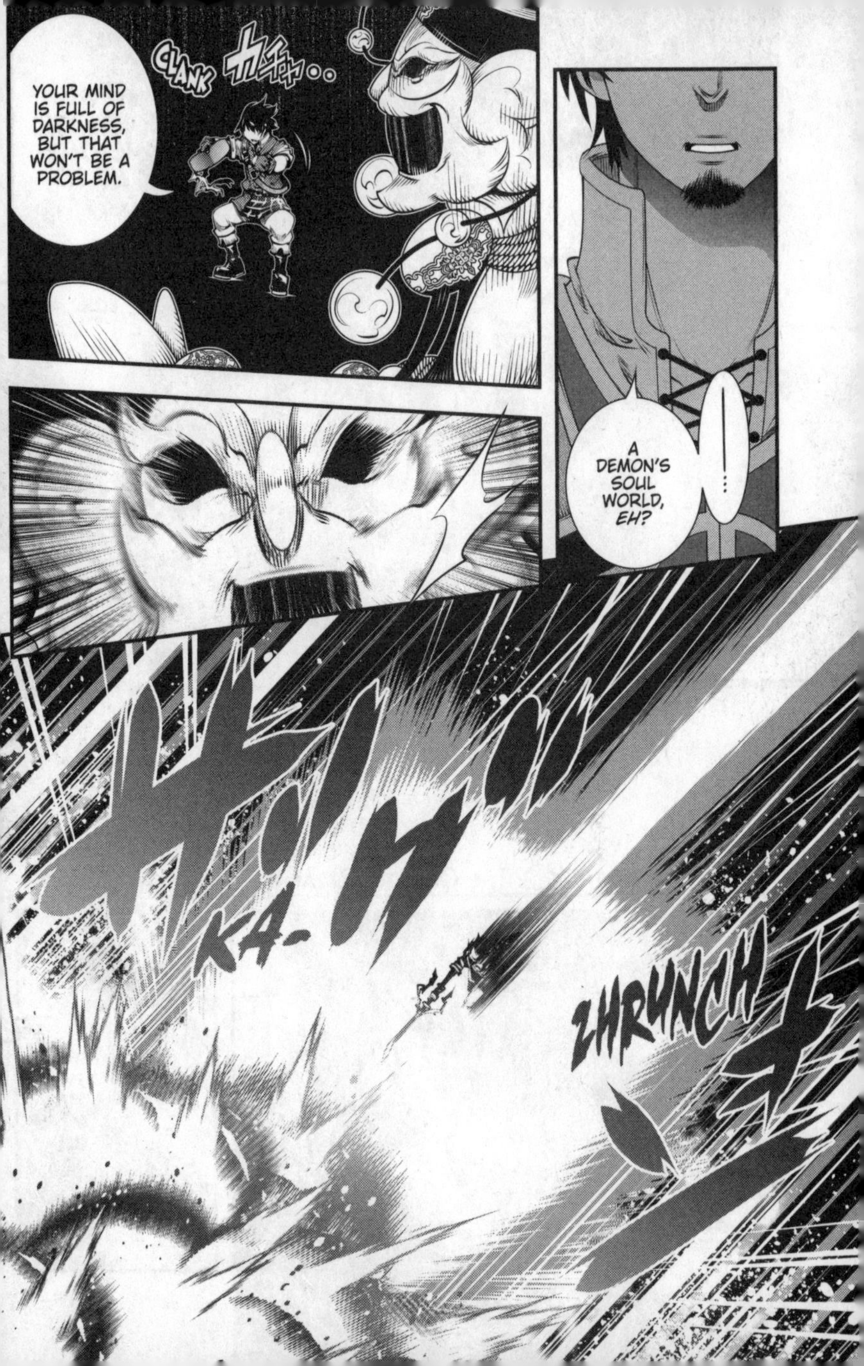
......
A DEMON'S SOUL WORLD, EH?
CLANK
YOUR MIND IS FULL OF DARKNESS, BUT THAT WON'T BE A PROBLEM.
ZHRUNCH
KA-

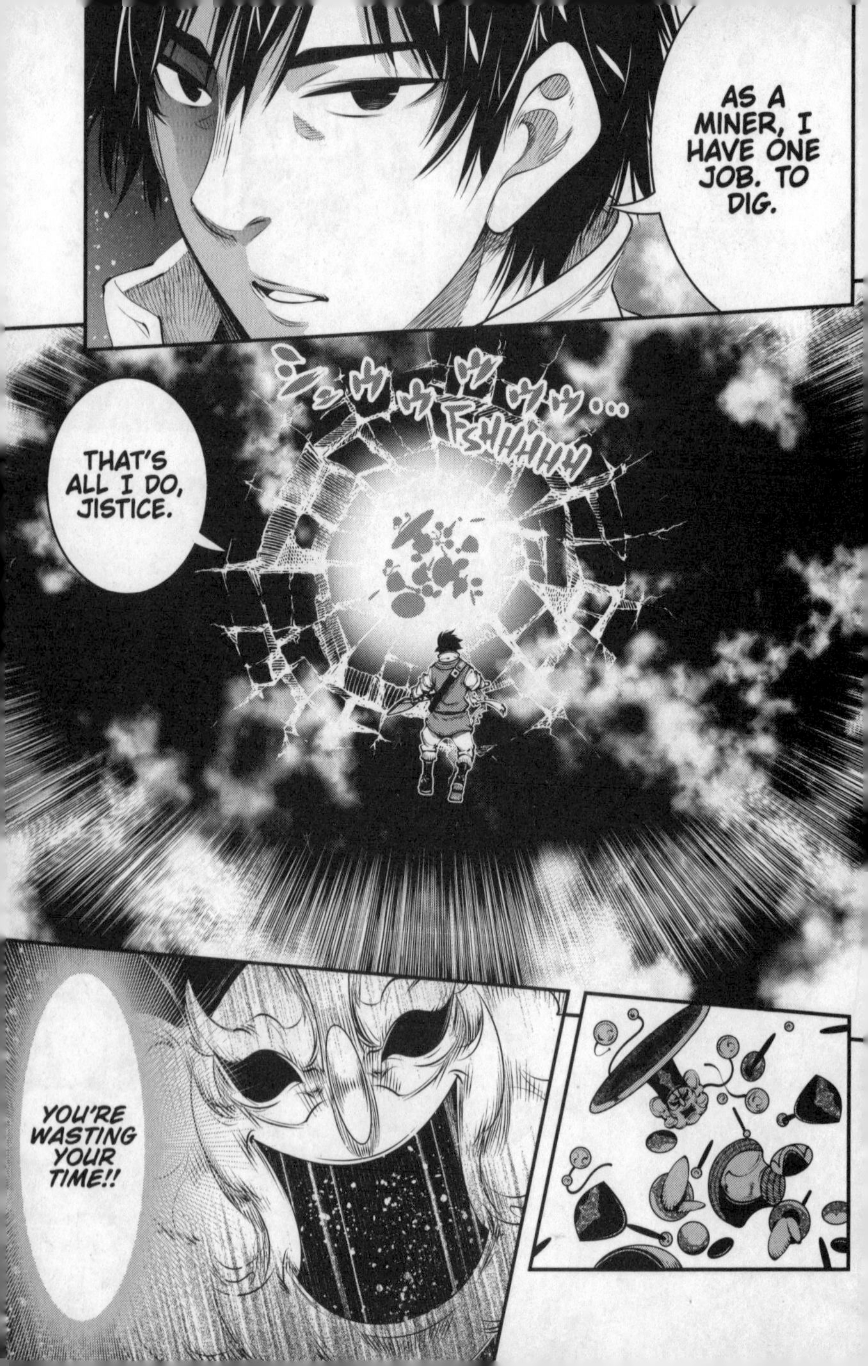
AS A MINER, I HAVE ONE JOB. TO DIG.
THAT'S ALL I DO, JISTICE.
FSHHHHHH
YOU'RE WASTING YOUR TIME!!

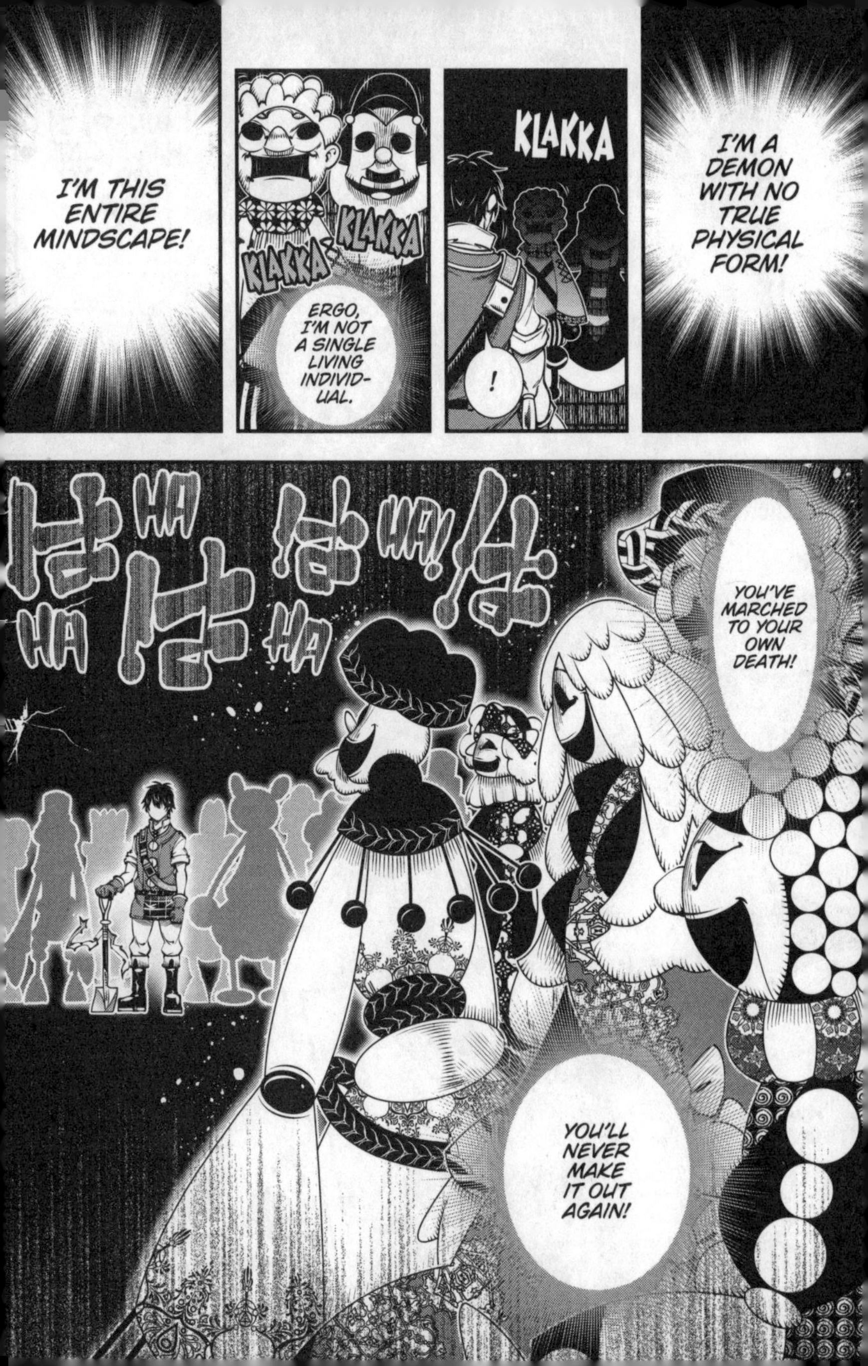
I'M A DEMON WITH NO TRUE PHYSICAL FORM!
KLAKKA
!
KLAKKA
KLAKKA
ERGO, I'M NOT A SINGLE LIVING INDIVIDUAL.
I'M THIS ENTIRE MINDSCAPE!
HA!
HA
HA
HA
YOU'VE MARCHED TO YOUR OWN DEATH!
YOU'LL NEVER MAKE IT OUT AGAIN!

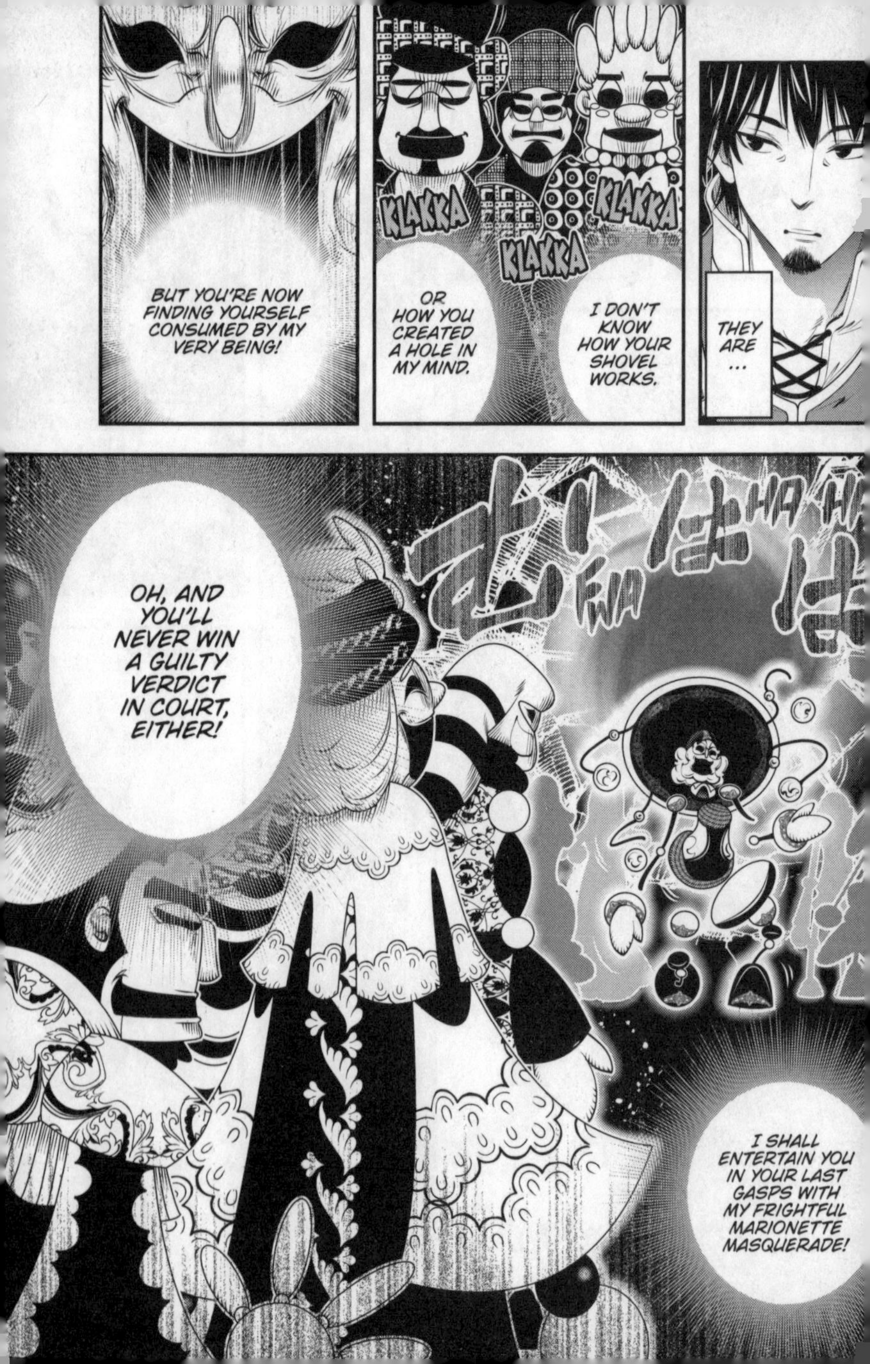
THEY ARE ...
KLAKKA
KLAKKA
KLAKKA
I DON'T KNOW HOW YOUR SHOVEL WORKS.
OR HOW YOU CREATED A HOLE IN MY MIND.
BUT YOU'RE NOW FINDING YOURSELF CONSUMED BY MY VERY BEING!
HA HA
FWA
OH, AND YOU'LL NEVER WIN A GUILTY VERDICT IN COURT, EITHER!
I SHALL ENTERTAIN YOU IN YOUR LAST GASPS WITH MY FRIGHTFUL MARIONETTE MASQUERADE!

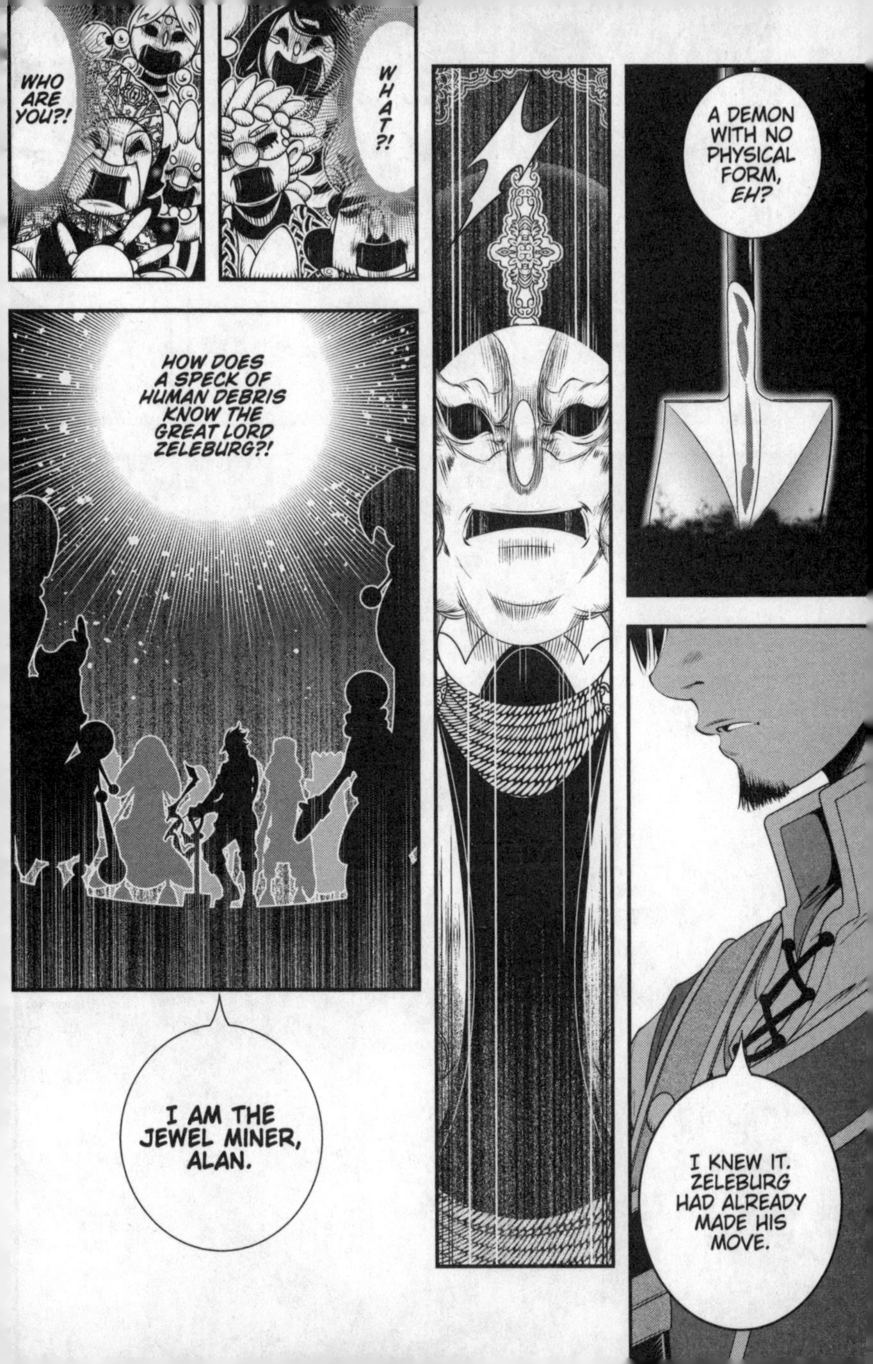
WHO ARE YOU?!
WHAT?!
HOW DOES A SPECK OF HUMAN DEBRIS KNOW THE GREAT LORD ZELEBURG?!
I AM THE JEWEL MINER, ALAN.
A DEMON WITH NO PHYSICAL FORM, EH?
I KNEW IT. ZELEBURG HAD ALREADY MADE HIS MOVE.

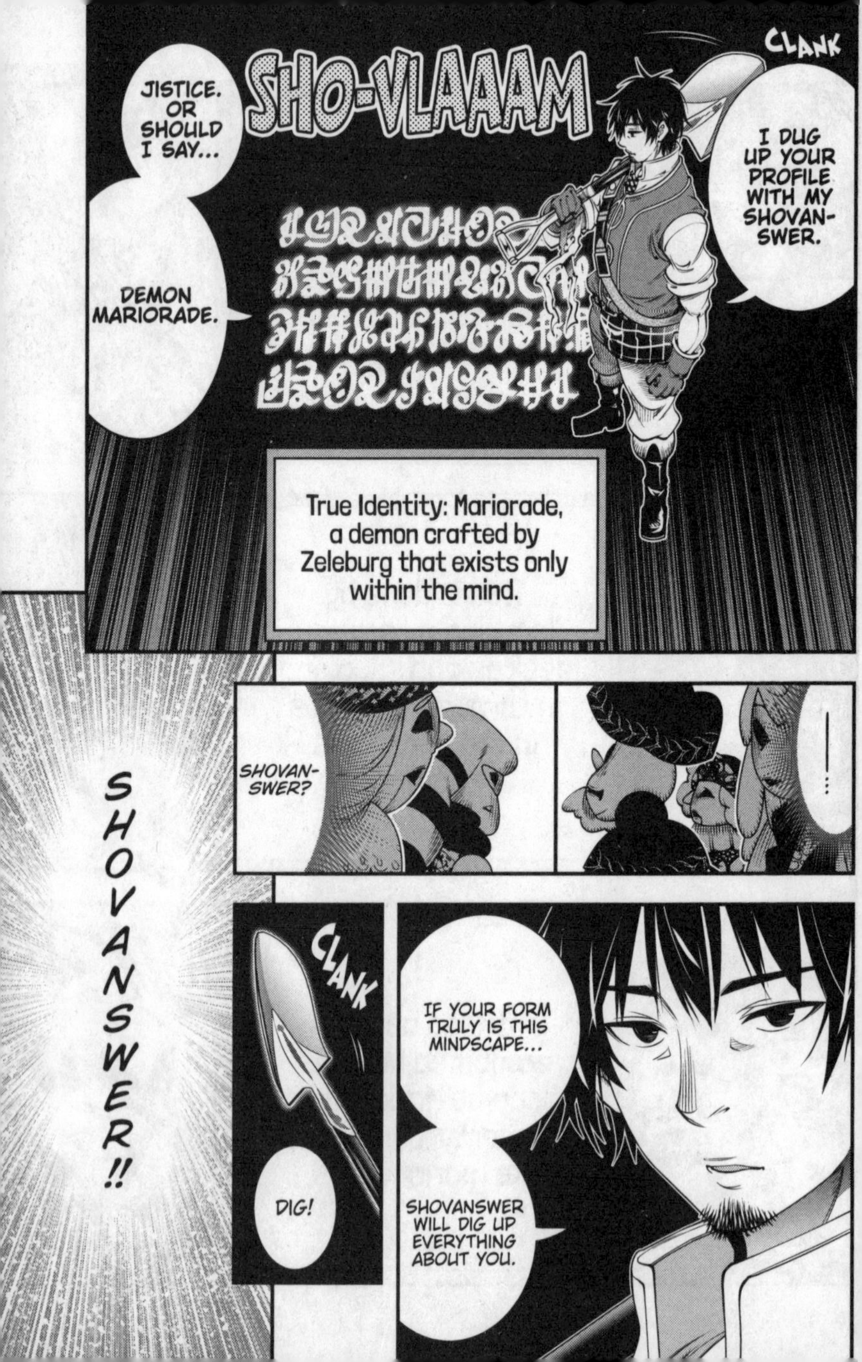
CLANK
I DUG UP YOUR PROFILE WITH MY SHOVANSWER.
SHO-VLAAAM
JISTICE. OR SHOULD I SAY...
DEMON MARIORADE.
True Identity: Mariorade, a demon crafted by Zeleburg that exists only within the mind.
...
SHOVANSWER?
IF YOUR FORM TRULY IS THIS MINDSCAPE...
SHOVANSWER WILL DIG UP EVERYTHING ABOUT YOU.
CLANK
DIG!
SHOVANSWER!!

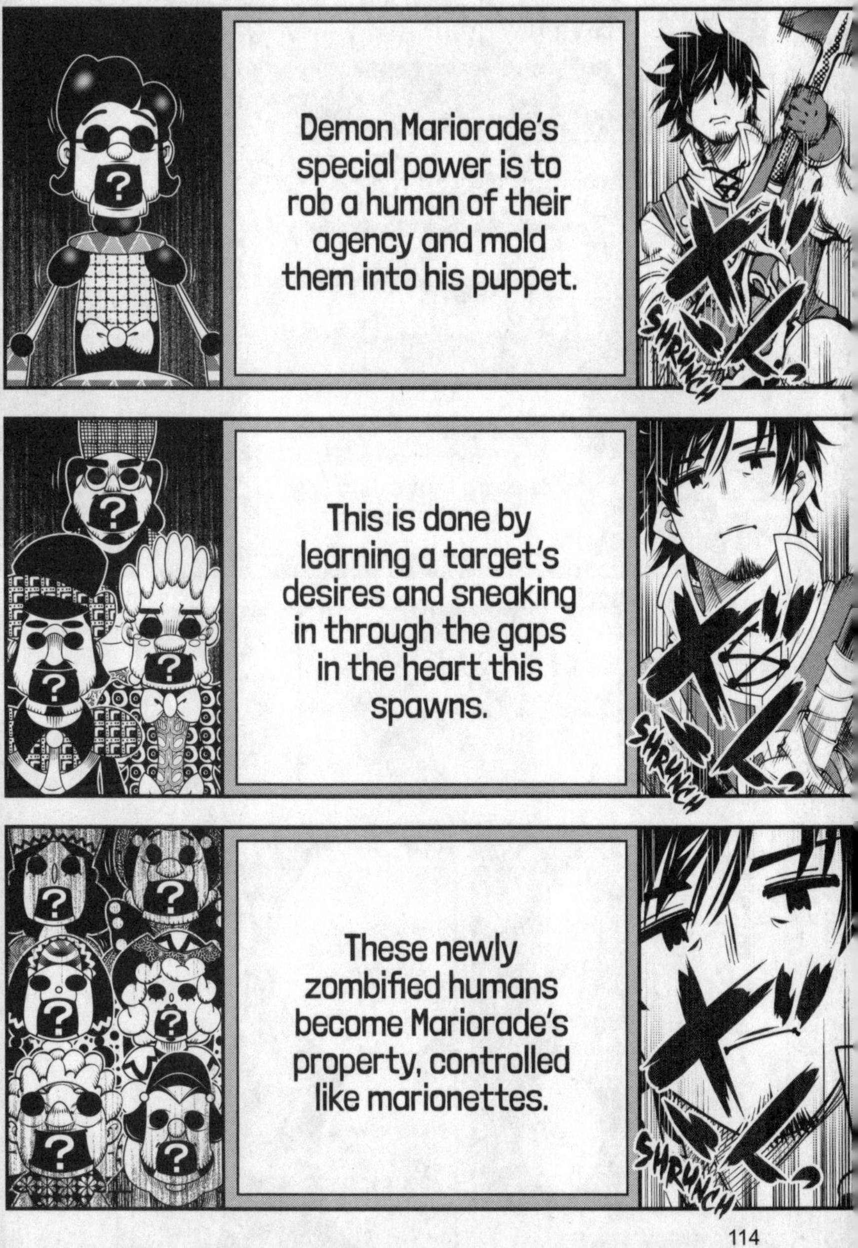
SHRUNCH
Demon Mariorade's special power is to rob a human of their agency and mold them into his puppet.
SHRUNCH
This is done by learning a target's desires and sneaking in through the gaps in the heart this spawns.
SHRUNCH
These newly zombified humans become Mariorade's property, controlled like marionettes.

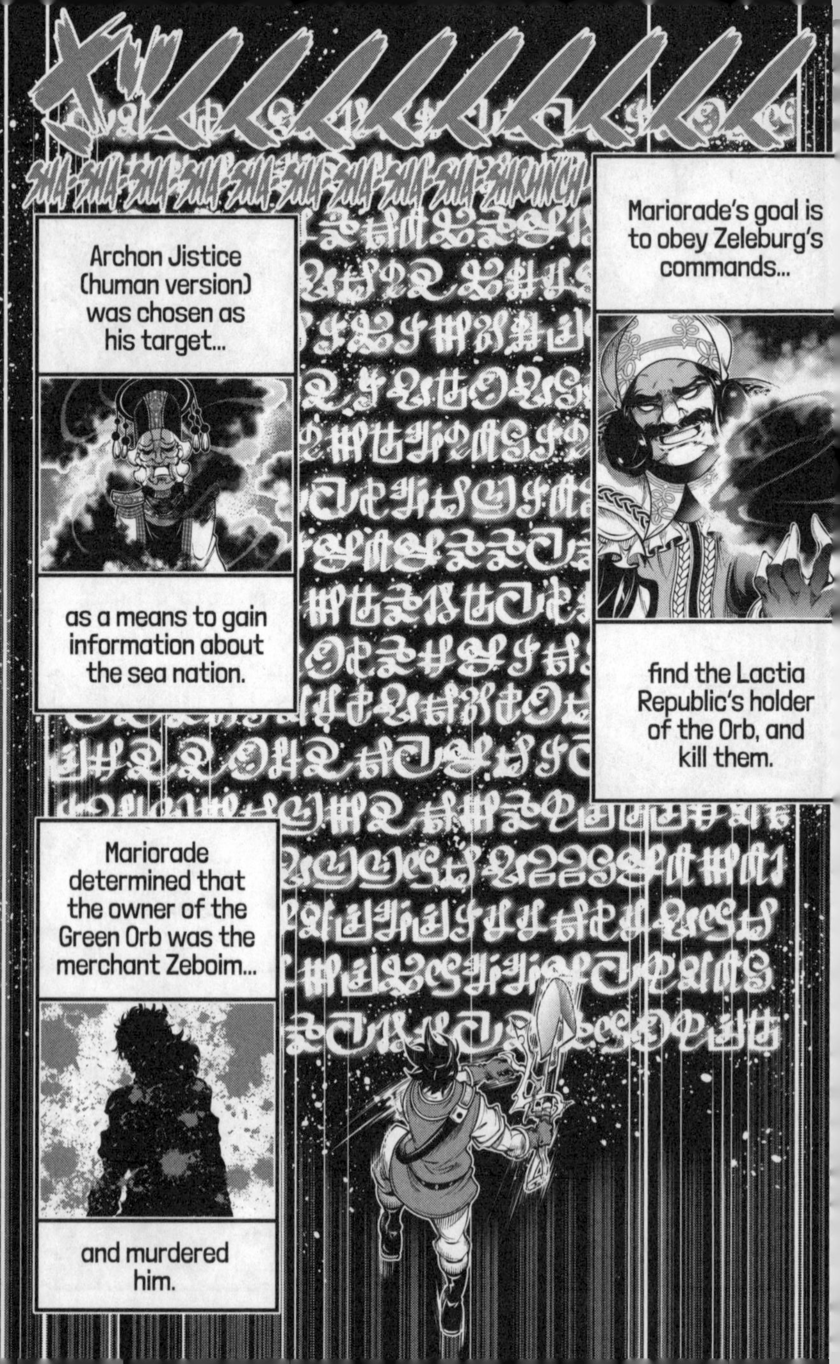
SHA-SHA-SHA-SHA-SHA-SHA-SHA-SHA-SHA-SHRUNCH
Mariorade's goal is to obey Zeleburg's commands...
find the Lactia Republic's holder of the Orb, and kill them.
Archon Jistice (human version) was chosen as his target...
as a means to gain information about the sea nation.
Mariorade determined that the owner of the Green Orb was the merchant Zeboim...
and murdered him.

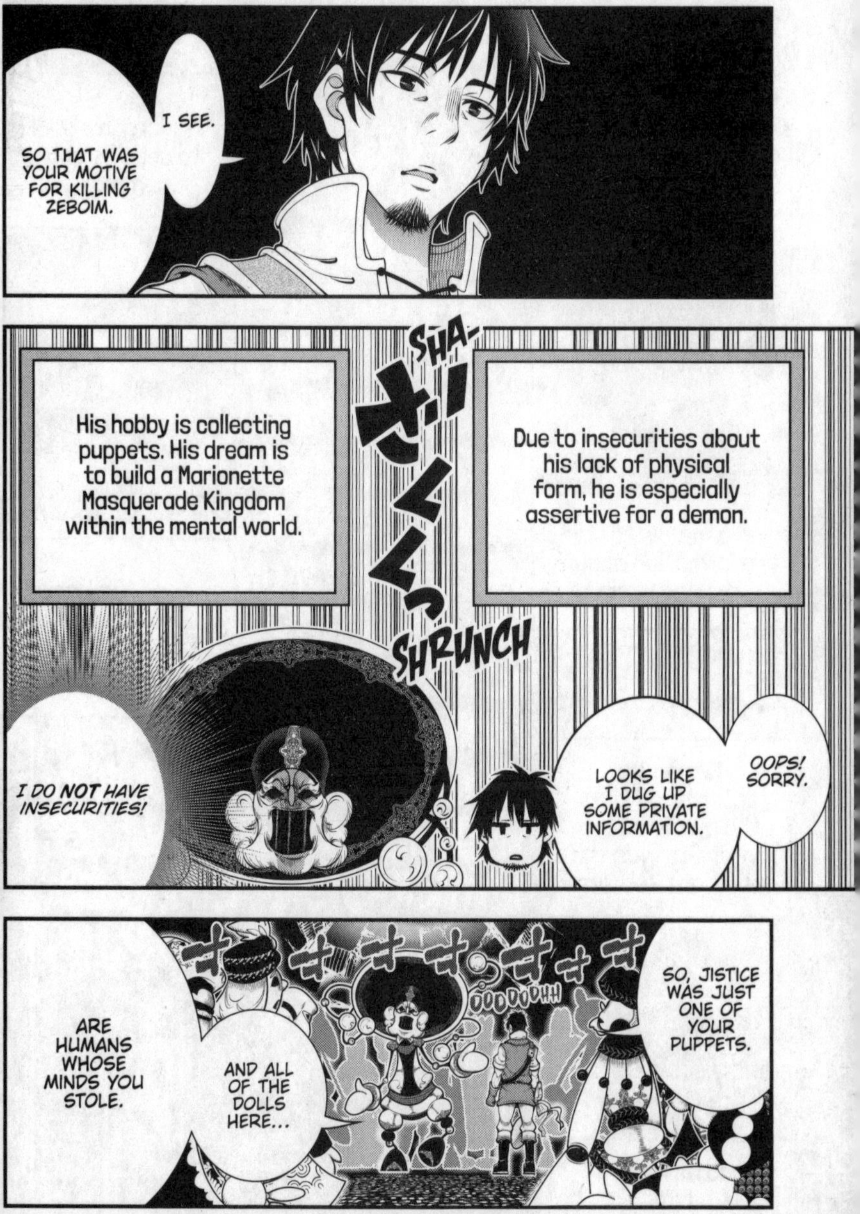
I SEE.
SO THAT WAS YOUR MOTIVE FOR KILLING ZEBOIM.
Due to insecurities about his lack of physical form, he is especially assertive for a demon.
SHA-
SHRUNCH
His hobby is collecting puppets. His dream is to build a Marionette Masquerade Kingdom within the mental world.
OOPS! SORRY.
LOOKS LIKE I DUG UP SOME PRIVATE INFORMATION.
I DO **NOT** HAVE INSECURITIES!
SO, JISTICE WAS JUST ONE OF YOUR PUPPETS.
AND ALL OF THE DOLLS HERE...
ARE HUMANS WHOSE MINDS YOU STOLE.

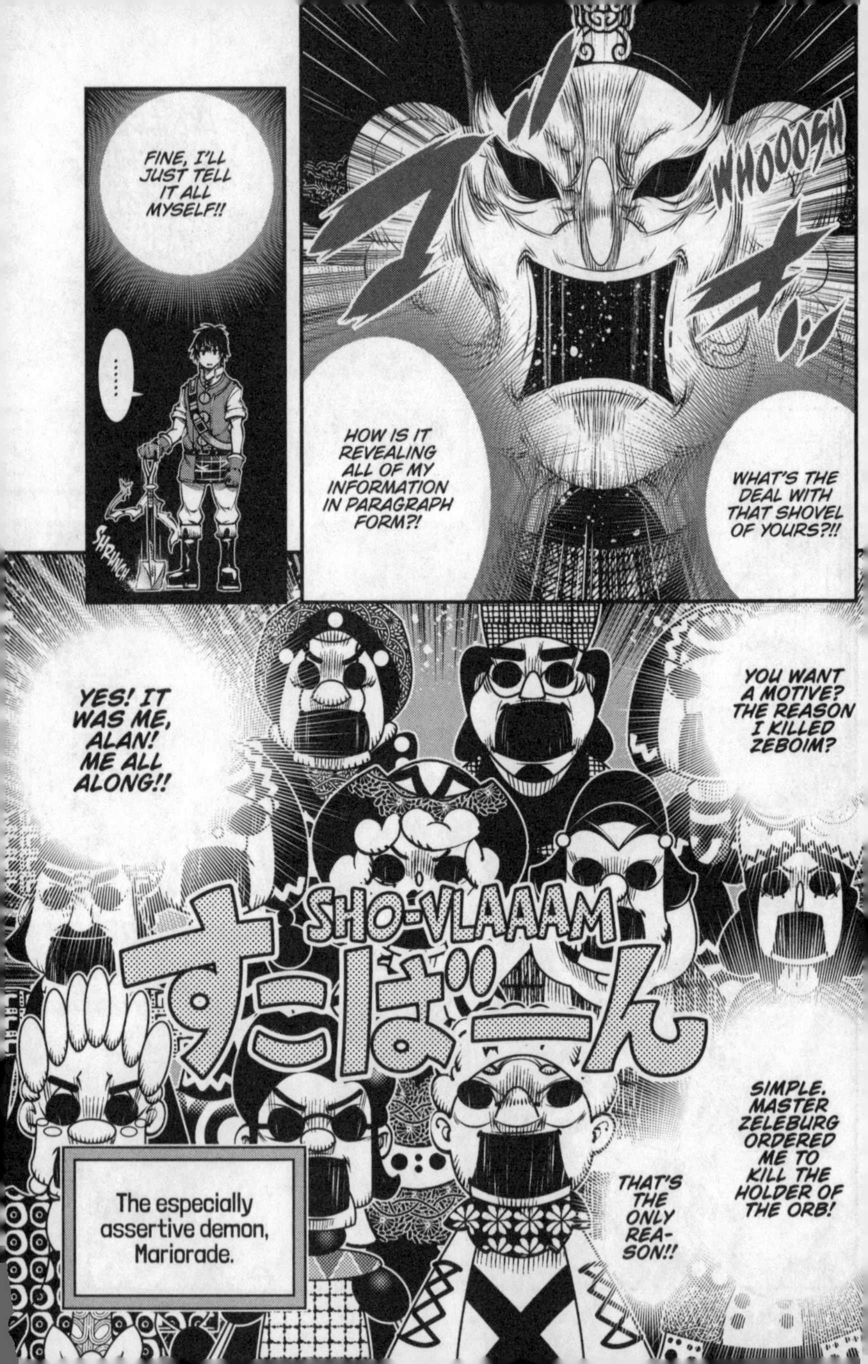
WHOOOSH
WHAT'S THE DEAL WITH THAT SHOVEL OF YOURS?!!
HOW IS IT REVEALING ALL OF MY INFORMATION IN PARAGRAPH FORM?!
FINE, I'LL JUST TELL IT ALL MYSELF!!
......
SHRUNCH
YOU WANT A MOTIVE? THE REASON I KILLED ZEBOIM?
YES! IT WAS ME, ALAN! ME ALL ALONG!!
SHO-VLAAAM
すばーん
SIMPLE. MASTER ZELEBURG ORDERED ME TO KILL THE HOLDER OF THE ORB!
THAT'S THE ONLY REA-SON!!
The especially assertive demon, Mariorade.

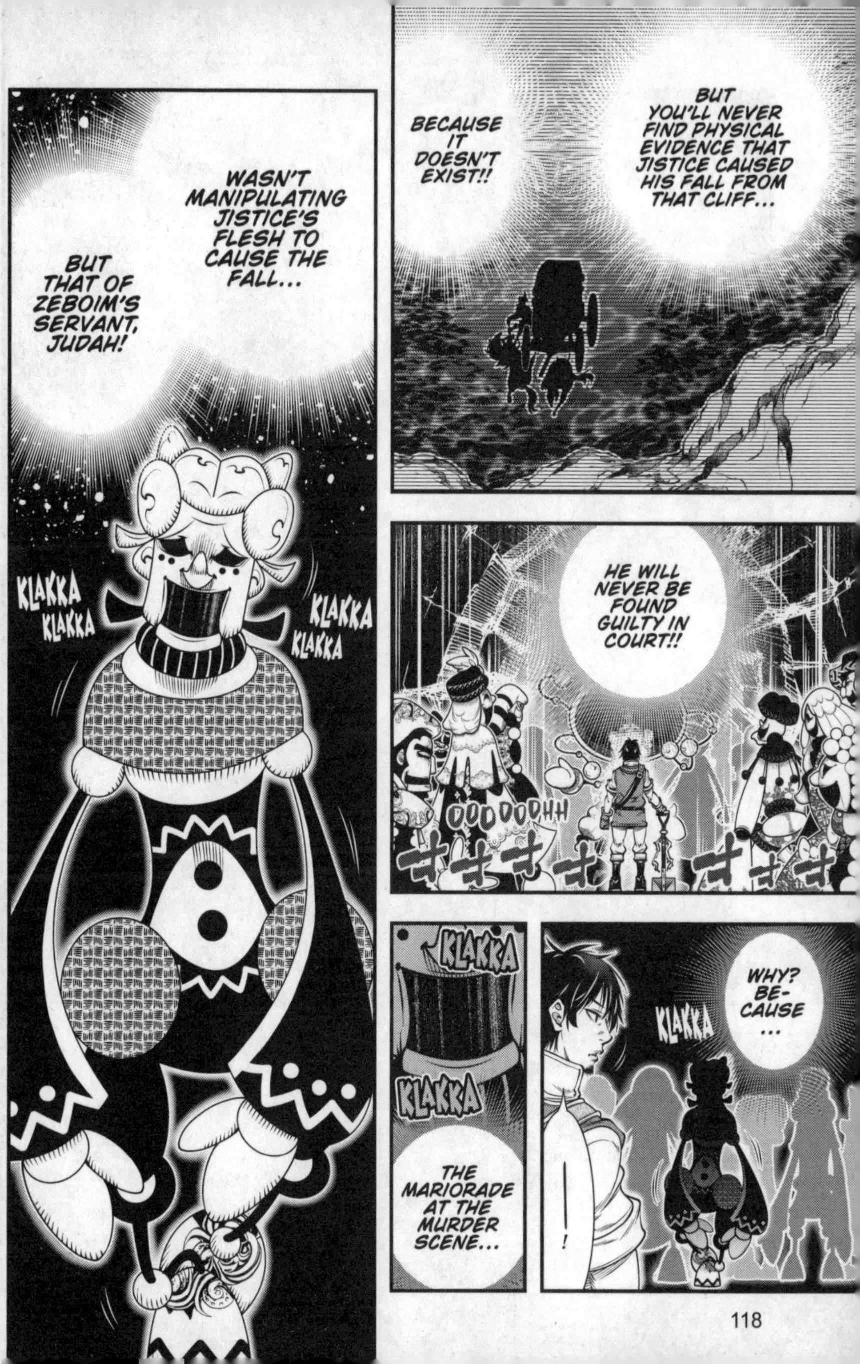
BUT YOU'LL NEVER FIND PHYSICAL EVIDENCE THAT JISTICE CAUSED HIS FALL FROM THAT CLIFF...
BECAUSE IT DOESN'T EXIST!!
HE WILL NEVER BE FOUND GUILTY IN COURT!!
OOOOOOHH
WHY? BE- CAUSE ...
KLAKKA
!
KLAKKA
KLAKKA
THE MARIORADE AT THE MURDER SCENE...
WASN'T MANIPULATING JISTICE'S FLESH TO CAUSE THE FALL...
BUT THAT OF ZEBOIM'S SERVANT, JUDAH!
KLAKKA KLAKKA
KLAKKA KLAKKA

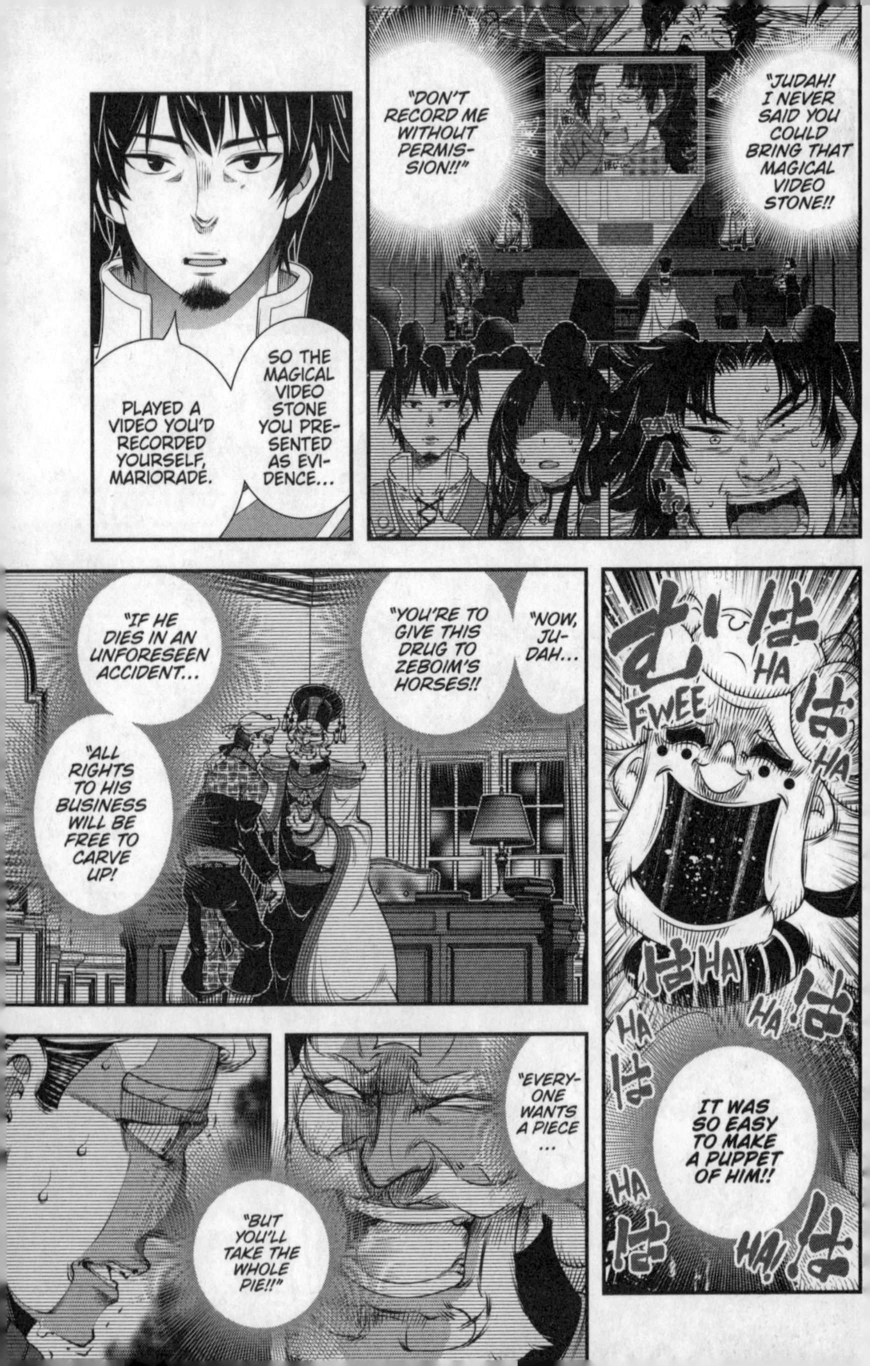
"JUDAH! I NEVER SAID YOU COULD BRING THAT MAGICAL VIDEO STONE!!
"DON'T RECORD ME WITHOUT PERMIS-SION!!"
SO THE MAGICAL VIDEO STONE YOU PRE-SENTED AS EVI-DENCE...
PLAYED A VIDEO YOU'D RECORDED YOURSELF, MARIORADE.
FWEE
HA
HA
HA
HA
HA
HA
HA!
IT WAS SO EASY TO MAKE A PUPPET OF HIM!!
"NOW, JU-DAH...
"YOU'RE TO GIVE THIS DRUG TO ZEBOIM'S HORSES!!
"IF HE DIES IN AN UNFORESEEN ACCIDENT...
"ALL RIGHTS TO HIS BUSINESS WILL BE FREE TO CARVE UP!
"EVERY-ONE WANTS A PIECE...
"BUT YOU'LL TAKE THE WHOLE PIE!!"

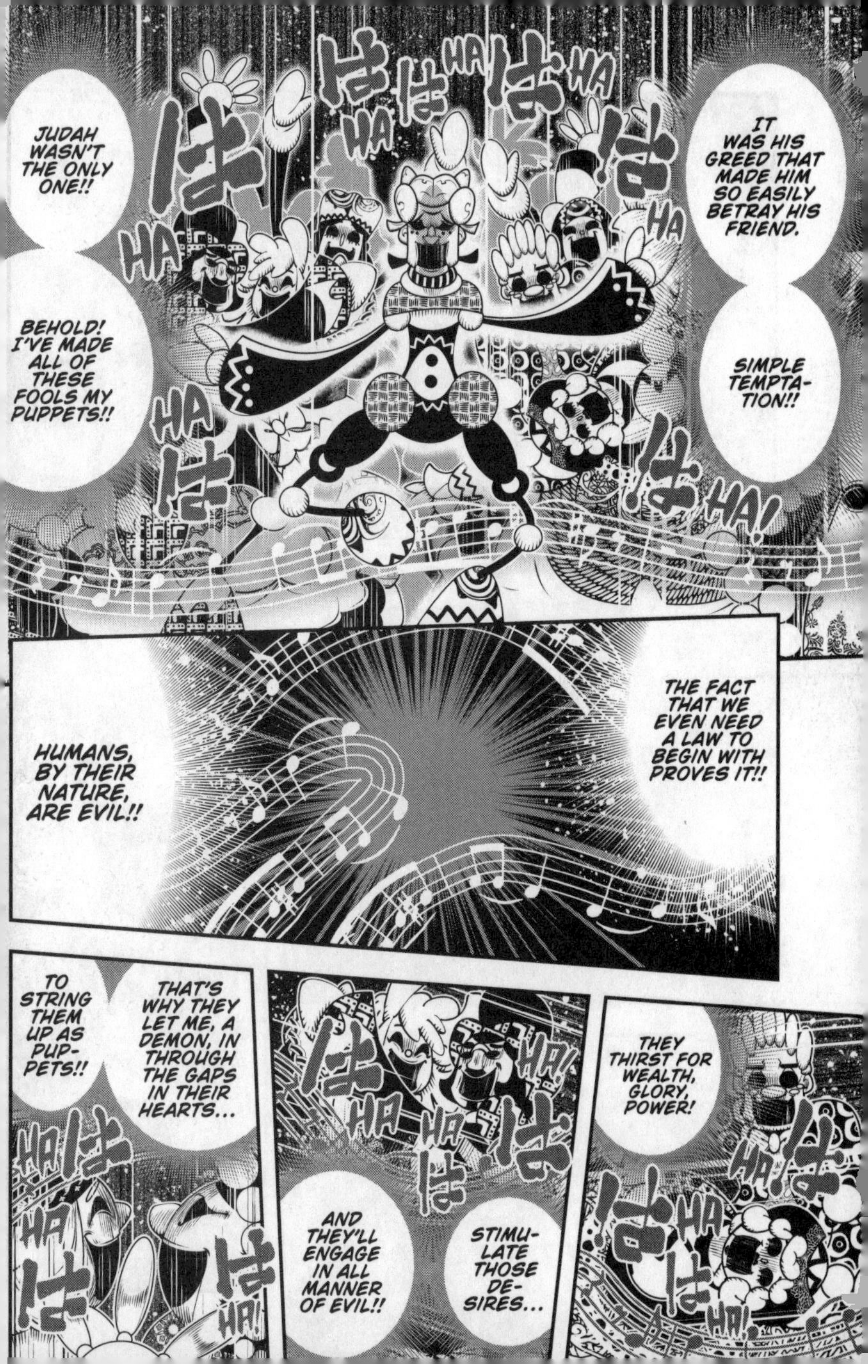
IT WAS HIS GREED THAT MADE HIM SO EASILY BETRAY HIS FRIEND.
SIMPLE TEMPTA-TION!!
JUDAH WASN'T THE ONLY ONE!!
BEHOLD! I'VE MADE ALL OF THESE FOOLS MY PUPPETS!!
はHAはHAはHA はHA はHA はHA HA はHA!
THE FACT THAT WE EVEN NEED A LAW TO BEGIN WITH PROVES IT!!
HUMANS, BY THEIR NATURE, ARE EVIL!!
THEY THIRST FOR WEALTH, GLORY, POWER!
はHA! はHA はHA!
STIMU-LATE THOSE DE-SIRES...
AND THEY'LL ENGAGE IN ALL MANNER OF EVIL!!
はHA! はHA はHA
THAT'S WHY THEY LET ME, A DEMON, IN THROUGH THE GAPS IN THEIR HEARTS...
TO STRING THEM UP AS PUP-PETS!!
HAは HA はHA!

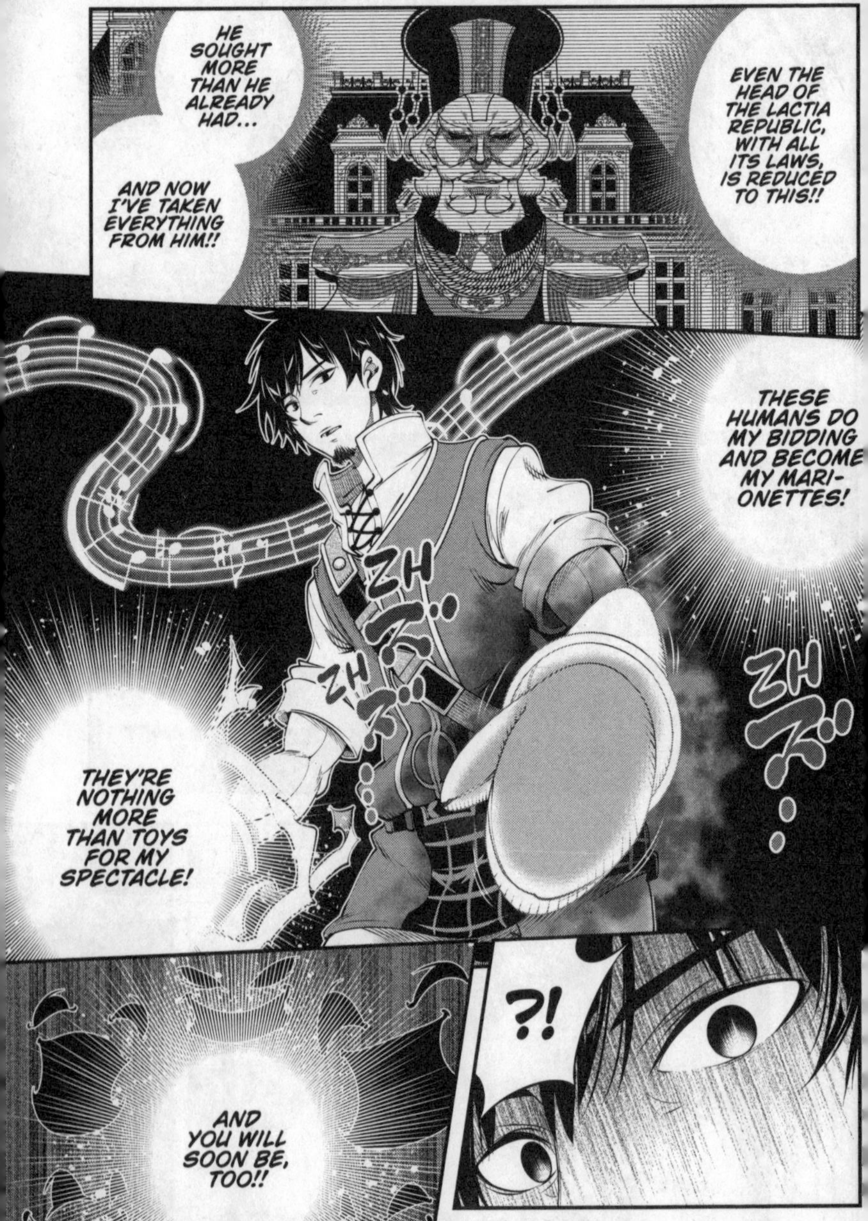
EVEN THE HEAD OF THE LACTIA REPUBLIC, WITH ALL ITS LAWS, IS REDUCED TO THIS!!
HE SOUGHT MORE THAN HE ALREADY HAD...
AND NOW I'VE TAKEN EVERYTHING FROM HIM!!
THESE HUMANS DO MY BIDDING AND BECOME MY MARI-ONETTES!
ZH ズ...
ZH ズ...
ZH ズ...
THEY'RE NOTHING MORE THAN TOYS FOR MY SPECTACLE!
?!
AND YOU WILL SOON BE, TOO!!

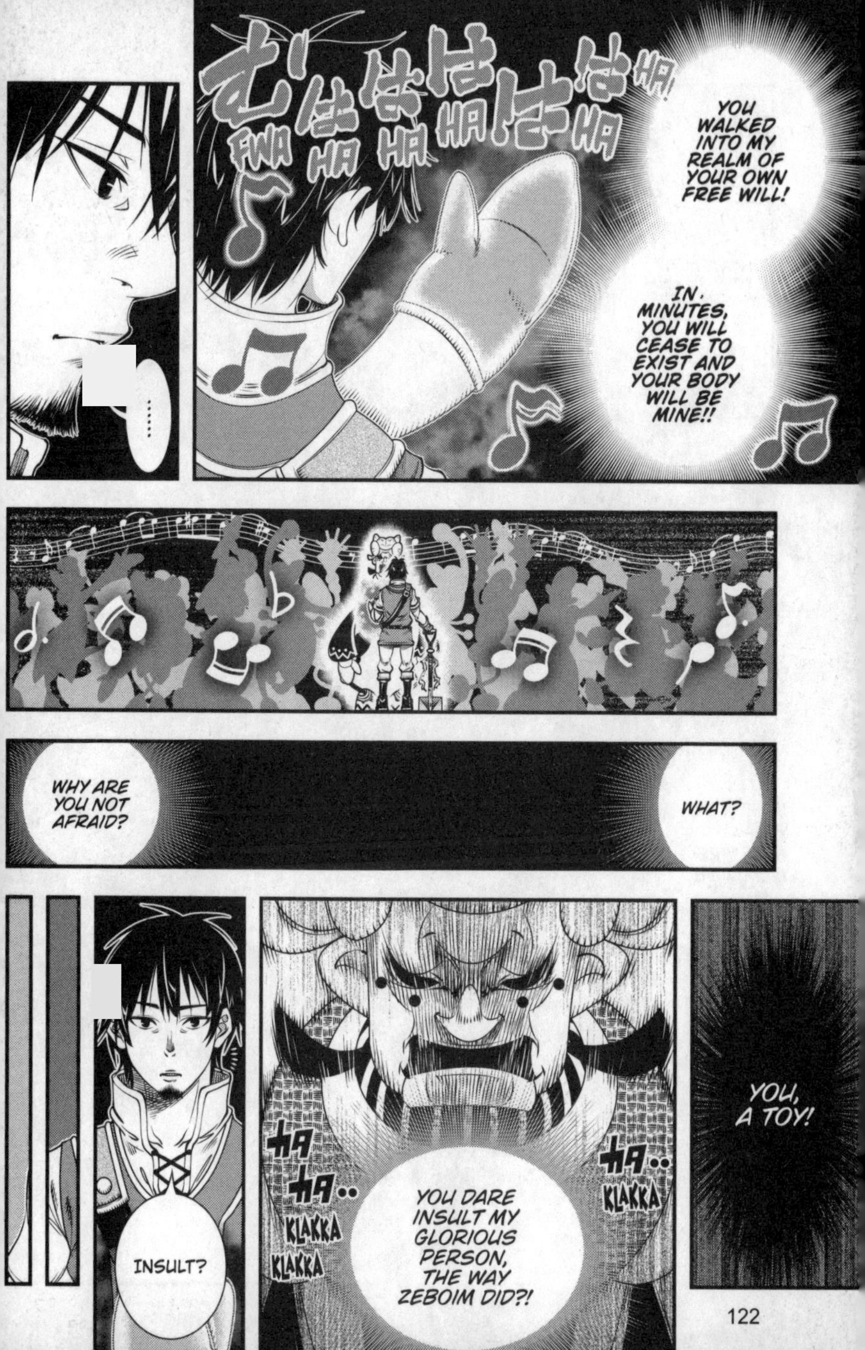

FWA~ HA HA HA HA HA!
YOU WALKED INTO MY REALM OF YOUR OWN FREE WILL!
IN MINUTES, YOU WILL CEASE TO EXIST AND YOUR BODY WILL BE MINE!!
......
WHAT?
WHY ARE YOU NOT AFRAID?
YOU, A TOY!
カタ‥ KLAKKA
カタ カタ‥ KLAKKA KLAKKA
YOU DARE INSULT MY GLORIOUS PERSON, THE WAY ZEBOIM DID?!
INSULT?

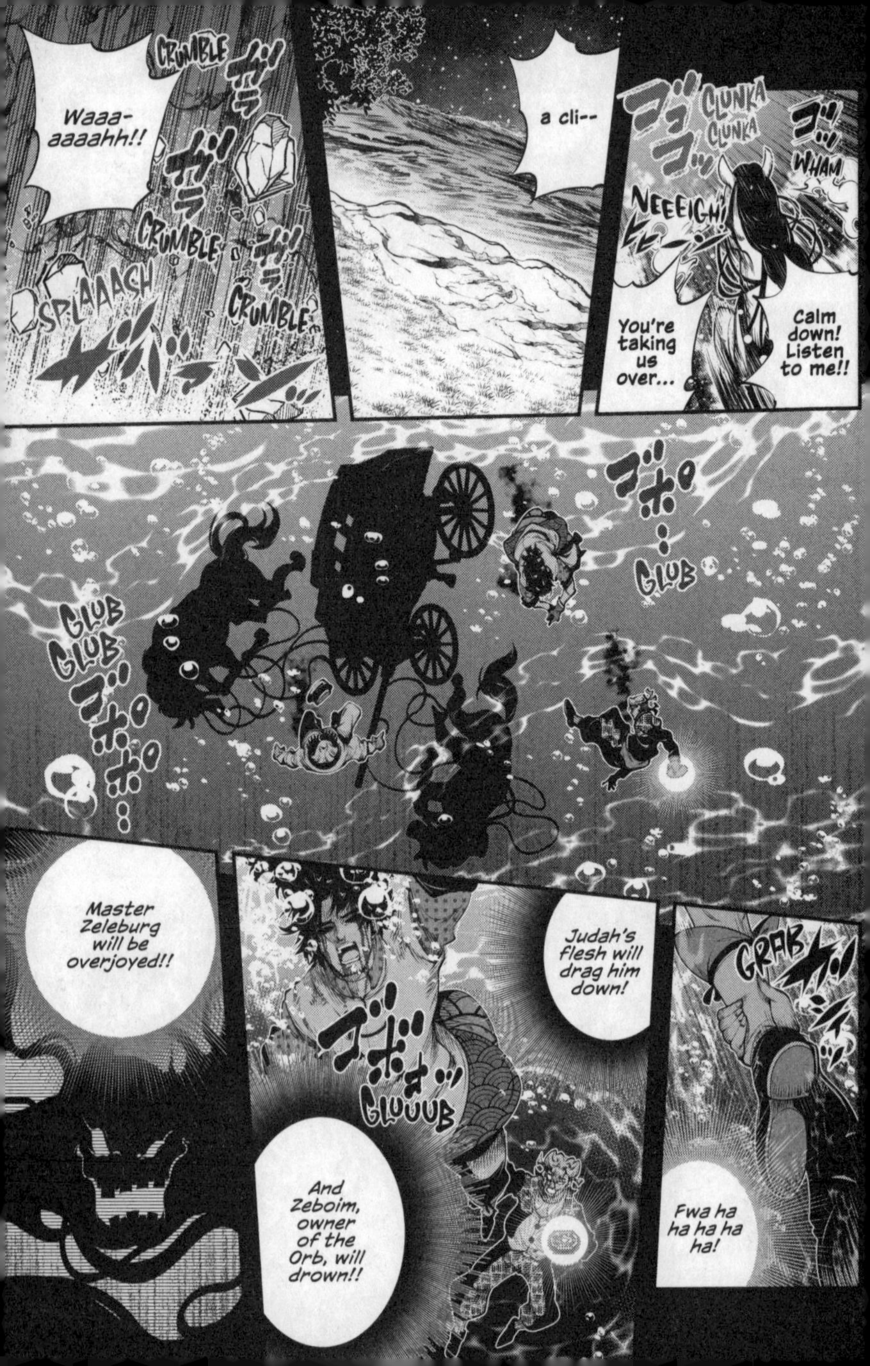
CLUNKA CLUNKA
WHAM
NEEEIGH!
Calm down! Listen to me!!
You're taking us over...
a cli--
Waaa-aaaahh!!
CRUMBLE
CRUMBLE
CRUMBLE
SPLAAASH
GLUB
GLUB GLUB
GRAB
Fwa ha ha ha ha ha!
Judah's flesh will drag him down!
GLUUUB
And Zeboim, owner of the Orb, will drown!!
Master Zeleburg will be overjoyed!!

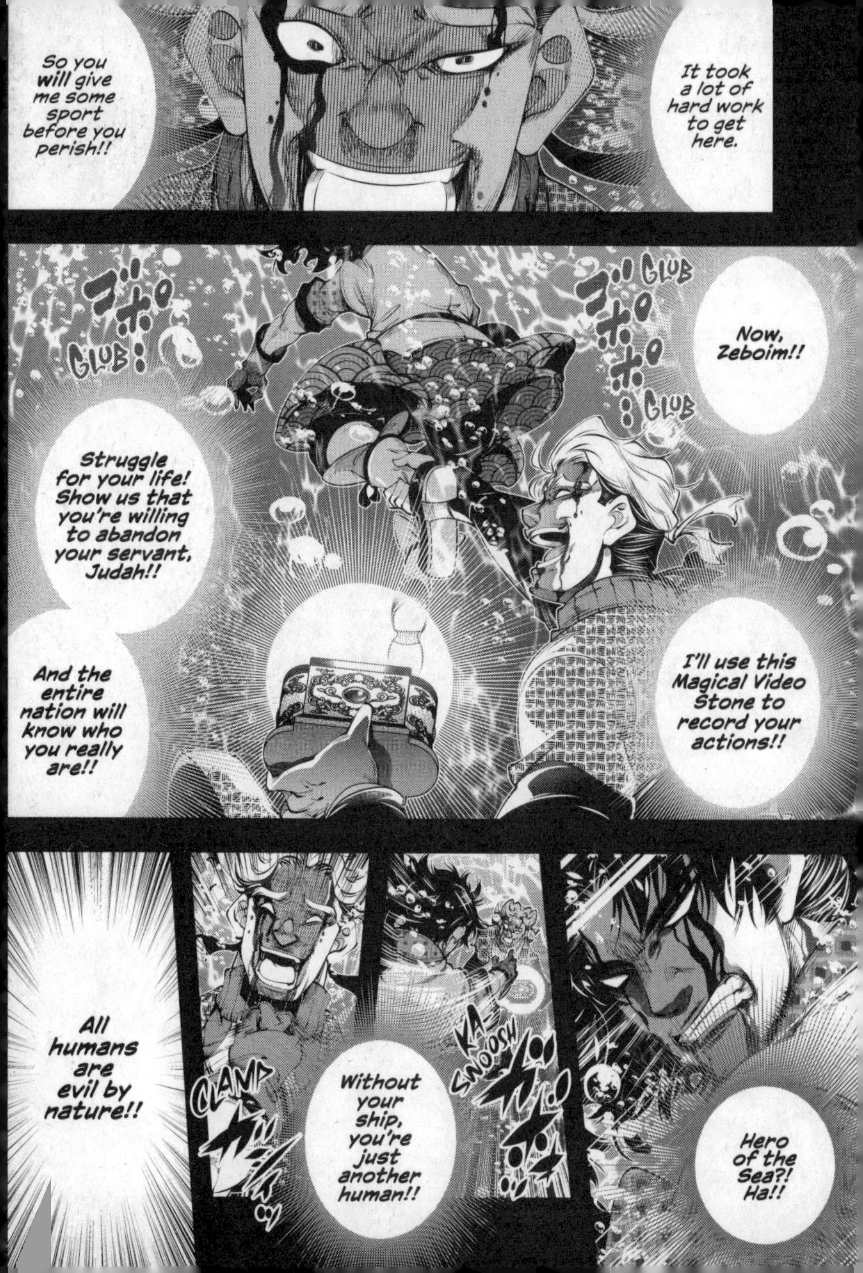
It took a lot of hard work to get here.
So you will give me some sport before you perish!!
GLUB
GLUB
Now, Zeboim!!
GLUB
Struggle for your life! Show us that you're willing to abandon your servant, Judah!!
I'll use this Magical Video Stone to record your actions!!
And the entire nation will know who you really are!!
Hero of the Sea?! Ha!!
KA-SWOOSH
Without your ship, you're just another human!!
CLAMP
All humans are evil by nature!!

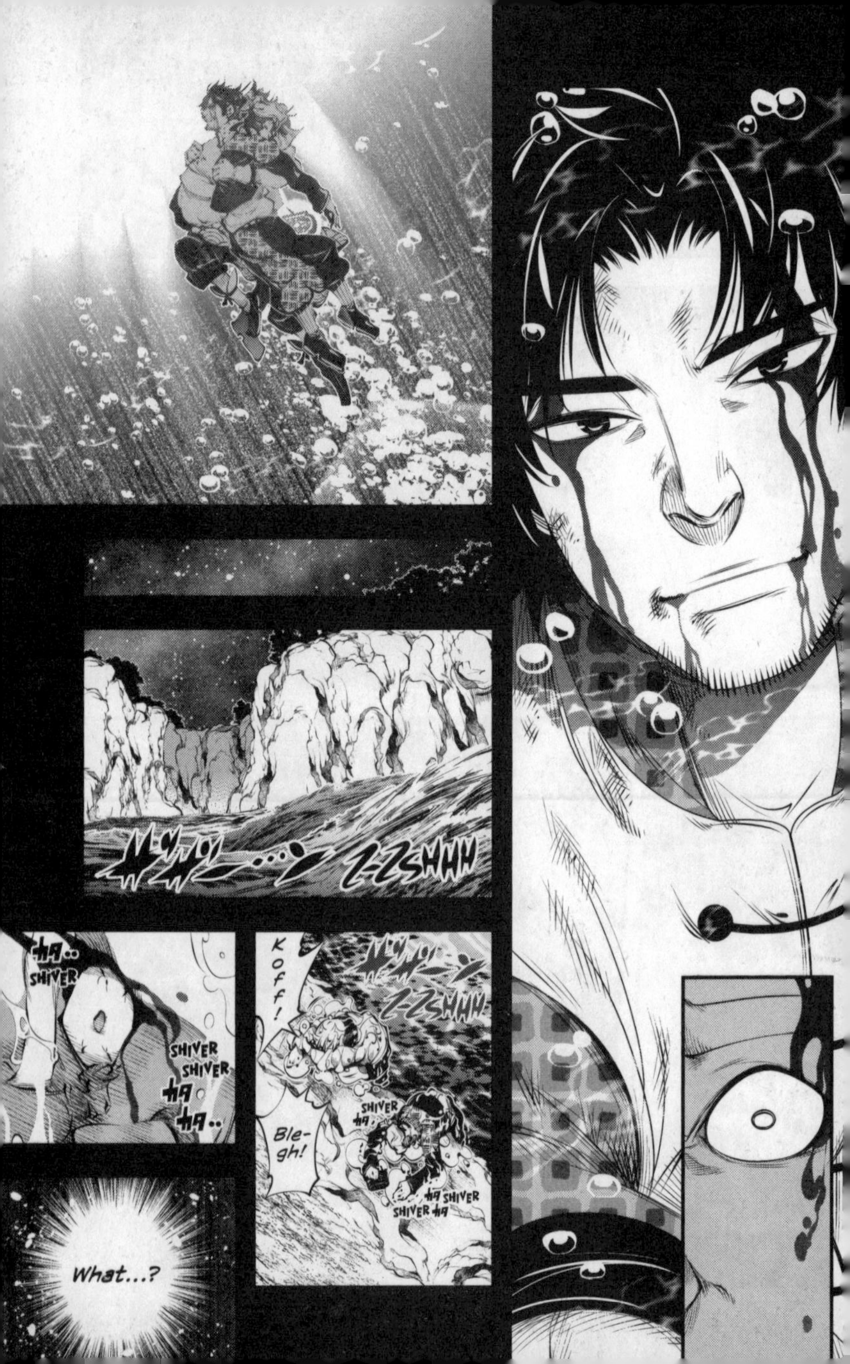
Z-ZSHHH
Koff!
Z-ZSHHH
SHIVER
Bleg-
gh!
SHIVER
SHIVER
SHIVER
SHIVER
SHIVER
What...?

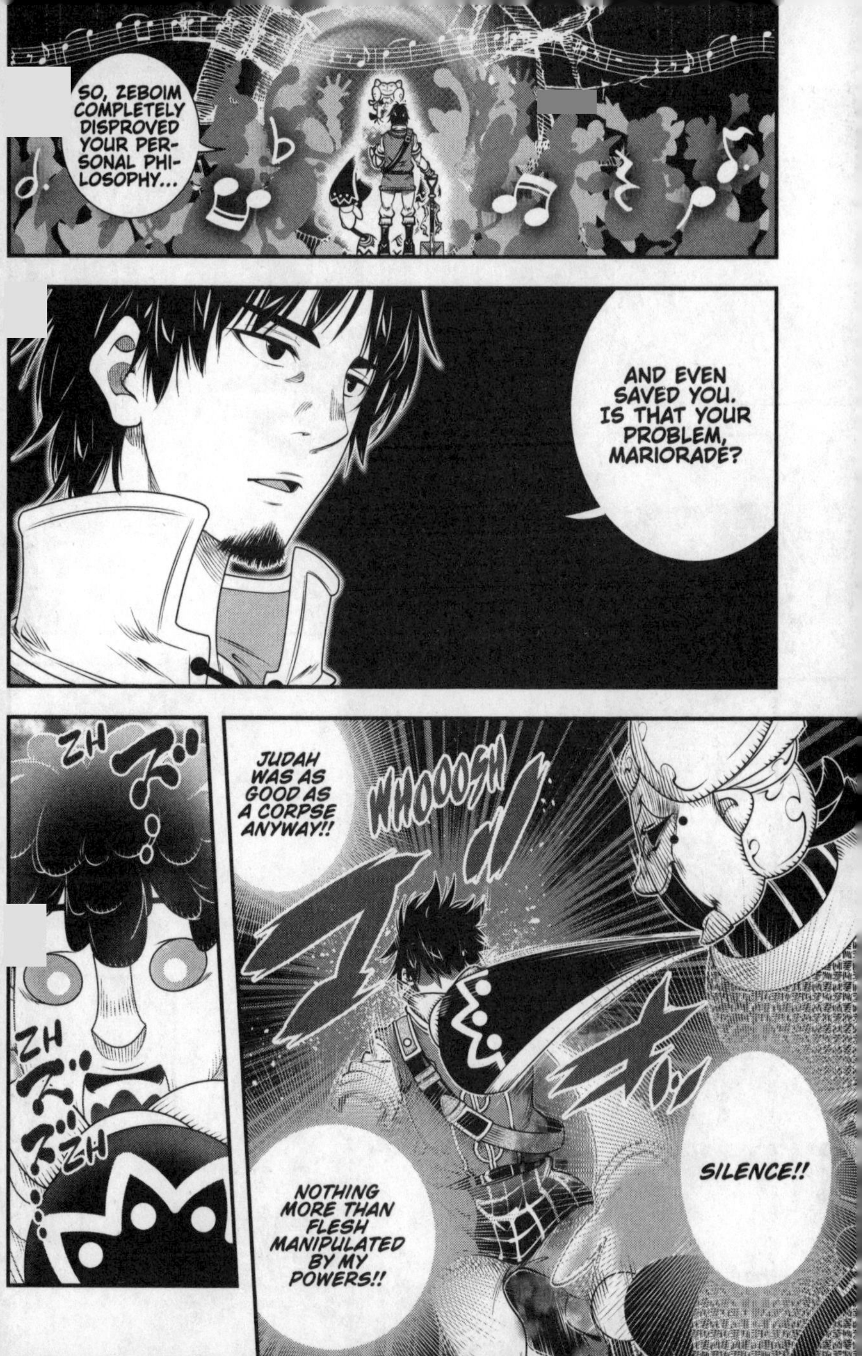
SO, ZEBOIM COMPLETELY DISPROVED YOUR PERSONAL PHILOSOPHY...
AND EVEN SAVED YOU. IS THAT YOUR PROBLEM, MARIORADE?
JUDAH WAS AS GOOD AS A CORPSE ANYWAY!!
WHOOOSH
SILENCE!!
NOTHING MORE THAN FLESH MANIPULATED BY MY POWERS!!
ZH
ZH
ZH

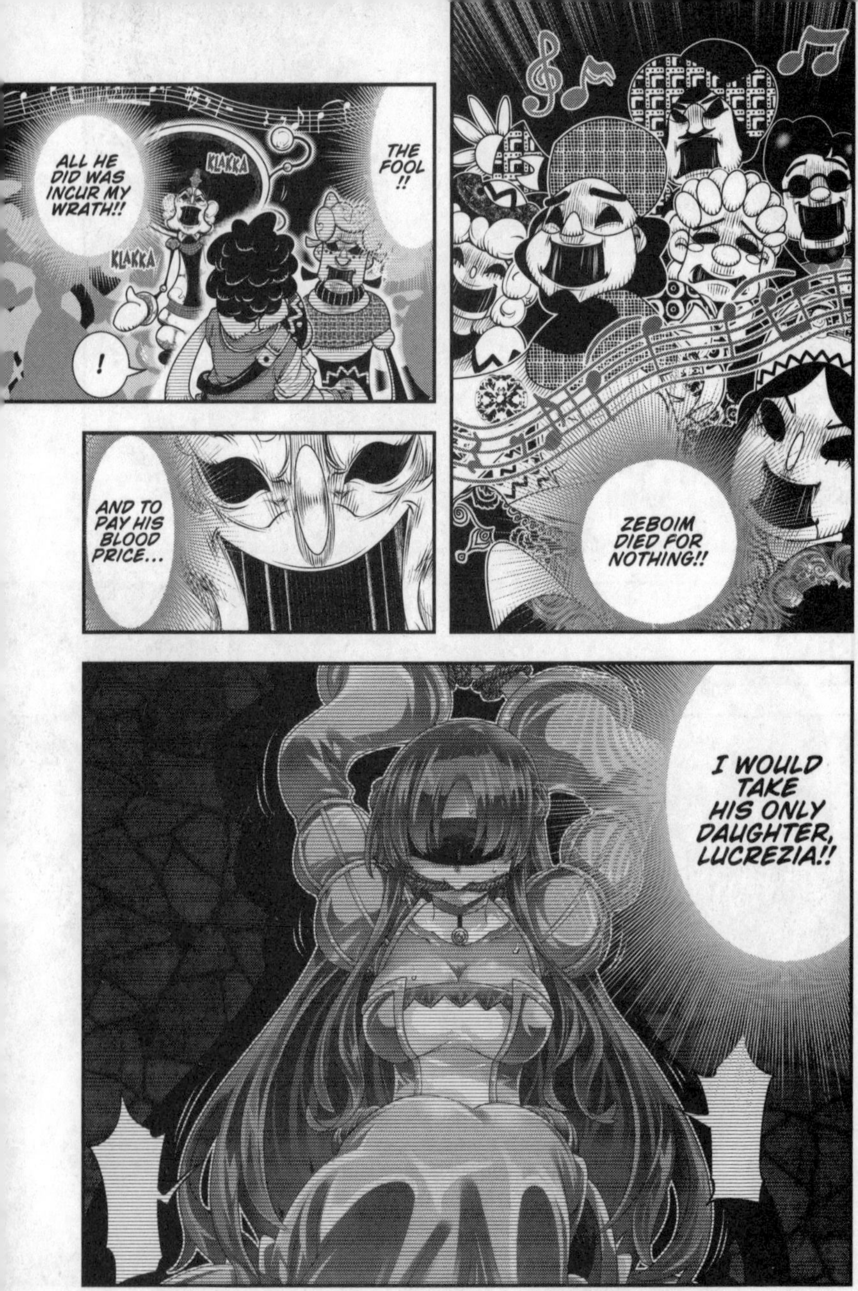
ZEBOIM DIED FOR NOTHING!!
THE FOOL!!
ALL HE DID WAS INCUR MY WRATH!!
KLAKKA
KLAKKA
!
AND TO PAY HIS BLOOD PRICE...
I WOULD TAKE HIS ONLY DAUGHTER, LUCREZIA!!

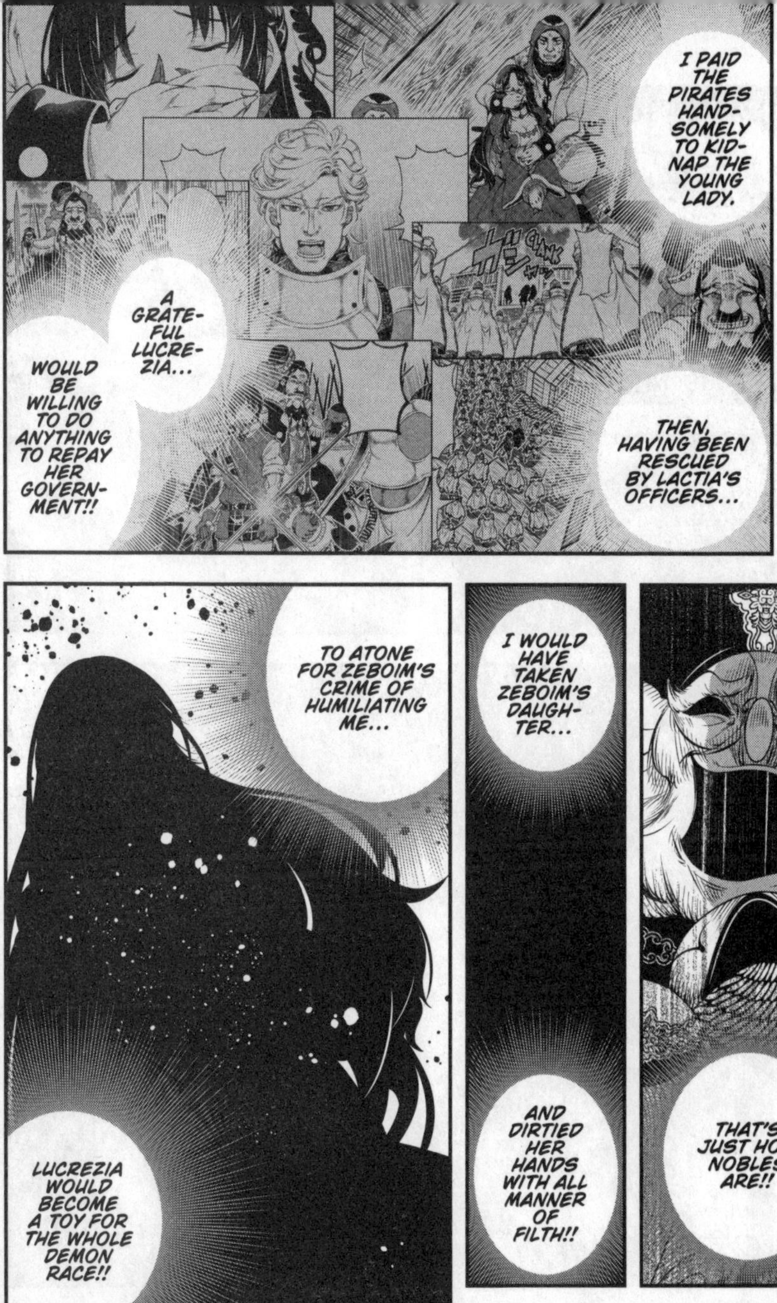
I PAID THE PIRATES HANDSOMELY TO KIDNAP THE YOUNG LADY.
CLANK
THEN, HAVING BEEN RESCUED BY LACTIA'S OFFICERS...
A GRATEFUL LUCREZIA...
WOULD BE WILLING TO DO ANYTHING TO REPAY HER GOVERNMENT!!
THAT'S JUST HOW NOBLES ARE!!
I WOULD HAVE TAKEN ZEBOIM'S DAUGHTER...
AND DIRTIED HER HANDS WITH ALL MANNER OF FILTH!!
TO ATONE FOR ZEBOIM'S CRIME OF HUMILIATING ME...
LUCREZIA WOULD BECOME A TOY FOR THE WHOLE DEMON RACE!!

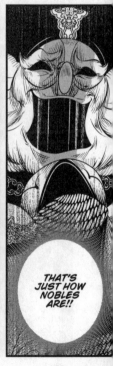

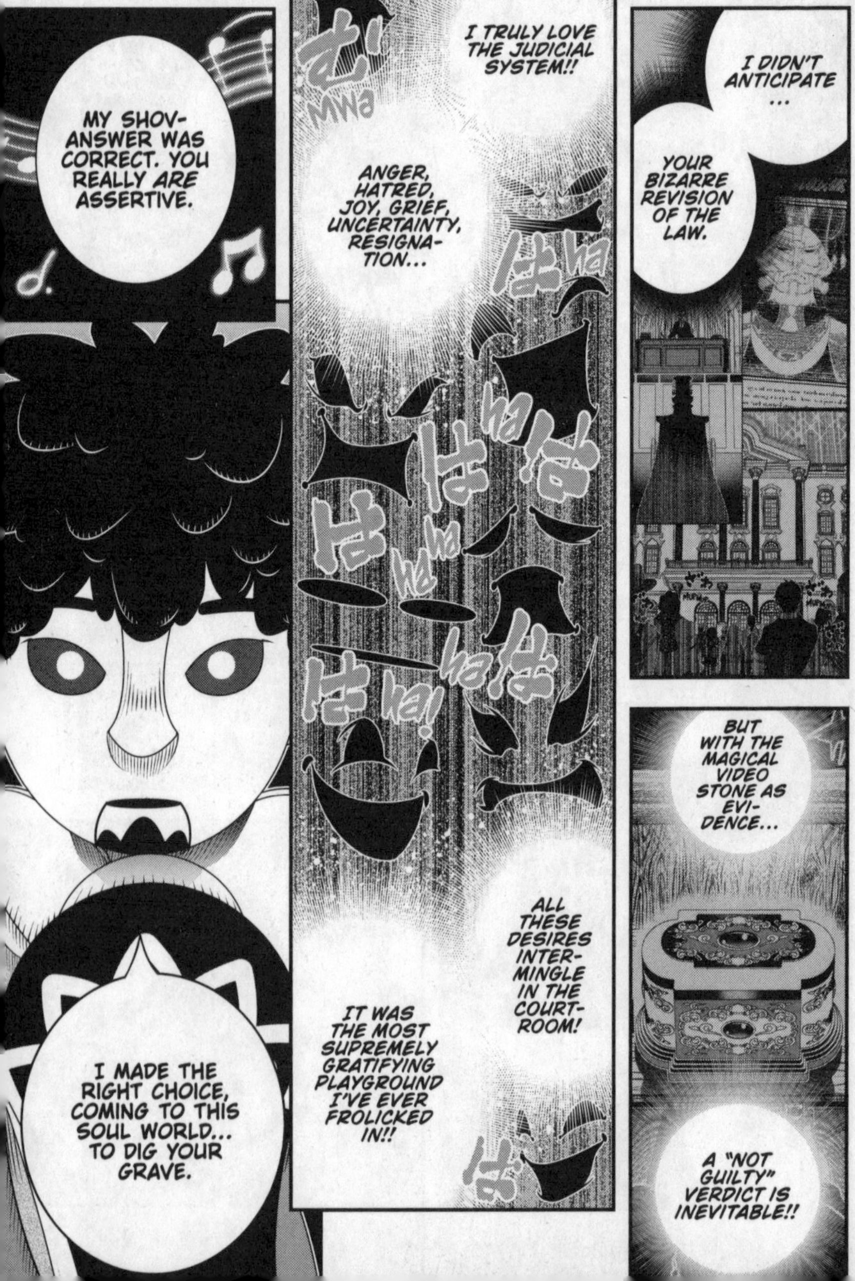
I DIDN'T ANTICIPATE ...
YOUR BIZARRE REVISION OF THE LAW.
BUT WITH THE MAGICAL VIDEO STONE AS EVIDENCE...
A "NOT GUILTY" VERDICT IS INEVITABLE!!
む MWA
I TRULY LOVE THE JUDICIAL SYSTEM!!
ANGER, HATRED, JOY, GRIEF, UNCERTAINTY, RESIGNATION...
は ha
は ha は ha は ha
は ha! は ha!
ALL THESE DESIRES INTERMINGLE IN THE COURTROOM!
IT WAS THE MOST SUPREMELY GRATIFYING PLAYGROUND I'VE EVER FROLICKED IN!!
は
MY SHOV-ANSWER WAS CORRECT. YOU REALLY ARE ASSERTIVE.
I MADE THE RIGHT CHOICE, COMING TO THIS SOUL WORLD... TO DIG YOUR GRAVE.

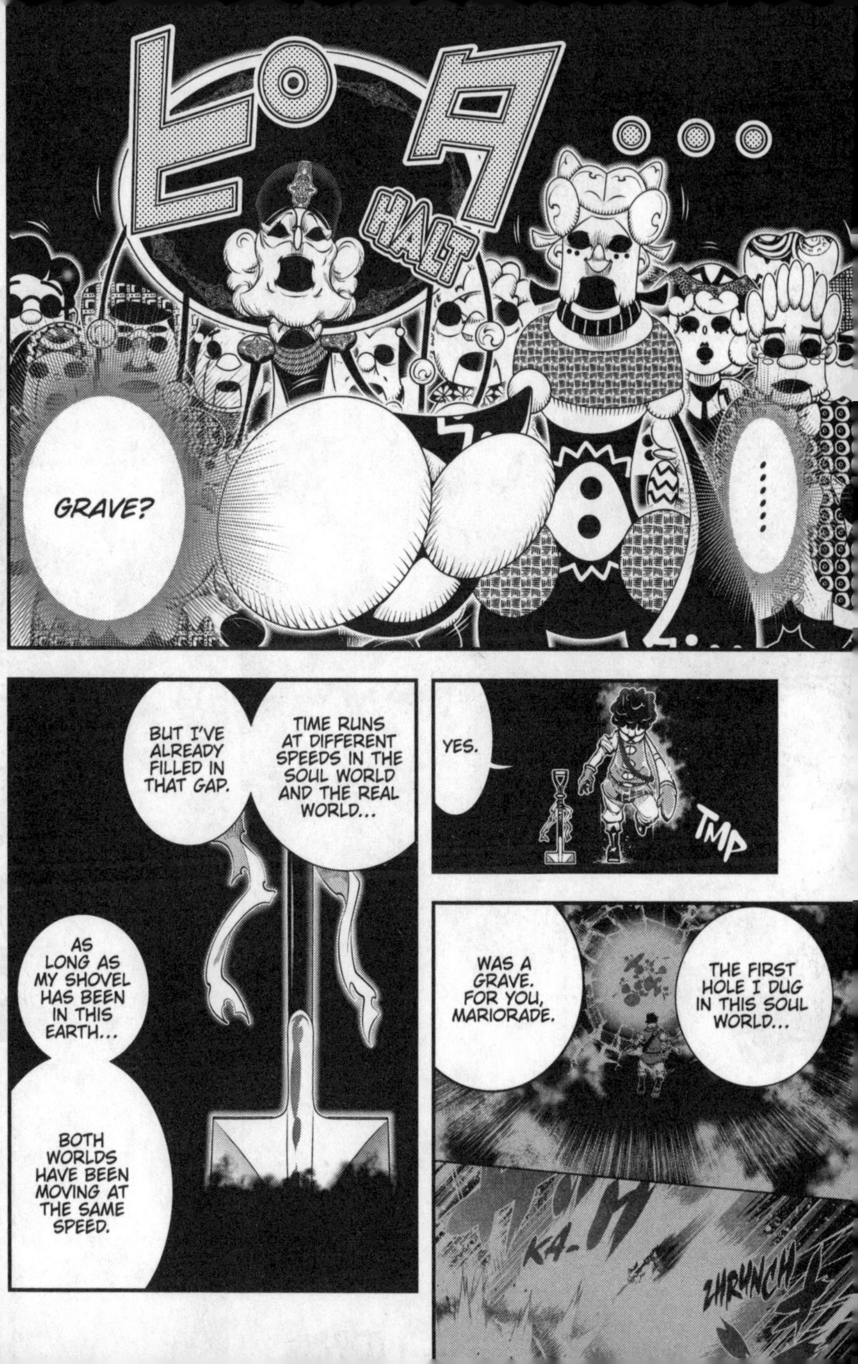
ピタ
HALT
......
GRAVE?
YES.
TMP
THE FIRST HOLE I DUG IN THIS SOUL WORLD...
WAS A GRAVE. FOR YOU, MARIORADE.
KA-
ZHRUNCH
TIME RUNS AT DIFFERENT SPEEDS IN THE SOUL WORLD AND THE REAL WORLD...
BUT I'VE ALREADY FILLED IN THAT GAP.
AS LONG AS MY SHOVEL HAS BEEN IN THIS EARTH...
BOTH WORLDS HAVE BEEN MOVING AT THE SAME SPEED.

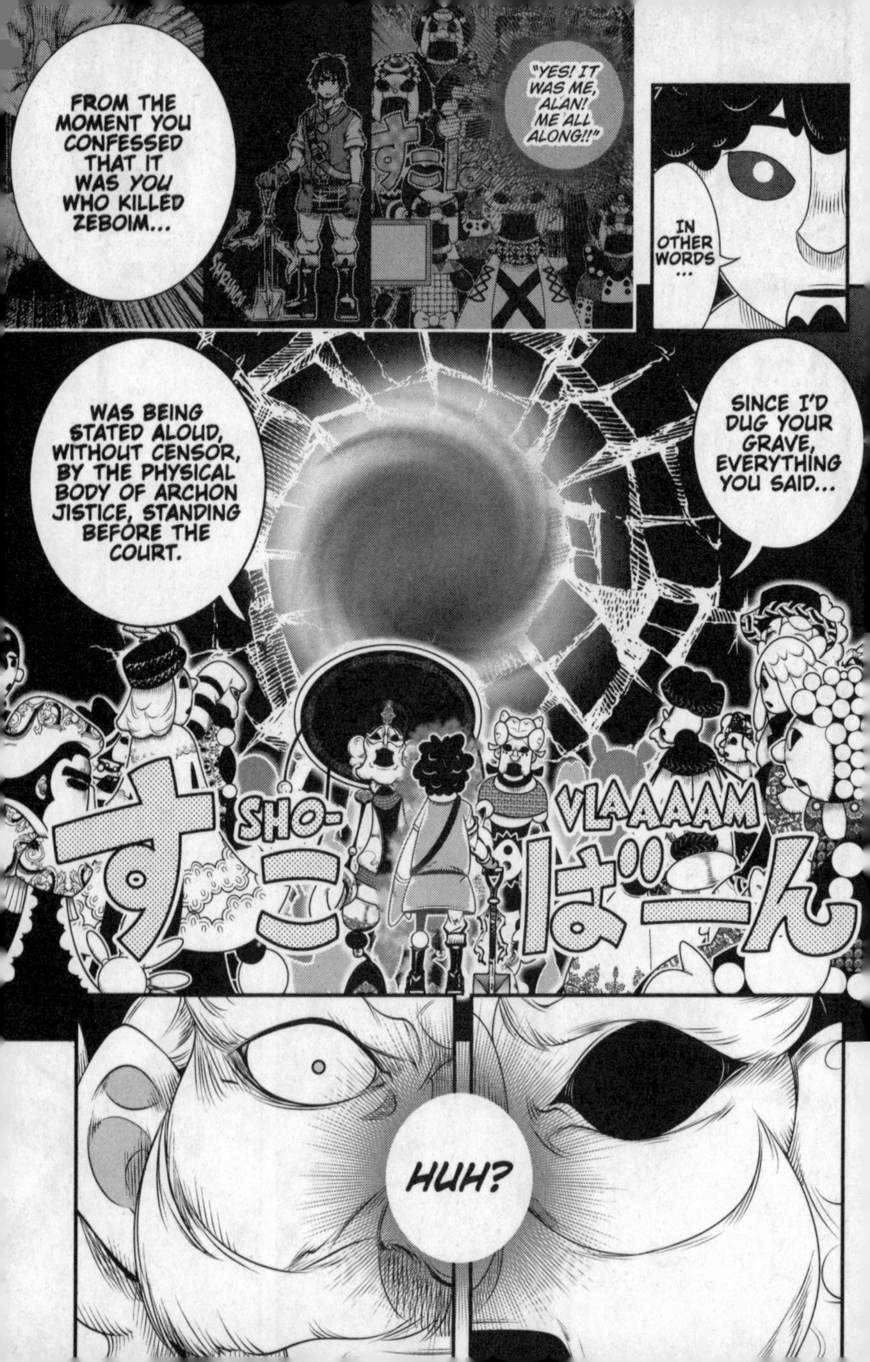
IN OTHER WORDS...
"YES! IT WAS ME, ALAN! ME ALL ALONG!!"
FROM THE MOMENT YOU CONFESSED THAT IT WAS YOU WHO KILLED ZEBOIM...
SINCE I'D DUG YOUR GRAVE, EVERYTHING YOU SAID...
WAS BEING STATED ALOUD, WITHOUT CENSOR, BY THE PHYSICAL BODY OF ARCHON JISTICE, STANDING BEFORE THE COURT.
SHO-
VLAAAAM
すごばーん
HUH?

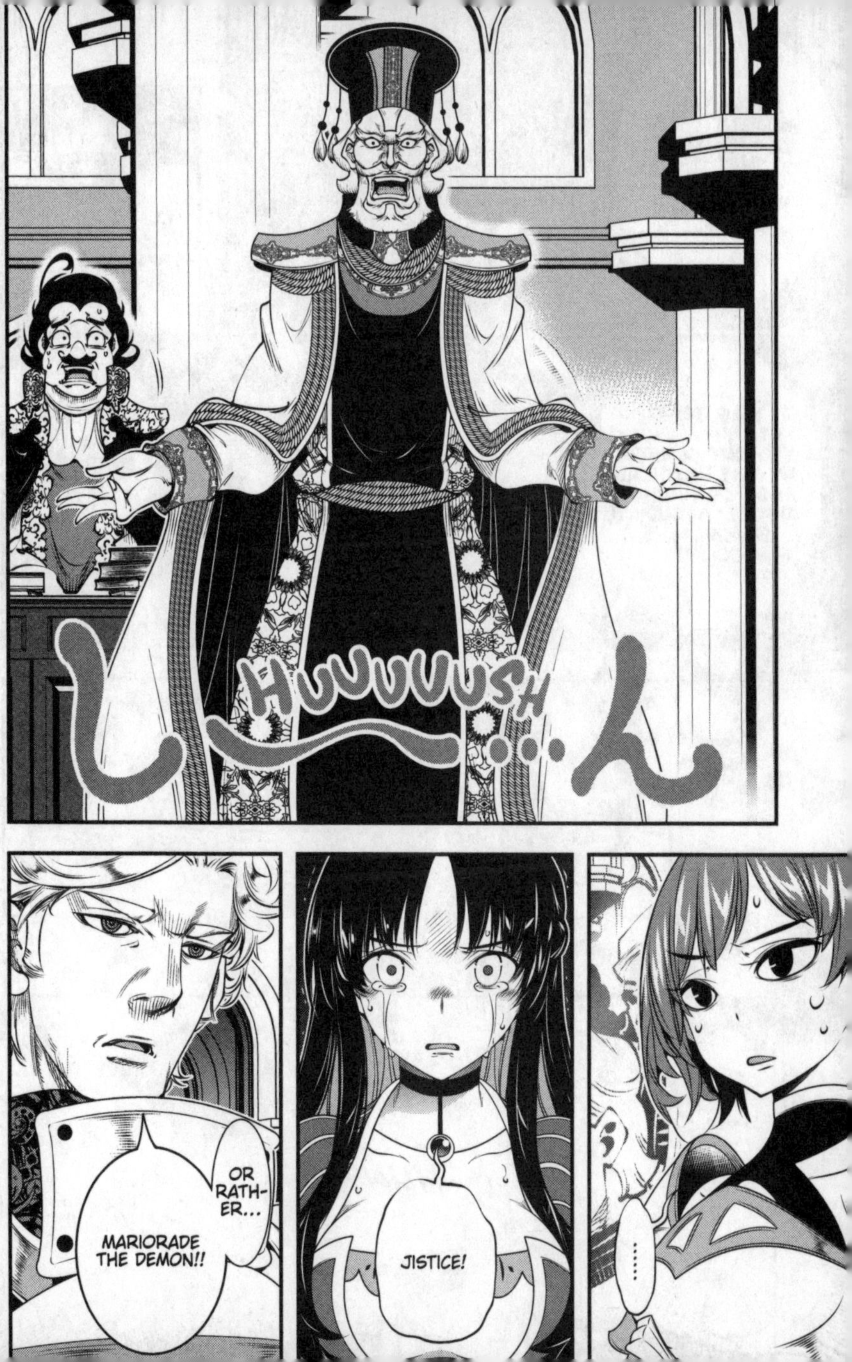
HUUUUUSH
し…ん
......
JISTICE!
OR RATH-ER... MARIORADE THE DEMON!!

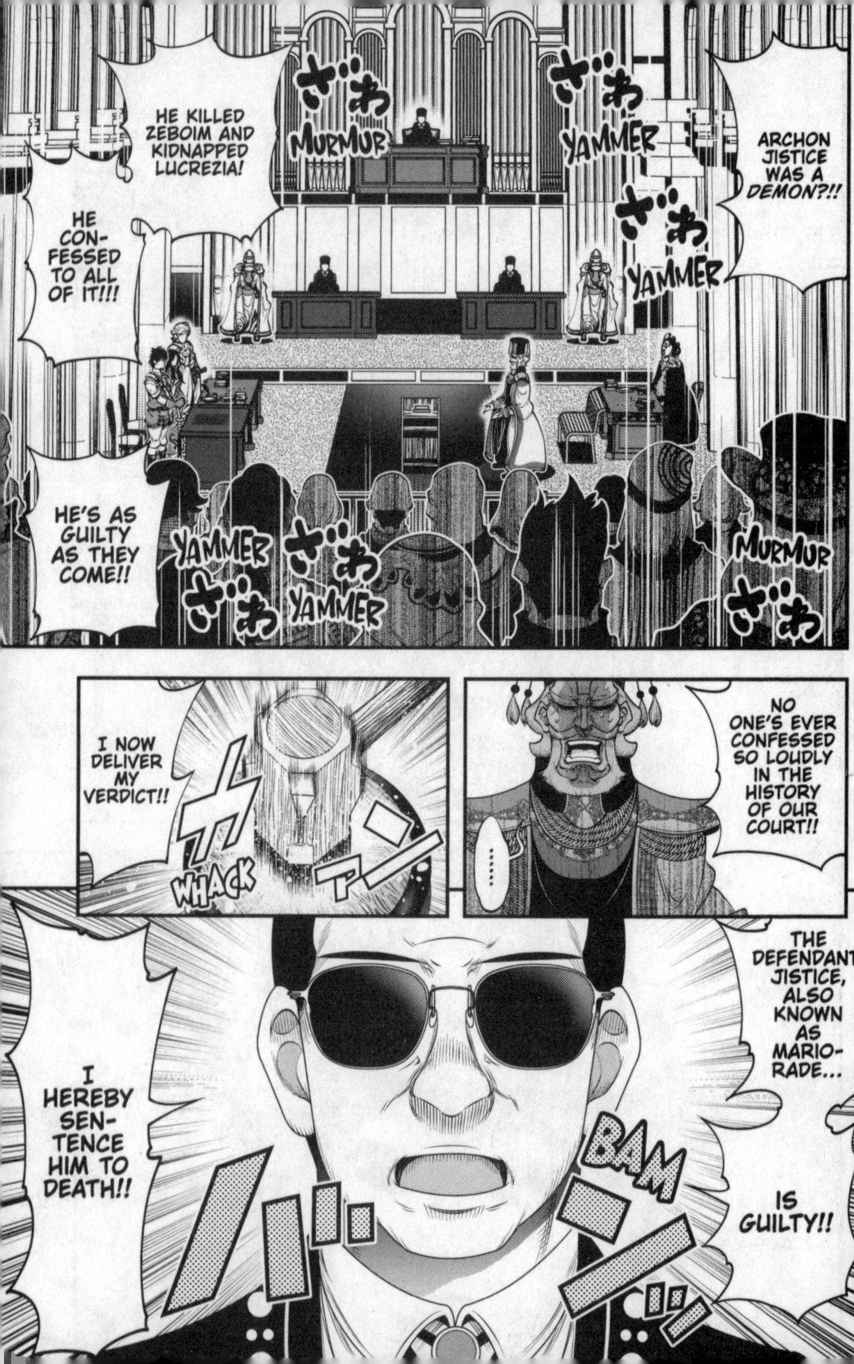
ARCHON JISTICE WAS A DEMON?!!
ざあ
YAMMER
ざあ
YAMMER
ざあ
MURMUR
HE KILLED ZEBOIM AND KIDNAPPED LUCREZIA!
HE CONFESSED TO ALL OF IT!!!
MURMUR
ざあ
ざあ
YAMMER
YAMMER
ざあ
HE'S AS GUILTY AS THEY COME!!
NO ONE'S EVER CONFESSED SO LOUDLY IN THE HISTORY OF OUR COURT!!
......
I NOW DELIVER MY VERDICT!!
WHACK
THE DEFENDANT, JISTICE, ALSO KNOWN AS MARIORADE...
IS GUILTY!!
BAM
I HEREBY SENTENCE HIM TO DEATH!!

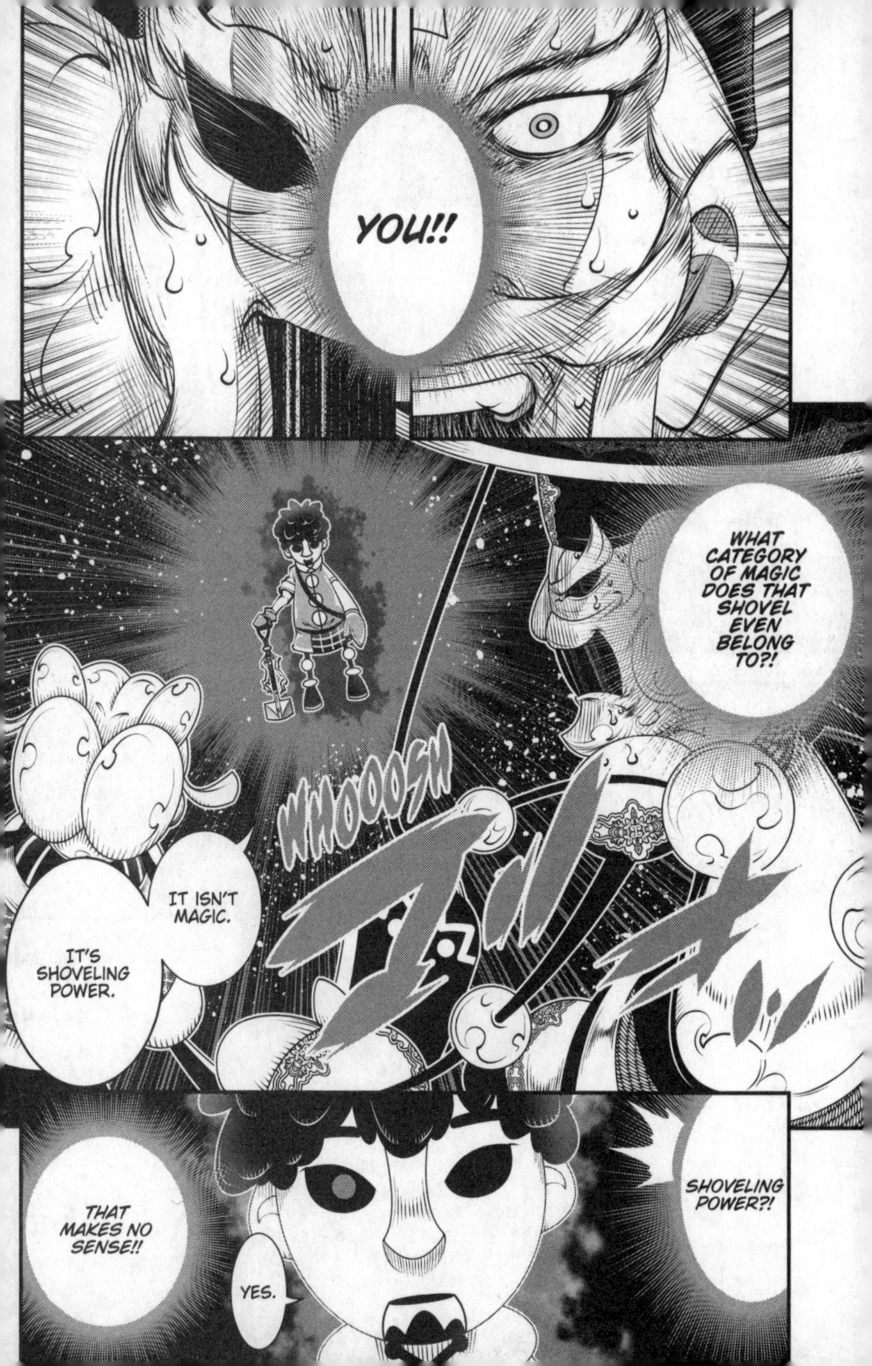
YOU!!
WHAT CATEGORY OF MAGIC DOES THAT SHOVEL EVEN BELONG TO?!
WHOOOSH
IT ISN'T MAGIC.
IT'S SHOVELING POWER.
SHOVELING POWER?!
YES.
THAT MAKES NO SENSE!!

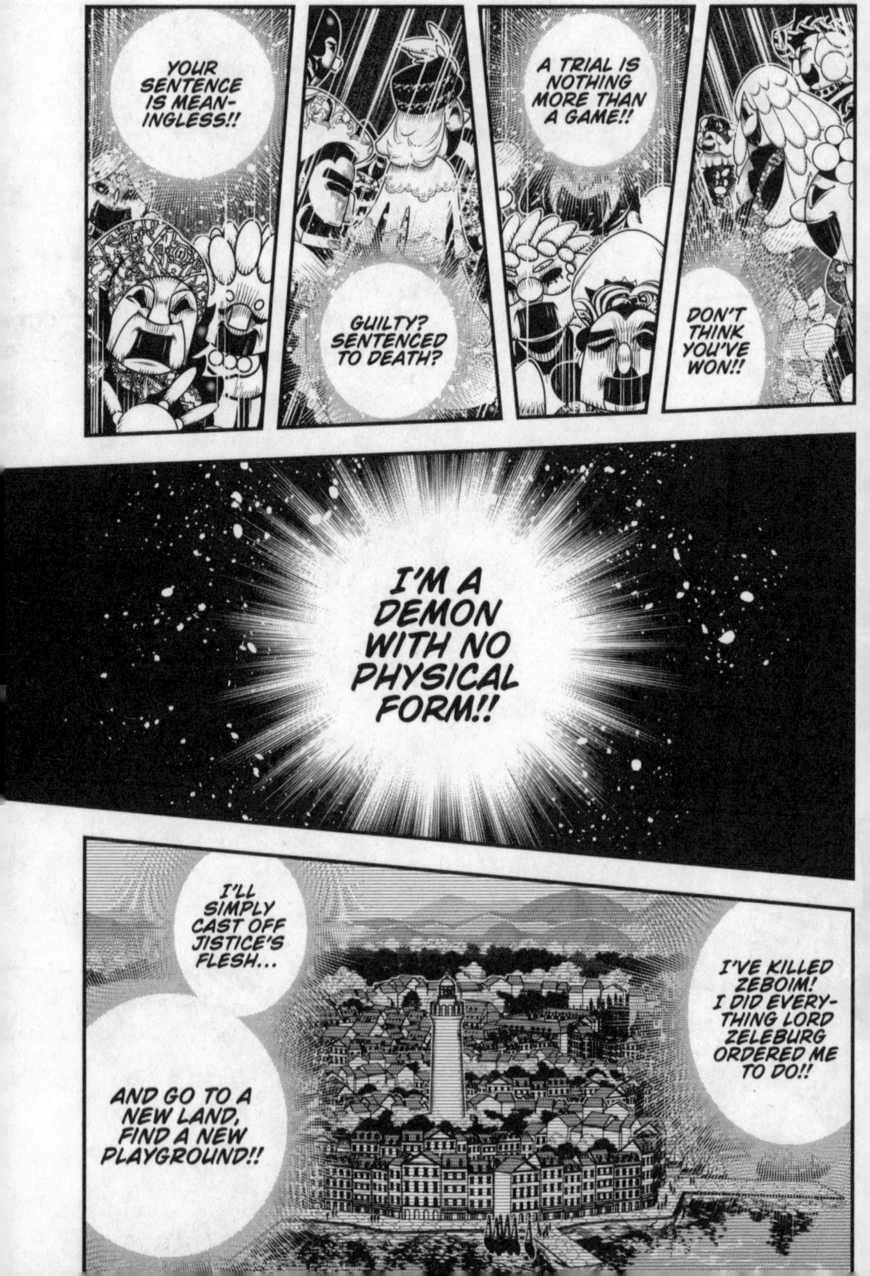
DON'T THINK YOU'VE WON!!
A TRIAL IS NOTHING MORE THAN A GAME!!
GUILTY? SENTENCED TO DEATH?
YOUR SENTENCE IS MEANINGLESS!!
I'M A DEMON WITH NO PHYSICAL FORM!!
I'VE KILLED ZEBOIM! I DID EVERYTHING LORD ZELEBURG ORDERED ME TO DO!!
I'LL SIMPLY CAST OFF JISTICE'S FLESH...
AND GO TO A NEW LAND, FIND A NEW PLAYGROUND!!

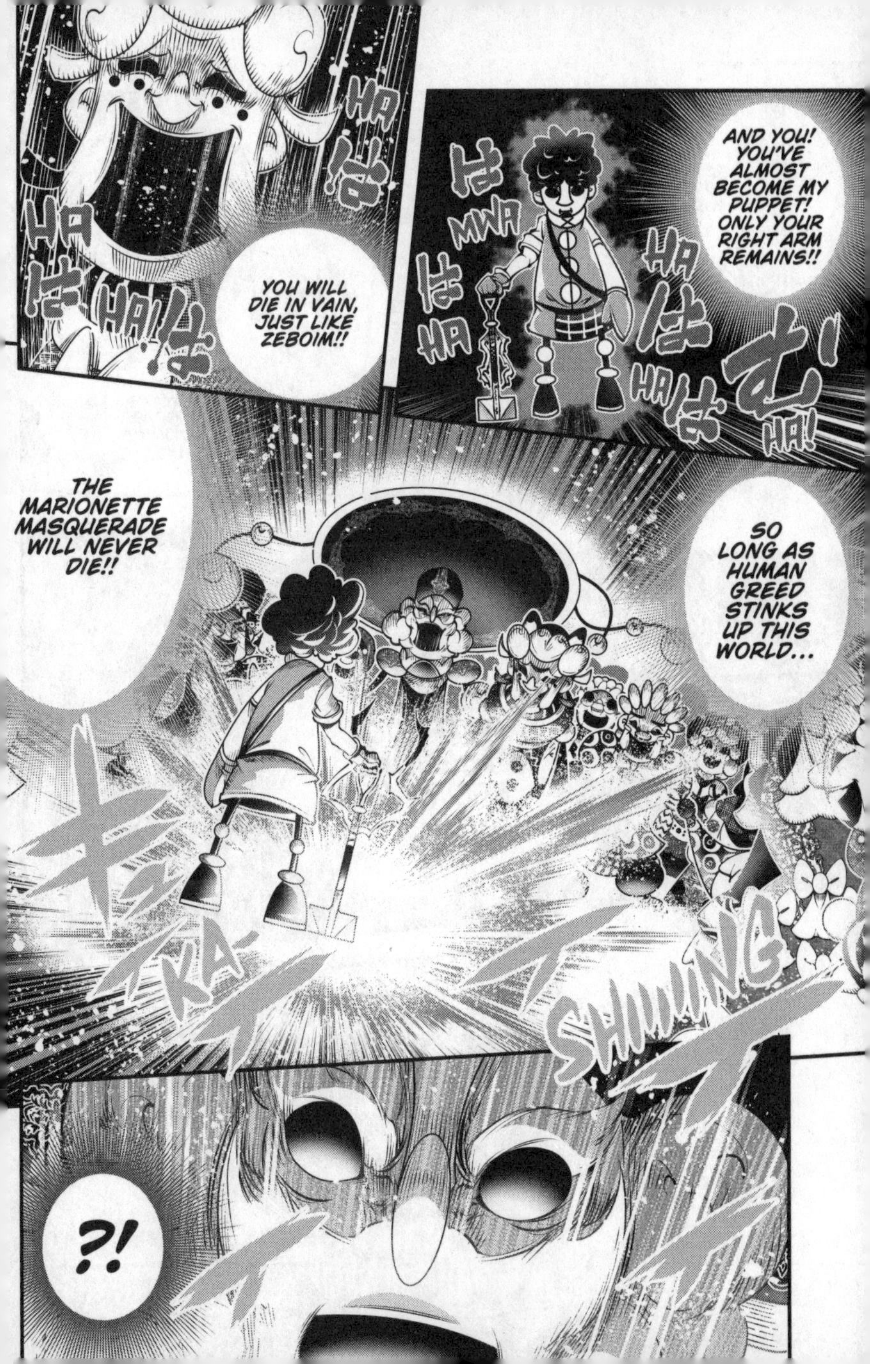
AND YOU! YOU'VE ALMOST BECOME MY PUPPET! ONLY YOUR RIGHT ARM REMAINS!!
MWA
HA
HA
HA
HA!
HA
HA!
HA
YOU WILL DIE IN VAIN, JUST LIKE ZEBOIM!!
HA!
SO LONG AS HUMAN GREED STINKS UP THIS WORLD...
THE MARIONETTE MASQUERADE WILL NEVER DIE!!
SHIIIING
KA-
?!

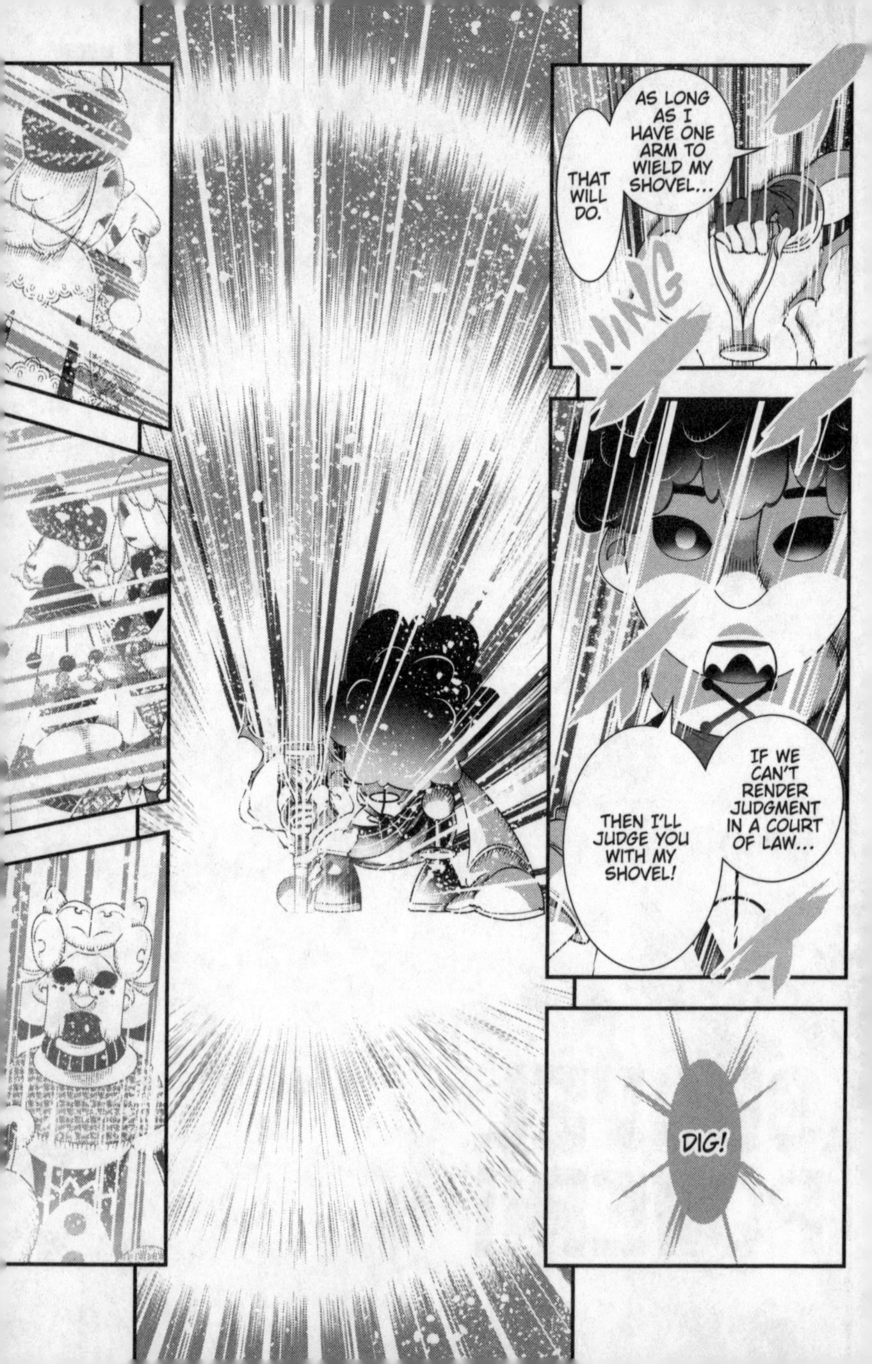
AS LONG AS I HAVE ONE ARM TO WIELD MY SHOVEL...
THAT WILL DO.
IF WE CAN'T RENDER JUDGMENT IN A COURT OF LAW...
THEN I'LL JUDGE YOU WITH MY SHOVEL!
DIG!

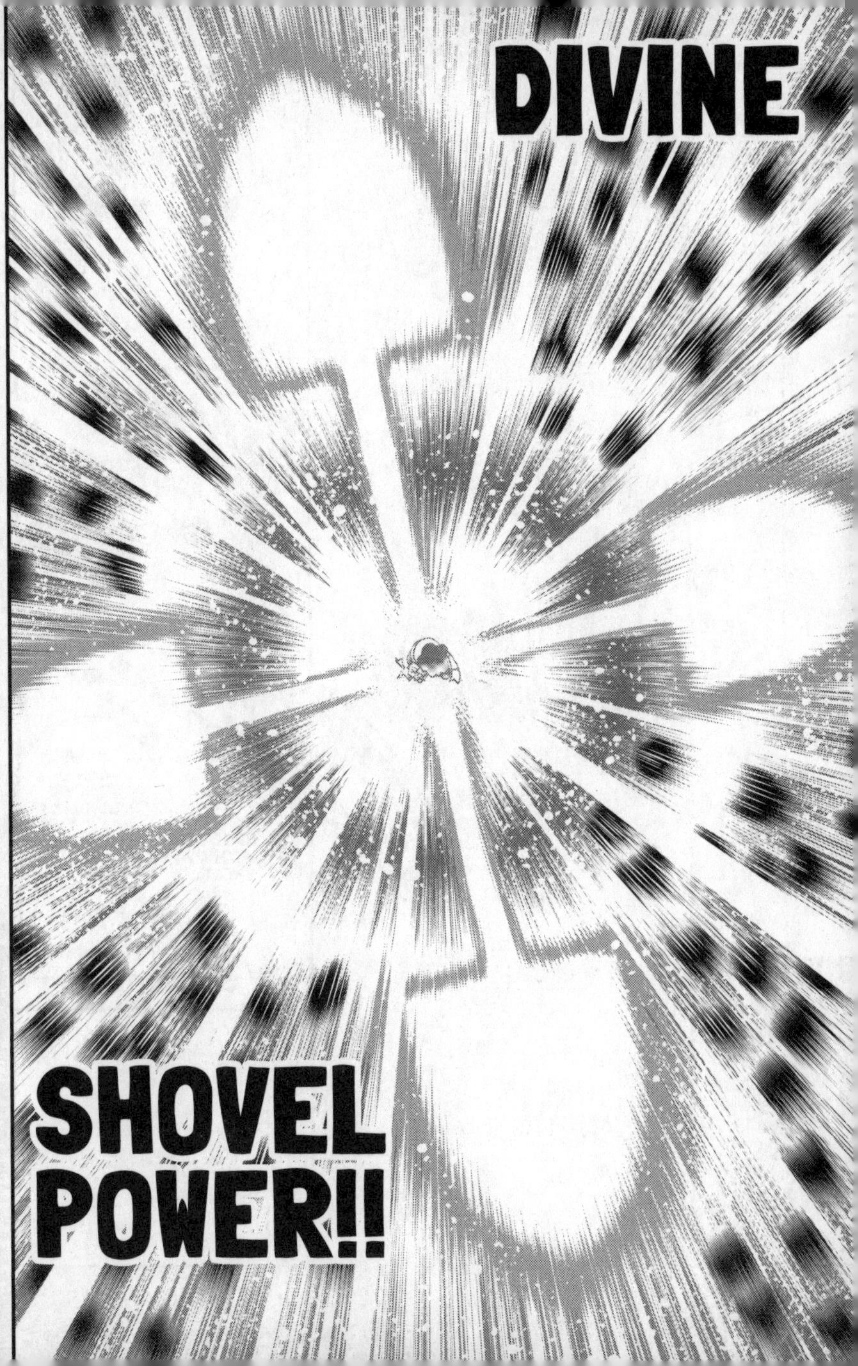
DIVINE
SHOVEL POWER!!

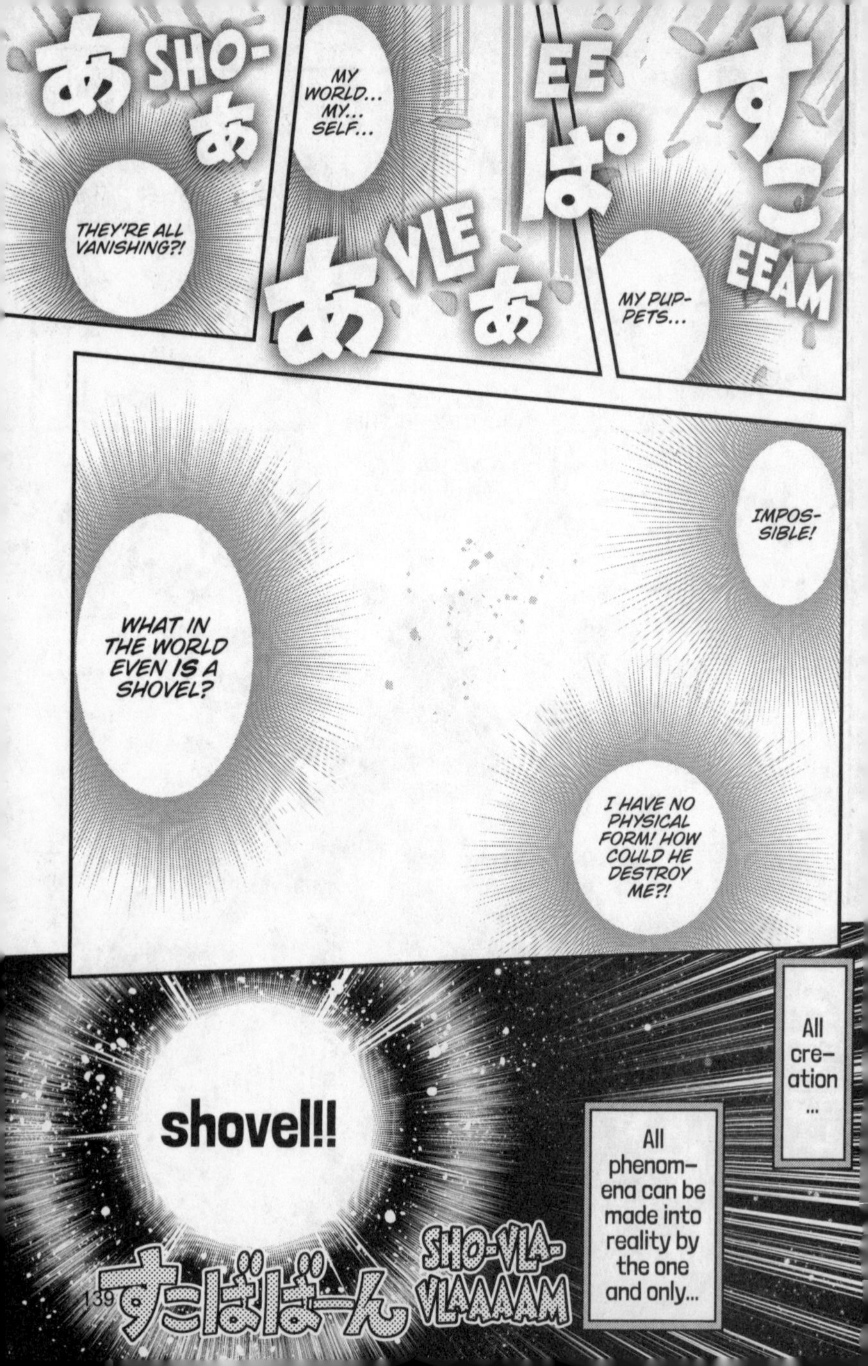

すこ
EEAM
ぱ
EE
MY PUP-PETS...
MY WORLD... MY... SELF...
あ VLE あ
あ SHO- あ
THEY'RE ALL VANISHING?!
IMPOS-SIBLE!
I HAVE NO PHYSICAL FORM! HOW COULD HE DESTROY ME?!
WHAT IN THE WORLD EVEN IS A SHOVEL?
All cre-ation ...
All phenom-ena can be made into reality by the one and only...
shovel!!
SHO-VLA-VLAAAAAM
すこばばーん

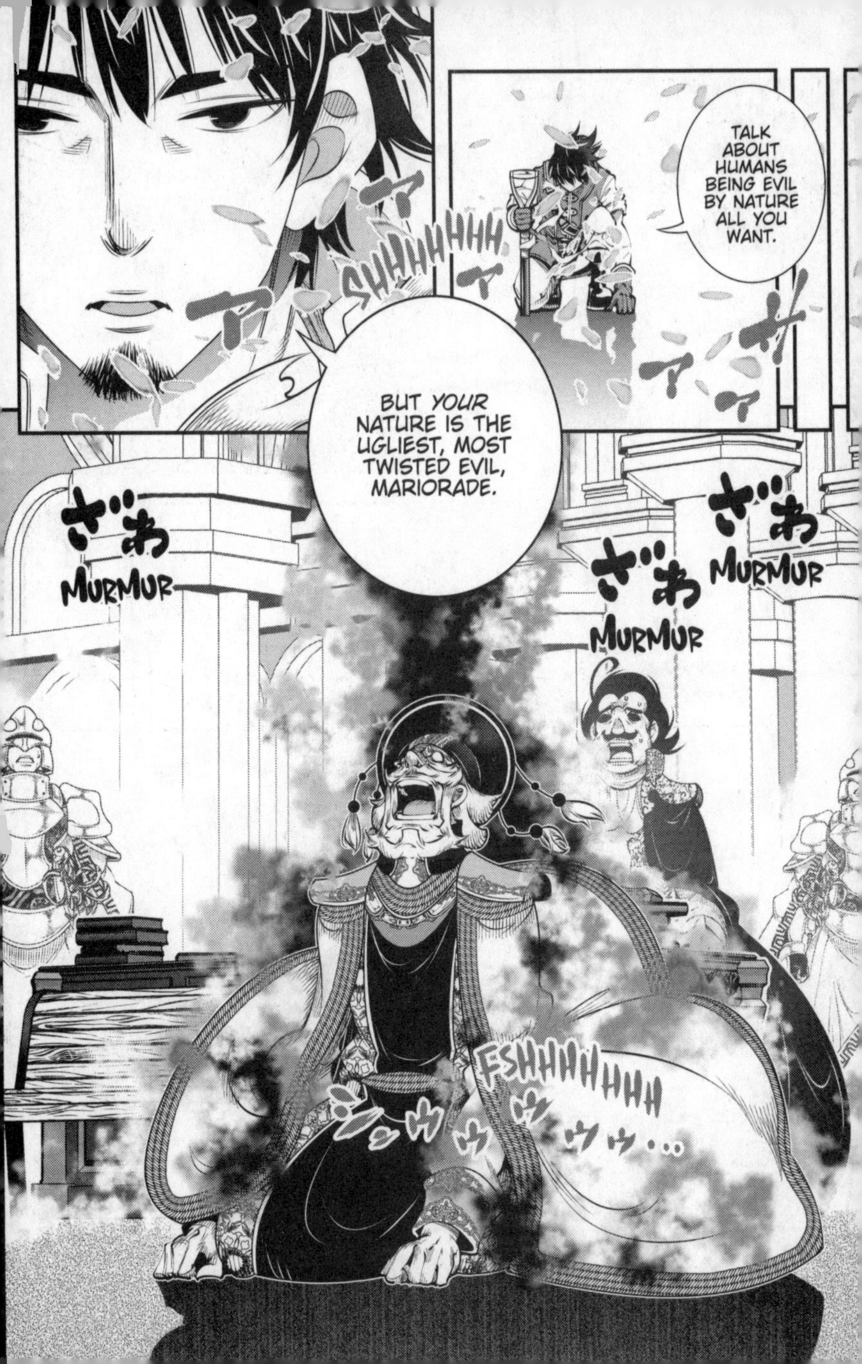
TALK ABOUT HUMANS BEING EVIL BY NATURE ALL YOU WANT.
SHHHHHHH
BUT *YOUR* NATURE IS THE UGLIEST, MOST TWISTED EVIL, MARIORADE.
ざあ
MURMUR
ざあ
MURMUR
ざあ
MURMUR
FSHHHHHHHH

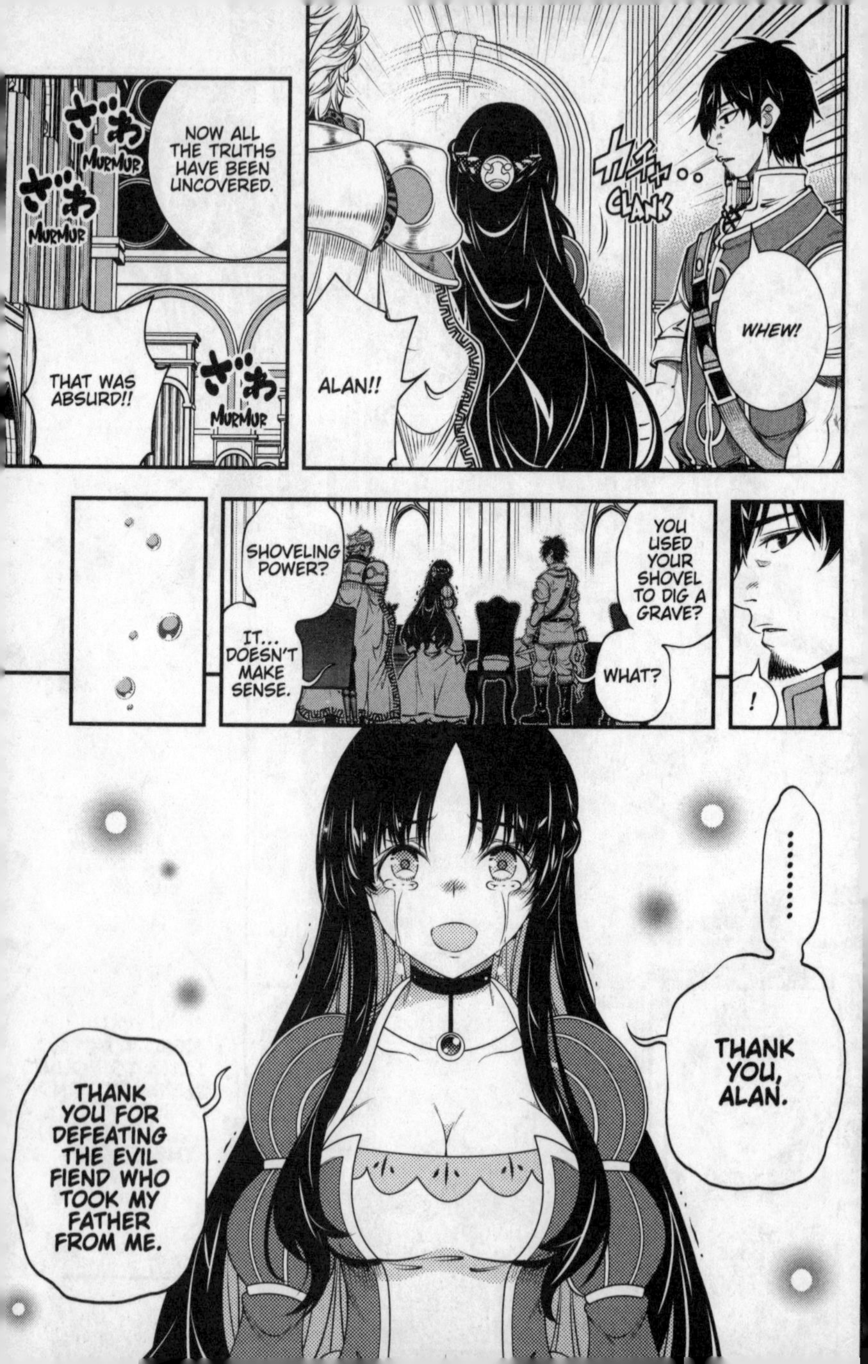

カチャ
CLANK
WHEW!
ALAN!!
NOW ALL THE TRUTHS HAVE BEEN UNCOVERED.
ざわ
MURMUR
ざわ
MURMUR
THAT WAS ABSURD!!
ざわ
MURMUR
!
YOU USED YOUR SHOVEL TO DIG A GRAVE?
SHOVELING POWER?
WHAT?
IT... DOESN'T MAKE SENSE.
......
THANK YOU, ALAN.
THANK YOU FOR DEFEATING THE EVIL FIEND WHO TOOK MY FATHER FROM ME.

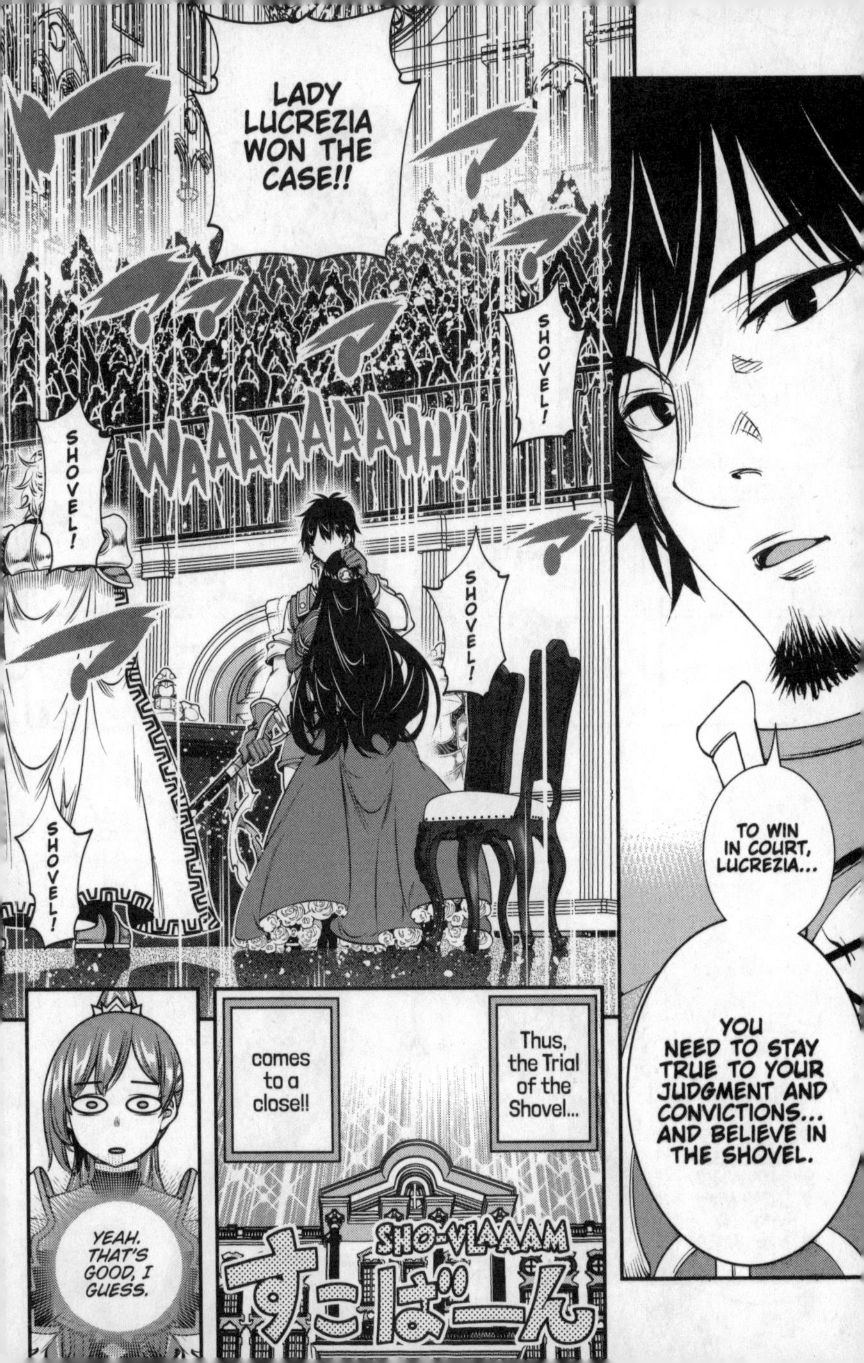
TO WIN IN COURT, LUCREZIA...
YOU NEED TO STAY TRUE TO YOUR JUDGMENT AND CONVICTIONS... AND BELIEVE IN THE SHOVEL.
LADY LUCREZIA WON THE CASE!!
SHOVEL!
WAAAAAAAHH!
SHOVEL!
SHOVEL!
SHOVEL!
Thus, the Trial of the Shovel...
comes to a close!!
SHO-VLAAAM
すこぱーん
YEAH. THAT'S GOOD, I GUESS.

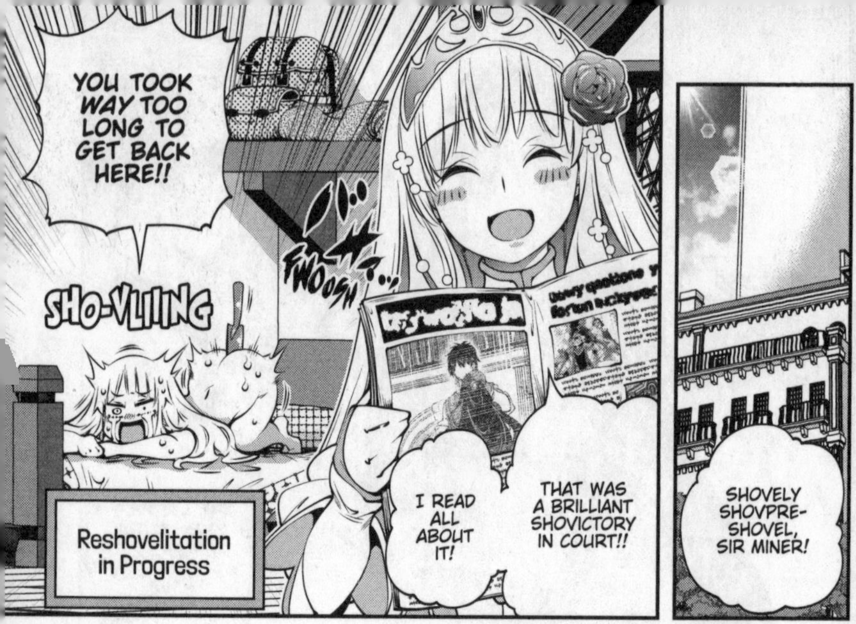
SHOVELY SHOVPRE-SHOVEL, SIR MINER!
THAT WAS A BRILLIANT SHOVICTORY IN COURT!!
I READ ALL ABOUT IT!
FWOOSH
YOU TOOK WAY TOO LONG TO GET BACK HERE!!
SHO-VLIIING
Reshovelitation in Progress

Chapter 21: Onward! Our Grand Shovoyage!

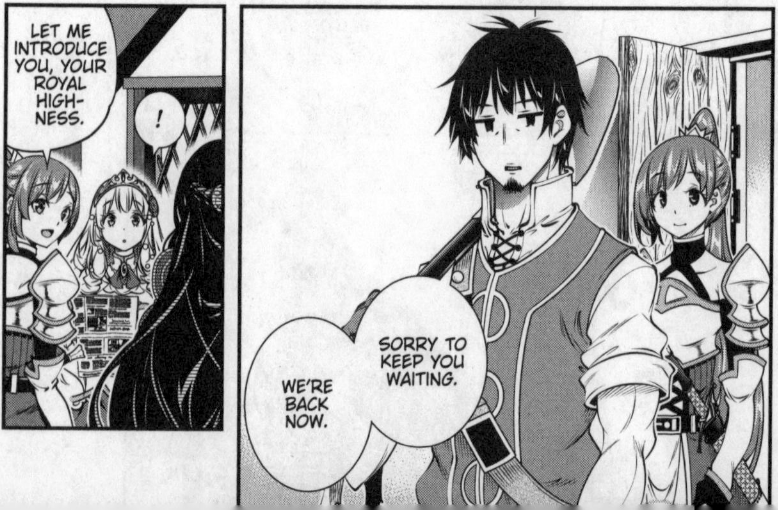
SORRY TO KEEP YOU WAITING.
WE'RE BACK NOW.
LET ME INTRODUCE YOU, YOUR ROYAL HIGHNESS.
!

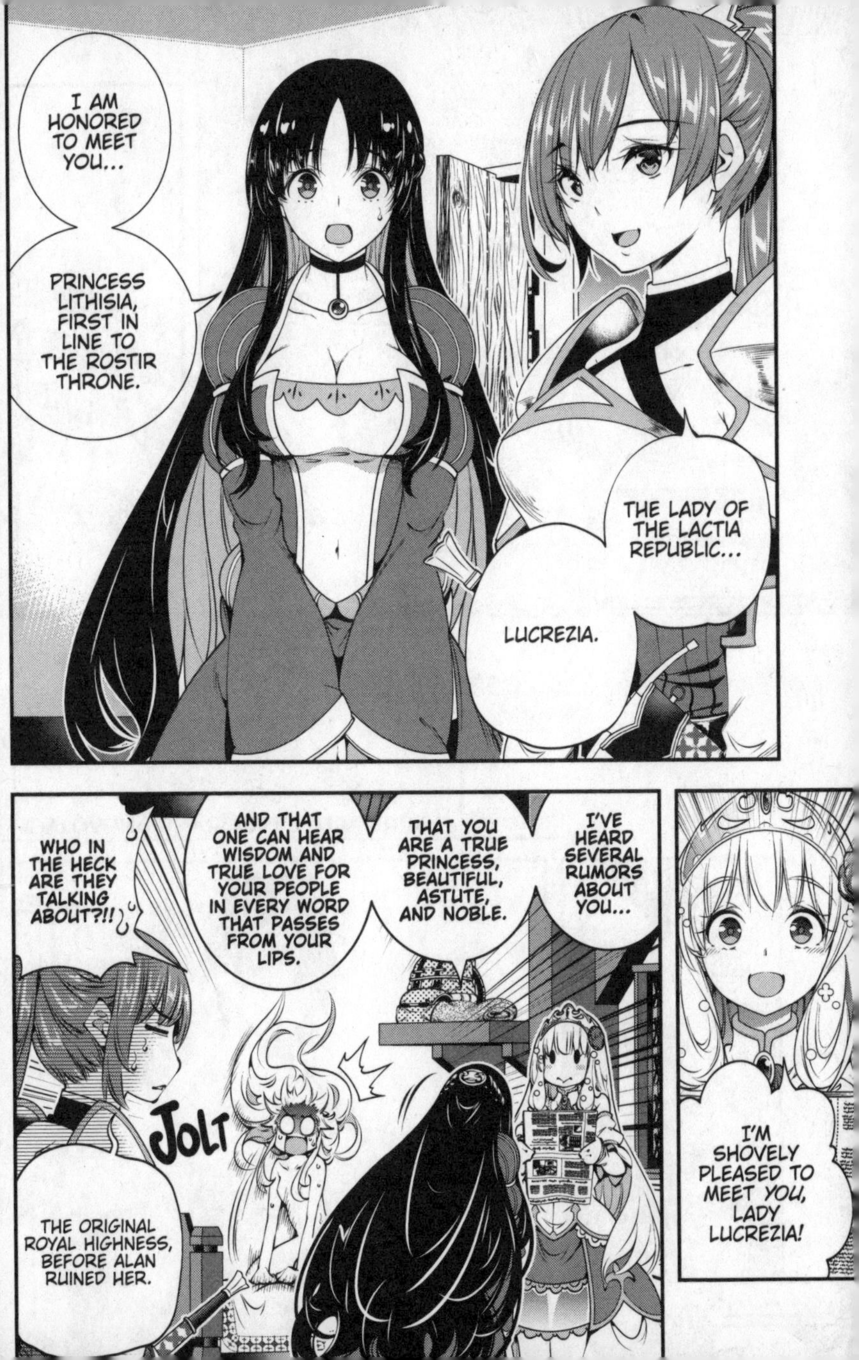
THE LADY OF THE LACTIA REPUBLIC...
LUCREZIA.
I AM HONORED TO MEET YOU...
PRINCESS LITHISIA, FIRST IN LINE TO THE ROSTIR THRONE.
I'M SHOVELY PLEASED TO MEET YOU, LADY LUCREZIA!
I'VE HEARD SEVERAL RUMORS ABOUT YOU...
THAT YOU ARE A TRUE PRINCESS, BEAUTIFUL, ASTUTE, AND NOBLE.
AND THAT ONE CAN HEAR WISDOM AND TRUE LOVE FOR YOUR PEOPLE IN EVERY WORD THAT PASSES FROM YOUR LIPS.
WHO IN THE HECK ARE THEY TALKING ABOUT?!!
JOLT
THE ORIGINAL ROYAL HIGHNESS, BEFORE ALAN RUINED HER.

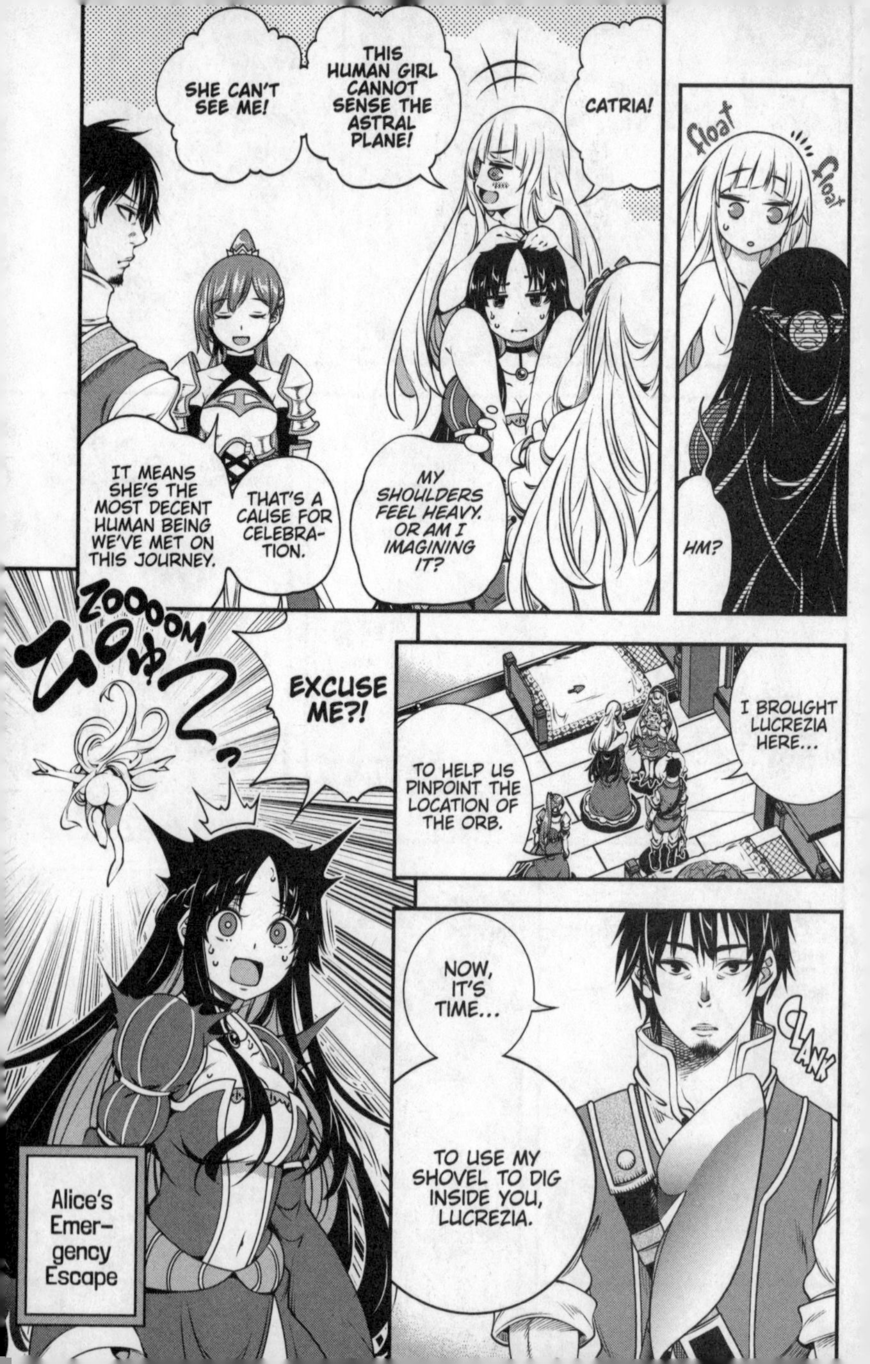
float
float
HM?
CATRIA!
THIS HUMAN GIRL CANNOT SENSE THE ASTRAL PLANE!
SHE CAN'T SEE ME!
MY SHOULDERS FEEL HEAVY. OR AM I IMAGINING IT?
THAT'S A CAUSE FOR CELEBRATION.
IT MEANS SHE'S THE MOST DECENT HUMAN BEING WE'VE MET ON THIS JOURNEY.
I BROUGHT LUCREZIA HERE...
TO HELP US PINPOINT THE LOCATION OF THE ORB.
NOW, IT'S TIME...
CLANK
TO USE MY SHOVEL TO DIG INSIDE YOU, LUCREZIA.
EXCUSE ME?!
ZOOOOM
ひゅっ
Alice's Emergency Escape

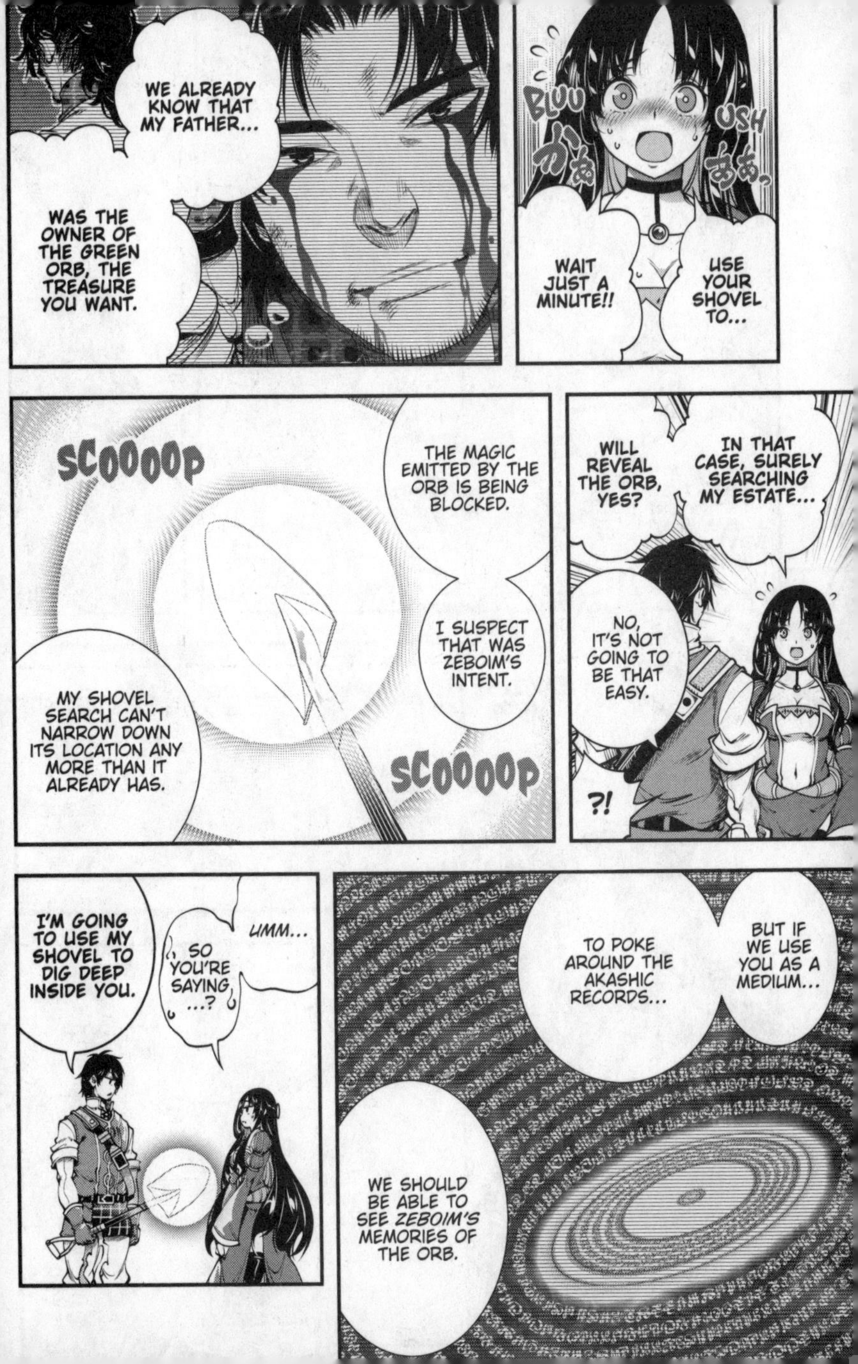
BLUU
かぁ
USH
ああっ
USE YOUR SHOVEL TO...
WAIT JUST A MINUTE!!
WE ALREADY KNOW THAT MY FATHER...
WAS THE OWNER OF THE GREEN ORB, THE TREASURE YOU WANT.
IN THAT CASE, SURELY SEARCHING MY ESTATE...
WILL REVEAL THE ORB, YES?
NO, IT'S NOT GOING TO BE THAT EASY.
?!
THE MAGIC EMITTED BY THE ORB IS BEING BLOCKED.
SCOOOOP
I SUSPECT THAT WAS ZEBOIM'S INTENT.
MY SHOVEL SEARCH CAN'T NARROW DOWN ITS LOCATION ANY MORE THAN IT ALREADY HAS.
SCOOOOP
BUT IF WE USE YOU AS A MEDIUM...
TO POKE AROUND THE AKASHIC RECORDS...
WE SHOULD BE ABLE TO SEE *ZEBOIM'S* MEMORIES OF THE ORB.
UMM...
SO YOU'RE SAYING ...?
I'M GOING TO USE MY SHOVEL TO DIG DEEP INSIDE YOU.

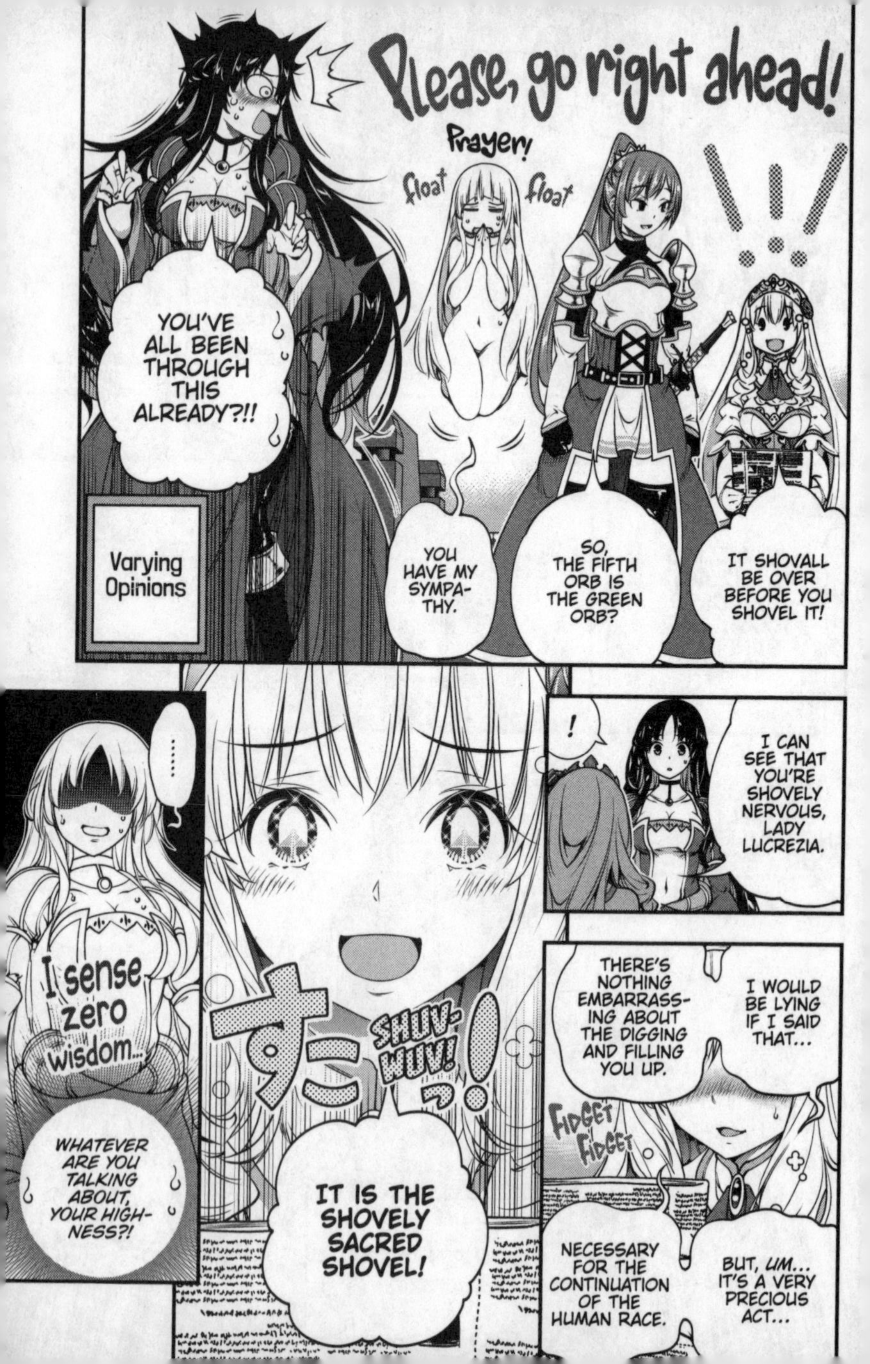
Please, go right ahead!
Prayer!
float float
IT SHOVALL BE OVER BEFORE YOU SHOVEL IT!
SO, THE FIFTH ORB IS THE GREEN ORB?
YOU HAVE MY SYMPA-THY.
YOU'VE ALL BEEN THROUGH THIS ALREADY?!!
Varying Opinions
I CAN SEE THAT YOU'RE SHOVELY NERVOUS, LADY LUCREZIA.
!
I WOULD BE LYING IF I SAID THAT...
THERE'S NOTHING EMBARRASS-ING ABOUT THE DIGGING AND FILLING YOU UP.
FIDGET FIDGET
BUT, UM... IT'S A VERY PRECIOUS ACT...
NECESSARY FOR THE CONTINUATION OF THE HUMAN RACE.
SHUV-WUV!
IT IS THE SHOVELY SACRED SHOVEL!
......
I sense zero wisdom...
WHATEVER ARE YOU TALKING ABOUT, YOUR HIGH-NESS?!

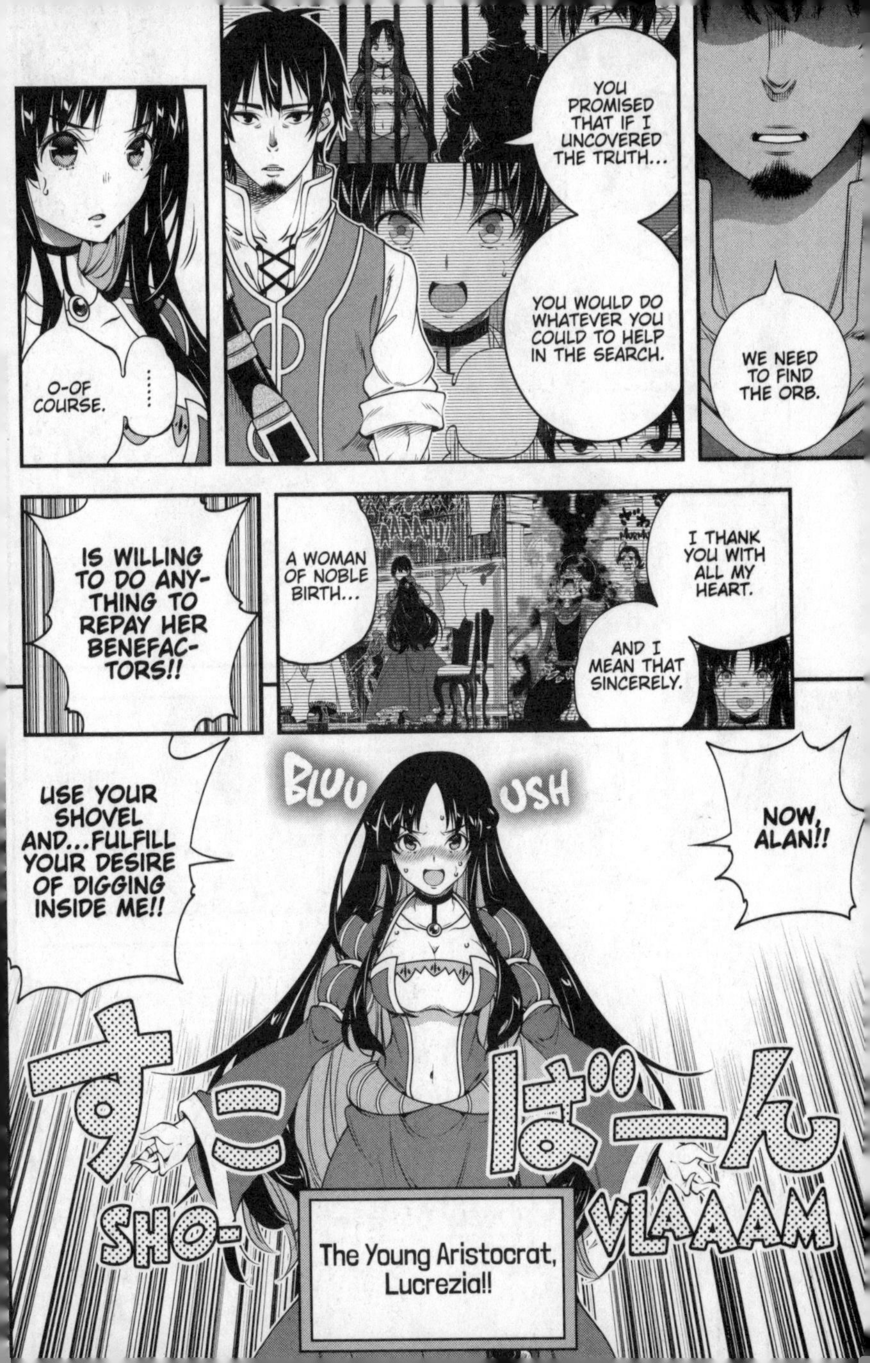
WE NEED TO FIND THE ORB.
YOU PROMISED THAT IF I UNCOVERED THE TRUTH...
YOU WOULD DO WHATEVER YOU COULD TO HELP IN THE SEARCH.
......
O-OF COURSE.
I THANK YOU WITH ALL MY HEART.
AND I MEAN THAT SINCERELY.
A WOMAN OF NOBLE BIRTH...
IS WILLING TO DO ANY-THING TO REPAY HER BENEFAC-TORS!!
NOW, ALAN!!
BLUU USH
USE YOUR SHOVEL AND...FULFILL YOUR DESIRE OF DIGGING INSIDE ME!!
すーばーん
SHO- VLAAAM
The Young Aristocrat, Lucrezia!!

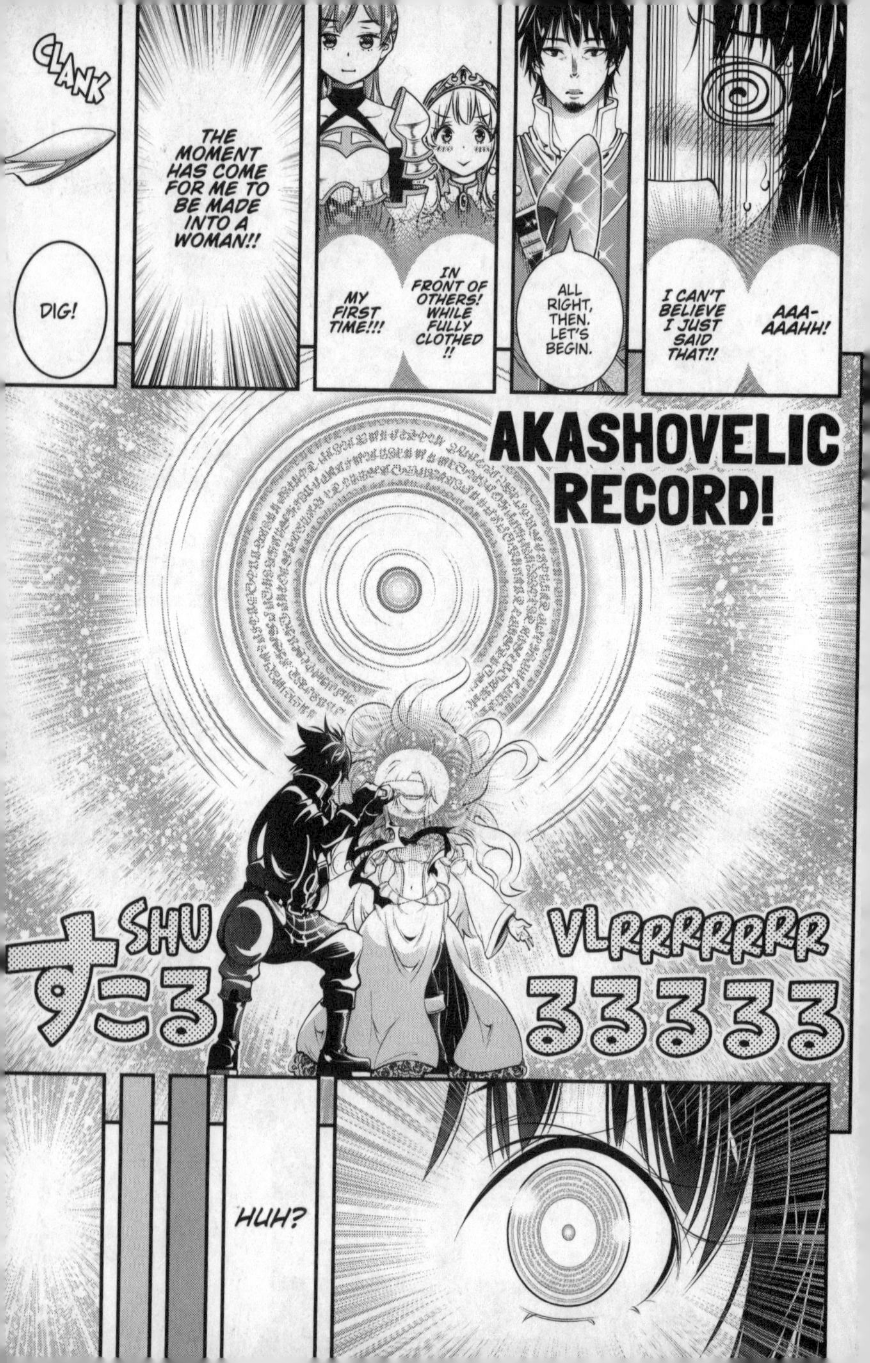
AAA-AAAHH!
I CAN'T BELIEVE I JUST SAID THAT!!
ALL RIGHT, THEN. LET'S BEGIN.
IN FRONT OF OTHERS! WHILE FULLY CLOTHED!!
MY FIRST TIME!!!
THE MOMENT HAS COME FOR ME TO BE MADE INTO A WOMAN!!
CLANK
DIG!
AKASHOVELIC RECORD!
VLRRRRRRR
SHU
HUH?

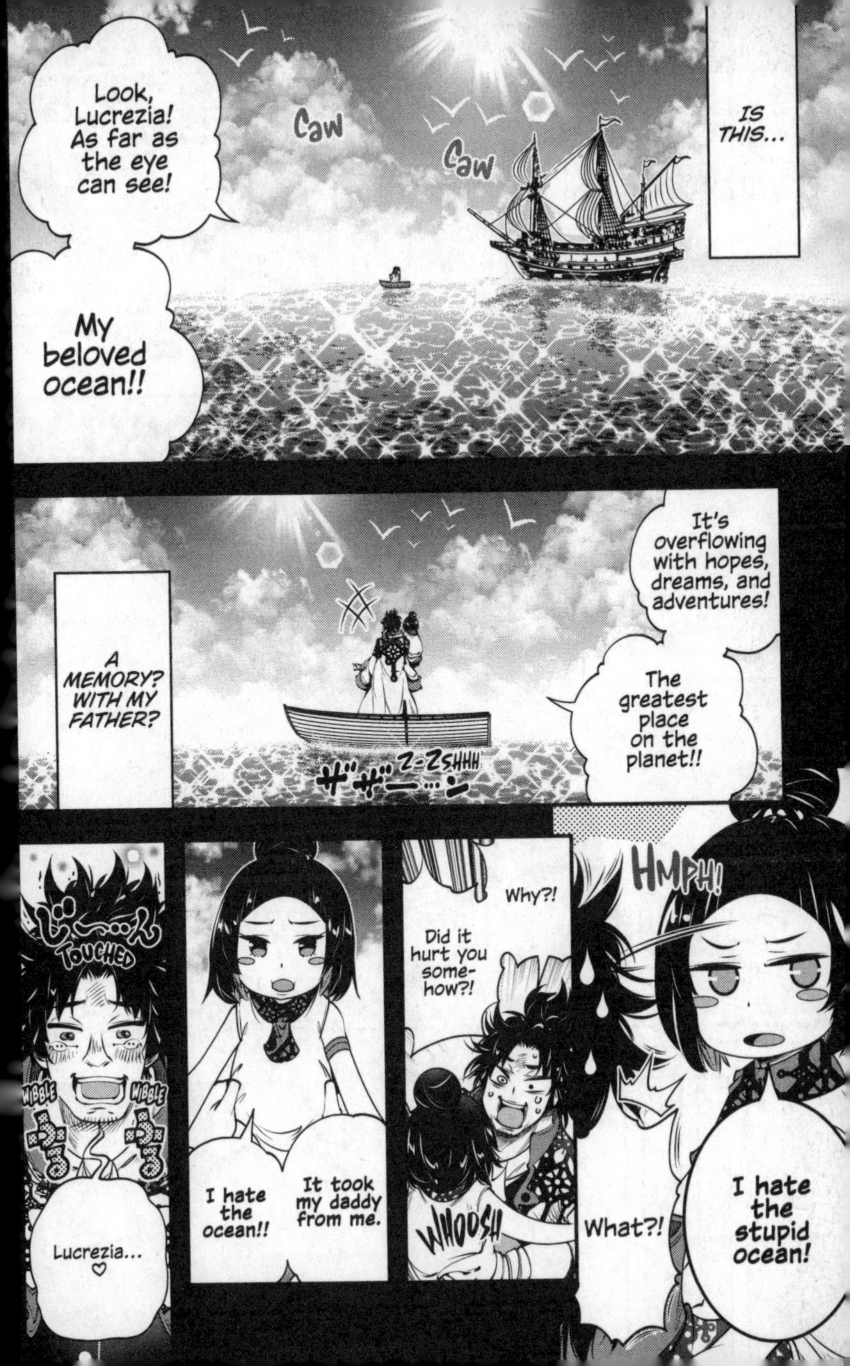
IS THIS...
Caw
Caw
Look, Lucrezia! As far as the eye can see!
My beloved ocean!!
It's overflowing with hopes, dreams, and adventures!
The greatest place on the planet!!
Z-ZSHHH
A MEMORY? WITH MY FATHER?
HMPH!
I hate the stupid ocean!
Why?!
Did it hurt you some-how?!
What?!
WHOOSH
It took my daddy from me.
I hate the ocean!!
TOUCHED
WIBBLE
WIBBLE
Lucrezia... ♡

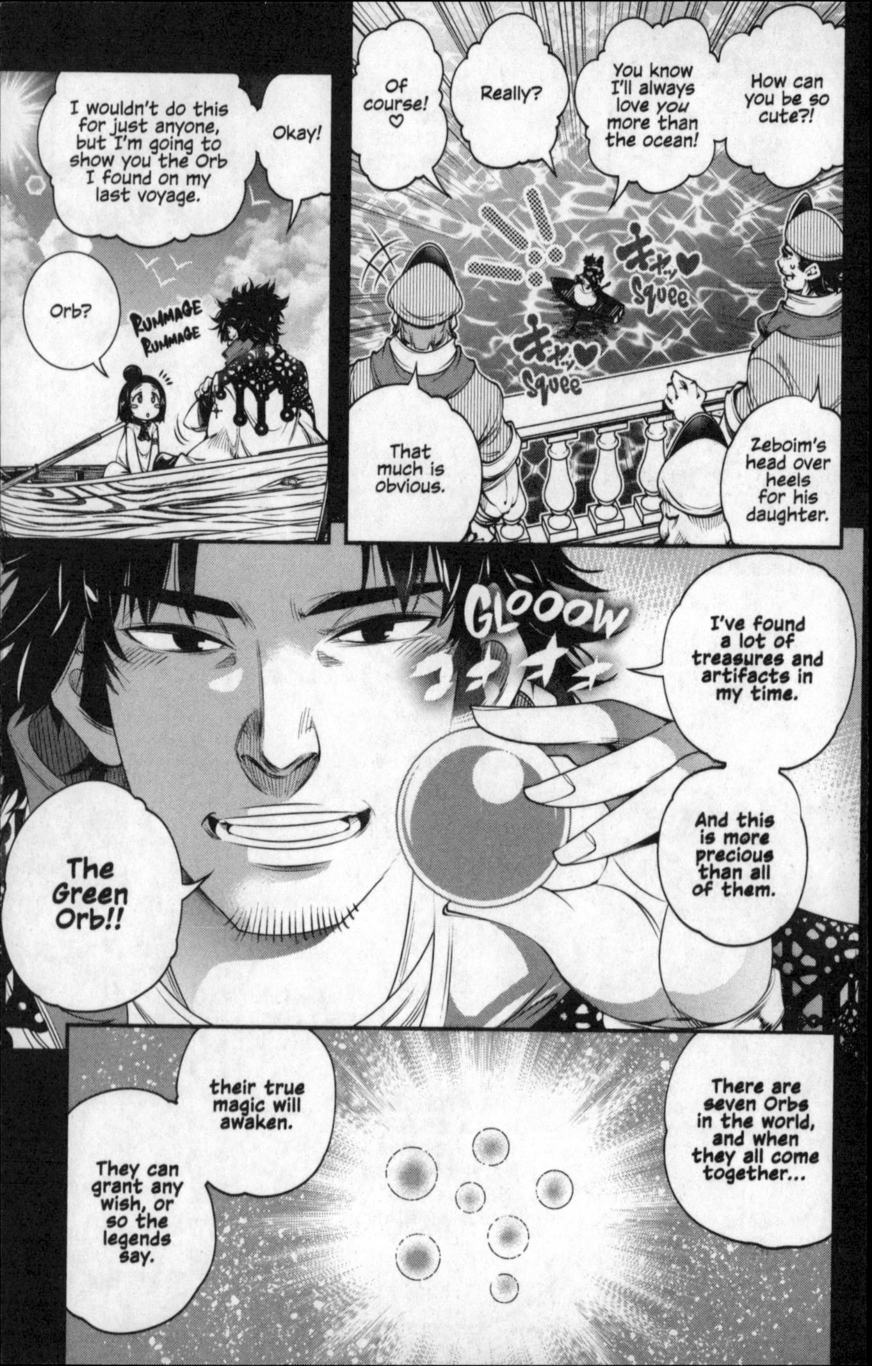
How can you be so cute?!
You know I'll always love you more than the ocean!
Really?
Of course! ♡
Squee
Squee
Zeboim's head over heels for his daughter.
That much is obvious.
I wouldn't do this for just anyone, but I'm going to show you the Orb I found on my last voyage.
Okay!
Orb?
RUMMAGE RUMMAGE
GLOOOW
I've found a lot of treasures and artifacts in my time.
And this is more precious than all of them.
The Green Orb!!
There are seven Orbs in the world, and when they all come together...
their true magic will awaken.
They can grant any wish, or so the legends say.

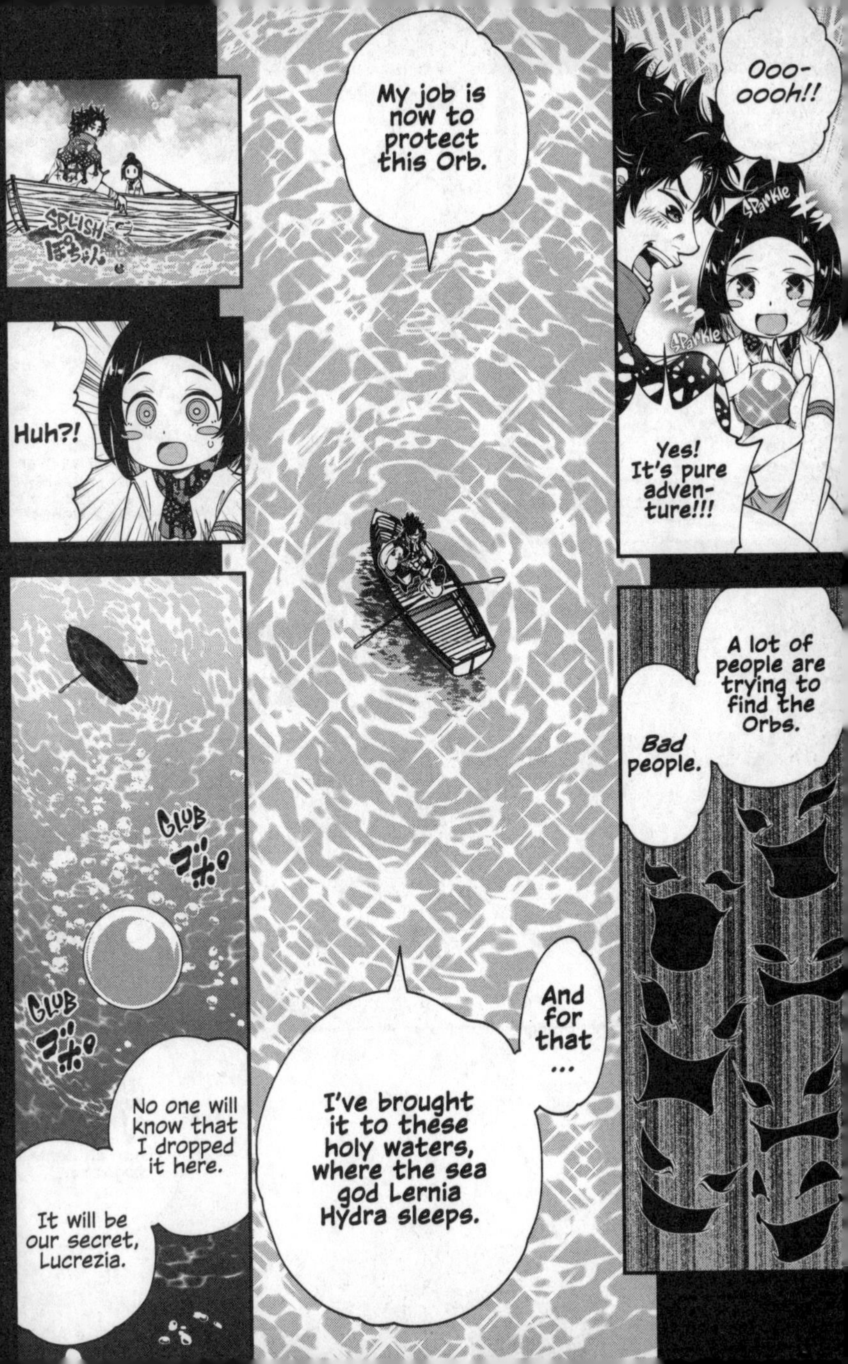
Ooo-oooh!!
SPARKLE
SPARKLE
Yes! It's pure adventure!!!
A lot of people are trying to find the Orbs.
Bad people.
My job is now to protect this Orb.
And for that...
I've brought it to these holy waters, where the sea god Lernia Hydra sleeps.
SPLISH ぽちゃん
Huh?!
GLUB ゴポ
GLUB ゴポ
No one will know that I dropped it here.
It will be our secret, Lucrezia.

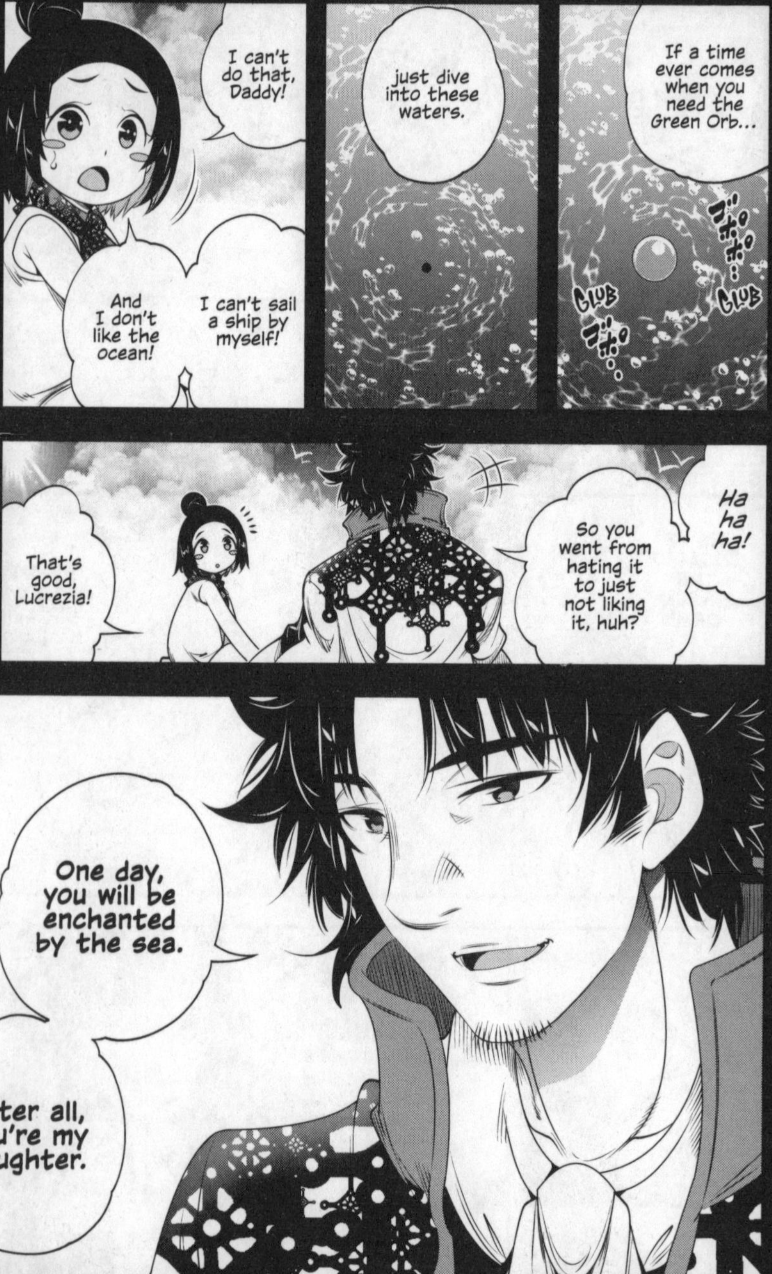
If a time ever comes when you need the Green Orb...
GLUB
GLUB
just dive into these waters.
I can't do that, Daddy!
I can't sail a ship by myself!
And I don't like the ocean!
Ha ha ha!
So you went from hating it to just not liking it, huh?
That's good, Lucrezia!
One day, you will be enchanted by the sea.
After all, you're my daughter.

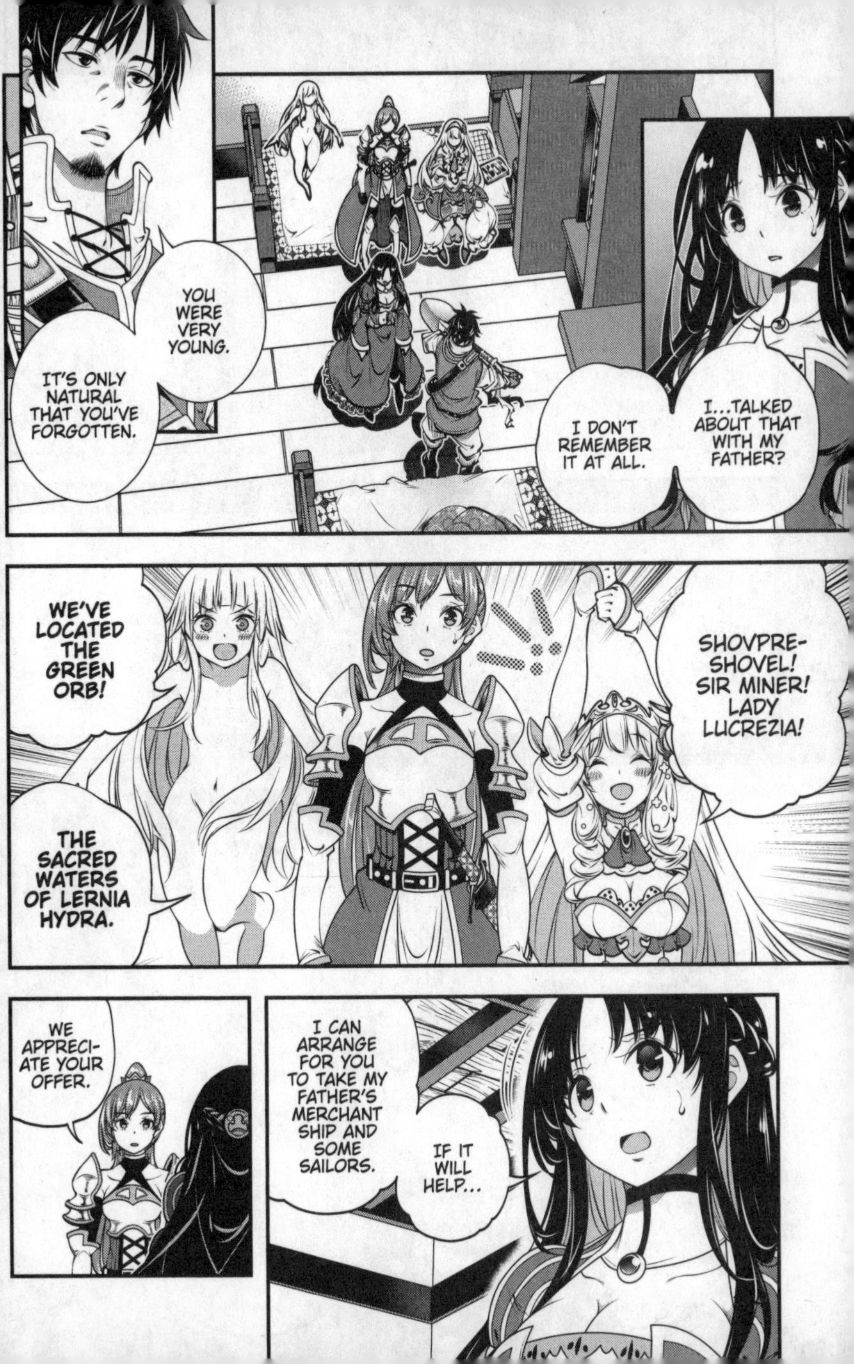
I...TALKED ABOUT THAT WITH MY FATHER?
I DON'T REMEMBER IT AT ALL.
YOU WERE VERY YOUNG.
IT'S ONLY NATURAL THAT YOU'VE FORGOTTEN.
SHOVPRE-SHOVEL! SIR MINER! LADY LUCREZIA!
WE'VE LOCATED THE GREEN ORB!
THE SACRED WATERS OF LERNIA HYDRA.
IF IT WILL HELP...
I CAN ARRANGE FOR YOU TO TAKE MY FATHER'S MERCHANT SHIP AND SOME SAILORS.
WE APPRECIATE YOUR OFFER.

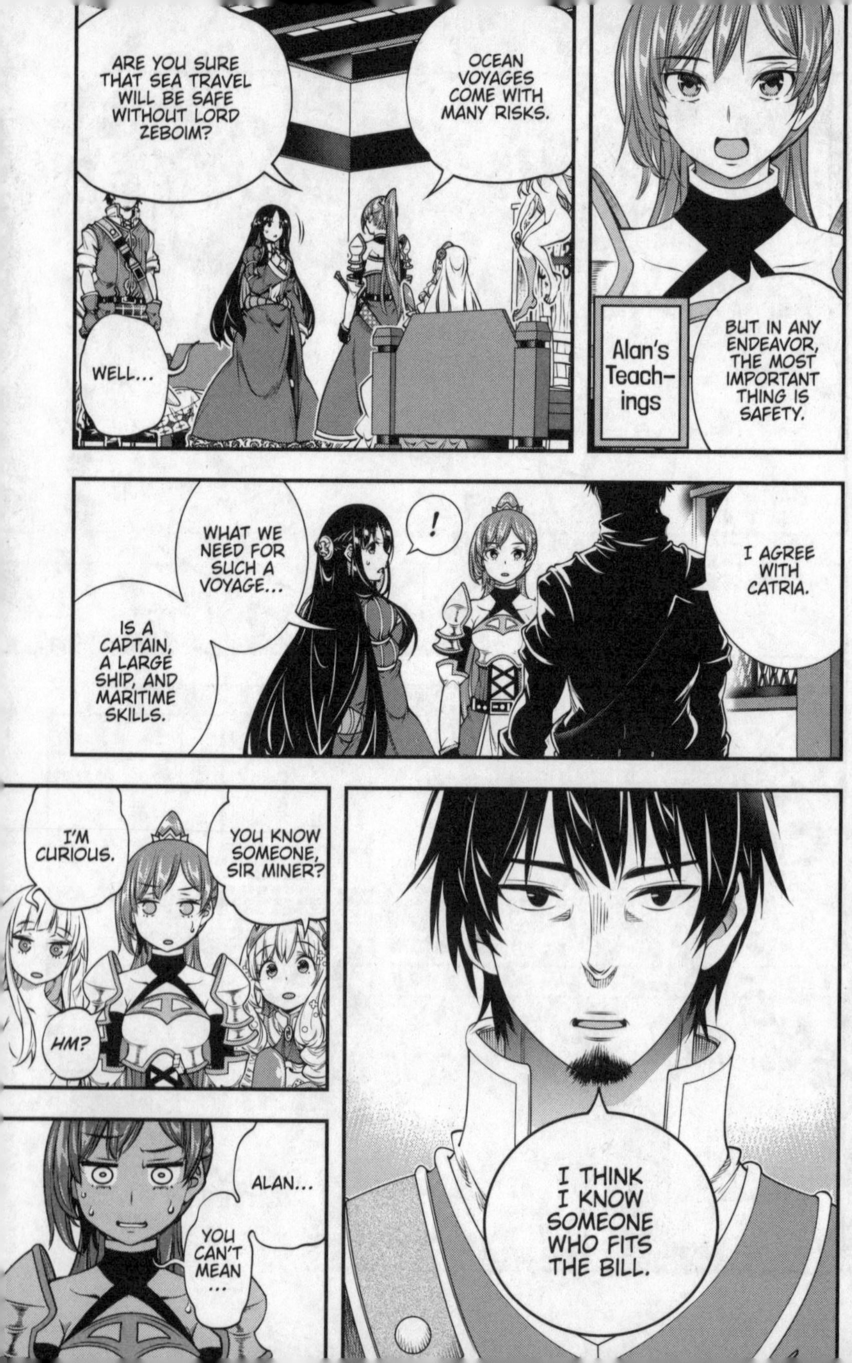
Alan's Teachings
BUT IN ANY ENDEAVOR, THE MOST IMPORTANT THING IS SAFETY.
OCEAN VOYAGES COME WITH MANY RISKS.
ARE YOU SURE THAT SEA TRAVEL WILL BE SAFE WITHOUT LORD ZEBOIM?
WELL...
I AGREE WITH CATRIA.
!
WHAT WE NEED FOR SUCH A VOYAGE...
IS A CAPTAIN, A LARGE SHIP, AND MARITIME SKILLS.
I THINK I KNOW SOMEONE WHO FITS THE BILL.
YOU KNOW SOMEONE, SIR MINER?
I'M CURIOUS.
HM?
ALAN...
YOU CAN'T MEAN ...

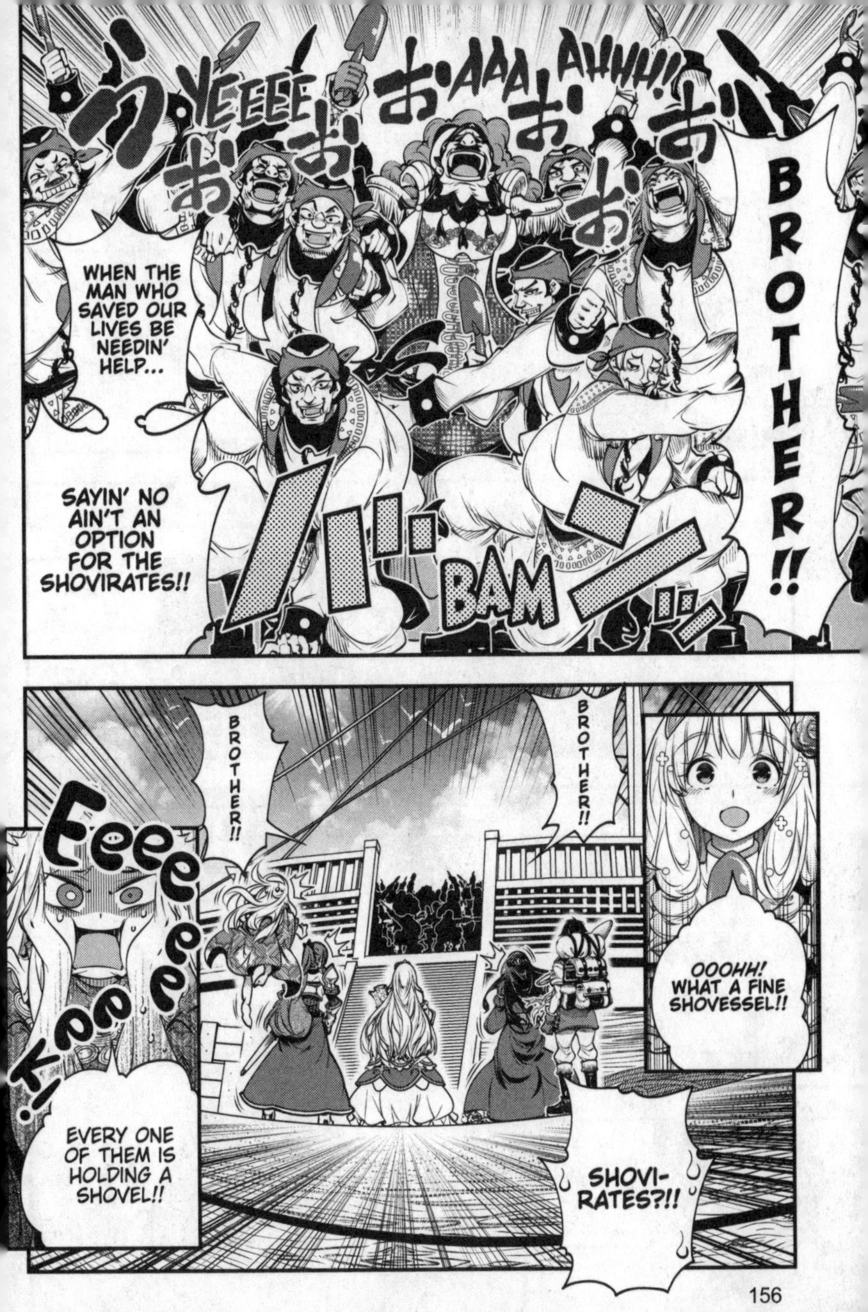
BROTHER!!
うおおおおお
YEEEEE AAAAHHH!!
WHEN THE MAN WHO SAVED OUR LIVES BE NEEDIN' HELP...
SAYIN' NO AIN'T AN OPTION FOR THE SHOVIRATES!!
バーン
BAM
OOOHH! WHAT A FINE SHOVESSEL!!
BROTHER!!
BROTHER!!
SHOVI-RATES?!!
EVERY ONE OF THEM IS HOLDING A SHOVEL!!
Eeeeeeeek!!

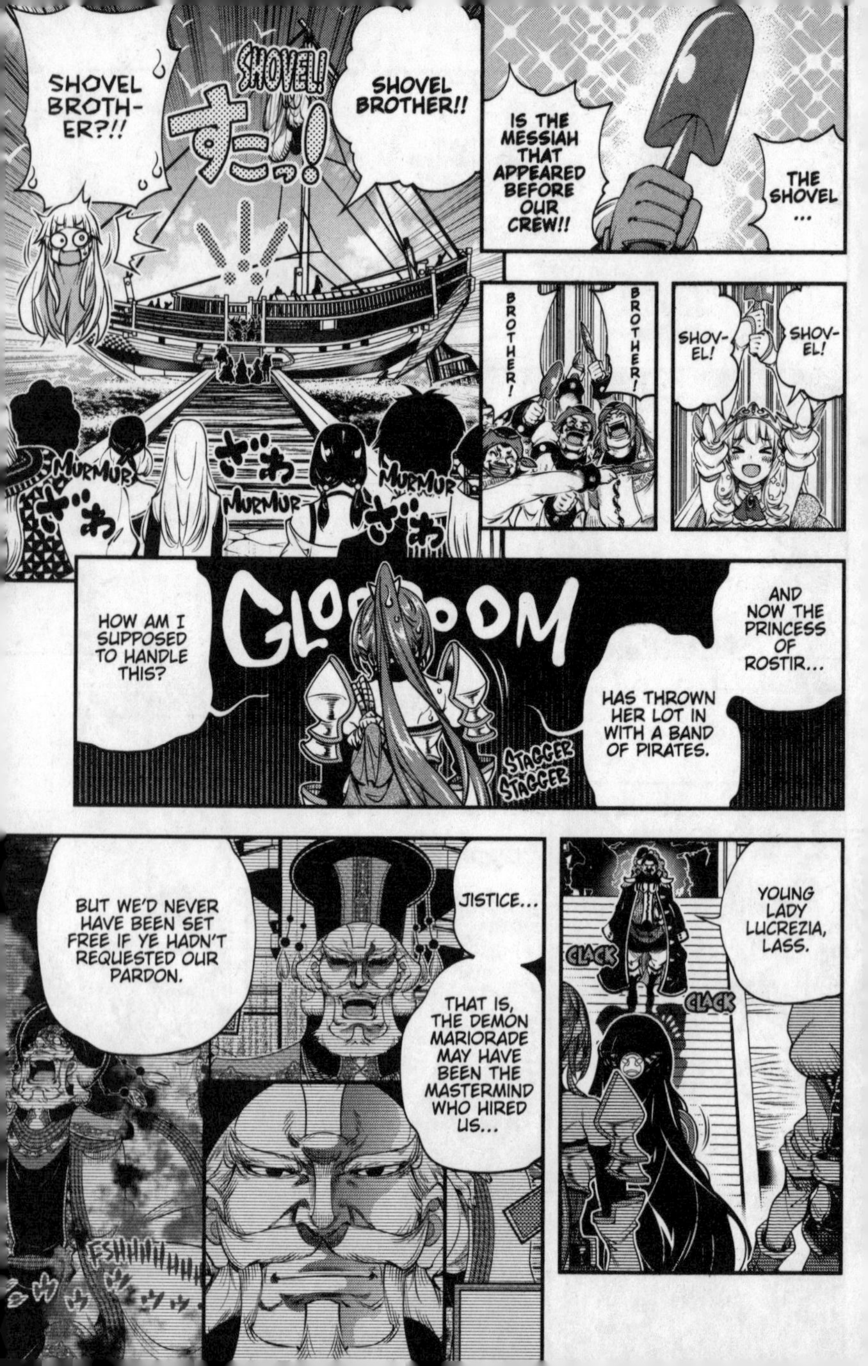
THE SHOVEL...
IS THE MESSIAH THAT APPEARED BEFORE OUR CREW!!
SHOV-EL!
SHOV-EL!
BROTHER!
BROTHER!
SHOVEL BROTHER!!
SHOVEL!
SHOVEL BROTHER?!!
MURMUR
MURMUR
MURMUR
AND NOW THE PRINCESS OF ROSTIR...
HAS THROWN HER LOT IN WITH A BAND OF PIRATES.
GLOOOOM
STAGGER STAGGER
HOW AM I SUPPOSED TO HANDLE THIS?
YOUNG LADY LUCREZIA, LASS.
CLACK
CLACK
JISTICE...
THAT IS, THE DEMON MARIORADE MAY HAVE BEEN THE MASTERMIND WHO HIRED US...
BUT WE'D NEVER HAVE BEEN SET FREE IF YE HADN'T REQUESTED OUR PARDON.
FSHHHH

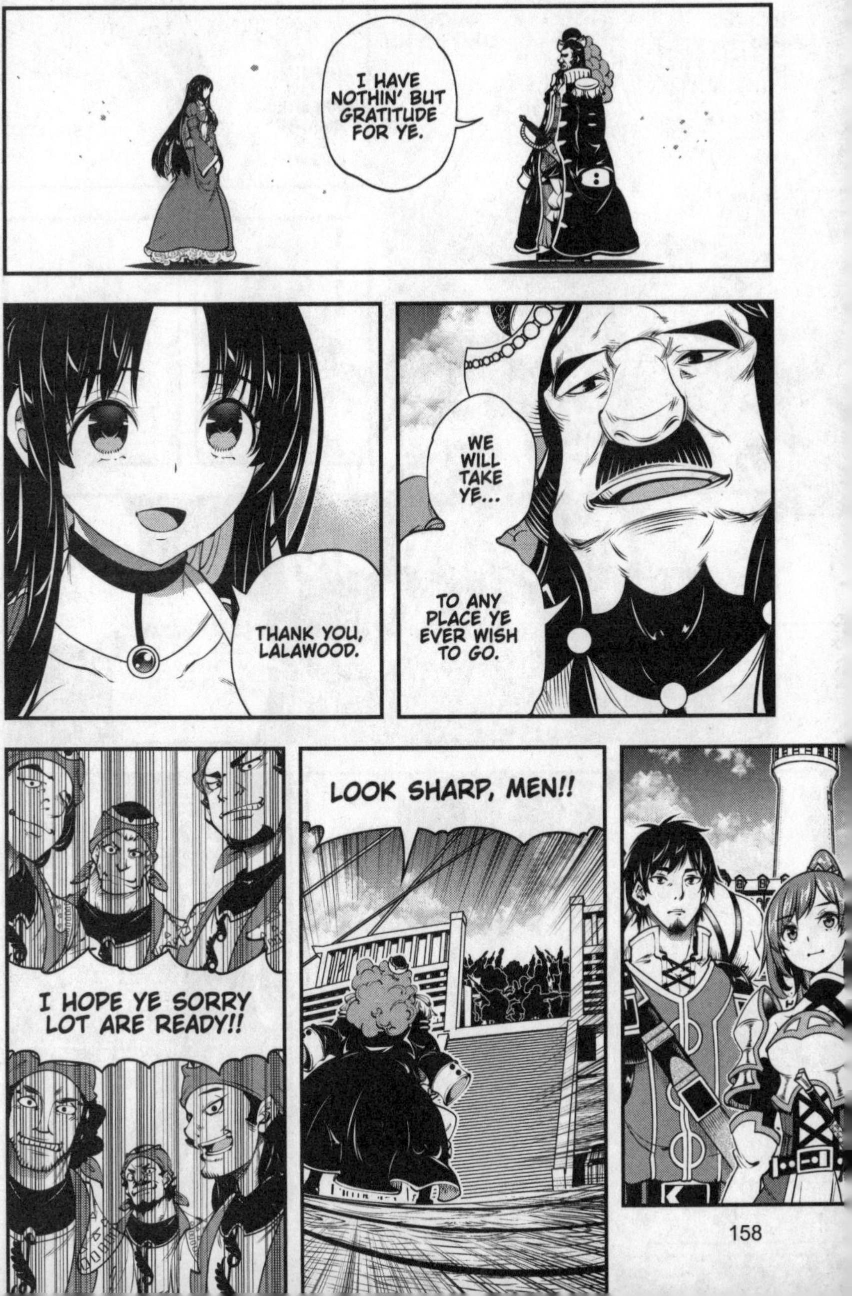
I HAVE NOTHIN' BUT GRATITUDE FOR YE.
WE WILL TAKE YE...
TO ANY PLACE YE EVER WISH TO GO.
THANK YOU, LALAWOOD.
LOOK SHARP, MEN!!
I HOPE YE SORRY LOT ARE READY!!

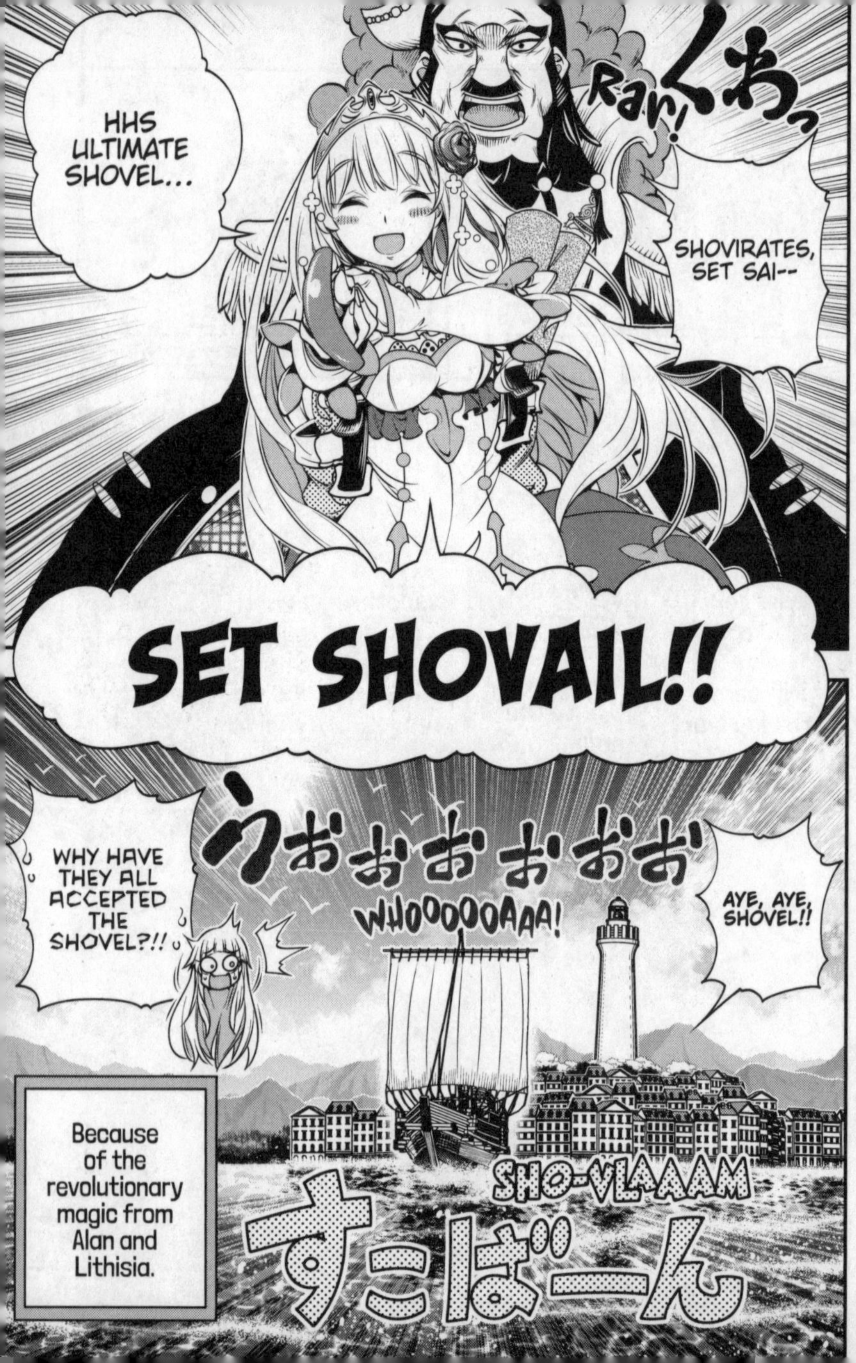
Rar! くわっ
SHOVIRATES, SET SAI--
HHS ULTIMATE SHOVEL...
SET SHOVAIL!!
AYE, AYE, SHOVEL!!
うおおおおおお
WHOOOOOAAA!
WHY HAVE THEY ALL ACCEPTED THE SHOVEL?!!
SHO-VLAAAM
すこぱーん
Because of the revolutionary magic from Alan and Lithisia.

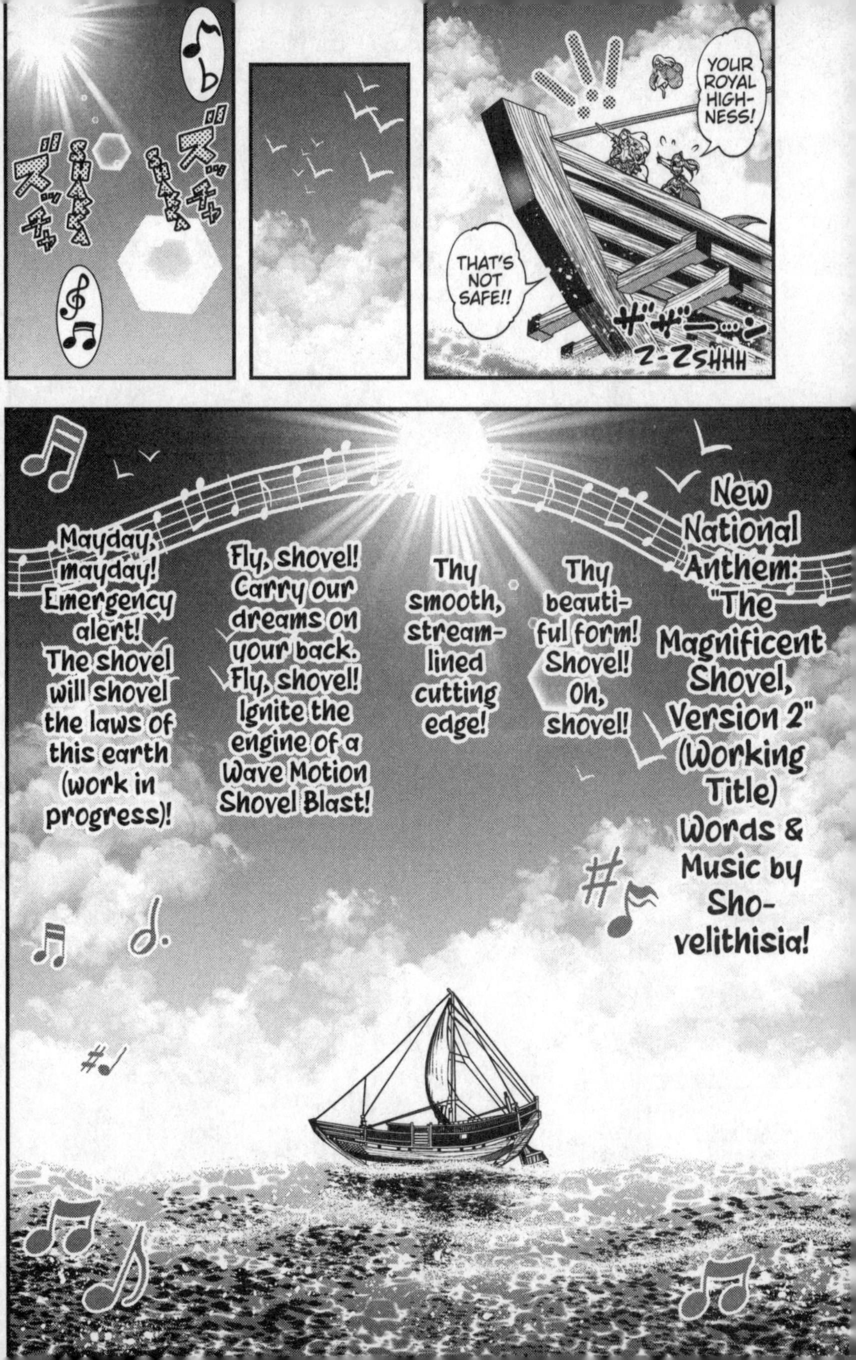

YOUR ROYAL HIGH-NESS!
THAT'S NOT SAFE!!
Z-ZSHHH
SHAKKA
SHAKKA
New National Anthem: "The Magnificent Shovel, Version 2" (Working Title) Words & Music by Sho-velithisia!
Thy beauti-ful form! Shovel! Oh, shovel!
Thy smooth, stream-lined cutting edge!
Fly, shovel! Carry our dreams on your back. Fly, shovel! Ignite the engine of a Wave Motion Shovel Blast!
Mayday, mayday! Emergency alert! The shovel will shovel the laws of this earth (work in progress)!

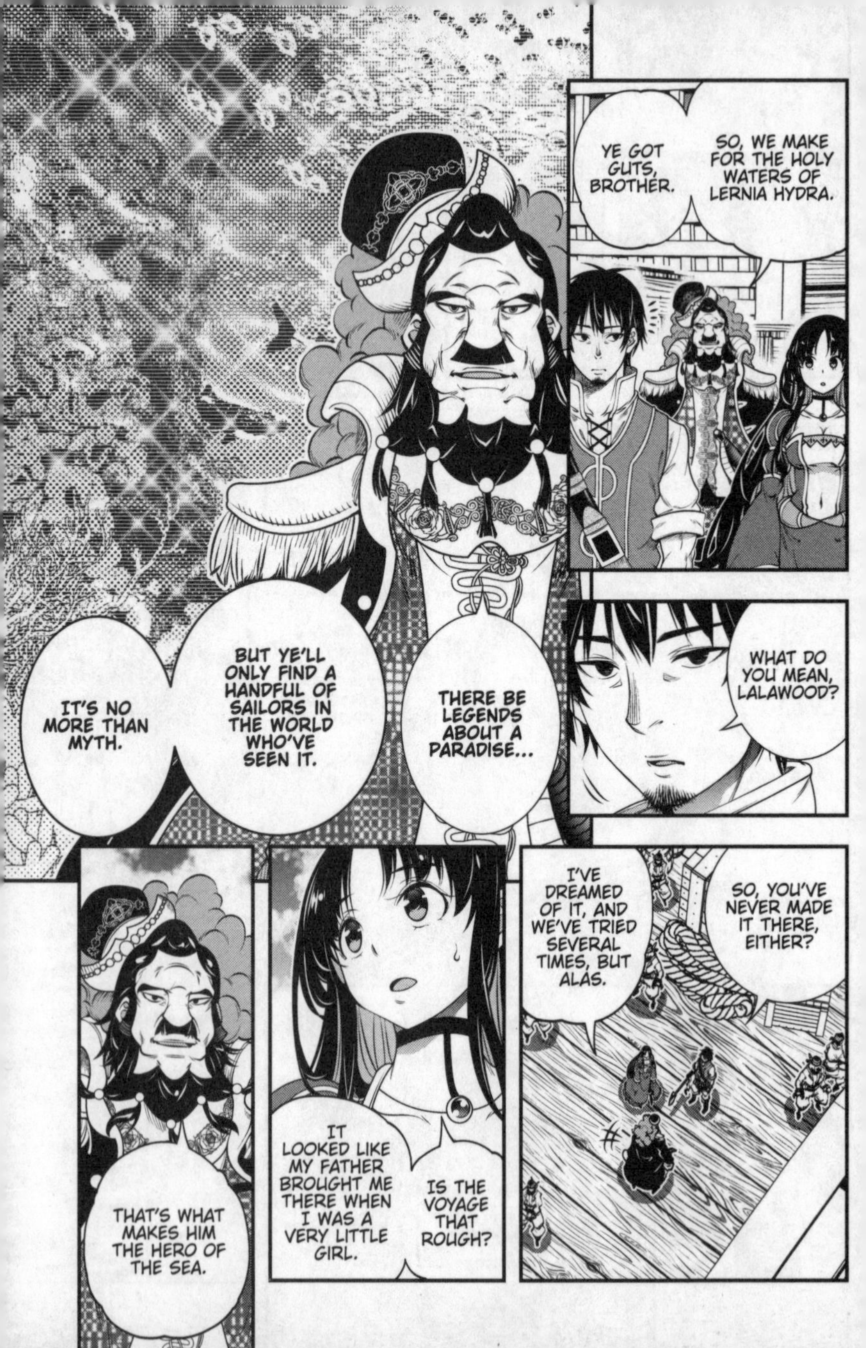
SO, WE MAKE FOR THE HOLY WATERS OF LERNIA HYDRA.
YE GOT GUTS, BROTHER.
WHAT DO YOU MEAN, LALAWOOD?
THERE BE LEGENDS ABOUT A PARADISE...
BUT YE'LL ONLY FIND A HANDFUL OF SAILORS IN THE WORLD WHO'VE SEEN IT.
IT'S NO MORE THAN MYTH.
SO, YOU'VE NEVER MADE IT THERE, EITHER?
I'VE DREAMED OF IT, AND WE'VE TRIED SEVERAL TIMES, BUT ALAS.
IS THE VOYAGE THAT ROUGH?
IT LOOKED LIKE MY FATHER BROUGHT ME THERE WHEN I WAS A VERY LITTLE GIRL.
THAT'S WHAT MAKES HIM THE HERO OF THE SEA.

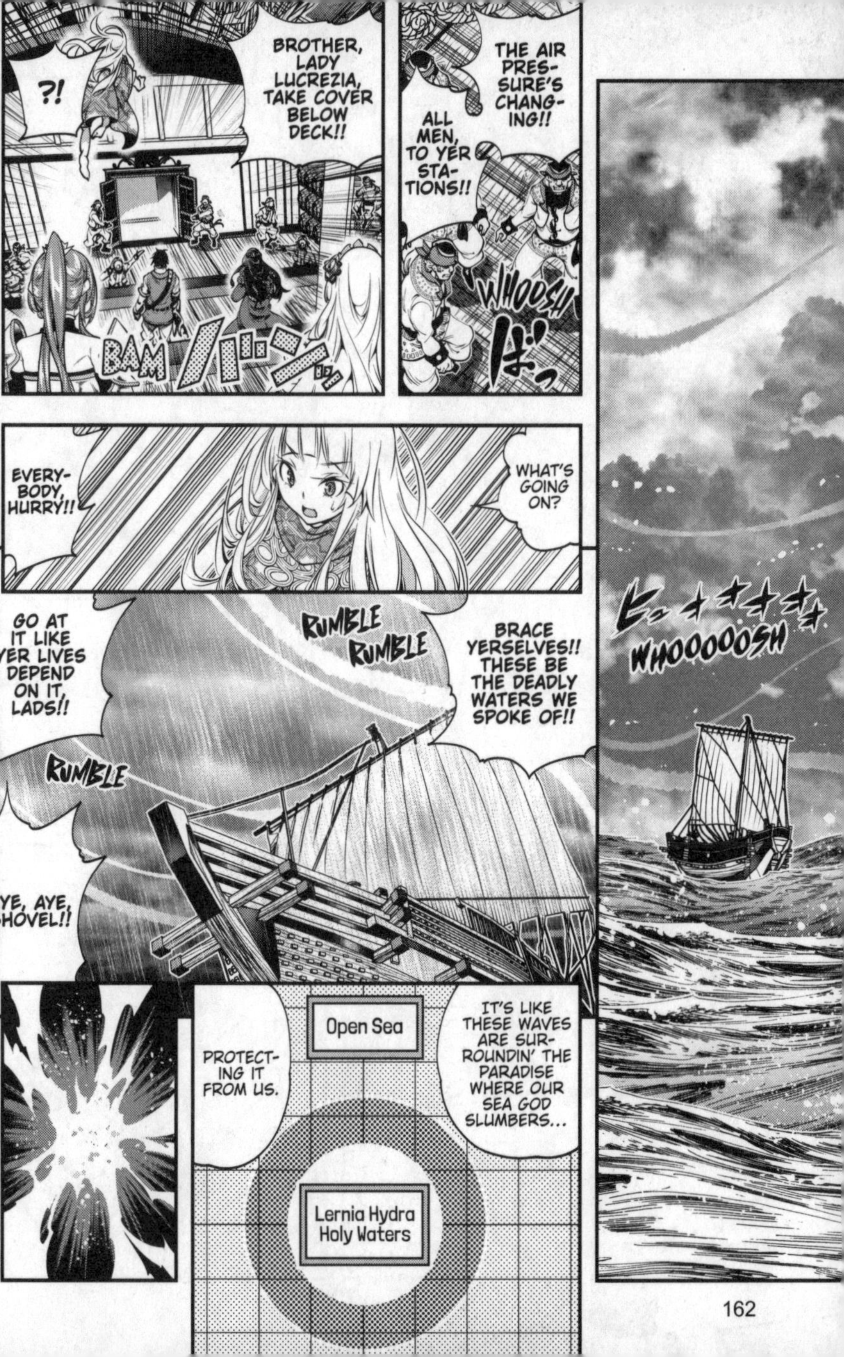
WHOOOOOSH
THE AIR PRESSURE'S CHANGING!!
ALL MEN, TO YER STATIONS!!
WHOOSH
ばっ
BROTHER, LADY LUCREZIA, TAKE COVER BELOW DECK!!
?!
BAM
バーン
WHAT'S GOING ON?
EVERYBODY, HURRY!!
BRACE YERSELVES!! THESE BE THE DEADLY WATERS WE SPOKE OF!!
RUMBLE RUMBLE
GO AT IT LIKE YER LIVES DEPEND ON IT, LADS!!
RUMBLE
AYE, AYE, SHOVEL!!
IT'S LIKE THESE WAVES ARE SURROUNDIN' THE PARADISE WHERE OUR SEA GOD SLUMBERS...
Open Sea
PROTECTING IT FROM US.
Lernia Hydra Holy Waters

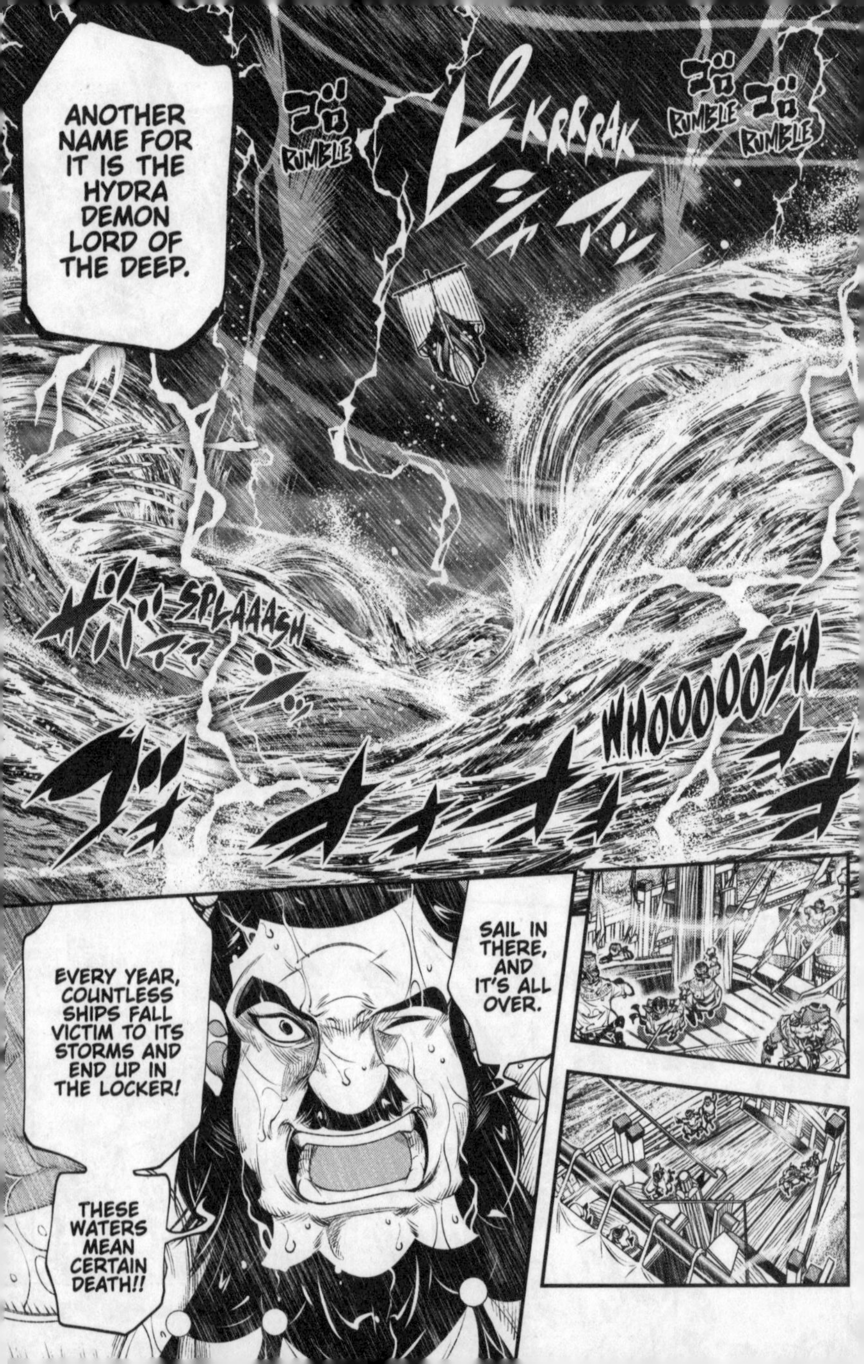
RUMBLE
RUMBLE
KRRRAK
RUMBLE
ANOTHER NAME FOR IT IS THE HYDRA DEMON LORD OF THE DEEP.
SPLAAASH
WHOOOOOSH
SAIL IN THERE, AND IT'S ALL OVER.
EVERY YEAR, COUNTLESS SHIPS FALL VICTIM TO ITS STORMS AND END UP IN THE LOCKER!
THESE WATERS MEAN CERTAIN DEATH!!

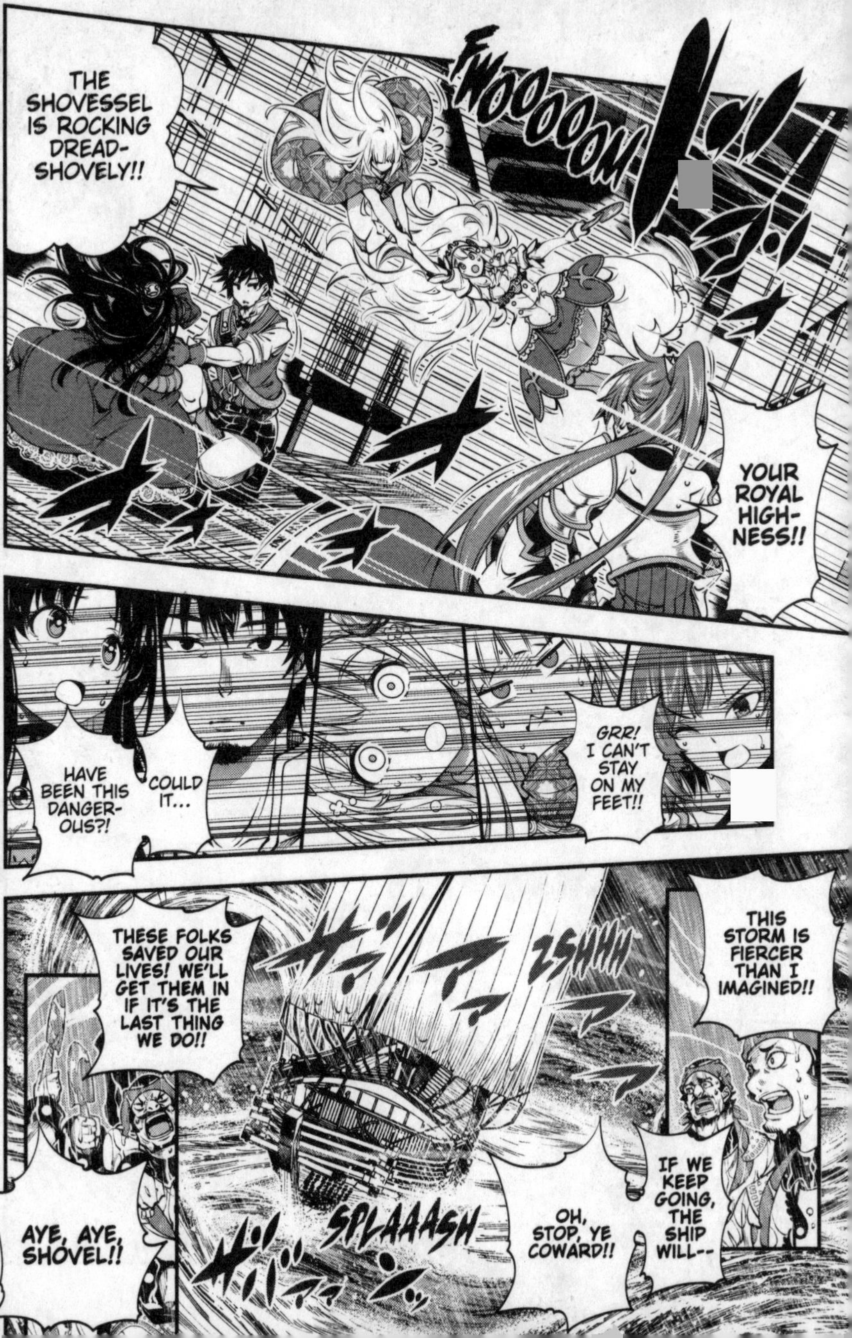
FWOOOOOM
THE SHOVESSEL IS ROCKING DREAD-SHOVELY!!
YOUR ROYAL HIGHNESS!!
GRR! I CAN'T STAY ON MY FEET!!
COULD IT...
HAVE BEEN THIS DANGEROUS?!
THIS STORM IS FIERCER THAN I IMAGINED!!
ZSHHH
IF WE KEEP GOING, THE SHIP WILL--
OH, STOP, YE COWARD!!
SPLAAASH
THESE FOLKS SAVED OUR LIVES! WE'LL GET THEM IN IF IT'S THE LAST THING WE DO!!
AYE, AYE, SHOVEL!!

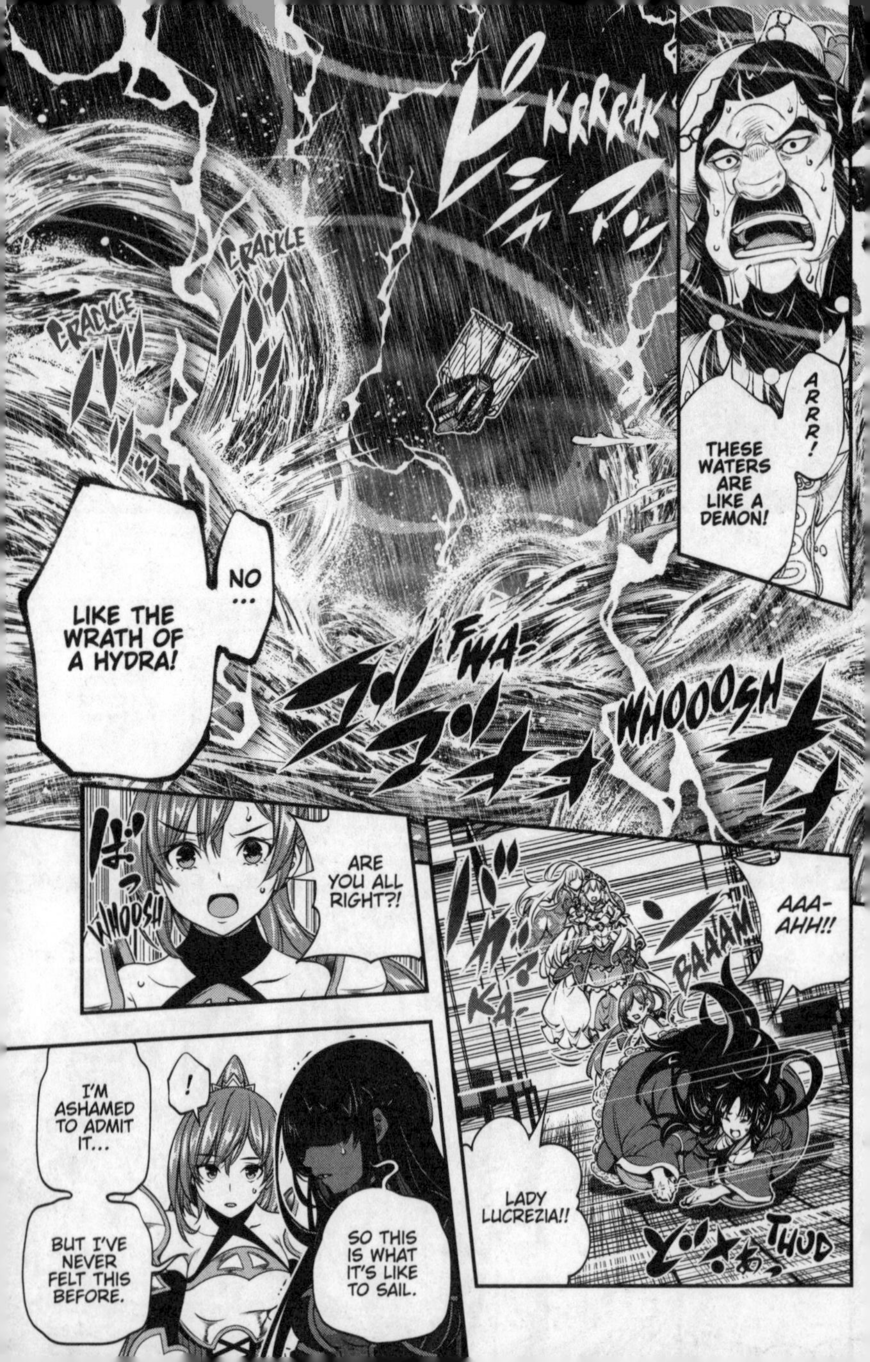
KRRRAK
ARRR!
THESE WATERS ARE LIKE A DEMON!
CRACKLE
CRACKLE
NO...
LIKE THE WRATH OF A HYDRA!
FWA-
WHOOOSH
AAA-AHH!!
BAAAM
KA-
LADY LUCREZIA!!
THUD
ARE YOU ALL RIGHT?!
WHOOSH
SO THIS IS WHAT IT'S LIKE TO SAIL.
!
I'M ASHAMED TO ADMIT IT...
BUT I'VE NEVER FELT THIS BEFORE.

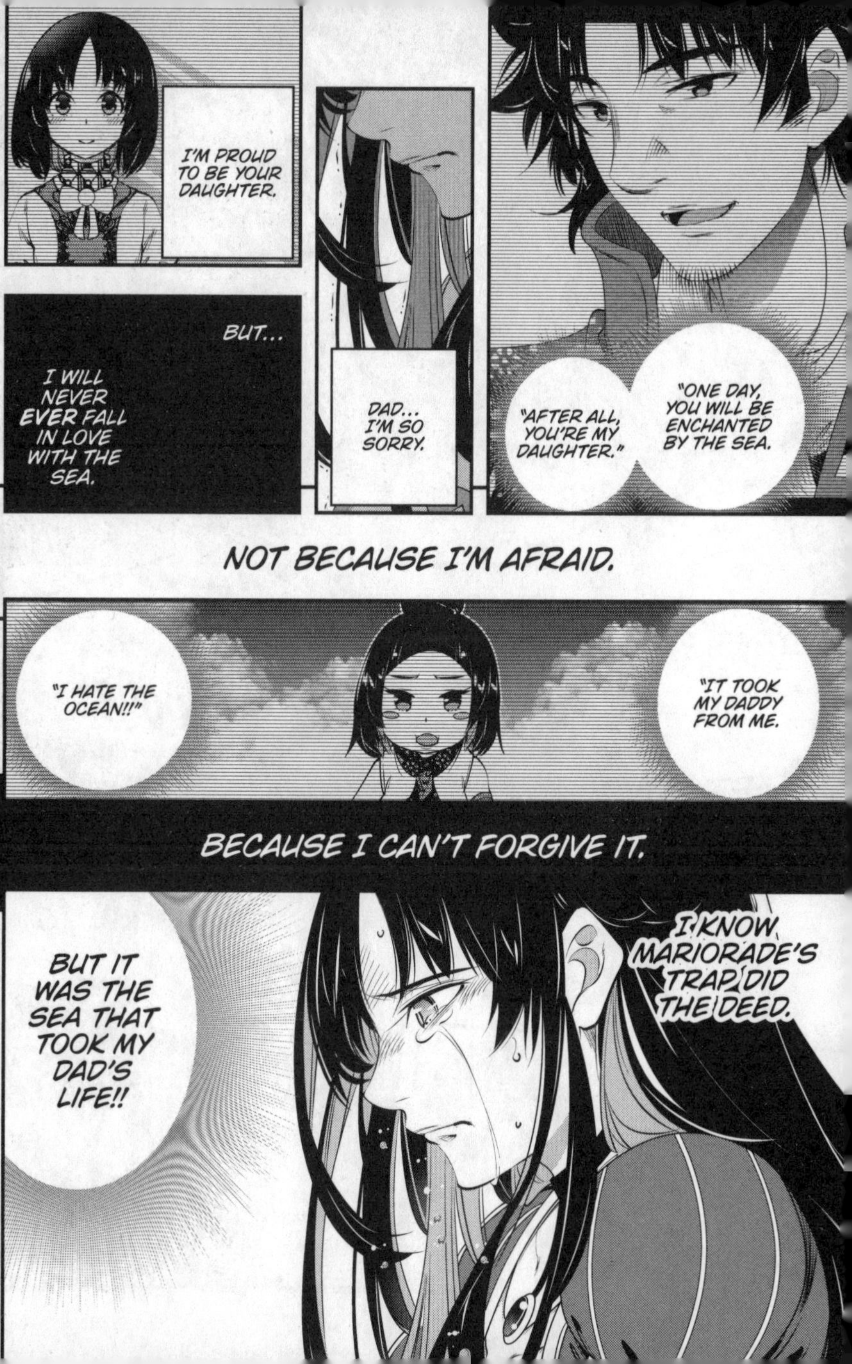
"ONE DAY, YOU WILL BE ENCHANTED BY THE SEA.
"AFTER ALL, YOU'RE MY DAUGHTER."
DAD... I'M SO SORRY.
I'M PROUD TO BE YOUR DAUGHTER.
BUT...
I WILL NEVER EVER FALL IN LOVE WITH THE SEA.
NOT BECAUSE I'M AFRAID.
"IT TOOK MY DADDY FROM ME.
"I HATE THE OCEAN!!"
BECAUSE I CAN'T FORGIVE IT.
I KNOW MARIORADE'S TRAP DID THE DEED.
BUT IT WAS THE SEA THAT TOOK MY DAD'S LIFE!!

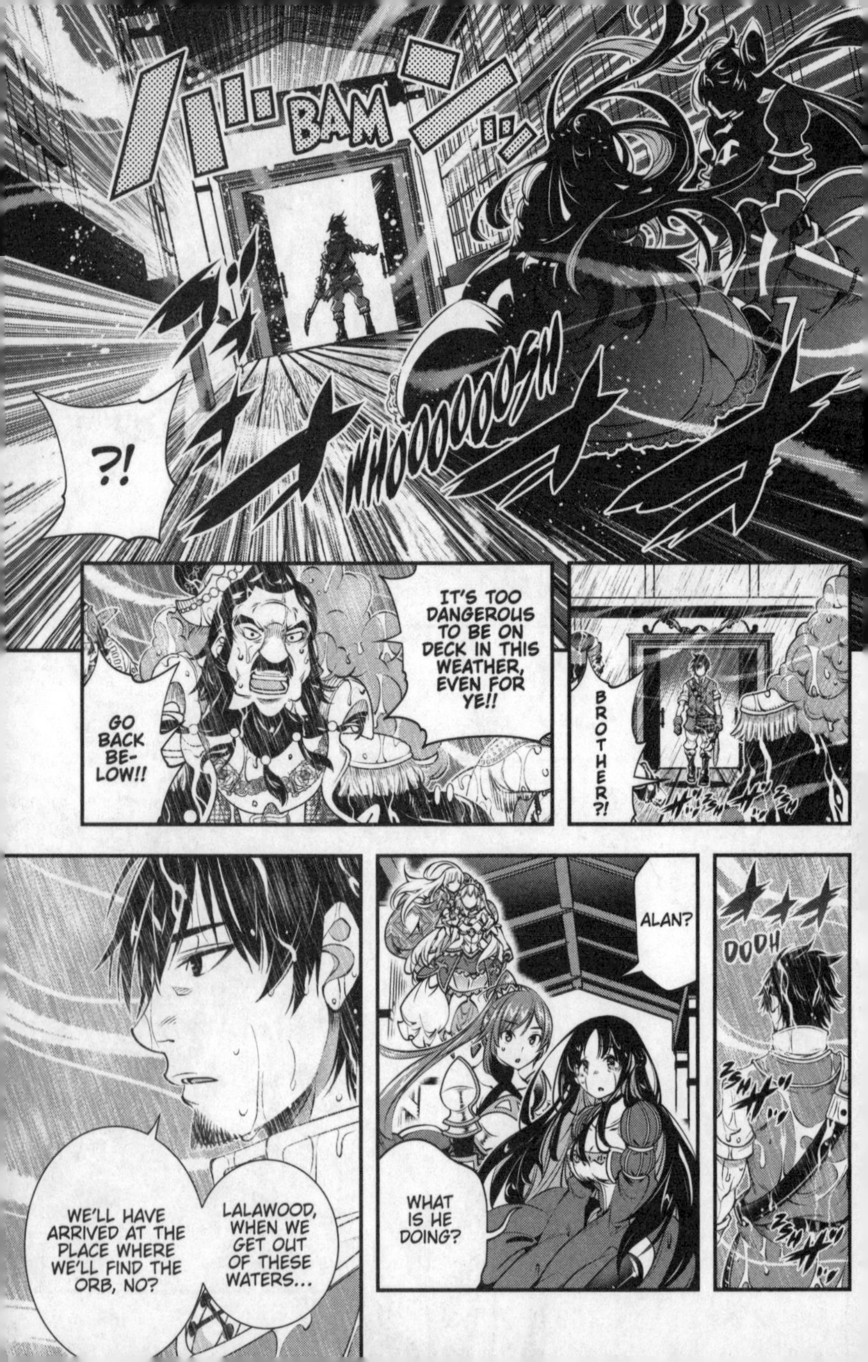
BAM
WHOOOOOOSH
?!
BROTHER?!
IT'S TOO DANGEROUS TO BE ON DECK IN THIS WEATHER, EVEN FOR YE!!
GO BACK BELOW!!
ZSH
ALAN?
WHAT IS HE DOING?
LALAWOOD, WHEN WE GET OUT OF THESE WATERS...
WE'LL HAVE ARRIVED AT THE PLACE WHERE WE'LL FIND THE ORB, NO?

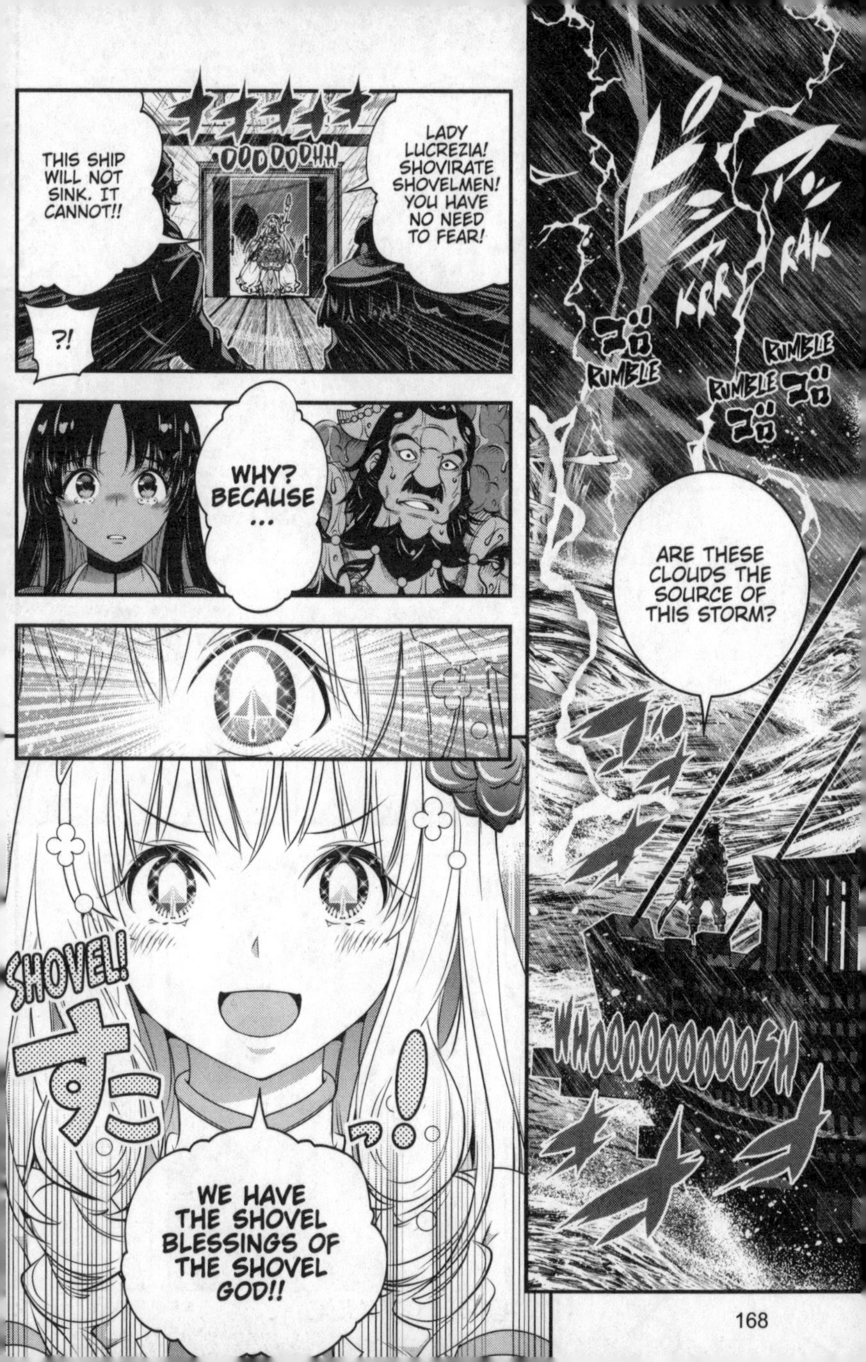
KRRRAK
RUMBLE
ゴロ
RUMBLE
RUMBLE
ゴロ
ゴロ
ARE THESE CLOUDS THE SOURCE OF THIS STORM?
WHOOOOOOOOOSH
LADY LUCREZIA! SHOVIRATE SHOVELMEN! YOU HAVE NO NEED TO FEAR!
DOODOODHH
THIS SHIP WILL NOT SINK. IT CANNOT!!
?!
WHY? BECAUSE ...
SHOVEL!
WE HAVE THE SHOVEL BLESSINGS OF THE SHOVEL GOD!!

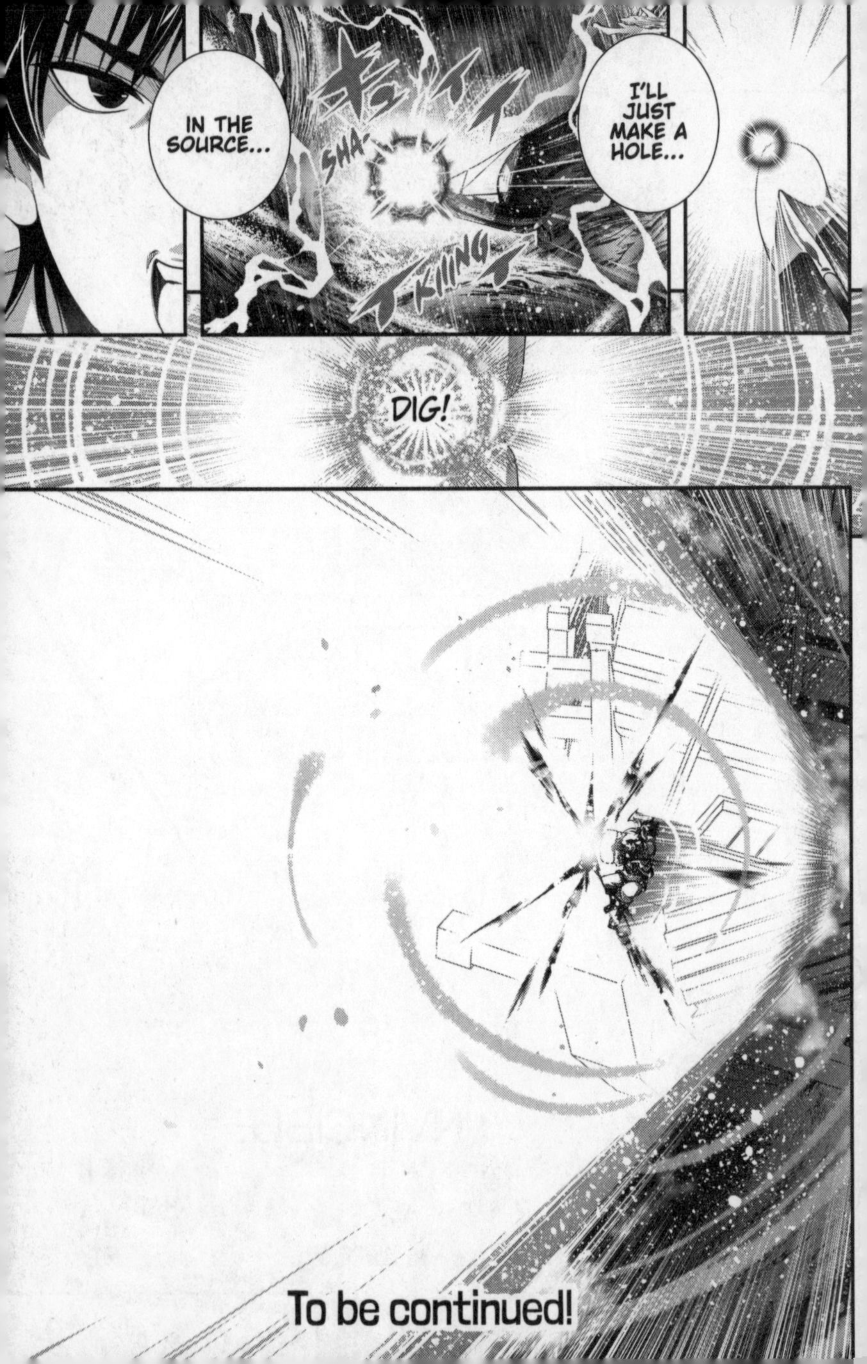
I'LL JUST MAKE A HOLE...
SHA
KIIING
IN THE SOURCE...
DIG!
To be continued!

THE INVINCIBLE SHOVEL

"WAVE MOTION SHOVEL BLAST!"

(˙ ･ω･ ˊ)♂====★(ﾟДﾟ ;;;).:∴ KA-CHOOOM

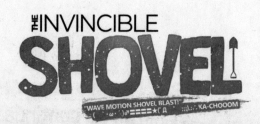

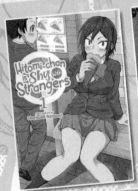
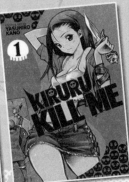
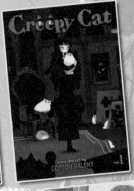
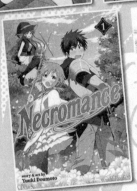
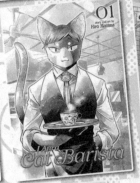
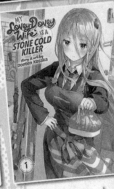
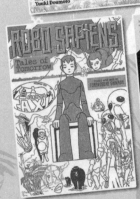
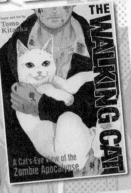
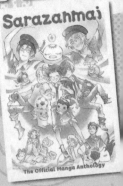

SEVEN SEAS ENTERTAINMENT PRESENTS

THE INVINCIBLE

VOL. 4

art by RENJI FUKUHARA / story by YASOHACHI T

D0652230

TRANSLATION
Alethea & Athena Nibley

ADAPTATION
Jamal Joseph Jr.

LETTERING
Arbash Mughal

COVER DESIGN
Kris Aubin

LOGO DESIGN
George Panella

PROOFREADER
Kurestin Armada

SENIOR EDITOR
Peter Adrian Behravesh

PRODUCTION DESIGNER
Christa Miesner

PRODUCTION MANAGER
Lissa Pattillo

PREPRESS TECHNICIAN
Jules Valera

PRINT MANAGER
iannon Rasmussen-Silverstein

EDITOR-IN-CHIEF
Julie Davis

ASSOCIATE PUBLISHER
Adam Arnold

PUBLISHER
Jason DeAngelis

First published in Japan in 2021 by KADOKAWA CORPORATION, Tokyo.
English translation rights arranged with KADOKAWA CORPORATION, Tokyo.

Seven Seas press and purchase enquiries can be sent to Marketing Manager Lianne Sentar at press@gomanga.com. Information regarding the distribution and purchase of digital editions is available from Digital Manager CK Russell at digital@gomanga.com.

ISBN: 978-1-63858-373-8
Printed in Canada
First Printing: July 2022
10 9 8 7 6 5 4 3 2 1

READING DIRECTIONS

This book reads from ***right to left***, Japanese style. If this is your first time reading manga, you start reading from the top right panel on each page and take it from there. If you get lost, just follow the numbered diagram here. It may seem backwards at first, but you'll get the hang of it! Have fun!!

1
2
3
4
5
6
7
8
9

Follow us online: www.SevenSeasEntertainment.com

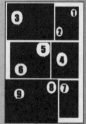